To The One I Love

To The One I Love

AVERY VOLZ

Tivshe
Publishing

Library of Congress Control Number 2021925339
Paperback ISBN 978-1-954175-23-5
Hardback ISBN 978-1-954175-29-7
Electronic ISBN 978-1-954175-22-8

Distributed by Tivshe Publishing
Printed in the United States of America
Cover design by Fay Lane Graphic Design

Visit www.tivshepublishing.com

For my mom and dad. Thank you for being patient; the wait is officially over.

For the person who feels stuck and has no clue what this next chapter of life will bring. Better days are coming.

Chapter One

DECEMBER 2080

The house was bitterly cold that night, but the fire in Abigail Reeve's heart kept her warm. She could not climb the stairs as quickly as she used to, but the excitement propelled her legs anyway. Her blood zipped through her veins; memories catapulted through her brain.

She supposed this idea had been looming in the back of her mind for decades, but it had only just now come to fruition. The letter she intended to write would be lengthy, but she had so much to discuss. So much she *needed* her children to understand. They needed to understand that they weren't alone in this odd rollercoaster of a life, even if it meant tearing open old excruciating wounds. And not to mention the closure Abigail would receive from this project. After all, a blank page was sure to be a better listener than some of her old acquaintances.

Finally in her bedroom, she approached the desk in the corner, finding that she remembered exactly where she placed the old journal. It was dusty now, having spent years in that drawer, and its sky-blue color was fading like daylight itself at sunset. Her fingers gingerly grazed the notebook's cover, and a dozen more memories flickered through her mind like fireflies illuminating a summer evening. A smile tugged on her lips-- thank goodness she purchased the journal after all. Now, it would act as her inspiration.

Abigail sat, her spine already aching from the low back of the chair. She reached for a pencil and said a silent prayer that arthritis would continue to spare her after this project. Just as she touched the pencil tip to paper, a small knock sounded at the door.

Aliana peeked her head in, and her soft green eyes narrowed as she spotted her mother at the desk. "What are you up to?"

Abigail shrugged. "I'm working on something I've been wanting to do for a long time now."

Aliana stepped further inside the room with curiosity written all over her face. "What's that?" The old woman glanced at her daughter, offering that same smirk Aliana knew all too well. "You're not going to tell me, are you?"

"Not yet," Abigail responded pridefully.

"When will I get to know?"

Abigail placed one withered finger to her chin and pursed her lips. "One day."

Aliana chuckled. "Can't wait. Hey, I think the kids are gonna watch a Christmas movie, and Mack and I are gonna make some cocoa. I think Gavin and Hope are already asleep, but do you wanna join us?" Her eyes flickered to the journal sitting on the desk.

"No, that's all right," Abigail replied. "I'm all Christmas-movied out. They've been running all day. But you guys relax and holler if you need anything."

"Are you sure? I could make an extra mug."

Abigail gave Aliana a humorously impatient look. "Scram, child. Let me work. Go be with your wife and children."

Aliana giggled. "All right. Goodnight, Mom. I love you."

Abigail accepted her daughter's hug without hesitation, for it seemed like the old woman's days were finally numbered, and each hug counted now more than ever.

"I love you, too, sweetheart," Abigail murmured.

As soon as Aliana left the room, the old woman returned her gaze to the blank piece of paper in front of her. A sudden wave of emotion coursed through her veins, stinging her eyes with tears. But even with the nostalgia surging through her body, she managed to smile. The wheels in her mind began to churn. Even at seventy-nine years old, she was still sharp as a tack. Every memory was accessible and clear, and for that she was thankful. Pressing the pencil tip to paper, she wrote the words, "Dedicated to the one I love," and began her letter.

Chapter Two

SARATOGA SPRINGS, NY (2012)

I was eleven years old when I first met him.

Colton Reeves was the standup comedian of the entire fifth grade, always trying to outdo his bogus jokes and make people laugh harder than ever. He often got in trouble for it, too, because our fifth grade teacher didn't find his disruptive behavior amusing. And neither did I.

I was never one to run around with the Hot Shots, as my friends and I called the oh-so-cool boys in our grade. Colton was the biggest hot shot of them all. He always hogged the foursquare spot on the playground for one thing, meaning I was forced to retreat toward the swings. He always took pencils from his friends, chewed gum instead of taking notes, and butted in line at lunch. Even the way he stood--arms crossed, head cocked, playful smirk--showed that he believed our entire elementary school belonged to him. But while I loathed him, my best friend Katy Marsh loved him.

"He's kind of cute," she said to me one day as I completed the monkey bars with break-neck speed.

I hopped down from the final bar and frowned at her. "You were supposed to be watching *me*, not the hot shot."

Ignoring my comment, she peered across the playground and stopped when her eyes landed on Colton. He was shifting side to side, bouncing on the balls of his feet, intensely focused on the foursquare game he was playing. His ashy blond hair shifted left to right as he moved.

"He's not *that* cute," I quipped.

Truthfully, I hadn't taken an interest in boys yet. Though I was starting to grow up, my mind was still much too focused on playing with my Barbie dolls and learning to braid my hair than trying to understand love or boys. Katy, on the other hand, had obviously beaten me to it.

"When I get older, I'm going to marry him. Just you watch," she said, chin high, hands on hips.

My fingers were starting to callous from the monkey bars, and I picked at one of the scabs. "Good luck with that."

"Oh, do you think *you're* gonna be with him?"

"Like I said, he's just not cute. You have bad taste in boys, Katy."

She glanced back at me, and I knew to start running because now her right eye was twitching and it only did that when she was aggravated. She chased me around the playground, and we ended up rolling through the grass and laughing until our sides burned.

"You can have him," I wheezed after my guffaws. "Colton means nothing to me."

A couple of years later, during one of the last days of eighth grade, Katy mentioned Colton a second time.

"You know, I heard that Colton and Hailey aren't together anymore. Can you believe it? They were dating for *so* long."

I ran my tongue over my braces and winced as I scraped it on a stray wire. "Do people even date in middle school though? I mean they probably only went to the movies on the weekends."

"I don't know, man." Katy shook her head and slammed her locker door shut. "I heard Hailey's pretty upset though. Colton must be a heartbreaker."

"Since when do you care about Hailey Binestra?" I laughed, but Katy shushed me immediately.

Colton had turned the corner and was walking down the hall with his other-half Ashton Rinoven. They were dying laughing over something. One time, Ashton spread a rumor that he was secretly gay for Colton and now they acted like they were soulmates. As they passed us, Colton's eyes touched mine for the briefest moment, but for some reason it felt longer.

"Tell me you don't think Colton Reeves is cute," Katy whispered when they were further down the hall.

I glanced back at him, cocking my head at his flopping blond hair and confident gait. My heart pursed its lips in consideration but made no effort to respond. So, I shrugged. "I don't know. Maybe a little."

To no surprise, our summer lasted about ten seconds, and then we put on our big girl outfits and walked into the high school as freshmen.

Once I joined the orchestra, I often hung around with the rest of my musical peers, so I wasn't exactly top-of-the-food-chain popular, but my connection to Katy made me cool by default because she had figured out how to get in with the right people.

Colton Reeves was in my honors English class that year, which downright shocked me. I assumed he never picked up a book in his free time. But as fate would have it, much to my dismay, his seat was right next to mine. Sometimes I wondered if Katy was jealous of my proximity to him since she still occasionally kept tabs on his life. But she had also since moved on to some other poor boy.

One Friday afternoon in September, I sauntered into the English classroom, copied the homework into my type A, color-coded agenda, and frowned. Of *course* Mr. Korrins had to assign us a partner project on *All the Light We Cannot See*...even though we already had a boatload of homework for every other class. My eyes flickered around the room, taking in the faces I'd known for years. I wasn't friends with any of these people, not really. I suddenly wished Katy had opted to take Honors English with me instead of College Prep. At least then I'd have a secured partner.

When the bell sounded, Mr. Korrins stopped clicking his pen and shuffled to the front of the room. "Good morning, good morning. 'Mkay, listen. You have until next Wednesday to complete your quote worksheet and create a poster board for your chosen topic. This will be part of your research project, which is half your grade for freshman year, so for the love of God, don't procrastinate." We all groaned, and he rolled his eyes. "Knock it off. I really don't feel like failing any of you. It's a lot of extra paperwork. Now get to it and work with your seat partners."

Oh, God. I inwardly cringed at the thought of working with Colton Reeves on anything. I knew exactly how this would pan out: I'd get stuck doing all the work and then he'd take all the credit for doing absolutely—

I froze when his eyes met mine.

Colton had grown up over the years. His quiffed golden hair sat in wispy loops on top of his head, no longer the shaggy mop of hair he had back in the day. His arms were also brawnier than the fifth grader I remembered. The sun-kissed shade of his skin put my weak, attempted tan to shame. And were his eyes always that vibrant? I noticed that they had little gold specks in them, glistening against the green of his irises. He sat hunched

forward, elbows pressed into the desk, shoulders hitched up.
The pose gave off a vibe of cool nonchalance. He had matured.
He had suddenly become handsome.

"What?" he asked after a moment. A deeper voice, too.

Vaguely, I wondered how I'd missed these changes, considering I'd known him most of my life.

For a moment, I felt self-conscious and touched a strand of
my toothpick straight brown hair. Did I look different from my
fifth grade self? My face was a lot more angular; I knew that
much. And I'd reached an outstanding maximum height of five-
foot-five, but was it noticeable?

Colton arched one golden eyebrow at me.

I cleared my throat. "I was just wondering what you thought
we should do for our project."

My voice was an octave too high. Here I was, talking with
Mr. Hot Shot...who apparently didn't act like much of a hot shot
anymore.

"Oh, I have no clue," Colton muttered with a shrug. "I wasn't
really into *All the Light We Cannot See*."

"Or did you just not read it?" I challenged, playfully
narrowing my eyes at him.

He glanced at me out of the corner of his eye — a perplexed
gaze that quickly became curious. And then he turned toward
me with one corner of his mouth tilted up. "I read *most* of it."

My first thought was to roll my eyes and chastise him like I'd
been doing for years, but something was different this time. His
reply actually made me laugh.

"What if we did our project on personal morality? Like,
Werner has orders from the Nazis, but he knows in his heart
that they aren't morally correct. He's always had good judgment."

It surprised me when Colton shook his head. "No way.
Werner got his good judgment from Jutta."

"What do you mean?"

"Well, he's *young* when he finds the radio, which means he

doesn't know a whole lot yet. But his younger sister reminds him of what's good. It's the same with Marie-Laure. Her dad was obviously a very righteous man who raised her well. I doubt those kids would be as moralistic if they were raised by actual Nazis."

I cocked my head at him. "You think environmental influence is a big thing?"

"For sure. People have the biggest impact on your life." His eyes touched mine again, and then as if he was embarrassed by his own analysis, he dropped his head and glued his eyes to the paper on his desk.

I resisted the urge to let my jaw drop. Who *was* this person I was speaking to? Perhaps I had misjudged.

Mr. Korrins leaned back in his chair and started clicking his pen again. He looked funny sitting there, red-faced and antsy, like he would rather be doing anything else than teaching a class-room of high school freshmen.

"I swear that man is a psycho deep down." Colton shook his head. "Who would ever willingly teach this class? English sucks." He began doodling on the side of his worksheet.

I retrieved the book from my backpack. "I like English."

"I'm more into engineering and architecture," he replied, glancing back at me. "I want to build cool places when I'm older. Hopefully I can make a career out of it. What about you?"

"I want to go into music."

"Oh, nice."

I started paging through my book to find some quotes and prove that what Colton had said about Werner and Marie-Laure was correct. Colton copied me, and for a couple minutes, the only sound between us was the flipping of pages. I found a good quote right away and scribbled it onto my paper. Colton gazed over my shoulder, and I giggled when he wrote the same quote on his worksheet.

Again, I was taken aback by how handsome he suddenly was. Where was that annoying little boy I used to know?

"So, what kind of music do you like?" he asked as I reread another passage from the novel.

"Oh uh..." I added a second quote to my list. "I guess I like pop music, but I've been listening to classical music for most of my life. I play the violin."

His face contorted. "Classical music? No way. Reggae music is where it's at." His grin widened when I rolled my eyes, but I was smiling, too.

And it was so unexpected that I shrank back slightly so that my hair would form a curtain between us. I didn't want him to see me blush.

"I bet you're pretty good at the violin," he murmured. "I played the saxophone for five minutes in sixth grade and then quit."

My laugh was audible this time. "You're missing out."

"I think I'll survive."

The clock was ticking, but I found myself wishing I had more time to talk with Colton. He was surprisingly easy to converse with.

"All right, listen up!" Mr. Korrins called three minutes before the bell rang. "Don't forget you need to have a finished poster by next Wednesday that shows all of your findings. We'll start presentations that day."

"Dammit," Colton hissed under his breath. "I freaking hate this class." He turned to me and retrieved his phone from his pocket. "Can I have your number?"

I stared at him, wide-eyed.

"For the project," he clarified quickly. "Just so we can be in touch about it."

I awkwardly shifted my backpack to my other shoulder. "Oh, sure."

As I listed the numbers, I took note of how his cheeks

flushed a light pink. Was he embarrassed about something? He typed quickly into his phone and then turned away from me.

"Thanks," I heard him say as he moved toward the door. "I'll talk to you later."

Returning home after school had become the bane of my existence. What was once a quiet, loving household was now a bloody battlefield between my parents. I could never tell what exactly they were fighting over, but it was a constant ambush of loud accusations and petty comebacks.

That afternoon, I met my dad in the driveway after school. He was fuming into his phone, hissing to someone I didn't know. The way his shoulders tensed up around his neck made me nervous. He nodded to me as I passed into the garage.

I could smell my mother's cigarette even before I found her. The putrid smell almost made me gag. Sure enough, Mom was sitting at the kitchen table in a cloud of smoke.

"Can you take that outside?" I asked spitefully.

I had little respect for my mom these days. Ever since the fighting started, she had transformed into the shell of someone I used to know. It seemed she only came back to life when she was trying to pick a fight with Dad. And I had heard her say some terrible, unforgivable things.

"Be quiet, Gail. Let me have a few moments of peace."

"Who's Dad talking to?"

"Lord knows."

I shook my head at her, and that was when the glint of light on metal caught my eye. I blinked a few times and entered the living room. If I wouldn't have been watching where I was walking, I would have stepped right in the mess. There was a pile of shattered glass on the hardwood floor, glowing in the afternoon sunlight. I knew those pieces well. It was the remains of an old vase my grandmother had given to my father before she passed away.

"What happened?" I shrieked.

"Your father aggravates me and doesn't understand when enough is enough."

Blinding rage struck a match in my chest. "*You* did this?"

She took another drag of her cigarette and exhaled a perfect smoke ring. "Clean that up, will you, Gail?" It didn't sound like a question.

My breath caught in my throat. That vase was one of the most prized possessions on my dad's side of the family. And now, I was ready to smack this woman to the floor. She stared at me emotionlessly, her cold eyes boring into mine. I quivered in all my fury.

"HOW COULD YOU DO THAT?" I demanded.

I knew their fighting was getting worse, but I never suspected it would take a turn like this.

"That's *ridiculous!*" I screamed, and adrenaline pulsed in my veins. Enough was enough.

Mom simply shrugged. I stomped toward her, ready to grab her by the hair, ready to shove that cigarette down her windpipe—

"Abigail!" my father roared before I could take another step.

I froze and glanced over at him.

He stood in the doorway with his cellphone clenched tightly in his hand. Though his expression was angry, the tear stains on his cheeks suggested otherwise. He was heartbroken, which was odd to see because he was my dad, and dads weren't supposed to cry. They were supposed to be strong forever. Unbreakable.

For a moment, I recalled the good old days, when my parents were sweet, civil, and dare I say, in love. The memory pierced my heart like a blade, and I felt my legs threaten to give out.

Without another word, I left the kitchen and ran toward my room. I knew a loud argument was coming, and I didn't know if

I could bear to listen. Hands shaking, I pulled out my phone and texted Katy. All I knew was that I had to get out of here before the storm hit.

SOS ! I texted.

I paced my room, blinking back tears. I didn't realize I was biting my lip until a sharp metallic taste grazed my tongue.

What's up bro? Katy responded shortly after.

Parents are at it again. Need to get out of here. Can I come over?

Of course!

My mom's harsh, accusatory tone cut through the silence, and I grabbed a jacket from my closet.

A small part of me felt guilty for leaving Dad to face Mom alone, but I knew he would prefer it this way anyway. Dad knew I despised the fighting, and though we rarely spoke of it, I was sure he wanted to shield me from the horror of it all.

Thankfully, Katy lived in the next neighborhood over, so it wasn't a far walk, but it was freezing in New York. People brushed past me, half of their faces concealed by hats and scarves. I shoved my hands into my coat pockets and started jogging.

Around here, the houses were all similar in color, size, and shape. It was like walking the same street over and over again. But as soon as I reached the big old oak tree on the corner, I knew I was close.

Katy didn't live in a bungalow like me. She lived in a symmetrical, three-story residence, constructed of maroon colored bricks and chipping white shutters. This place was basically my second home. The thick patches of ivy and the dust-covered porch chairs just made it even more homey.

It was near sunset when I knocked on the door and was greeted by Katy's mom. Mrs. Marsh was always wearing her painting apron, which was covered in splotches of every single color. The entire living room to the right of the front door was filled with her impeccable artwork. But I didn't have the patience to observe and compliment right now.

I found Katy upstairs, bending over her toes and applying a fresh layer of blue nail polish. She glanced up at me and concern pinched her doll-like face. "Gail, what's going on?"

I sat down in her fuzzy desk chair, which was like a therapy seat for me, and tried to calm my breathing. The thought of my parents' argument sent my heart into overdrive, and I looked around nervously at Katy's lilac-colored walls.

"I'm not your mom, bro. You can talk to me," she said after a moment, sensing my hesitation.

The comment nearly made me burst into tears.

I had to resist the urge to spit my words. "My mom broke my grandma's vase."

Katy gasped "Wait...Granny Silvia's vase?"

My friend had been in my life long enough to know which heirlooms were most important to my family. I nodded.

"No offense, but your mom's kind of a bitch."

"Yes, and the sky is also blue."

Katy frowned and sealed up her vial of nail polish.

"I don't know," I said after a few minutes. "We used to be one big happy family, but everything changed when I got to high school. It's like...I want to hate my mom, and I *do*...but it's hard when I have all these happy memories of her." I stared down at the fluffy carpet beneath my feet. "She's just someone I don't know anymore."

Katy was quiet for a moment, contemplating my words. "She *has* changed, I'll give you that. But it's not your fault. People fall in and out of love all the time, Gail. It's not anything you can control, it just...happens."

"They're going to get a divorce."

My statement hung in the air, and after a few moments of deafening silence, Katy said, "It's probably for the best."

I knew she was right. Mom and Dad's relationship had turned toxic over the years. It was far better to leave than stay and add fuel to the fire. But then...why did that hurt so much to consider?

I pressed my clammy hands together and tried to focus on the orange and gold trees outside the window. I didn't know why my heart was beating so fast, but each thump was like a punch to my ribcage. Panic whirled through my chest, and I felt lightheaded.

"You'll be okay, Gail, I promise," Katy said, fiddling with a nail file. "Everything will turn out fine."

My phone buzzed in my pocket. I pulled it out and stared blankly at the screen.

```
Hey Abigail, it's Colton. Sorry to
bother you but I'm at the store getting
supplies for the project now. What do
you think we should get?
```

I blinked at the message, and as I read it over a few times, my shallow breathing returned to normal. The broken vase and my parents' argument miraculously faded into the background.

"Who's that?" Katy wanted to know.

An unexpected grin split my face in half, and I shook my head. "You'll never guess."

Katy was shocked when I revealed my connection to Colton. And being the nosy, curious friend she was, she didn't let the subject drop for months.

Thankfully, Colton and I had received As on our research presentations, and in the meantime, I'd been talking to him a lot more. He had a sort of dry humor that made me giggle uncontrollably, which felt good in the midst of so much family drama. As the year passed, Colton and I grew even closer as we raved about music, made fun of teachers outside of class, compared our grades, and fantasized about summer vacation. And when summer finally did roll around, we continued to text and Snapchat even as we went about our own lives. Needless to say, by the start of sophomore year, we'd become best friends. And it drew the attention of our entire grade.

"Are you and Colton dating?" Matt Lastin asked me one afternoon in algebra class. I felt half the class lean in to hear my response.

"No," I laughed, but I knew I was blushing, and I knew they wouldn't believe my answer.

I couldn't hide the truth from myself; Colton had definitely grown on me. He made the drama with my parents dissolve like a dream. But Colton and I didn't talk about our home lives very much anyway. Music was an ever-present topic of conversation, but now we also discussed my violin and Colton's part on the school's volleyball team. He told me that he was always happiest in the moments that his team scored.

I liked listening to him talk. His smooth voice wrapped around me like a warm blanket on a frigid winter day. It was an expressive cadence, one that grew louder and faster every time we got on the subject of something he was passionate about.

He was unbelievably polite, too, always asking how I was doing and listening to me speak just as intently as I did for him. It dawned on me that this boy I knew now was nowhere near the shallow jerk I'd once imagined him to be. *Thank God.*

It was through all of this that no one, not even Katy, was

surprised when Colton asked me to hang out one weekend in December.

"Christmas lights?" I asked as we walked down the hall after eighth period.

Colton flashed me a grin that I was getting to know quite well. "They always put lights up at Yaddo Gardens around the holidays. I haven't been there in a while, but...I thought maybe you'd want to go this year."

"Of course! I'd love to go!"

The way his smile widened did funny things to my heart.

"If you want," he continued as we stopped outside my German classroom, "we could go to the Brook Tavern afterwards."

It was one of my favorite restaurants to go to as a kid. My parents used to take me there almost every Friday night; it was our family hangout. But given my recent home situation, I was more than eager to make new memories there. Especially with Colton.

"I love that place!"

Always unwilling to part, we hovered outside the room until Frau Hartlin called me inside.

As I sat down next to Katy, she gave me a quizzical look.

"What?" I asked.

"Why don't the two of you just date already?"

I blushed again.

The night I accompanied Colton to Yaddo Gardens was also the night I met his mother. The resemblance was uncanny. She had her honey-colored hair wound up into a tight bun, and her eyes were the same emerald shade as Colton's.

"It is *so* nice to meet you." Mrs. Reeves beamed at me as we climbed out of her Jeep. "My son's been going on and on about you for weeks!"

"Oh my gosh, Mom." Colton shoved his hands into his pockets and looked away.

I just smiled politely. "It's great to meet you, too, Mrs. Reeves."

"Oh, honey, please," she said. "Call me Sandy."

Colton waved at her and then motioned me toward the gates.

"Sorry about that," he said breathlessly. "My mom can be a little forward sometimes."

"What're you talking about? She's great," I assured him.

"I guess," he said, stifling a laugh.

I froze in my tracks as I spotted the top of a massive Christmas tree just beyond the gate. It must've been at least ten feet tall with shining red bulbs hanging off nearly every branch. A giant sleigh hung on the top of the gate, and a robot Santa waved at us as his reindeer twinkled.

"Whoa." My breath created a cloud of smoke.

Colton nodded. "Oh, just wait. That's not even the half of it."

He guided me through the gate, and we went around the colossal Christmas tree to a lookout point. My jaw dropped to the ground. Marble walkways were lined with dancing lights that were intricately woven through bushes. Candy canes glowed from treetops, signs for cocoa glimmered in the distance, Christmas trees of every color dotted the lawns. Wired outlines of reindeers flashed on repeat, giving off the illusion that they were leaping through the air. I couldn't even move. I was frozen in awe.

Colton grinned at my expression. "Come on."

Bundled tight in our coats, Colton and I navigated the maze of beauty. We took pictures beside the Christmas trees and stared wide-eyed at the lights and tinsel that were woven down light posts and tree trunks. Every time I spotted mistletoe, my heart did a cartwheel.

Sharing these moments with Colton was like freefalling from an airplane. All of my worries were gone, nonexistent. I felt like

I was floating. I knew the moment we walked past the shimmering fountain and he suddenly took my hand that I truly did care about him. It was more than a crush now, and the realization overwhelmed me with joy.

By the time Sandy came back to pick us up, I was blowing on my hands to keep them warm.

Colton chuckled as we climbed into the backseat. "Your nose is pink."

"Your whole face is pink," I retorted with a laugh.

"Touché."

It was a quick drive to the Brook Tavern, and Sandy helped the time go faster by inquiring about my taste in the violin.

"I actually haven't practiced in a while," I admitted somewhat sheepishly.

Colton theatrically pressed a hand to his heart and pretended to faint. "Oh, the horror!"

It felt so good to laugh.

"Text me when you're finished," Sandy told her son when she let us out at the restaurant's doors. "And hey." She wagged a finger through her open car window. "Be a gentleman." There was an authoritative ring to her voice.

"Always am." Colton gave her a reassuring wink.

He then spun on his heel and held the door open for me.

A blast of memories hit me the second I entered the tavern. My eyes flicked to the tiny table in the back, the place we always used to sit as a family. Something heavy materialized in the pit of my stomach, and I drew in a deep breath. Colton offered me a soft, sweet smile, which instantly boosted my mood.

"Two please," he told the hostess.

She appraised both of us, and a wide smile appeared on her face. It was a look that screamed, *Awww*.

"How old are you guys?" she asked as we sat down in a booth.

"Fifteen," Colton and I answered in unison.

I couldn't believe the strength of her curiosity. We were just two close friends getting dinner together. It wasn't any of her business.

When she finally left to grab our waters, I took off my coat. It felt strange being here without my parents, but I was also overtaken by a sudden giddiness. Colton's hair was slightly windswept, but it made him look even more handsome. We didn't speak for a few minutes as we looked at the menu, but with each passing second, my heart squealed louder.

"The burgers here are *so* good," he commented.

"I was thinking of getting the spicy buffalo shrimp celery," I replied matter-of-factly.

He looked up at me. "You like spicy stuff?"

"I was kidding," I clarified.

"Oh." The skin around his eyes crinkled when he smiled.

"Do *you* like spicy stuff?" I inquired.

"Nah. I like sour things."

I made a mental note of this information. Any new fact about him always made me want more. It was like binge watching an amazing TV show—I was entirely invested in whatever he had to say.

An older couple entered the restaurant and sat down at the table that always used to be my family's.

I didn't realize I was frowning until Colton said, "Hey, are you okay?"

Family talk wasn't something I liked, but I decided Colton should know, given how close we'd gotten.

"My parents are...in a bad place right now. Or...they have been for a long time. My mom just constantly harasses my dad. Like verbally harasses him." I watched my hands as I spoke. "They've been fighting for a long time now. Maybe two years, but um...I used to come here a lot with them when I was younger. When they were happier."

Colton was quiet for a moment. "My parents have been

divorced since I was in elementary school. My dad's an alcoholic and suffers from PTSD."

"Oh my God. I'm sorry."

Colton shrugged. "He was physically abused by his dad when he was young, like really bad. And he never got over it. That's why I never knew my grandpa. He destroyed my dad's life."

I smacked a hand to my forehead and apologized for even mentioning our parents.

"It's all right. My mom kicked my dad out when I was nine. But stuff like this happens, I guess. It's out of our control."

Either because I was overdue for a vent session or because Colton was the best listener I knew, the words suddenly poured out of me like a waterfall. "I just feel like I'm *part* of the reason. My parents never used to fight. You know, maybe if I...talked to them a little more—"

"Abigail," Colton whispered, his gold-green eyes boring into mine, "that is *not* your fault. Your parents have their own issues that have to be worked out, but I *guarantee* you are not one of them!"

"But I feel *guilty* for always running off, not stepping up. I—I start to shake, and my stomach gets into knots—"

"That's anxiety," Colton answered in a softer tone. "It's normal. You're experiencing the tension, too. That's nothing to be ashamed about. Trust me, I felt the same way! When I found my dad drunk and passed out on the kitchen floor, I almost lost it. He always made my mom cry because she didn't know how to help him through his episodes or how to get him to quit drinking.

"I would lock myself in my bedroom for the rest of the night because I couldn't handle what was going on. That doesn't mean their loss of love was my fault though. It just means my dad had issues that my mom couldn't resolve."

I wanted to rebuttal, but the way his lips set into a straight line told me the point wasn't worth arguing.

"Gail, you have so much going for you. You're so talented and *kind*. And loving. How could anybody ever hate you?" His eyes dropped to my hands, which were resting on the table.

Slowly, he reached out and took one of my hands in his own. I felt butterflies fill my stomach, and I almost couldn't look into his eyes.

"You are...probably the most amazing girl I've ever *met*," he continued. There was a flash of color in his cheeks. "I find it funny how...we've been in school together all these years, and yet, we're just now connecting."

"We got lucky," I murmured.

He chuckled. "But I'm so glad that I know you now. And...I want to be with you."

The soft trill in his voice made the butterflies take flight.

"Gail, will you be my girlfriend?"

I found it adorable that even though he was showing that sweet smile, the nervousness was still distinguishable in his eyes. I found it so adorable I almost cried out.

"Yes," I breathed. "Yes!"

He exhaled and squeezed my hand.

Colton and I sat in that booth, talking for what felt like an eternity. Our food came and disappeared into our bellies, but I didn't remember eating. I just recalled laughing and gazing into those gorgeous eyes.

When Sandy dropped me off at home, I wished her a good night and said goodbye to Colton. Then I scampered into the garage and resisted the urge to scream out gleefully. But the euphoria didn't last long because Mom's car was missing from its place next to my father's.

I found Dad in the living room with his nose in a book. It was a thick book, entitled *God—the Giver of All*. I felt sick when I saw the look on his face.

"Hi," he muttered. "You should know that your mother and I have officially filed for divorce."

Chapter Three

MARCH, 2081

G randma!"
　　Abigail glanced up just in time to see her three grand-kids barreling toward her before they enveloped her in a bear hug. Abigail squeezed them tightly.

"Geez, I didn't know college students still knew how to hug their grandparents."

"We wanted to stop by and surprise you," Andrea said, flicking her white-blonde hair over her shoulder.

It always amazed Abigail how much Andrea and her sister Trinity looked alike. They were identical twins — perfect clones of each other. The only way Abigail could tell them apart was by the way they dressed. Andrea favored skirts and fancy dresses over the athletic shorts and T-shirts that Trinity wore. But if they *both* decided to dress up, forget about it. Abigail would mix them up all day.

"We come home for spring break, and we can't even tear you away from your writing." Her grandson Kota sighed. "Seriously,

Grandma, what're you doing in here? It's sixty-eight degrees and gorgeous outside!"

"I thought you kids would be at the beach partying with your friends."

"We were," Trinity laughed, "but after a week, we decided to come home."

"Whatcha writin'?" Andrea leaned over the couch to look at the paper in Abigail's hand. "Divorce? Who's getting divorced?!"

"Buzz off, kid!" Abigail hissed, turning the paper over so her grandchildren couldn't read anymore.

"Who's getting a divorce, Grandma?" Kota pressed.

"No one, relax."

"Then what is that you're writing?"

"Geez, you'd think college would've mellowed you kids out, but you're just as hyper as you were when you were little," Abigail huffed.

"Some things never change." Kota flopped down on the couch beside her.

The girls followed, and soon, they were all squished together on the cushions.

"Do your parents know you're here?"

"Yeah," Trinity said. "We told them we were coming home yesterday."

Abigail laughed. These kids were the three musketeers of the family — cousins and best friends for life. They did everything together, apparently even spring break.

"So come on, spill," Andrea insisted. "Why're you writing about a divorce?"

There was no controlling the three musketeers once they wanted to know something.

"It was my parents," Abigail murmured. "Your great-great grandparents."

Trinity pulled her legs to her chest. "What about them?"

"They got divorced when I was fifteen."

"Ooh, who broke up with who?" Kota asked, and Andrea smacked his arm.

"It wasn't that simple," Abigail said with a tiny chuckle. Sure, it was easy to laugh about now, but back in the day, it had ruined her life.

"You don't seem so upset about it now," Trinity said, as if reading her Grandma's mind. "Besides, you never really talk about your parents. What were they like?"

"They were..." Abigail trailed off when she thought about what she had just written. Even now, fifty-four years later, it was still hard to put into words. She'd had such a hard time navigating that divorce. "Well, if you really want to know, you'll just have to read this when I'm done."

"What even is it?" Andrea asked.

"A story," her grandmother answered. "A story about love, loss, family, and friendship."

Three pairs of eyes gave her blank stares.

"So, are you actually writing a romance book?" Kota asked distastefully.

Abigail sighed impatiently. "One day, you'll see."

Silence followed, and it was obvious she'd lost her grandkids' attention. Damn this new generation with their goldfish-like attention span.

"I made cookies yesterday," Abigail said then. "They're in a tin can in the pantry. Help yourself."

"Aw, *yes!*"

All three kids shot off the couch and sprinted for the kitchen. Abigail couldn't help but laugh as she watched them. They were so young—only juniors in college; they didn't understand how much of the glorious world was still ahead of them.

Abigail took a swig of orange juice, listening to her grandchildren laugh and carry on. Then she set her pencil tip back on the piece of paper and continued to write.

Chapter Four

SARATOGA SPRINGS, NY (2017)

Separation is an odd thing, even if you are not the one in the relationship. It's strange to see two people who used to be so in love suddenly glaring into each other's souls.

In the coming weeks, my parents' divorce was finalized. The sight of Mom's moving boxes cluttering the living room made me shrink three sizes. This wouldn't be *our* house anymore; it would either be Mom *or* Dad's house. Except Mom didn't tell me where she was going. She just continued to strip our home of her belongings and seal them away.

By the first week of January, she was gone. Something inside of me died when her Subaru disappeared around the corner, and the house immediately felt emptier. I tried not to think about the open seat at the table or the gaping hole on the couch between me and Dad. And I really tried not to think about all the times my mother used to smile at me when I was younger. Wherever she was, she wasn't *that* person anymore. I was just clinging to a ghost.

The only person that kept me even remotely grounded was

Colton. His charming grin was medicine. And when I cried—as I often did when the good memories of my mother resurfaced— he'd gather me into his arms.

"It's gonna be okay," he'd whisper. And because it was him who said it, my brain automatically believed it.

After a few months with Colton, the pain numbed to a dull ache. Dad was getting better, too. He was talking more, laughing more. We shoveled the snow-covered sidewalks together and watched countless movies and NFL games. He sat front-row at every single one of my violin recitals and always bought me a cake pop from Starbucks afterward. Little by little, we crept toward acceptance together. And though he wasn't exactly thrilled that his little girl was seeing a boy, he welcomed Colton into the house anyway.

Somehow, some way, winter ended. I was feeling a lot better when I took my finals in June. The only thing on my mind now was a summer romance. Even after six months, my heart still stuttered for Colton.

As the bell rang on the last day of school, I caught up with Katy at her locker. Colton was busy with his volleyball team, so I'd made plans to go out for a celebratory feast with my best friend.

"Let's have a bonfire," she suggested, slamming her locker door shut.

"A bonfire?"

"You know, to burn all our notes." She wasn't joking in the slightest.

I laughed. "We might need some of that stuff next year too, in case we forget. It's a good reference—"

"What happens during sophomore year stays in sophomore year!" she exclaimed. "I couldn't care less anyway. Let's get out here!"

She drove us to a Chick-Fil-A with the windows rolled down, allowing the summer breeze to play with our hair. I only had my driver's permit and was supposed to get my license this coming December, but it was a plus to be friends with one of the oldest people in our grade. Katy was one of the few who'd gotten their license early, like Colton who was supposed to get his next month.

"So," Katy began, turning down the volume of the radio, "summer love, huh?"

I grinned. "Mhm."

"Have you guys done it yet?"

I whipped my head to look at her. "No, Katy! Of course not!"

She laughed. "You act like it's a bad thing. But you guys have been together for a long time now, and sooner or later...if he hasn't already, he's going to start dropping hints."

I swallowed loudly. "What kind of hints?"

Katy grinned, loosened her hold on the steering wheel, and adopted the intelligent tone of a psychologist. "Well, when a boy wants to move to second base, you'll start to notice some things. And—wait...you've kissed, right?"

"Yeah."

I recalled my first kiss with Colton. The cold starry night, the movie playing in the background. How his phone lit up with a text message from his mother, saying she'd arrived to pick him up, and the way he'd pulled me into his lap and pressed his warm lips to mine. A swirling sensation filled my chest, and I forced myself to refocus on Katy.

She pursed her lips indignantly. "Okay, I'm just gonna ignore the fact that you didn't tell me about that. But have you guys made out?"

"Uh...no." Not that I didn't want to. "He's sixteen now, and I'm still fifteen, Katy. We're moving slow."

"And there's nothing wrong with that." Her voice held the sound of a Cheshire Cat grin. "But like I said, the hints are going to start dropping. If he...looks at your lips while you talk. If you catch him checking you out. If you've hugged, and you can feel his—"

"Okay!" I shouted, instantly uncomfortable. "I get it. Thank you for the insight." A nervous laugh escaped my lips. "How do you know all of this?"

She looked at me like I was crazy. "Earth to Gail. *Everyone* knows this stuff. Where've you been?"

I rolled my eyes. So what if I was a little out of the loop when it came to sensual innuendos?

Katy just laughed. "Don't worry, bro, that summer romance of yours is gonna really heat up. I guarantee it."

And like usual, she wasn't wrong.

My favorite nights were the nights I spent by the crackling fire with Colton. He had a pit in his backyard, and Sandy always had fresh marshmallows for s'mores. One night at the end of June, we sat on blankets in the yard with a roaring fire to gaze into. My head rested on Colton's shoulder, and his arms were wrapped around me like the walls of a castle. As we stared into the withering orange flames, the cicadas sang a lullaby in the trees.

"I think it's official," he murmured.

"What?"

"You're making this the best summer ever."

His words spread through me like a wildfire, even hotter than the actual flames in front of us. I sat up to look at him, my breath catching at the site of his glowing gold-green eyes. For a few moments, that was all I could do—just stare.

"I feel the same," I said eventually. "Never in a million years did I think I would be sitting here with Colton Reeves." I scooted closer to him. "But I wouldn't want to be anywhere else."

His eyes touched mine, traveled over my cheeks, down the length of my nose, and stopped on my lips. When the fire spewed a shower of orange sparks, so did my heart. Colton leaned into me. This kiss was different from the past ones. The way his lips molded themselves to mine, I felt my walls weaken, and just like magic, I melted into him. His hands found their way into my hair, and my heart was beating so fast it might have exploded. Before I knew it, my back was pressed to the blanket, and Colton was on top of me. Apart from the dizziness that was clouding my head, I didn't want it to end. I'd never wanted Colton so close, but I found that I wanted him even closer than this. When his lips touched my neck, the fire in my body gave me goosebumps.

A small bit of embarrassment pinched my stomach. Whatever we were doing—it was entirely foreign to me. I didn't know what to do or what to expect. But my love for Colton outweighed my hesitancy, and I kissed him back fiercely.

When the sliding glass door squeaked open, Colton slid off me so fast it made my head spin. I sat up, a little lightheaded, and tried to look normal despite the erratic thumping of my heart.

"Here's the stuff for s'mores," Sandy announced, setting a tray of goodies on a tree stump. "Skewers are in the garage. Help yourself."

She gave me a gleaming smile before returning to the house.

Neither of us spoke for a moment. We couldn't even look each other in the eye. In the back of my mind, I questioned what had just happened. But even though I couldn't think of an answer, my body asked for a second round.

"Do you think she...saw?" I wondered out loud. My voice was cringingly high-pitched.

Colton shook his head. "She would've said something."

I risked a glance at him and found him staring at me already. Not even a second passed before we were howling with laughter.

"I'll be right back, love," he said as he rose to retrieve the skewers.

Before going, he kissed me again. It was a gentle kiss this time though, as if he was afraid to let it escalate and risk getting caught once more.

I was busy during July. In addition to my many hours of private violin lessons, I had also gotten a small job at my father's medical clinic. Organizing papers, mopping floors, and showing patients around wasn't exactly my idea of a thrilling summer. But the days seemed to pass quickly because as soon as my shifts were over, I spent the rest of the evening curled up close to Colton.

Every moment spent with him was like running on a sugar high. When he laughed, I laughed. When I smiled, he smiled. We moved like one being, always intertwined—hand-in-hand or with linked arms. Lost in an alternate, happier universe.

On the days I had off work, we went for bike rides and ice cream runs. We spent hours passing a volleyball back and forth, and I even agreed to accompany him on a jog around the neighborhood even though I came back smelly and drenched in sweat and probably totally unattractive. Some days, he begged me to play my violin for him, which I gladly did. He would sit and listen, seeming so lost in the melodies my instrument made. But when the sun went down, we became entirely different people.

His basement was our private universe. I found myself under him almost every night, sighing as his lips teased my neck. And here I was, kissing him back, like my body automatically knew what to do even though I'd never made out with anyone before Colton. I liked the thought of his and my body getting acquainted. I liked the thought of Colton's body, period. And I was getting addicted to the stirring sensation in my chest. Our clothes stayed on, only because his mother was right upstairs. But we promised each other that one day, we would take them off and take things further.

I was fantasizing about what that might be like one afternoon as I was labeling files at the clinic. Dad came around the corner with his white lab coat swishing behind him.

"I feel so bad for that poor kid. He had to get a few shots."

I'd heard a toddler crying a few minutes ago, but my mind was so preoccupied with Colton that I barely registered it.

Dad sighed and pressed his palms against the countertop. "Looks like you're almost done."

I capped the Sharpie and eyed the leftover files that still needed labeling.

"How about we go to dinner tonight? Six o'clock. You can pick the place."

My jaw set on edge. I didn't want to go out to dinner with my father. I wanted to spend the evening binge-watching old movies and making out with my boyfriend. But as that realization struck me, shame effloresced in my chest. I used to love going out to dinner with my father, even when Colton and I first started talking. So I decided to go with Dad after all. What was a few hours away from Colton? I could handle it. I just had to ignore the empty, aching feeling in my torso.

The rest of July sped by as if it all happened in the span of one day. August was no different. I was sad to see summer leave because junior year was shaping up to be pretty crappy. I didn't get first chair of the orchestra; no amount of practicing could have compared me to Kasey Green's unbelievable talent with the violin. But Colton wasn't in any of my classes either. The only time I got to see him was during lunch, and the distance killed me.

"You two could use some time apart," Katy commented one day in history. "You've literally been attached at the hip since summer started."

I bit my lip. "Is that a bad thing?"

"Well, I'm glad your romance is still alive and well, but I haven't seen you in ages, so yes!"

"I'm sorry, Katy," I replied. And it was the truth.

When someone else spoke on the matter, it was easy to see that I had been spending too much time with Colton lately. The thought set me on edge, and I suddenly felt obligated to change something. I didn't feel comfortable neglecting Katy, so something had to be done. But as I considered this, that aching sensation hollowed my chest again. What was it? Withdrawal?

I was nervous as I waited for Colton after the last bell. He'd promised to meet me in the lobby before going to work out with his friends. I stood in the swarm of students, contemplating all the ways this discussion could roll out.

"Hey, gorgeous," he said once I spotted him. He flashed that sweet smile I loved so much.

Already, my confidence was dwindling. I waited until the lobby cleared a little to broach the subject. "So, I've been thinking recently. Today at lunch, I realized I haven't seen Katy in forever."

Colton dropped his gym bag into a nearby chair, and the remainder of a smile was still lingering on his face.

"I think...I think you and I are spending too much time together."

The smile vanished.

I watched him as he glanced at a group of soccer players heading for the west end doors, and I tried to make sense of his expression. But his face was unreadable. It felt like a stone was dropping through my stomach.

"Okay," he said after a few minutes. "Maybe you're right."

An awkward tension filled the air between us, and I didn't like it.

"So, what do you want to do then?" Colton asked. Even though his face was composed, his somber tone betrayed him.

I had to resist the strong urge to hug him, to comfort him, even though I was the one who brought it up.

I tried to keep my voice positive when I spoke. "We should

make time for our friends, too. I mean...come on, when was the
last time you saw Ashton?"

"Two hours ago in eighth period."

"Seriously."

"I don't know."

My eyes dropped to the patterned tile of the floor. "Exactly.
We should just try to make time for our friends, too. Nothing
wrong with that."

When I felt Colton's hand wrap around mine, I knew the
conversation was over.

"I love you. You know that right?" he said.

The words still made my heart skip several beats. "Of course,
I do. I love you, too."

Unfortunately, our resolution lasted about a week and a half. It
was football season, and Colton and I attended every game
together, laughing and cheering for our team. It was like we'd
completely forgotten our plan, but a small selfish part of me was
okay with that. Katy and I saw enough of each other in school,
but Colton and I only had these sweet, cherished moments on
the weekends. I couldn't give them up.

Here, in the midst of the roaring student section at the football game, Colton was the only person I was aware of. No one
else existed. When he wasn't shouting at our team to pull up
their defense, he was whispering into my ear and making me feel
beautiful. I had no idea I could feel so light on my feet.

In no time, the school was abuzz with details about
homecoming.

"Look at my dress!" Katy squealed the following week after
math class.

She shoved her phone in my face, and I glimpsed the shimmering two-piece gown that fell to her feet in a puddle of blue
ruffles.

"That's so pretty," I complimented.

"What about your dress?" she inquired, jumping all around me like a child.

"I don't have one."

She stopped bouncing, and I shrank back from her sharp gaze.

"Didn't Mr. Perfect ask you yet?" she demanded.

"I don't know if we're going," I admitted.

"Well, he better get a move on! The dance is in two weeks!"

I tried not to let her comments get to me. I would have been perfectly content skipping the dance just to see a movie with Colton instead, but...if I was being honest, a small part of me *did* want to dress up and dance with Colton.

That afternoon, Colton and I sat at the dining room table in my house with our homework cluttered all around us. After nearly twenty minutes of silence, the lead in Colton's mechanical pencil snapped, and he heaved a frustrated sigh.

"I hate school, did I ever mention that? I mean, who *cares* about the amount of protons that Nitrogen has!"

"Seven," I answered.

He gave me a pleading look, and I giggled. "What's wrong, Colt?"

He looked out the window, into the sheeting rain. The look on his face suggested something really was on his mind.

"I want to kiss you," he said, but his tone was so dismal, I took offense to it.

"What—"

"I mean...all I ever want to do is kiss you. So, I wonder how I'm going to be able to keep my hands off you next Saturday night."

I stared at him.

"Abigail, will you go to the homecoming dance with me?"

"Yes!" I threw my arms around his neck, knocking his chemistry binder right off the table.

He laughed against me, holding me tight to his chest.

"Still want that kiss?" I inquired with a grin.

His eyes suddenly widened, and he nodded. I giggled and leaned in, but my lips barely brushed his before my father entered the room.

"Everything okay in here?"

"Guess who's going to homecoming?" I declared in a sing-song voice.

My father tensed. "Ohhhh...congratulations." His tone wasn't as excited as I thought it would be.

Colton and I looked at each other.

"Dad, you know I'm going to need a nice—"

"Yeah, yeah. I got it. My wallet was doomed the day you were born."

My first homecoming was one of the best nights of my life. Dressed in a powdery purple dress, I posed on my porch for a few solo pictures. Dad held the camera in front of me, clicking away. Sandy and Colton stood off the side, watching. Colton especially couldn't take his eyes off me.

"Oh, Gail, sweetheart. You look absolutely gorgeous," Sandy gushed.

My hair was woven into two waterfall braids that connected in the back and cascaded into the rest of my hair, which had been curled into massive waves. After posing for several more pictures, Colton announced that if we didn't leave we would be late.

Just last week, he'd passed his drivers test and had taken possession of his mom's old Sedan. He held the passenger door open for me with a heartwarming smile.

"Have fun, kiddos," Sandy called as she climbed into her own Subaru.

Dad waved goodbye from the porch.

Inside the school, colorful lights were strobing to the beat of music. People from all grades crowded the dance floor, convulsing with the rhythm, but we turned several heads with our arrival. Though he would never admit it, Colton was a bit on the popular side, which meant affection was now being poured over *me*, too. We maneuvered our way through the mob of sweaty bodies and met up with our friends at one of the tables. Katy had come with Allister Brugan, a senior on the varsity basketball team. I still wondered how she'd managed to catch his eye. But as Allister pressed a tender kiss to Katy's temple, she gave me a mischievous wink, and I realized their relationship was more of a friends with benefits type. Typical.

At first, I was a little uncomfortable in this chaotic club-like scene, but Colton was a comforting force at my side. And when the DJ started a slow song, he practically swept me off my feet and led me to the dance floor.

"I'm literally incapable of dancing," I warned him.

He waved my comment away and smiled. "Good thing we just have to sway."

With his hands resting on my waist, we swayed along to the methodical sound of strings. In that moment, with our eyes locked on each other, the world seemed to fade away. The song played on—a gorgeous combination of cellos and violins—and as I danced with my love, the butterflies in my stomach dissolved.

Colton shook his head, almost like he was trying to clear it from a daze.

"Gail?"

I leaned closer to hear over the music.

"You are so beautiful. I love *every* part of you, you know that? I think I want to marry you someday."

My eyebrows shot upward. "What?"

"You're my entire world," he continued. "I don't know if I could ever live without you. I don't *want* to." Maybe it was just the dim lighting, but I swear I saw his eyes glisten with tears. "I want to love and protect you forever. If anything ever happened to you—"

"You really want to marry me?" I asked. My heart was drumming so loud it was starting to compete against the music.

He nodded and gazed at me with such strong affection that I wanted to melt into him entirely.

"I want to marry you, too," I whispered, and the truth of the statement scorched my bones.

Our foreheads touched as we considered such a blissful future. My love for him was so overwhelming. I felt it pulse beneath my organs, threatening to erupt inside me.

"I'm in love with you, Abigail Ferr. My heart is yours forever."

With that, he pressed his lips to mine. The chorus of the song played once more, and the speakers shook with a massive crescendo. Colton's lips moved with mine, dizzying both of us with a welcomed headrush. My heart cried out his name. My grip on his arms tightened. This was passion. This was pure. This was love.

For the rest of the night, I couldn't take my eyes off Colton. I wanted to be with him forever and never let go. He was my other half, and my love for him was limitless.

And I thought we could live forever in that small bubble of happiness. The world was ours; there was no way it would crumble under our feet. But I was wrong. Little did I know that with the coming spring, I would inspire him to make a decision that would change everything between us for good.

"I talked to your mother recently," Dad said one cold December afternoon as I drove us home from the DMV. I'd just passed my driver's test.

I glanced over at him, wide-eyed. "*What?*"

He nodded. "One thing that I've learned over the years is

that life's too short to hate people and hold grudges — even if they've hurt you."

"What did she say?"

"Not much," he admitted with a ghost of a smile. "But I just wished her well and told her I hoped she had a good Christmas." This news was shocking. A year and a half ago, my father would have cringed at the thought of ever talking to Mom again. But his growth was exceptional. And inspiring. I felt somewhat relieved to know that his hatred had dissolved. I almost entertained the thought of them getting back together and me finally having two parents again. But Dad's tone was perceptive. His relationship with my mother was in the past, where it belonged. I figured that if Dad had the strength to forgive Mom, I guess I could forgive her, too. After all, I had loved her once.

I decided to share this news with Colton that night after driving alone to my boyfriend's house for the first time.

"Wow," Colton said after I finished the story.

"I know! I mean, yeah, my parents weren't in a great place for the longest time, but...that's in the past. I'm ready to move on. I think I can finally let it all go."

Colton was quiet as he stared at the carpet. His kitten, Lulla, hopped up into his lap and he stroked her fur absentmindedly.

"What's wrong?" I asked softly.

He hesitated for a few seconds and then shrugged. "I've been thinking about my dad a lot recently, just about what happened all those years ago. And...I think I want to forgive him. Like you said, I — I'm ready to move past it. I'm sick of holding this grudge. He used to love me and take care of me for crying out loud. But his stupid alcohol addiction and PTSD just got the better of him."

I scooted closer to Colton on the couch and laid my head on his shoulder.

"Then forgive him."

Colton shifted his position, and Lulla jumped from his lap.

"But I haven't talked to him in years. I don't know...who he is now or—"

"Well, you never know unless you call him."

"What if he doesn't answer?" I'd never seen Colton so bewildered.

I had to collect my thoughts. "Then it's not your fault. He may still have issues that he needs to work out, but it'll be okay. And I'll be here with you."

I wrapped my arms around him and squeezed him tight. Colton rested his head on mine and sighed.

"You really think I should do this?"

I sat up straight and offered a firm salute. "Colton Reeves, I, Abigail Ferr, fully encourage you to reach out to your father in an attempt to make peace."

He laughed and pulled me to his chest again. "All Right, all right."

All week, I had to feed his confidence. He chickened out once twice on Tuesday and again on Wednesday, coming up with all of these illegitimate excuses.

"My mom will probably think I'm insane."

"For wanting to see your own father?"

Colton shrugged. "He did have his issues. During one of his episodes, Mom said he couldn't even talk. He was just mumbling and shaking from head to toe."

"He was harshly abused, Colt. That's what PTSD does to a person."

"I know that. I just hope he found the help he needed."

Colton inhaled through his nose, and I watched his body tense.

"You. Can. Do. This," I urged. "You're the man!"

Finally, that brought a smile to his face. "Okay, okay. You're right. I love you, thank you." He kissed me once and then touched his forehead to mine. "In the meantime, what should we do for New Years?"

. . .

Two weeks later, I had the displeasure of organizing the children's play area in my dad's clinic on a Friday night. An old Led Zeppelin song blasted through the speakers — one that I knew because of my father — and I got to work on picking up stray toys and books. The song was halfway over when my phone vibrated in my pocket with Colton's picture on the screen. I risked a glance at the control-freak receptionist who was technically my boss. Thankfully, she was occupied with a patient. I answered the phone and pinched it between my cheek and shoulder.

"Hey."

"I did it!" Colton exclaimed. "I talked to him!"

I dropped the book I was holding and shifted my phone to my other ear. "Yay! What happened?"

"He answered on like the third ring, and he sounded so happy to hear from me. Can you believe that?"

"I told you it would work out!"

"Yeah, he asked me about school and volleyball, and he even wants me to come visit sometime!"

"Are you?"

Colton paused for a moment. "Well, when I told my mom, she was proud of me for reaching out, but she said she doesn't want anything to do with Dad...which I guess I understand." I listened to him exhale. "But a part of me really misses him, so...I think I will go see him, yeah."

I fully supported his decision. After what happened with my mom, I believed he could find the same closure. So, when April rolled around, he made plans to go to his father's house for spring break. Thankfully, Mr. Reeves lived in Wilton, a small county that was only a thirteen-minute drive from Saratoga Springs.

The Wednesday before spring break, I invited Katy to come

watch one of Colton's volleyball games. We sat on the bleachers with the rest of our peers, watching our team take on their opponents.

"Why couldn't he play an outdoor sport?" Katy complained, fanning herself and sucking on a lollipop. "It's too hot in here."

"Relax," I murmured, patting her arm while not taking my eyes off the ball. "The game's almost over."

The score was tied with fifty seconds left, and I sat on the edge of my seat with my hands balled into fists. I gnawed on my lower lip and watched the action play out. Colton's friend Ashton dove to save the ball, and the crowd erupted. My eyes flickered between the ticking clock and the white jerseys that blurred in front of me. Colton's face was pinched in concentration. He was crouched low on the balls of his feet with his arms spread out. Even from here, I could see the sweat glisten on his brow. A member from the opposing team sent the ball soaring over the net, and quick as lightning, Colton jumped into the air and spiked the ball as hard as he could. It hit the ground with a resounding *crack*. We all leapt to our feet and screamed for Colton. Seconds later, he was swarmed by his team.

As soon as the gym cleared, I ran to Colton with Katy hot on my heels. Ignoring his sweat soaked jersey, I jumped into Colton's arms and congratulated him on the win.

"Stay there! Let me get a picture!" Sandy shouted. She raised her iPhone and snapped a dozen.

"Thanks for coming, love," Colton said and nodded over my shoulder. "What's up, Katy?"

"Hey, good job out there. That spike was sick."

"Thanks! I need to run home and take a quick shower, then I'm off to my dad's house."

"You'll have to tell me all about it," I said.

His smile stretched from cheek to cheek, which melted my heart, so I had to kiss him.

"Ew, no gym PDA! Especially when he's covered in sweat," Katy said, groaning.

Easter weekend passed quickly. My cousins flew in from Florida, and Dad finally got to hang out with his brothers and sister again after six months apart. As a family, we played endless card games and watched almost every NBA game that aired. I didn't hear much from Colton — just a few text messages every now and then. I figured he was hanging out with his father, rekindling their lost relationship.

However, when I got to school the following Tuesday, he wasn't there. Which was odd. Normally, if he wasn't going to be in school, he texted me bright and early to let me know. And he didn't miss class often — only if he was sick or traveling. But as far as I knew, none of that was happening since he was supposed to have gotten home on Sunday night.

"Have you seen Colton?" I asked Katy in math class.

"Nope. Why, is he ditching?"

"No!" I exclaimed and then bit my tongue.

No. He wouldn't ditch. That wasn't like him. But why wasn't he here then? Uneasiness sank through my chest.

"You don't think he's...hurt, do you?"

"Yeah, hi, little miss worries-too-much, the phones for you." She held her hand out to me, and I smacked it away.

This wasn't a time for jokes.

She sighed. "Bro, I'm sure he's fine. You can't stress yourself like this. It might give you pimples."

"He went to see his dad this weekend..." A thought occurred to me, and I gripped Katy's arm so hard she screeched. "What if his dad did something? He used to be an alcoholic, and—"

"Hold on! One, people are starting to stare, so please take a chill pill. Two, that's ridiculous. You said his dad was a changed man. Maybe Colton just ate some bad ham, was up all night puking it out, and is just sleeping the day off! Maybe that's why he hasn't texted you. *He's sleeping off the poisonous ham!*"

"Okay, okay!" I took a deep breath, willing my nerves to calm. "You're right, it's probably nothing."

But Colton wasn't in school the following day either. I checked my messages and my voicemails repeatedly every hour, but there was nothing from him. No assurance, no "I'm okay." Not a thing.

By the time the final bell rang, I couldn't take it anymore. I shut myself in my car and called Sandy. I was worried sick, out of my mind. I didn't know what to think.

"Hello?" she answered on the fourth ring.

"Miss Sandy," I nearly shouted into the phone.

"What's wrong, Gail? Are you okay?" I was confused by her tone. She sounded perfectly normal, like her usual cheery self.

"Uh...Colton hasn't been in school the last couple of days. I'm wondering if *he's* okay."

"Oh, yes. He's here. Poor thing hasn't been feeling well for days."

"What's wrong with him?"

"He says he's been having terrible migraines. Personally, I think it's from all the stress he gets from volleyball."

"But he had the entire spring break to rest."

She laughed. "Gail, my son doesn't stop playing just because it's spring break."

I held the phone against my ear, not knowing what to say. Sandy took advantage of the silence to reassure me.

"Don't worry, honey. He'll be back tomorrow. I hear there's a big math test or something, and I'm not letting him miss that."

I didn't remember thanking her or hanging up, but before I knew it, I was home.

The evening crawled by. Dad made spaghetti for dinner, but I hardly tasted it. I ignored his questions to see if I was okay because I wasn't okay. Something wasn't adding up, and I needed to see Colton as soon as possible.

By the next morning, I still didn't have any messages from him, which made my insides churn sickeningly. So, when I *finally* saw him in the hallway on my way to English, I pulled him away from his friends and shot daggers at him with my eyes.

"What?" he asked.

"*What?* First of all, you don't even tell me how your weekend went, but then you all of a sudden disappear off the face of the earth, and I don't hear from you."

He shrugged. "Sorry."

When he moved to walk away from me, my body turned ice cold in disbelief. I caught his arm and pulled him back to me, but to my surprise, he thrashed his hand free from my grip and glowered at me. He'd never acted like that before.

"Are you okay?"

He *looked* perfectly normal. Nothing seemed out of the ordinary. He was dressed in light-wash jeans and a faded old Nike T-shirt.

"I'm fine," he hissed, and without another word, he walked away.

I was so shocked, my mouth hung open as I stared after him. I watched as his friends clapped him on the back, and I watched when he winced ever so slightly.

For the rest of the day, I sat in my classes feeling numb. I was still shocked that he'd spoken to me that way, and for what? *What was going on?* By ninth period, my stomach was roiling so sharply, I considered ditching my final class to go vomit in the bathroom. Something didn't feel right. How dare he treat me like this after I encouraged him to make peace with his father?

As always, I waited for Colton at the end of the day. Biting my lip, I scanned the current of the student-body, freezing when my eyes landed on his face. But he didn't look happy; he seemed annoyed. I lifted my chin an inch higher as he approached.

"Hey," he said monotonously.

I stared into his eyes, feeling my own eyes narrow.

"Hey." It came out sharper than I intended.

When he didn't say anything else, I threw my hands up in frustration.

"*What* is your problem?" I demanded.

He shifted his backpack on his other shoulder, flinching as he did so, and my eyebrows furrowed.

"Nothing's wrong," he answered curtly.

We stood at the school gate. People were moving past us, too lost in their own conversations to notice the tension in the air.

"No, no, no. Something's definitely wrong with you. Since when do you act like you hate my guts?"

I didn't expect him to shrug, so when he did, I felt a knife twist in my heart.

Who was this boy I was speaking to? *Whoever* he was, he was wearing Colton's face as a mask. Adrenaline sparked through my veins, and I resisted the urge to scream at him. I felt the anger rising in my chest.

"Did I do something to piss you off?" I wondered, spitting the words like they were acid on my tongue.

Colton shook his head and turned to walk away, but I sprinted and butted in front of him just as he made it to his car.

"Stop walking away from me! What has gotten *into* you?" My voice was slightly pleading.

It felt like I was talking to a brick wall. His eyes were bottomless, emotionless, and they made me nervous.

"Just drop it, Gail," he warned, tossing his backpack into the passenger seat.

"Drop *what*? I don't even know what *it* is!"

He didn't answer me and walked around the tail end of his car to the driver's side. As he passed me, I peeked at his face. It was a look of disgust, of pure fury. I'd never seen him look like that before. It frightened me, and I suddenly found myself blinking back tears.

Before he could climb into the driver's seat, I reached out to stop him again. But I missed his arm and instead got a fistful of his T-shirt. When the material crinkled in my hand, I caught a glimpse of his back, and what I saw made me feel like I was punched right in the gut.

Swollen black and blue slashes streaked across his skin. Bruises flowered his entire back. I gasped at the sight, and Colton spun around to pull his shirt down.

There was no stopping the tears now. I pressed a quivering hand to my mouth. My eyes were wide, filming with tears. I knew I was shaking, but somehow, my body felt numb. Colton was seething now, his face florid with anger.

He roughly grabbed my arm and pulled me around the side of his car, away from any prying eyes. The force of his action scared me, and I swallowed a yelp.

"Gail," he said darkly.

I shook my head, trying to clear it. But the more I tried, the dizzier I got. Tears streamed down my cheeks. I trembled beneath Colton's harsh grip.

"Colton," I managed, swallowing the bile in my throat, "what happened to your back?"

I had a hunch, but I was hoping—*praying*—that I was wrong. When Colton hesitated, I squeezed my eyes shut and hung my head. My tears cascaded down to the asphalt.

"My dad happened," Colton said.

A million thoughts buzzed around my brain. "W-what? How?"

I didn't think it physically possible, but his eyes darkened even more. "Turns out a person with PTSD can get help and still have really bad episodes." He paused, swallowed, and blinked several times like he was trying to hold back tears. "Well he must've mistaken me for an enemy or something because...he-he grabbed his belt and..."

I hunched over and pressed my hands against my knees, ready to vomit right here, right now. Black spots dotted my vision; bile surged up my throat. I even convulsed a few times, but somehow, my stomach held back.

We had to tell Sandy. I had to tell my father. We had to call the cops, alert the school. But all of these very rational ideas took a back seat when an even worse realization struck me. It hit me straight through the heart—a fatal bullet wound.

"I—I'm so sorry that I said you should go," I sobbed.

I was choking on my own voice. The sound of it made me want to rip my ears off. How could I have let this happen? The guilt crashed down on my shoulders.

"He was screaming at me," Colton muttered in a strange, hollow tone. "He-he said...'If you ever tell anyone...I'll kill you.'"
He took a few deep breaths and glanced around like he was trying to get a bearing on his surroundings.

"Colton," I said, pressing a shaky hand to his cheek.

But at my touch, he backed away, almost like an abused animal who was kept in a cage. When his jaw unclenched and he seemed slightly more in control of his actions, he glanced over across the football field with shimmering eyes.

"You encouraged this," he whispered.

"No!" I answered quickly, stepping toward him. I shook my head fiercely. "No, Colton, I had no idea, I swear!"

"It doesn't matter now."

I was shaking so hard it must have looked like an earthquake was passing through me. "W—we have to call the cops. Tell y— your mom. I'll tell my—"

"I think you've done enough."

When I looked back at his face, it was emotionless again. It was cold. It was terrifying.

The reality of his words slowly sank in, and my heart stopped. "Wait...what are you saying?"

"I'm saying I can't do this right now, Gail."

A numbing buzz spread throughout my body like a poison. It stung, but my brain was slow to comprehend.

"Are you...breaking up with me?"

"Yes."

"No," I heard myself say. "No. Absolutely not."

"Yes."

"No! Not now! Not when you need me—"

"You are one of the reasons I'm in this mess!" he bellowed, stepping so close that our noses were inches apart. He towered over me, and for the first time ever, his height was frighteningly intimidating.

"Colton, please," I whispered. More tears spilled down my cheeks, and it felt as if my heart had snapped in two. "Please!"

His face held its callous expression. He shook his head and climbed into the driver's seat of his car. "Leave me alone."

He backed his car out of the space and drove past me without another look.

I didn't remember driving home. I wasn't even sure I got in my car. The only thing I was aware of was that my lungs were suddenly burning for oxygen. But I didn't take a breath.

Chapter Five

SARATOGA SPRINGS, NY (2019—2020)

I t was the worst summer of my life. Unfortunately, I didn't have the pleasure of numbness; I felt each emotion with stunning clarity. The anger, the confusion, the profound sadness, and the guilt. The crushing guilt.

I'd heard multiple news stories over the summer, updating the public about Mr. Reeves' trial. He was sentenced to one year in prison, which I didn't think was nearly enough time, but he pleaded mentally unstable. I always wondered how Sandy reacted when she found out. I also wondered *how* she found out, considering Colton was threatened for his life not to tell anyone.

Colton never texted or called me. Aside from the news stories, it was like he didn't exist anymore...and that destroyed me. I never slept. Instead, I stared up at the ceiling fan as my eyes continued to drown in tears. When I wasn't crying, my face was blank. I hardly ate either. It horrified my father, and eventually, he forced me onto over-the-counter medication for the depression. I took the pills willingly, praying that it would take this gut-wrenching pain away. But I still found myself wrapped up in bed, tortured by the thought of someone violently harming Colton—and his father at that.

More than anything, I just wanted to hold Colton in my arms so that we could fight off the demons together. I couldn't imagine the pain he must have been enduring. I wanted to kiss him and keep him captive in the space between my lips so that no one would ever hurt him again. But we were broken up now. There was nothing I could do.

Some days the pain was so dreadful, I wanted to die. I would sit in my room and stare at the wall as fresh tears stung my cheeks. I felt so ugly inside, so *worthless*. He had turned away from me, made me feel like I was powerless. Of course I knew that Colton was going through something far worse than a stupid little heart break. But I just couldn't ignore the pain that was rotting my soul.

I just kept wishing I would hear from him. Hear *anything*— even if it was some rude, unforgiving comment because even then, at least he was talking to me. But there was nothing. Pure silence. It was absolute torture. Some nights, I even came so close to texting him myself, but I couldn't do it. I was too afraid to face him. Instead, I would throw my phone across the room and curl up in a ball while the insufferable pain gnawed on what was left of my heart. Maybe that was what real torture was, loving someone so deeply and then receiving absolute silence.

One night in early August, as I was trudging back up the stairs after an untouched dinner, my father called me back into the kitchen. He stood by the fridge, crossing his arms, and I could tell by his expression that he was struggling to find the right words.

"I just wanted to let you know that Sandy called."

At the mention of her name, my heart lurched in my chest. "What did she say?"

"She said Colton's been going to physical therapy for weeks now, and well, he's going to be just fine."

The relief was dizzying. I spun on my heel, ready to race up the stairs to text him and congratulate him on his return to health. But I stopped dead in my tracks, and my torso twisted sharply. We were still broken up. Nothing had changed really.

Dad caught my realization and cleared his throat. "Listen, kiddo, first heartbreaks are tough. Trust me, I know. And to be honest, you never really forget your first love. I mean, I still remember mine and that was like, a hundred years ago."

I didn't laugh.

"Anyway, I'm always here if you need to talk. Just remember this though. That pain that you're feeling right now—you're not going to feel it forever. I *promise* you." I rolled my eyes. "I know! I *know* you think I'm insane for saying that. But you're going to be okay. Try to remember that, all right?"

"Mhm."

I escaped to my room before another wave of emotion could hit me.

My senior year was absolute hell. Colton wasn't even in school a lot of the time, and I chalked it up to the fact that he just wasn't ready to return to normal yet. But when he *was* here, his eyes wouldn't even drift in my direction. In fact, he seemed perfectly oblivious to my presence. And it infuriated me because *I* was still stuck on the sour aftertaste of his absence.

I also discovered that Katy wasn't the type of person to play therapist anymore. She only listened to my complaints when she felt generous enough to do so. And in the meantime, she found a new group of friends, slowly disappearing from my life until suddenly, I was all alone.

Life lost all of its color.

"Gail!" my father shouted one night while I was having a staring contest with the wall. "Delaney called and said you haven't been to your last two private violin lessons."

I knew he was waiting for an answer, so I gave half a shrug, not breaking eye contact with the wall.

"You need to keep at the violin! It's very good for you right now!"

I didn't see his point. Playing the violin reminded me of Colton, and I couldn't bear to have him in my head for more than five seconds though he never really left my thoughts anyway.

The year passed painstakingly slowly. Each day left me more mentally exhausted than the last. And in my depressing world of solitude, I was starting to lose my mind. I felt trapped in my own life, so out of loop with what was going on around me. As much as I wanted to open my heart and discuss the pain I was in, I was terrified the information would get back to Colon.

I came to the conclusion in late November that I was now afraid of Colton and his opinion. I couldn't bear to think that he might still despise me for what happened, and I was scared that if I let any true emotions show, he would take advantage of my vulnerability as a way of revenge. Plus, he just didn't need to deal with my spiraling emotions right now. He had his own trauma to work through.

What a strange thing, I pondered one cold Saturday afternoon as I gazed out the window into a light snowfall. *How strange it is to be afraid of someone you love.*

By Christmas, my father had had enough. He stomped up the stairs and entered my room with a gruff, determined expression. In his hand was my violin case that I'd stashed in the basement a long time ago. It still had a heart-shaped sticker on it, where I'd written Colton's name. The sight brought a fresh chill over my bones.

Setting the case beside my bed, Dad turned to me. "Remember that?" Judging by his tone, I could tell he wasn't in the mood for excuses.

"Uh-huh," I answered curtly.

My lack of emotion only seemed to make him angrier. "You're going to start playing again." He held a hand up when I started to protest. "I remember when this house used to be filled with that beautiful music of yours. Now it's gone. What happened to it, Gail?"

"It died with my interest."

"Wrong answer. It's just been *buried* with your interest. Sweetheart, you are so talented with the violin. Why not give it another go?"

"Dad, I just don't want to." This conversation was starting to make me anxious. I wiped my clammy palms on the blanket I was wrapped up in.

"Colton can't judge you now, Gail."

His name was a knife plunged deeply into my side.

"You're safe here! There's no one but you and your violin."

I stared at him and raised my eyebrows.

"I'll even leave," he added after a moment.

He moved toward the door, obviously happy with himself for what he'd done.

"You're wasting your time, Dad!" I called after him.

Love you, sweetheart!"

I made a face at the closed door and sighed. The room suddenly felt very empty without Dad here. Snuggling deeper into my blanket, my eyes landed on the violin case.

It was old and covered in dust, water stains, and memories. But they were happy memories...of my bow sailing smoothly from string to string, of the melodies flowing from the violin like blood through a maze of veins. The audience cheering for me, my father's smiling face visible from the stage. Colton praising me for my talent...

I moved closer to the case, suddenly overtaken with an urge to feel it in my hands again. Unlocking the latches, I realized that after trying so hard to forget such memories, I never truly wanted them gone.

Inside the case, my violin seemed to glow. Even with its faded maple color, finger marks, and rosin-covered strings, it was still beautiful. I grazed my fingers over its smooth dusty surface, marveling at the feeling.

Wariness crept through my brain. With all the time I'd spent mourning the loss of my relationship, I was suddenly worried that I had unintentionally flushed all of my talent down the drain. I hurried over to my bookshelf and chose one of the composition books my private instructor gave me. I flipped to an open page and found the sheet music for Leonard Cohen's "Hallelujah." It was one of my favorite pieces to play growing up, and I decided it was a perfect way to start again.

I took my time. Months in the cold basement had set the strings out of tune. Luckily though, matching the pitches in my mind was still as easy as breathing. I rosined my bow and then positioned myself so I could read the notes from my book.

Carefully, almost hesitantly, I began to play. An angelic alto melody poured into the room, swelling with each stroke of my bow. My fingers moved effortlessly over the fingerboard. A foreign feeling clutched my heart in a fist, and each time my fingers spoke hallelujah, I could feel the joy pulsing inside me, growing stronger than before.

I suddenly wasn't alone anymore. The music was a physical entity, singing to me in its sweet, soft voice. I even closed my eyes, finding that I knew the notes by heart. And for the remainder of the song, I allowed its gorgeous melody to carry me off to a sweeter place.

Music healed me. When I was playing the violin, I wasn't worrying myself sick over what Colton was thinking or enduring. I wasn't sitting in rage over the fact that Katy never talked to me anymore. When I was playing, I was healthy...happy.

I devoted myself to the orchestra then, playing every spare

moment I had. My instructor welcomed me back with open arms, and I even made first chair when I auditioned at the start of the second semester. The more I played, the more confidence I regained.

But as much as the violin helped me, the guilt was the hardest thing to shake. The music was like medicine now, but that seemed like a betrayal to Colton. I shouldn't have been moving on, I should've been down and depressed like I knew he probably was. I should've been advocating against physical abuse on social media and joining mental health clubs at school. But I wasn't because I also knew that it was far better to just step away from all of that for a little while, for my own well-being. Why did self-care all of a sudden feel incredibly selfish?

The very sight of Colton still made my heart quicken. In school, every time my eyes locked with his, I felt a swift jolt of energy, like a flickering light. I wanted to ask him so many questions. *How was he doing? Was he finding peace? Could he find peace after something as traumatic as parental abuse?* I would never know because his distant expression always warned me to keep my distance. So, the light would fizzle out, and we would go about our day, trying to ignore each other.

Luckily, I'd made some new friends in the orchestra — girls who were much nicer than Katy had ever been. We often hung out on weekends. The one girl, Erica Trevins, was easily the kindest person I'd ever met. Only a junior, she was already the head of the second violin section. And even though she was a year younger than me, her wise remarks and sensibility basically qualified her as a senior, too.

That winter, my dad got his wish. The house was filled with music once again. I practiced four to five hours a day and sometimes more. I just couldn't get enough of the beautiful cords on my lovely violin. Color was slowly bleeding into my life once more.

Dad was thrilled that I'd turned to music after all, and the only time he forced me away from my instrument was when he insisted that I visit a few more college campuses while I had time.

"I like the Curtis Institute of Music," I said one night at dinner.

Dad gave me a funny look. "But that's so far away."

I shrugged. Music had become the new love of my life, and I wanted to pursue it.

Dad sighed. "You're going to be some famous violinist one day, you know that? Remember me when you make it big."

"I do love the violin," I said, "but I think I might want to study music theory and be a conductor one day."

He nodded. "That would be easy for you since you're so driven, sweetheart. With your work ethic, you can do anything you put your mind to."

I auditioned at the Curtis Institute of Music in early February and was still awaiting a response. I checked the mail every day after school, but it wasn't until the end of April that I spotted a bright letter in the mailbox. When I read the stylish calligraphy, I was stunned.

Congratulations, Abigail Ferr! You have been accepted to attend the Curtis Institute of Music next fall!

I read it and reread it, hoping my eyes weren't playing tricks on me. When I was sure I wasn't hallucinating, I ran up the porch steps, screaming, "Dad! Dad, guess what!"

When I called Erica later to share the news, she didn't sound as enthused.

"What am I supposed to do without you?" she whined.

"I'll come visit all the time," I insisted through laughter.

And I vowed to myself that I would. Erica had gotten me

through some very tough times, and I wasn't quite ready to leave her behind. She was far too important to me.

"The real question is what am I going to do without *you?*" I asked.

"Good question. No one could ever replace me."

"True."

When May came around, there was only one thing people discussed in school: prom.

"I think I'm gonna get the green dress," Erica decided in orchestra. "It'll bring out my eyes."

"Definitely green," I agreed. "It'll accent the highlights in your hair, too."

"Right."

We packed up our cases and hung outside the door for a few minutes before the bell could dismiss us.

"I got that blue dress from the gown shop," I said.

Erica squealed. "You're going to look *so* gorgeous in that! Make sure you get those silver heels I sent you. Remember?"

She pulled out her phone to find the picture of a pair of sparkling silver stilettos. But her face suddenly drained of color.

"Erica?" I asked, alarmed.

Her eyes practically popped out of her head and a crease formed between her eyebrows. For a moment, I was worried she was going to be sick.

"What is it?" I demanded.

"Uh..." She shook her head, trying to find the words.

I couldn't stand the suspense any longer. I snatched the phone from her hand to see for myself, and my heart plummeted to my feet.

She had logged into Instagram and the first picture to pop up was of Colton...kissing someone else. The account belonged to

Destiny Raklin, another junior like Erica. In the photo, they were posing under a breathtaking sunset — Colton with his hand cupping Destiny's cheek, and Destiny with her hair frozen in some billowing wind. The caption read, *Wouldn't want to kiss anyone else.*

A blast of white hot fury rose in my chest, and I nearly crushed my friend's phone. My lungs seemed to close up. I desperately sucked down oxygen, but it burned. When the room started spinning, I stumbled to the bathroom across the hall, about ready to puke up my lunch.

Erica followed quickly behind me. She knew how much Colton had meant to me, thanks to all of our late-night talks over FaceTime. But now, I slammed the stall door in her face. It didn't occur to me that the gesture was rude; all I could feel was my anxiety finally surfacing after a long, dormant sleep. Squeezing my hands into fists, I threw my head back, gasping for air that wouldn't come. My body convulsed, trembling fiercely with each passing moment.

I hadn't even considered the fact that Colton was capable of loving someone else, especially with what he'd just recently been through. I always thought his heart was mine. But reality had to slap me in the face.

I clenched my jaw shut to hold back a scream. Tears dripped down my cheeks, quivering on their path.

Why, the little voice in the back of my head asked. *Why are you this upset over it?* It had been ten months since the breakup, and I had been doing so much better. Why did this one little thing send me spiraling again? What did it mean...and what did it say about my character?

"Gail?" Erica asked in a small voice.

I ignored her for a second, forcing air into my raw lungs and trying to block Destiny's face from my mind.

I wanted to yank her face away from Colton's. I felt myself seething with rage, and it frightened me. *Envy*, my conscience whispered. *It's just the jealousy. It'll pass.* But why was I even jealous to begin with? I thought I was over Colton.

"Gail, are you okay?" Erica asked louder this time.

I wasn't sure if I was. An overwhelming epiphany glimmered to life inside my brain. I sucked in a sharp breath. I was still in love with Colton Reeves; I'd simply been burying the feelings this whole time.

Erica kept me sane. On the days when my jealousy soared, she gave me healthy reality checks.

"Okay, but do you understand that Destiny doesn't even play a sport? She also didn't make it through the first round of student council elections. Oh, *and* I heard she sleeps around. So, stop thinking she's superior. She doesn't hold a candle to you, Gail, believe me."

"Then why does Colton like her?"

"If I had the answer to that, I'd be exposing his ass right now, not sitting here talking to you."

Erica even persuaded me to attend the prom, even though Colton and Destiny had definitely already gotten tickets.

On the night of the big event, it was downpouring.

"Ew!" Erica whined as she hauled up her long sequined skirt and tried to jump over a murky grey puddle on the concrete. "This *sucks!*"

I held my dress up, too, shivering in the thirty-three degree weather. I made a mental note to strangle the juniors who suggested prom be held on the football field under a semi-large party tent without first consulting a weather app. Erica and I stood in line with our tickets, feeling the moisture in the air ruin our curls.

"I swear, if they play 'Old Town Road' before we get in there, someone's gonna die tonight," Erica grunted.

The space heaters in the corners of the tents made no impact against the wind and rain. I trembled off to the side while more and more people crammed into the tent. My eyes flickered to every face, and I couldn't ignore the mounting hysteria boiling in my stomach. He was gonna be here soon.

Fortunately for Erica, "Old Town Road" was one of the first songs they played. She shot her arms up into the air and pulled me into the growing circle on the dance floor. Ella and Brie appeared in the chaos, and I pulled them in for a hug while we exchanged the usual, "Oh my gosh! You look so gorgeous!"

"Look here, ladies!" a photographer called, signaling for us to link arms.

I smiled as best I could. And then Colton walked through the entrance.

For a moment, the music died away and the faces around me became just a wash of blurred color. His black suit was striking, and the dark blue satin bow tie, of course, matched Destiny's dress. I caught her eye before I caught Colton's. She did a double-take and scrutinized my gorgeous poofy gown that belonged in a Disney museum. Then she rolled her eyes and pulled Colton along toward the photo booth. I dropped my eyes as he passed, but I could feel his presence like he walked right up to me and slapped me in the face.

The night went by surprisingly quickly, although the music was mediocre at best, and my dress was stepped on more times than I could count. I tried desperately to lose myself in the excitement and dance my heart away with Erica, but my eyes kept straying to the front of the tent where Colton and Destiny were laughing and looking utterly in love. Meanwhile, I wanted to die.

"If I don't get water soon, I'm gonna shrivel up," Erica called over the bass of Ariana Grande's "7 Rings."

I followed her through the crowd and took a cup of water for myself. Pink lights danced to the beat, and I watched the student body jump like one being and shout all the profanity that was bleeped out of the song. After Ariana sang her last line, "The Cupid Shuffle" blasted through the speakers. Immediately, the clump of students shuffled into several neat lines.

"Come on!" Erica screamed, towing me into one of the lines.

We did the basic dance however many times over, and I tried to scan the crowd for Colton. But he was suddenly nowhere to be found. I did a second look through as I kicked my feet four times, but still couldn't find him. It was only eight o'clock. We still had a whole other hour yet. Where had he gone?

We did the rest of the popular line dances—"The Cha Cha Slide" and "The Cotton Eye Joe"—and then came back together to pump our fists in the air in time with Post Malone and Swae Lee's "Sunflower." Colton and Destiny had simply disappeared.

By the time nine o'clock rolled around and the DJ played "Party in the USA," I had had enough. Deep in my heart, I knew that the reason I wasn't having fun anymore was because Colton wasn't here to watch me have a great time without him.

"Totally worth it," Erica said as we rushed through the rain to the parking lot.

I climbed into the passenger seat of her silver Sonata and gathered my enormous train into my lap. Erica threw her heels in the backseat and twisted her keys in the ignition.

"Did you see Colton and Destiny leave?" I asked as nonchalantly as I could.

Erica pulled out in front of a red Corolla and was rewarded with a honk. "No. Aren't they leaving now?"

"I think they left earlier." I squinted my eyes through the window to try to spot either of their cars. But again, they were nowhere to be found.

"They probably left to go have ugly sex," Erica admitted, craning her head left and right before pulling out onto the main road.

My heart stopped. "You think they have sex?"

"Do I think Destiny uses her body to brainwash Colton into

having sex? Yes, yes I do. I told you, Gail, that girl gets what she wants. Now, do you wanna go to the Midnight Diner for some milkshakes?"

I nodded and waited for my stomach to solidify. They say you never forget your senior prom, but I was gonna try real hard.

In school, Destiny clung to Colton like a cheap spray tan, whispering in his ear in a way that was almost scandalous. The rumors were the worst part though. People came to me with stories of Colton and Destiny skipping class together to go Juul in the parking lot. I'd also heard that she had gotten Colton into drinking and partying, which was extremely difficult to believe when I thought of Colton as the angel I used to know. But that was just it. He was a stranger now, and even though I'd never physically caught him doing these things, it was sad to admit that I wouldn't have been surprised if the rumors were true.

Destiny was also painfully aware of *my* existence. She gave me dirty looks in the hallway and muttered to her friends, and then they would glare at me as well.

Something seemed off though. Every time Destiny leaned into him, Colton's eyes would quickly touch mine and then flicker away. Having no other choice but to grin and bear it, I managed to bite my tongue and take the high road.

"She's a total rebound," Erica concluded one morning. "He's just using her to fill the void *you* gave him. Trust me, they won't last."

And she was right.

By June, their relationship turned to dust. Destiny didn't seem to be coping very well, pouting all over social media about "a certain someone." But one look at Colton suggested he was completely unaffected, maybe even relieved by his decision to end things. I wondered why that was.

He and I still never talked, but there was an unspoken war

raging between us. It seemed he was pleasant to everyone on the face of the earth except me. Sometimes, it made me angry, and I couldn't resist the urge to glare at him as we crossed paths in the hallways. But most times, I was left feeling mentally exhausted. I wanted to let this whole thing go. I wished it would blow away like the sweet spring breeze. The only time Colton truly left my mind was when I was playing my violin, and I did so with every available opportunity.

Graduation loomed over us like a limitless rainbow.

I couldn't seem to process the fact that I was days away from closing this chapter of my life. As close as it was now, I found that I wasn't ready to say goodbye to these people yet. Saying goodbye meant growing up.

Colton, of course, remained a question mark, but I figured it was better to let that be than force a halfhearted goodbye. Even Katy crossed my mind in the final days.

She had made a negative reputation for herself. Her clothes were now either too short or too tight—anything to attract the eyes of our male peers. And I heard that she'd gotten addicted to weed, which my mind couldn't fathom. Both she and Colton had become complete strangers. But Colton, on the other hand, was the one person my heart stubbornly refused to release.

On the morning of graduation, the sky was a cloudless sheet of blue. I woke up with an unusual energetic jitter. It was the end of an era, and my stomach was already filled with butterflies.

Seniors weren't required to attend the full day of school, so I went out with some other senior girls who were in the orchestra with me. We went to my house for a couple of hours to curl and braid and tease our hair, and then we spent the rest of the afternoon at a Starbucks downtown.

"I can't believe this is it!" Brie exclaimed, almost spilling her mocha frap in all her excitement.

"I know!" Ella replied. "High school went way too fast, but I'm glad we get to leave. Can't wait to get to Villanova and meet all those cute guys!"

I kept Brie and Ella around for comic relief when I couldn't talk to Erica. They were living normal teenage lives where the biggest issue was a broken nail. And I was going to miss them more than they could ever imagine.

After four o'clock, we all parted ways to spend our final hours as high school students with our families. Even though I was grateful for the sunshine, it had become unbearably hot outside.

"I'm literally gonna melt in my cap and gown," I complained as I darkened my lashes with more mascara.

My father scurried between his own bedroom and the mirror at the top of the stairs. He kept readjusting his tie, studying his appearance from every angle. "Join the club. At least you won't have to be crammed tight into the bleachers."

"Try sitting in the middle of two hundred other students," I quipped.

"Touché."

Applying one last layer of my favorite lip gloss, I exited the bathroom and stood before my father with my arms extended at my sides. "So? What do you think?"

I was wearing a white knee-length dress accompanied with matching heels, and I topped it all off with the glittering pearl jewelry I'd bought that afternoon with Ella and Brie.

My dad shook his head slightly and crinkled his nose. It was almost funny; I'd never seen him cry before. But before any actual tears could escape, he cleared his throat.

"You look beautiful, sweetheart. I can't believe my little angel is actually *graduating*! I remember the day you were born—"

"Oh geez." I rolled my eyes. "Not this spiel again."

"Dear Lord, please freeze this moment," he prayed, and I had to laugh.

Dad insisted that he drive me to the ceremony himself.

When he dropped me off at the door, I ran inside and was immediately caught in a sea of red and gold—our school colors. Bright red graduation gowns filled the hallway wall to wall. Everyone was shouting, laughing, crying. It was hard to take in.

I'd been going to school with these people since the first grade, and after today, I would probably never see them again. The thought almost made me tear up. Despite the drama, the extensive amount of work, and the tiring determination to make distinguished honor roll each marking period, I undoubtedly had some of the best times of my life in high school. After today, we would go our separate ways. After today, life would truly begin.

A sudden fear exploded in my chest. *Stop!* my conscience screamed. *I'm not ready to grow up!*

"Okay, students, please listen up!" the principal called over the dull roar of my peers. "We are about to head outside to the football stadium. Please arrange yourselves in alphabetical order by last name just like we rehearsed!"

I stood next to Jake Faren. He had been in my math class four years in a row. He turned to me, pushing his glasses up the bridge of his nose.

"I can't believe this is it," he exclaimed.

"Me either." My voice sounded an octave too high, and I wondered if I was more nervous or excited.

Jake's voice floated into my brain, but I suddenly couldn't hear him. I found Colton standing at the back of the line. It stunned me to see him in a cap and gown. To me, he would always be the sweet teenaged boy I'd grown to love. In a way, he was even still the whimsical boy from our youth. But he was all grown up now. A man who, personally, I still thought was roguishly handsome.

Our gowns made things feel too official, too final. I hated it.

For a split second, he caught my eye, and a rush of memories passed between us. The strength of our affection, the intensity of our connection, the destruction of our breakup—it all surged through me in that second. I wanted to run to him. I wanted to grab his hand, ditch these gowns, and run away. I wanted to stay young with him forever.

And then he looked away, and I was forced back to the present.

Unsurprisingly, the setting sun still cast a hot, orange glaze over the football field. Together, my peers and I marched down to our seats, trying to shield our eyes from the sun's rays. I briefly scanned the bleachers, looking for my father, but instead spotted Erica as she flapped her arms wildly and blew me a kiss.

"We are here today to celebrate the class of 2020 and their amazing achievements," the principal greeted the crowd.

After a few speeches from our teachers and both the valedictorian and salutatorian, they began to call names. I attempted to appear calm and collected, but really my body was abuzz with nerves. This was all happening so fast I couldn't bring myself to truly enjoy the moment. To make matters worse, the heat nearly had me sitting in a pool of my own sweat.

When the principal began the F section of last names, I felt my stomach somersault and land at my feet. I discreetly wiped my moist hands on my gown and started gnawing on the inside of my cheek, which was another nervous habit I'd developed in the last year. They called Jake, and I clapped for him. And then my muscles went razor tight.

"Abigail Marina Ferr."

The crowd erupted. I couldn't tell who was cheering louder — my father or Erica. I climbed the steps of the stage, shook each of my teacher's hands, and accepted my diploma with a radiant smile. My legs felt numb as I walked off, and my brain was still spinning by the time I returned to my seat.

I screamed for Ella and Brie when they were called, and I laughed as the principal teased Brie by pulling her diploma back before she could take it. There was an elated, festive mood in the air as each of my peers crossed that stage. Even though I wasn't friends with everyone, I suddenly felt the urge to wish all of them goodbye and good luck for the future.

Deep down, I knew I was waiting for one single name to be called. And until it was, I shifted restlessly in my seat. Finally, the principal reached the R section, and it was like a shock to my spine because I sat bolt upright.

"Colton Orion Reeves."

He rose from the crowd and high-fived his friends on his way to the stage. The smile on his face grew several inches when the crowd screamed for him, and I clapped as loudly as I could.

I drank in the sight of him, trying to commit it to memory. His smile was so gorgeous it made my heart flutter. After everything he'd been through, that smile was like a shimmering little trophy. Again, I felt the urge to reach for him, keep him in my arms, and maybe even kiss him.

"Yeah, Colton!" a familiar voice screeched from the audience.

I looked up to see Sandy waving her arms over her head. I missed her terribly, missed her soothing voice and her sweet, welcoming nature. In many ways, she'd been the mother I desperately wanted back in my life. But she was in my past now, too. I smiled up at her and then glanced back down at my own diploma.

All too soon, they finished calling names and the principal stood tall at the podium once again.

"Congratulations class of 2020!"

With that, we tore off our golden caps and tossed them into the air. They all soared, glimmering in the fading sunlight before falling back to the earth. In that moment, life was truly amazing. A ribbon of euphoria coiled inside me, wrapping my heart in a tight hug.

Afterwards, I was bombarded by my father and the rest of my friends. Each of them wrapped their arms around me and told me how much they loved me.

"One last picture," Erica squealed as we turned to face my father again.

Dad held the camera up before us, and as he started to count to three, my eyes flickered down the field. Colton was taking a picture with his friend Ashton. Unexpectedly, his eyes touched mine, and Colton flashed me a private smile—the one he never seemed to give anyone else, even Destiny. The one I hadn't seen in so long. My heart flooded with joy.

My father finally counted three and snapped the picture. I'd never look happier in a photograph.

Chapter Six

CURTIS INSTITUTE OF MUSIC, PA (2020-2021)

I spent my nineteenth birthday with my toes curled in the sand at Bethany Beach in Delaware. Erica had begged me to accompany her family there for vacation at the end of July, which just happened to fall on my birthday. Despite the scraggly discomfort of sand and salt coating my legs, the soft breeze and heavenly ocean fragrance was enough to lull me to sleep. But just before my eyes could close, Erica poked my arm.

"Did you ever get to hang out with your roommate?"

"Oh yeah," I said, adjusting the sunglasses on my nose. "She's awesome. We each drove halfway and met up for lunch at a Panera."

"What's her name again?"

"Cara."

I pictured the girl I'd met. She had rivulets of pale honey hair that had ginger highlights. I remembered her picturesque brown eyes and her tall, lean stature. She was going to the Curtis Institute of Music for songwriting and singing.

"So is she actually good at singing?" Erica asked. "Like, is she the next Ariana Grande?"

"I haven't heard her sing yet, we were just eating lunch. But she's super nice."

"Good. I won't allow some lousy roommate to mistreat my best friend."

"That's why I love you, Erica."

"Well then you're about to love me a whole lot more. I got something for you."

I pursed my lips. "You didn't have to."

"No, no, no." She waved my comment away. "Don't go all modest on me now. You turn nineteen today, and you leave for college in like, what? A month?"

"A month and three days," I answered forlornly.

"So..." She reached around her chair and nestled around in her backpack until she found what she was looking for.

She pulled out a small silver gift box, complete with glitter and a sparkling bow.

"Cute," I said, taking it carefully in my hands.

"Wait till you see what's in it."

I untied the neat ribbon and peered into the box. She grinned at me and clasped her hands together under her chin.

My breath caught in my throat. It was an elegant bracelet that held a single charm with a heart engraved on it like a fingerprint. It was refulgent, twinkling in the hot afternoon sunlight.

"Erica, this is gorgeous! How much was it?" I exclaimed.

"Don't ask me about a stupid price. I just wanted you to have something to remember me by when you go off to college. All the way to Philadelphia, I still can't believe it." Erica frowned.

I knew that I couldn't throw her in my suitcase and have her come with me, but the sinking feeling never really surfaced until now. The sinking feeling of...having to say goodbye. As I stared at the bracelet, a wistful smile played at the corners of my lips.

"Thank you," was all I could manage before I collapsed into my best friend's arms.

She giggled in delight. I don't know how long my head remained on her shoulder, but I didn't want to move because I was suddenly afraid to let go. I wondered how I would fare without her. Who would I run to when things got stressful or difficult? I tried to shove the thought out of my mind and focus on the present moment instead, while she was still here beside me.

A few feet away, the waves splashed lazily onto the sand and a seagull cried above our heads. As the tide rolled in, it pooled at my feet, sending instant chills over my body.

It was a four hour drive from Saratoga Springs to Philadelphia, Pennsylvania. But despite this, my father was more than eager to make the drive down to help me get settled into my new dorm. I was staying in Lenfest Hall — the suit-styled living quarters in association with Curtis.

Students stood in the lobby with their parents, gazing at maps and looking almost as confused as I felt. Others were hugging their friends, and some even looked antsy, like at any moment the ceiling would collapse on them.

"I'm on the third floor," I told Dad, glancing at my papers again.

Dad huffed as he shifted my toiletries bag to his other shoulder. "Alright, let's get a move on then."

Lenfest Hall had suite rooms that were to be shared among four individuals, and each person had to share a dorm with a roommate.

We trailed behind the mass of students heading toward the elevator, and after two rounds of waiting, we finally boarded and headed up to the third floor. The crowd dispersed up here, and

Dad and I navigated the hallways to room 223. That was when I saw her.

"Cara!"

My new roommate stood beside the door, and when she saw me, a wide grin illuminated her face. Today she was dressed in a pink Nike shirt with black shorts, but even in this casual attire, she could've easily passed for a professional model. Her mother was a spitting image of Nicole Kidman and dressed to impress in current-date Dior fashion.

"Hi, Gail!" Cara exclaimed.

Dad dropped my toiletries bag and held out a hand, plastering a friendly smile on his face. "Hey, how are you?"

Nicole Kidman's twin shook his head. "Hi, nice to meet you. I'm Jen."

"Albert," my dad replied.

Cara glanced at me. Her warm, luminous brown eyes seemed to absorb all the light in the hallway. She offered me a kind smile.

"Well, go on," Jen said excitedly. "Open the door!"

Inside was a fairly large living room area, accompanied by a side kitchen. Closet doors were ajar and two hallways extended off the main seating room.

"Ah, well this is nice," Jen complimented in a buttery voice.

I thought so too. I just wondered how I would fare living with three other girls — two of which I had yet to meet in person. We had all connected months ago on Instagram, but these other girls were too busy to meet before moving in.

Cara lightly bumped my shoulder. "Come on," she said as our parents scrutinized the common area. "Let's go see the bedrooms."

She moved gracefully down the right hallway, and I followed on her heels.

Our beds were styled like bunk beds, complete with steel ladders at the end to climb up and down. Under the beds, however, were wide wooden desks.

"Sweet," Cara exclaimed, dragging the word out as she looked around.

She tossed her teal Adidas bag onto the left desk and wandered over to the window. It really was a spectacular view: an overlook of the city of Philadelphia. Skyscrapers jabbed the sky, and cars zipped by on the street below. I almost felt at home.

As if she was reading my mind, Cara asked, "You said you were from New York, right?"

"Saratoga Springs," I answered politely. "In New York, yeah."

"Right. I'm from Michigan. Maybe I told you that, but I forget." Her laugh was silvery like a windchime. "I'm just super excited to get to know you more and become great friends."

"Me too," I admitted. "It's nice to be able to come out to a new place and change my surroundings."

"Tell me about it," she answered, her chocolate dough eyes bulging for emphasis. "My brother and I aren't exactly on the best terms right now."

I raised my eyebrows at her.

"It's a long story," she replied, pretending to rummage through her bag for something.

She hid her frown quickly and changed the subject to her love for music and performing arts. Particularly singing. I remembered that when we'd met for lunch, she explained that she had started singing as a young girl and had joined multiple choirs since. I'd replied with the fact that I was a violin player, looking to become a conductor one day, and she had said that she could totally see me in that role.

It wasn't long before our other roommates arrived with their mothers, who already appeared to be friends. They poured in through the door with too many suitcases to count. The one girl was named Julia Blake. She was a short brunette who had a strong love for vibrant eyeshadow even though it made her porcelain skin seem even more pale. Maybe that was why she carried a small compact in her hand like it was an extension of her body.

The other girl was Maya Gray. She had a very angular face that was beautiful in its own unique way. Her eyes were a striking hazel color, appearing almost gold in this lighting. Her skin was the pretty color of mocha. She looked like she belonged in the 70s with the other hippies, protesting war and advocating for peace. She wore psychedelic pants matched with a denim shirt and a tie-dye headband. The tips of her dark hair were dyed a pastel pink.

"Hey, guys. I'm Cara," she greeted them in a smooth voice.

"Hi, Abigail," Julia said to me, tossing her wavy brown locks over her shoulder. With the motion, an unexpected waft of strawberries filled my nose.

"Hey, yeah, it's just Gail."

But she didn't seem to hear me. She'd already turned back to Cara, chatting away about the expensive sneakers Cara was wearing. Maya even said she was jealous. Already, I could tell I would be the odd one out just because I didn't own designer clothes like these girls did. But then, those possessions might go to my head, and I didn't want to be like that anyway.

It reminded me of how Colton had climbed the popularity ladder after the news of his father's abuse leaked to the public. It went to his head. It turned him into a stranger.

A stranger...

No, I told myself. Colton was a part of my past. I'd decided it would stay that way. His father was in jail and Colton was safe. After all, I wouldn't see him again, so what did it matter?

"Oh, thank you!" The sound of Cara's voice broke me from the thoughts. "I just got them actually."

As our other roommates gushed over this, Cara shot me a quick look, and I was surprised to see the plea in her eyes. It almost made me laugh. She was good at appealing to her audience, but maybe that was a gift and a curse.

I'd all but forgotten our parents until I heard Dad cut the conversation short, saying he had to get back home for a meeting at work. I knew there was no meeting; he just didn't want to chat with the ladies anymore. I curled a hand around my mouth to keep from laughing.

When he escaped the conversation, he called me to the doorway and pulled me into a hug. A lump materialized in my throat, and I tried to swallow around it.

"I'll miss you, Dad."

"I'll miss you too, sweetheart. Promise to keep in touch. I can't *wait* to hear about all your success. And I'll come to every concert!"

"That's a four hour drive every few weeks."

He paused. "Do they have a livestream link I can watch?"

I laughed and hugged him once more. He kissed the crown of my head and said, "Work hard. Don't be stupid. And I'll see you later. I love you."

With that, he squeezed my hand and disappeared down the hall. I stared at the door for a moment, trying not to let my emotions probe my heart any further. Cara tapped my shoulder, and I turned to see that Maya and Julia had retired to the common area to talk with their parents. Cara's mom had also joined them.

"Alright," Cara said, her voice so low I had to lean in to hear. "It's clear they're going to be a handful. But I'm not worried. At least we have each other."

"Thank goodness for that."

She smiled and then sucked in a sharp breath. "Oh my gosh, I almost forgot! There's a party tonight on the terrace. It's kind of like a get-to-know-you type of thing. I think we should go."

"Oh, definitely," I said.

I was suddenly eager to escape our suite and explore Curtis. Classes didn't start until Monday, which meant I would have a great deal of time to look around and make some new connections. This was college after all, not high school. No one knew who I was. It was the perfect opportunity to step out of my comfort zone and into the world.

The terrace was decorated with bulbs of lights that lined the balcony railing and snaked along the thresholds. A game of ping-pong was set up in the corner and already occupied by a group of shouting boys. Lounge chairs dotted the perimeter and toward the back of the terrace sat a long table filled with an array of snacks. It was a warm August night, and from this height, you could see the sunset in its full glory. A thick line of orange streaked the horizon while the rest of the sky was covered by dark clouds, like smoke. As if the sun decided to set the horizon on fire.

A warm breeze carried through the terrace, playing with my braid. Cara had generously decided to do my hair and makeup.

"You never know who you're gonna meet at these things," she'd said as she brushed through my wavy hair. "You've gotta look your best."

Now, I was dressed in a velvet crop top with skinny jeans that were rolled up at the ankles. And I had to admit that I did feel pretty.

"Oh, I know that girl!" Cara said suddenly, pointing to a group of females cluttered around the lounge chairs. "I'll be right back."

Not even five seconds after she left, my stomach started growling. Just as I gravitated toward the food table, I was stopped by a strawberry redhead with glasses. She peered up at me, offering a courteous smile.

"Hi, I'm Dalia, the head of floor three. You're Abigail Ferr right?"

"Yeah, Gail."

She stuck out a pale hand, which I shook politely. "Hey, Gail.

Nice to meet ya. Welcome to the terrace party, first off. I'm in charge of things on our floor, so don't hesitate at all to ask if you have any questions!"

There was a nametag clipped to her shirt with the words *Resident Advisor* printed across the top and a picture of her smiling face.

"Cool, thanks," I said.

I turned to grab a plate and started filling it with some cheese cubes.

"So, what have you chosen to major in?" she inquired.

I added some pretzels to my cheese mountain. "Well, I play the violin, but I want to be a conductor."

She clapped her hands together. "You are going to *love* our orchestra. Mr. Autrie, the conductor—he is the *best!*"

I liked how she had so much school spirit; it was a refreshing change from the listless, blasé student body of high school. Before I could respond, a boy tapped on Dalia's shoulder and she turned toward him.

"Someone over there needs your help, Dal. They asked for you," he said.

Before departing, she flashed me another gleaming smile and encouraged me to enjoy myself. Then she spun on her heels, fluffed her strawberry curls, and sauntered off.

"Don't mind her," the boy said with a careless wave of his hand. "She takes her job very seriously."

I watched as he poured himself a glass of lemonade.

"Are you two close?" I wondered.

"Well, everyone's sorta close with Dalia. She makes it her *priority* to become friends with the entire student body." He took a sip from his red solo cup and turned toward me.

He had several inches on me—maybe two feet. His charcoal colored hair had the slightest curl to it. His skin tone resembled Maya's as a mix between cinnamon and copper.

"At least she cares about her peers, you know?" I popped a

cheese cube into my mouth.

"Oh, yeah. Dal's the best. I got here early for the summer program, and she was a huge help." The corners of his lips tilted upward and he shifted his cup to his other hand to shake mine. "I'm Elijah, by the way."

A lot of new greetings tonight. "Gail."

His eyebrows furrowed. "Gail? That's an old name, isn't it?"

"It's short for Abigail."

He considered this for a moment and then turned his bright hazel eyes back to me. "I like it. You don't hear it often."

I surprised myself by laughing. "Elijah's not common either."

He shrugged. "My parents are big on biblical names. They're some serious church goers."

"So is my dad."

He took another swig of lemonade and hid his smile behind the rim of his cup. "So did I hear you're a violin player?"

"Have been since I was seven."

"Damn. I started playing the cello in sixth grade. Never even made first chair in my section, can you believe it?"

"Well you must be good if you got into Curtis."

A blush warmed his cheeks. "Actually, it's my fault I didn't get first chair. I just didn't really want the attention."

"Then why go to a school that demands competition?" I asked through a mouthful of pretzels.

"It was my parents' dream," he replied with a sad smile. His eyes dropped into the contents of his drink, and he drew a deep breath. "But I'm glad to be here. It's a great school, and tuition is free." He gave a mischievous wink.

"Room and board's definitely not," I groaned.

"It's all in how you look at things."

I found that I liked talking with Elijah. He was quiet and reserved—completely different from the hollering boys gathered around the ping-pong table.

· · ·

My classes were not large at all. In fact, my Music Theory class had about as many people in it as my algebra class from freshman year of high school. I was thankful though because *this* I could manage. A class of four hundred would doom me to daily anxiety attacks.

What was better was that Elijah was in most of my classes, too. He usually sat next to me, talking until our professor entered the room. And with each passing day, I found that I liked Elijah more and more. He was my dose of positivity.

With all the courses I was taking, I had to admit that my actual conducting professor was my favorite. Victor Autrie was an elderly man who descended straight from France. He came to America as a boy with a strong love for the luscious sound of string instruments. His passion showed through his animated conducting style.

"You will do well here, *ma chérie*," he told me one chilly after-noon as the class was wrapping up.

He set his baton back on the stand and turned toward me, the natural sunlight streaming off his silver hair.

"Thank you, professor."

"I assume you've joined the orchestra?"

"Of course. First practice is today, isn't it?"

He laughed heartily and nodded. "I will see you there!"

As the weeks passed by, I started to gain confidence in my new surroundings. By now, I'd gotten used to Maya and Julia, meaning I'd gotten used to their interest in gossip and makeup. I discovered that Julia was here for piano, and Maya was pursuing composition. Our interest in music was what brought us all closer together, and before long, we were living like an actual family.

Some nights, Cara would sing for us while Julia played the keyboard in the common area. As many times as I'd heard her voice by now, Cara's vocal ability still shocked me. She was an alto, performing effortless scales through a velvet-like tone, and her vibrato always gave my soul chills.

"Cara, you could go so far with a voice like that!" I nearly shouted as I scrubbed a makeup wipe over my eyes. "I'm serious."

We were in our dorm, closed off from the others, and it was a quiet Wednesday evening. Cara glanced up from her song book and laughed.

"Thanks. Imagine if I won a Grammy one day."

"I can totally see it happening."

She beamed for a moment, but then her smile faded.

"What's wrong?" I ventured.

"I don't think I could go *that* far. Getting a Grammy is like a...one in a trillion chance."

"But not impossible," I countered, climbing the ladder to my own bed. "Where's this coming from?"

She closed her song book and let go of a sigh.

"Remember when I told you that my brother and I aren't on the best of terms?"

I nodded.

"Well...he's a voice major, too, but he ended up going to Julliard. When we were kids, we had this plan that we would become the top recording duo in the country. And we were dead set on it, too. We were gonna go straight to LA, walk right into a recording studio, and play them what we had." She stopped for a moment, gazing off into space like the memory was replaying right on the wall. "That's crazy, I know. We were just two kids with insane dreams. But then we grew up, and we realized that the chances of making it, especially as a duo, were next to none. Being a musical influencer is a solo game. Every man for himself. You think the people who have your back are with you forever, but...they aren't."

"Cara, what are you saying?" I urged.

"Jack realized that before I did. He realized that this industry survives on reputation and talent. And before I could do anything, he packed his bags and went to Julliard, leaving me behind to fend for myself."

When she hung her head, sorrow invaded my heart. I knew she wasn't lying. Music *was* a tough major, but it must have been even harder for her to move here after what happened with her brother.

"So now, I'm kind of...scared of him," she continued. "Jack is *extremely* talented. He's going to be the one to get the Grammy, not me."

"Wait, hold on. Stop. You're extremely talented, too! I'd kill to have a voice like yours! Any recording academy would be lucky to have you!"

"But it would just make matters worse." She squeezed her eyes shut and fiddled with the cover of her song book.

I wasn't seeing the point. "Cara, your voice—"

"I don't want to be recognized for something if it means I can't have my brother with me."

A deafening silence filled the room.

At that moment, a whole new light fell over Cara, and I suddenly understood her. Understood her humbleness and her compassion. It all stemmed from her brother. She would trade her talent to have him back in a heartbeat. Not only had she been plagued by loss and betrayal, but her heart was kinder because of it.

"We were supposed to be a team. What is success if you can't have the people you love with you?" she whispered. "What makes an award special if it would just deepen an ongoing silent war? And I know I shouldn't care. I have my own life to worry about. But...he's my brother, and I just wish we didn't have this stupid feud. Love is weird, Gail."

For the first time in weeks, Colton flashed to my mind, and my breath caught in my throat. The clarity of my memory was astonishing. I pictured his stunning gold-green eyes, his breathtaking smile. I pictured all of this, and that same feeling of extreme loss pulsed through my veins. It felt like I'd just carved open a sealed wound, and I pressed my lips together, resisting the urge to cry. I wondered why after all this time his loss still cut me in half.

"I know," I managed through clenched teeth.

Cara was quiet for a moment, staring through the blinds and out into the glittering city. "I just wish I could *talk* to him, you know?"

Now she was the one blinking back tears.

"Have you tried to call him?" I suggested softly.

She laughed once, but it lacked any real humor. "I can't do that. I know myself, and I know him. We're both...stubborn. It would turn into a fight before we even started talking. I just mean that I wish we could be adults and keep things civil."

I gnawed on the inside of my cheek, knowing what I had to do. Reopening the wound may help Cara, and she needed to know she wasn't alone with these feelings.

"I, uh...I had a boyfriend two years ago who meant...a *lot* to me."

She glanced at me, ears perked.

"Things were great for a long time, but...our parents were pretty messed up people." At the thought of my mother—wherever she was now—tears stung my eyes like daggers. "My mom turned into a...jerk and left me and my dad. And I later found out that my boyfriend's father was an alcoholic with PTSD...who ended up beating him." With great effort, I blinked back my tears and ended up choking on my own words. The wound began to bleed again.

Cara pressed a hand to her mouth. "Gail."

"My boyfriend dumped me because of that," I continued, fighting to control my quivering voice. "I guess he just couldn't handle his emotions and...went off the deep end. I didn't want to break up, but he changed and pushed me away with every chance he got."

"So...does that mean you never reconciled?" Cara asked gently.

I shook my head, feeling the pain squeeze my heart. "Not really. I think time healed us, but we never had the guts to face each other again. So I *know* what being stubborn feels like. And I know that missing someone you love is absolute hell."

"I am *so sorry*, Gail," Cara whispered.

I shrugged and drew in a shaky breath. "It's like you said. Love is weird. You keep wishing you could make things right, but...it never works out."

"Yeah, I mean, I don't think Jack's ever going to speak to me again—"

"Hold on," I cut in. "You didn't let me finish. Things are different for you, Cara. He's your brother. You're literally bound by blood. There's nothing stronger than that. He'll come around someday, I promise."

She sniffled and tried to smile. "Thanks."

Even though I was happy to see her content again, I felt stuck in a sudden panic. Colton was racing through my mind, and I couldn't stand to see his face. It was making me sick. It was making me miss him.

"I'm going to step out for a little," I said, climbing back down the ladder.

Cara's concerned eyes cut through mine. "Are you okay?"

I nodded. "Just need some air. I'll be fine."

Aside from a small group of chatting girls, the hallway was deserted, which wasn't unexpected considering how late it was. I strode toward the empty lounge area, my heart pounding faster with each step. I collapsed into one of the armchairs, forcing oxygen through my nostrils and into my lungs. Absentmindedly, I toyed with the charm bracelet Erica had given me months ago.

I wanted to cry, but now the tears were avoiding me. Anxiety was stirring in my chest, and I wondered what the problem was. I hadn't had an anxiety attack like this in a long time. Why now? I tried to stop my hands from shaking. I stared at the gray ash in the fireplace, willing myself to concentrate on the color of it, the texture, the smell of the gas still hanging in the air from when the fire was on earlier today. I wanted to shut my eyes until this spell passed. I wanted to go home. I wanted Colton.

"Gail?" a voice cut through the silence.

I whipped around and exhaled when I saw Elijah standing in the hallway. I must've looked pretty upset because he rushed to my side.

"Are you okay?"

I swallowed loudly. "Just anxious."

"About?"

I couldn't tell the story again. It hurt too much. "I — I don't know. It comes and goes when it wants."

"You have nothing to be worried about, Gail. You're safe. And I'm here. I won't let...whatever it is you're worrying about hurt you. I won't let anyone hurt you. Just breathe."

He spoke calmly as if he knew exactly how to deal with this. Maybe he had helped someone else through an anxiety attack before. He gathered me into his arms, which turned out to be surprisingly warm. He smelled nice, too, like a mix between lavender and pine. And suddenly, I wasn't thinking about Colton anymore. I could feel Elijah's heart beating steadily in his chest. It soothed me.

He sighed. "You seem a little better already."

I allowed my eyes to meet his. They were a lovely shade of blue-green like the ocean. I don't know how long we stayed like that, gazing into each other's eyes. But when my mind woke up, I found that my lips were on his. I didn't remember leaning in, I didn't remember that initial touch. But now, suddenly my hands were gripping his shirt.

I wasn't an impulsive girl. Whatever I was doing, it scared me because I knew this wasn't me. But at the same time, a rush of heat was spreading through my body. And I found that I'd missed the sensation.

When I finally pulled away, he stared at me, wide-eyed.

"Gail."

I couldn't bring myself to speak. I didn't know what I would say anyway if I tried. All I knew was that I had been missing this intimate connection for some time, and I needed someone to fill that space.

Before I knew it, we were locked in another kiss.

Chapter Seven

CURTIS INSTITUTE OF MUSIC, PA—SARATOGA SPRINGS, NY (2021-2022)

Elijah and I had developed an odd relationship. By day, he was my go-to study partner, but by night, he ignited a fire in my belly. We often found ourselves mouth to mouth in a private space, away from peeping eyes.

Tonight was no different.

My back was pressed against the wall, and Elijah's hands were roaming. His lips were saccharine, coating my lips in sugar-like kisses. I pulled his shirt up over his head to expose his toned torso, but before I could pull him back to me, he went rigid in my arms. There was a question in his hazel blue-green eyes—a suggestion. It was the same look he always gave me around this time. *Can we take this a step further?* And just like always, the flames engulfing my heart were extinguished. I gave him my usual response: an apologetic smile and a small shake of my head.

"Gail," he said after an awkward moment of silence. "If I'm making you uncomfortable—"

"No." I ran a hand through my tangled hair. "I like what we're doing, I just don't want to...you know. Not yet."

He glanced toward his bed and then at his roommate's empty bed and sighed. "We don't have to do this."

"Do what?"

"This." He gestured between his body and mine. "If I'm making you feel like you have to kiss me and stuff, that was never my intention. You're an amazing person. I don't want to take advantage of you."

"No, Elijah," I shook my head. "You're not taking advantage of me. I just..."

"Your heart's not in the right place?" His voice was gentle.

Something inside of me twitched. "Yeah, you could say that. But it has absolutely nothing to do with you, I swear."

He stared at me for a moment and brushed his thumb across my cheek. There was an emotion in his eyes that I couldn't name, but it made me feel all warm inside, and then I was on my tip toes and kissing him again. He groaned slightly when I bent to kiss his neck.

"So, just to clarify, we're *not* having sex tonight?" he asked breathlessly.

I pulled back to look at him. "No. I just want this, plain and simple. Uncomplicated."

"Yes, ma'am." He flashed me a handsome, genuine smile and I dove at him again.

December arrived at last, forcing some excitement out of the frosted windows and annoyingly frigid weather. The student body wasted no time decorating Lenfest Hall for Christmas.

"The holiday party is this Friday. You don't want to miss it!" Dalia announced as our peers moved around her.

Cara and I had just gotten back from lunch, and we watched our redheaded friend press festive fliers into people's hands.

"Oh, Gail, Cara! The holiday party is this Friday. You don't want to miss it!" she exclaimed when she spotted us.

I took a flier from her.

"Thanks, Dal," Cara said. "Should we bring something?"

"Just your beautiful self," Dalia replied, readjusting her glasses. She then motioned to someone behind us. "Elijah! You're coming, right?"

He took a flier from her and quickly scanned its contents. "I wouldn't miss it for the world," he said with a wide grin.

When Dalia giggled, he turned to us and winked.

"Oh, Elijah, great job on your cello solo the other day," Cara complimented.

"Thanks." His eyes fell back on me, and I beamed.

Cara hadn't questioned me about my unique relationship with Elijah. She said it wasn't any of her business but if I needed someone to talk to, she was always there. I was so lucky to have a roommate like her.

"You'll be there, right?" Elijah asked.

"Wouldn't miss it for the world," I echoed, and he chuckled.

The dining hall was spruced up for the occasion, adorned with wreaths and elegant candelabras. A grand tree stood in the back corner, its shiny ornaments twinkling in the light. It must have been a real tree, too, because the scent of rich pine permeated the air. Each table had a vase of Christmas poinsettias and burgundy candles. Christmas music flowed from the speakers at the front of the room. Dalia and her fellow student council members stood under the threshold, greeting each of us as we entered the hall.

Our evening was filled with gift-giving and pleasant conversations. But the best part of the night was when Professor Autrie serenaded us with his stunning violin solo.

He stood before the crowd of students, perfectly poised,

brushing his bow across the strings. He played an enchanting medley of *Silent Night* and *Mary, Did You Know?* which was performed so well, I even saw the Dean's jaw drop. Professor Autrie's talent was otherworldly. When he finally finished and lifted his bow from the strings, I was stunned speechless. He bowed, and the audience's uproar turned his smiling face bright pink.

"I'll admit," Elijah whispered. "Dude's still got skills."

"That's an understatement," I said, shaking my head in wonder.

Later, when things were winding down, I sat in a circle with Cara, Elijah, Maya, and Julia. Sometime throughout the night, Maya and Julia had both attracted the eyes of Jessie and Sean, two boys from our music theory class.

"Hey, why don't we get out of here," Julia suggested, glancing around the dining hall.

Most of our peers had left. Some were still slow dancing with their sweethearts, and the members of the student council were beginning to clean up the wrapping paper that had been absentmindedly discarded.

"And do what?" Jessie inquired, leaning into Julia with a mischievous gleam in his eye.

"Pretty sure you know what," Julia said. She pulled him up from his seat, gave us a swift nod, and they both dashed for the door.

"They better not be going to our suit," Cara said. "I'm going to practice some scales."

"At ten at night?" Elijah asked.

"It helps me relax before bed," Cara replied in a matter-of-fact tone. "Goodnight." She smiled and waved to both of us.

"Night, Care," I called after her.

Maya was practically already in Sean's lap, loudly expressing her desires. So before I knew it, I was alone with Elijah.

This was our last night at Curtis before we would return

home for holiday break. I was more than excited to get home and see my father and Erica. But as I glanced at Elijah, I found it difficult to say goodbye.

"I'm glad I came tonight," he murmured, watching a boy swipe used cups off a table.

"Me, too. You can never go wrong with a Christmas party."

"Yeah," he responded and I felt the weight of his glance. "But I'm just glad that I got to spend the night with you."

I watched as his eyes traveled over my glittering dress then froze on my lips. A cold feeling slid through me like ice water, settling like ice chips in my stomach. When he leaned forward to brush his lips against mine, I froze. His hand curled around my neck, drawing me closer. His lips were warm, inviting, but I couldn't bring myself to respond. I didn't know how I truly felt about Elijah, but kissing him in the public's eye made me anxious. Suddenly the spark was gone. He sensed my disapproval and broke the kiss.

Elijah leaned back in his seat, pinching the bridge of his nose. "Oh, God," he whispered. "I'm sorry."

"It's okay." My attempt to comfort him sounded flat, and I could've kicked myself.

I really liked Elijah, but maybe not in the way I thought I did. Confusion swirled through my brain like a thick fog.

"No, I *am* sorry." He pinned me with an intense gaze. "But...I just had to kiss you like that at least once."

"Like what?"

"Harmlessly without it escalating into another makeout session. I figured if I showed some class, you would respect me more, but...I guess I read you wrong." His apologetic tone made me frown.

"What're you talking about?"

He hesitated before saying, "Someone really hurt you, didn't they?" When I flinched, his lips became a hard line. "It's okay. You don't have to talk about it. It's just...more obvious when we get closer. Every time we kiss, you kind of go cold. When we make out, you're distant. It's like you're *there*...but your heart's not in it."

I couldn't bear to hear these words. Colton flashed in my mind like a neon sign, refusing to go unnoticed. My heart started into a nervous stutter, as if it was preparing to feel the onslaught of loss again.

"The problem is...I think I'm actually starting to fall for you," Elijah muttered. His tone was guarded, and his face was unreadable. "I like *more* than just your body, Gail. You're smart, and funny, and talented. But I'm not going to try to make this work if your head is still wrapped around someone else."

I felt sick. He spoke so nonchalantly, it was as if we were discussing the weather.

"And there's something else." He inhaled slowly. "I'm transferring over break."

"*What?*"

Elijah nodded. "I've been thinking for a while, and music just isn't for me."

I stared at him like he had three heads. "You're incredibly gifted! You have such a natural talent with the cello—don't give that up!"

And don't leave me, I wanted to say.

He had a point: my heart was still in recovery over Colton's absence, and maybe I really was with Elijah just to fill a void. But that didn't mean I didn't wish I could love him more. There was just a massive strain settled over my body. I understood that our connection wasn't pure, and that was what made me loathe myself.

But above all, Elijah was one of my closest friends. Had I ruined this friendship already by not being able to love him in the way he wanted? Time had run out to tell because now, to my complete horror, he was transferring.

"W—what are you pursuing instead?" I stammered.

"Don't laugh," he began, a pinkish tone painting his cheeks. "I want to be a tabloid journalist."

He'd never even mentioned his love for journalism before, and I couldn't picture it. I could only see him seated behind a cello, fingers tickling the strings, bow sailing.

"I won't stop playing," he assured me. "I don't think I ever could. But when I was in high school, I took all these creative writing classes, and I loved it. But my parents wanted me to pursue music so badly. The thing is I don't really like the competitive atmosphere for music. We're all constantly competing for the conductor's attention or for a solo at each performance. Truthfully, the only thing keeping me here was you."

My head fell into my hands. How could I have been so blind? I should have noticed Elijah's discomfort, but I was too distracted by my own problems. So wrapped up in my heartbreak that I coveted Elijah in the wrong way...which wasn't fair at all.

"So where are you going?"

"Ashford University."

My breath caught in my throat. "But that's in—"

"California." He nodded.

The room started to tilt.

"Gail, I'm sorry for kissing you like that. I should've just said goodnight and left."

"Without telling me?"

He rose from his seat, but I caught his arm, suddenly feeling panicked. This was the last time I would see him. Come January, he will have flown to the opposite coast.

"So that's it?" I demanded. "You're just *leaving*? I'm sorry about being distant, but I'm *not* sorry about what we did! You mean a lot to me!"

Elijah looked distraught. He gently eased his arm out of my grip and closed his eyes. "As much as I would like to believe that...we could be something more, your heart still belongs to someone else, and I don't want to be in a one-sided relationship."

My mouth snapped shut.

"That being said, I still want to be friends. I'm always one call away if you need me."

"Yeah, one call and like five hours away by plane."

He bent down to my height and chuckled.

"I'll always care about you, Gail—you can count on that."

"Is this all life is?" I asked, fighting to control my tone. "Forming relationships only to lose them?"

Elijah thought for a moment and then shook his head. "No. Life is about meeting new people and cherishing your time with them, no matter how long it lasts. And if it does end, well, you take what they gave you and move forward."

"What if you can't let someone go?"

He pursed his lips. "Then that just proves that what you had was real."

I hung my head, trying to stop the wound from reopening. I could feel it starting to tear.

"You're gonna be okay, Gail," Elijah murmured, slowly nodding his head. "Whatever you've been through — it'll pass eventually. And I'll miss you a lot, but I hope you can find peace."

His smile was as soft as a sunset. I had to find a way to be happy for him; I had to respect his decision to leave. I took a little comfort in the fact that Elijah would find his own happiness in California. If you love something, set it free...

He sighed and stood back up. "I hope you and your family have a merry Christmas."

I gave him the strongest smile I could manage, though my lips quivered slightly. "You too."

. . .

The first thing I did when I pulled into Dad's driveway was take a deep breath and allow myself to take it all in. I stared up at the house—at it's fading, stained stucco and chipping blue shutters. At the pale stone walkway and the festive wreath hanging on the door. It was so nice to be home, to be back in familiar surroundings.

I jumped out of my car and hauled my suitcase out of the backseat. Just as its wheels hit the pavement, the front door swung open. Dad appeared, wearing a charming ironed shirt, and I almost laughed. I'd never seen him wear that before. But then a thin brunette stepped out behind him.

"Hi, sweetheart!" Dad enveloped me in a tight hug, but my eyes stayed trained on the stranger.

She looked to be about his age with big green eyes and two dimples that didn't match in size. She folded her hands patiently behind her back, smiling at our embrace.

"Oh, Gail. I'd like to introduce you to Jamie."

The woman's smile widened. "Hi, it's so nice to meet you. I've heard so much about you." Her voice was sweet and friendly.

"Are you guys...friends?" I asked, trying to feign indifference.

Dad wrapped an arm around Jamie's waist, securing her to his side. They gazed into each other's eyes for a second and then looked back at me, and I would've had to be an idiot not to recognize the affection they seemed to share.

"A little more than that," my father answered jovially.

He looked happy. Actually, he looked ecstatic. And Jamie kind of reminded me of a Disney princess—someone who you can tell is kind and heartfelt just by the look of them. She, too, was beaming. I smiled and extended my hand toward her.

Over dinner, Dad explained that he'd met Jamie at work.

"I'm new to the area," she added before taking a sip of water. "When I graduated from med school, I moved out to Minnesota and worked as a child psychiatrist for ten years. But then my ex-husband and I went through a rough patch, and things fell through, and well...fate brought me here to New York. And it just so happens that your dad's clinic was looking for a new psychiatrist." Her dimples poked holes in her shining smile.

"Lucky for me, right?" Dad had spaghetti sauce smeared across his chin, and I couldn't keep myself from laughing.

It was nice to know that after all these years my father had found love again. And Jamie was quiet, observant. She only spoke when she had something insightful to say, and I found myself clinging to every word. Even her voice was mellow and delicate. She was a perfect match for my father, and that reminded me that even the most broken of hearts could be mended.

Dad helped himself to another plate of spaghetti and then gestured toward me. "So who are your new friends? Do they play instruments, too?"

I gushed about Maya and Julia and Professor Autrie and Cara. Especially Cara's voice.

"You'd literally cry if you heard her sing." I shook my head.

"She's that good, huh?"

"Yeah! And my other friend, Elijah —" I stopped, remembering that Elijah was supposed to board his flight to California next week.

Dad and Jamie raised their eyebrows.

I cleared my throat. "My friend Elijah plays the cello, but...he's transferring."

"Why's that?" Jamie asked.

"He doesn't think music is for him." There was no mistaking the sadness in my voice. Elijah and I hadn't talked since the Christmas party, but I knew that he had other things to take care of now anyway.

The next morning, I made Dad a veggie omelet and saved the rest for myself. Jamie had gone home for the night, but she was supposed to come back over this afternoon for lunch. As my father and I sat down to eat, sunshine poured in through the kitchen windows, glinted off our plates and nearly blinded us.

"Plans today?" Dad inquired with his mouth full.

"I'm going to see Erica."

She and I had been in touch for the last week and a half, discussing what we would do when I got home. After some debate, it was decided that we would go Christmas shopping and then swing back around to get some delicious cookies from the bakery.

"Have fun," Dad said. "After lunch, I'm taking Jamie downtown to see a band play."

"You guys are cute together," I commented, stabbing a piece of egg with my fork.

My father's face lit up. "You think so?"

"No doubt! I'm happy for you, Dad."

And I was. He'd been through so much with my mom; it was nice to see him smile at someone else for a change.

"Thanks, kiddo. Oh, Gail," he said just as I got up to rinse my plate. "I heard that they're calling for snow tonight, so make sure you drive safely. I don't want you out all night in that mess."

"Aye, aye, captain."

My phone was constantly buzzing in my pocket. The screen showed text message after text message of Erica's excitement. She was just as thrilled to have me home as I was to be home.

`I'm kinda craving Starbucks.` she texted as I pulled my parka on over my shoulders.

`Should I stop by and get u something on the way?` I texted back.

`If you insist. Tall peppermint mocha please—w/ extra whip!`

Naturally, the line at Starbucks was so long, it stretched out the door and down the street. I tugged on my mittens, and tried to remind myself that Erica was worth the wait. By the time I finally made it to the register, I was shivering something fierce.

"Can I help you?" the barista asked.

I repeated Erica's order and then listed my own, watching the barista's coworker combine the ingredients as I spoke.

When the order was up, I took the two coffees in both my hands and turned toward the door. But just as I started to walk, my heart flipped inside out, and I stopped breathing.

There, sitting at an empty table and scrolling through his phone in the back corner of this tiny Starbucks, was Colton Reeves. He sat hunched forward with his elbows on the table, one hand around his coffee, the other wrapped around his phone. I could do nothing but stare. My mouth hung open slightly; I was lost in shock, pierced by memories as they flashed through my brain.

He really didn't look all that different — brawny arms, a smooth and flawless face, sun-kissed hair with hints of gold. The only difference was that today, his hair was gelled back into a stylish swoop, which I hadn't seen since he was my date to homecoming sophomore year.

My eyes took in every inch of him while my mind spun.

I recalled the feel of those lips on mine, the warmth of those arms, the shape of those hands. The strength of that heart. I remembered his eyes as they gazed into mine. The sound of his voice. *I'm in love with you, Abigail Ferr. My heart is yours forever.* The breathtaking purity of it all. The scars on his back and the indescribable pain of loss. Inside my body, there was a monsoon of emotion.

He was just a boy sitting alone in a Starbucks. Just another face in this crowd. But to me, he was my first love. The one that got away. The one that, even after all this time, still sent me spiraling. I considered running to him, hugging him. Even kissing him. But my legs didn't work.

Someone brushed past me and hit my shoulder, and I almost dropped Erica's coffee.

"'Scuse me," the man said gruffly.

"Sorry," I squeaked, hardly hearing myself.

I didn't even realize I was walking until I was two feet away from Colton. He still hadn't noticed me, and I almost turned away. It was funny; I felt like a young teenager again, plagued by uncertainty and endless what-ifs. What if he was still upset? What if he had moved on?

"Colton," I said before I could stop myself.

He glanced up at me, uninterested at first, but then his eyes widened and his jaw clenched tightly. For a fraction of a second, he paled, and it seemed he too stopped breathing. But just as quick as this expression appeared, it was gone. He replaced it with a polite smile and stood up to greet me. I'd forgotten how good he was at masking his emotions.

"Abigail," he said. His eyes briefly scanned my face. "It's been a while."

"Yeah. I was just passing through, and I saw you, and I couldn't leave without saying hi." It was difficult to keep my breathing under control.

He nodded. "Where, um...where are you going to school?"

"Curtis Institute of Music. Playing in the orchestra."

"Wow. I bet you're doing well." His cheeks scorched pink with the compliment, and I felt a smile blossom on my lips.

I wanted to discuss everything that had happened since I saw him last. I wanted to ask him how he was doing, learn every detail of his life since we broke up. This was the first time we'd spoken since then after all. My throat nearly closed up. My heart swelled at the sight of him. It pounded faster with each passing second, gleefully crying, "It's my Colton!"

"What about you?" I asked. "Where are you going?"

"Penn State," he answered. "Great school for architecture."

I'm more into engineering and architecture, he told me once in Mr. Korrins' class during freshman year. I smiled softly at the memory. It was good to know that he was pursuing his dream too.

"Well, it was really nice talking to you," he said.

"Yeah, are you...?" My voice trailed off when I spotted the second coffee waiting on the table.

He followed my gaze, and I watched the wary look cross his face before he could conceal it with indifference.

"I'm waiting for someone," he explained smoothly.

Jealousy prickled inside me, and I hoped it wasn't showing on my face.

"Oh cool." The statement didn't sound as nonchalant as I would've liked.

Colton's face faltered again, failing to keep its unperturbed mask. His lips sagged into a frown, and there was a slight plea in his eyes. But then he noticed the second coffee in *my* hand.

"For a friend," I clarified, which wasn't a lie.

He swallowed and his jaw twitched again. "Nice."

We stared at each other for a moment, and it was all I could do to hold back my hundreds of questions and conceal my emotions. But I was stubborn and so was he.

"Good to see you, Abigail," he murmured and sat back down to return to his phone.

Why don't you call me Gail? I wondered. It almost annoyed me that he didn't.

"You too. Merry Christmas."

He looked back up at me one last time, and I could've drowned in those gold-green eyes. "Merry Christmas."

There was that smile...the smile that made me want to kiss him forever. The smile that made my heart stutter. It was so pure, so innocent, and it reminded me of the time I was sixteen — a sophomore in high school. The time where college majors didn't matter yet, and we were free to live in our youth. Colton simply awakened that teenager in me, and I didn't want to go back to real life.

But Erica was waiting...at least that was the excuse I told myself to get away before I did something I would regret. Colton was in my past, and I had to accept that. So I turned away and strode toward the door, each step as painful as a knife to the gut. My lungs felt shriveled and useless all of a sudden, and I forced air into them. Outside, the wind bit at my cheeks, but I hardly noticed.

I inspected every female I passed, wondering which one was going to meet Colton. They were too tall, too overdressed, or wearing too much makeup. I hated every one of them, and the envy burned beneath my bones.

No! my conscience screamed. *He hurt you when he broke your heart! Why do you care?* But my heart was already mourning, wishing to have its original love back.

Four hours later, Erica and I entered a Forever 21 store, our arms already aching with several other bags. A pair of blazing red joggers immediately caught my eye, and I rushed toward them. Erica reached for a pair of ripped skinny jeans. It was then, as I was checking the price tag on the joggers that I decided to tell Erica about my encounter with Colton.

"Damn, that boy does not know how to *disappear!*" she huffed, squinting at the tag on the jeans.

"Well it's not really his fault. We're both home for holiday break," I reasoned.

She hardly heard me. "Do you still like him? I thought you had a new boyfriend. The one you texted me about, remember? From college?"

"Elijah wasn't my boyfriend. Besides, he's transferring, so—"

"Do you still like Colton?" Erica dropped the jeans and bored her into mine with so much intensity I almost had to look away.

"No! Well...n—I don't know!" I exhaled.

Erica lowered her eyes, lost in thought. Her expression was almost sympathetic and I felt chagrin set my cheeks on fire. When she glanced back up at me, her face was scrunched up in concern.

"Why do you think that is?" She walked a few paces over to a rack of cashmere sweaters.

I ditched the joggers and followed her. "I don't know! I mean, we were sixteen when we dated. That was three years ago. And I've been focused on my music, plus I've made a lot of great new friends at school. I don't know why all I have to do is take one look at Colton and melt. He's a jerk after all."

"You're right, he *is* a jerk. He blamed you for something that wasn't even your fault!"

I shook my head. "Erica, if it was anyone else, I wouldn't care."

My friend frowned and looked back at me. I could see the wheels churning in her mind. After a few moments, she sighed.

"Alright, I'm gonna tell you a story." She walked further into the store, beckoning me to follow. "A week and a half ago, I was going through my mom's old jewelry box because she's gonna sell it, and she wanted me to pick some things to have. In the back of the box, I found this *gorgeous* necklace. It was a heart locket, but I'd never seen my mom wear it, so I asked her about it. She said that the necklace was given to her by her first love, and she kept it all these years. Apparently, she'd forgotten it was in the jewelry box. Mind you, she and my dad have been married for like, twenty-some years."

She was momentarily distracted by a Pink Floyd T-shirt.

"The point is, Gail...there's something about that first love that stays with you forever. When I showed my mom the necklace, she took it and put it somewhere else for safe-keeping, even though she must've dated that guy when she was my age! It's like...you grow up and move on, but that one person lives in your heart forever—no matter how you change."

I let her words sink in while simultaneously wondering if Colton was still thinking about me.

"Besides, everyone grieves differently," Erica continued with a shrug.

"But it's been years."

"Did you not just hear me recite that entire story about my mother?" Erica laughed. "It's okay, Gail. It's normal to have a soft spot for him, even though he...dumped you out of sheer stupidity."

Her bluntness actually made me laugh.

"So what do I do if I have to go through life permanently hooked on someone?"

Erica added the Pink Floyd T-shirt to her already full arms and shook her head. "You won't be permanently hooked, Gail. Time's gonna push you to move on, trust me. There will come a day when that blond loser won't even cross your mind. So when the time is right and you feel ready, you can get back out there."

"You're saying I should go date the first guy I see?"

"Stop twisting my words," Erica warned, and I giggled. "Elijah was a good start, but just keep focusing on yourself for the time being. You're in college now, for heaven's sake. No more high school shit."

I bit my lower lip. "So what do I do?"

"First off, just hope to God you don't see Colton again. That boy causes more drama than you have time to handle. But if you *do* end up seeing him...well, just remember that you're always gonna have feelings for this person, and there's nothing you can do about it. But I wouldn't worry about that. It's a big world, and you guys are only home once every so often."

. . .

When I returned to school in the middle of January, I wanted nothing more than to just live my life as a single woman. Erica was right, boys were a distraction I didn't need. Curtis did feel slightly less vibrant without Elijah's warmth and kindness, but I found a way to manage. We talked every once in a while, and he sent me pictures of the towering buildings at Ashford University. But for the most part, our communication slowly died out.

In the meantime, Maya and Julia became party animals. Blame it on the time cooped up indoors for the winter, but they were suddenly stir crazy and gone almost every night. The first couple times they went out, I stayed home, but then Cara got hooked and insisted that I join them. Too many times I found myself in a packed mansion, nearly high from secondhand smoking marijuana, as it seemed the entire house reeked of it.

But I didn't go for the dope and drugs, I went for the music and the vibes. Since we started going to the parties, I'd developed a love for dancing. When the music was so loud it shook the ground, I got lost in my own world. Who knew dancing in a room of strangers would be the adrenaline spike I'd been searching for.

By spring, I was working harder than ever in my classes. Professor Autrie noticed my improving grades and acknowledged me in front of the entire conducting class, complimenting me for my hard work.

Dad came to Curtis in late May for the orchestra's annual spring performance. The crowd rewarded us with a standing ovation. Afterward, Professor Autrie approached me and my father to recommend me for the Young Artist Summer Program. It was a suggestion my father *had* to cave to. My happiness was worth burning a hole in his wallet for. Besides, he was well aware that working with Professor Autrie would help me improve my skills to become a famous conductor one day.

The end of my freshman year came sooner than I expected. Before I knew it, Cara and I were packing our bags, and our dorm room suddenly looked more like a storage unit than a place to sleep. It was hard to believe we already had one year under our belts.

"It was so nice meeting you, Gail," Dalia whimpered as I wobbled down the hallway with my suitcase and other bags.

She kept my pace easily though and didn't seem to notice that I was struggling with my luggage.

"You, too, Dal," I huffed.

"You signed up for the Young Artist Summer Program, right?"

"Of course."

It was so easy to cheer Dalia up. It was like flipping a switch; she was suddenly all smiles, jumping around me like a little kid in a candy shop. "Oh, yay! You're going to *love* the program!"

I dropped my bags by the elevator doors and tried to ignore the stabbing pain that was pulsing in my wrists and biceps. Dalia flashed her sweet, innocent smile, and I shook my head.

"Did anyone ever tell you that you're really good at your job?" I inquired.

She shrugged. "Only a lot."

I laughed and drew her in for a hug, thanking her for making my first year at Curtis so wonderful. She took the compliment like it was a shiny badge.

"Congrats on graduating, by the way. We're gonna miss you," I said.

"Not as much as I'm gonna miss you." Dalia adjusted her glasses and blew me a kiss before disappearing down the hall.

I met Cara downstairs in the lobby. Her hair was pulled up into a messy bun, with a few golden strands spilling down the sides of her face. I threw my arms around her.

"Promise to stay in touch," I demanded.

"Absolutely! We should look into buying an apartment next

year. Oh, and good luck with the program this summer. I know you'll be amazing."

"Yeah, I'm really excited."

I had tried to get Cara to sign up for the program with me, but she shyly declined, saying that she needed the summer off. And I knew she had something more important to do anyway. I could see it now in the worry that was filling her eyes.

"Hey, don't worry, Care, your brother will come around. Just tell him everything you told me. It'll be alright."

She exhaled and gave me a brave smile. "Thank you, Gail."

After one last hug, we parted ways and I hauled my suitcase outside.

The warm air kissed my cheeks as I hurried toward my car. I always loved the summer. It was the time to be free, to breathe again. The sun glittered in the sky, like a large jewel casting fractions of light onto the earth. I felt it graze the crown of my head like a gentle caress.

Yes, summer was the time for living, and until I would check back into Curtis in one month, I planned to experience the world for what it was: a massive kingdom of opportunity. But as I tossed my suitcase into the trunk and climbed into the driver's seat, something weighed down on my heart. It was an old familiar ache, like a fist was clamped around my chest. Going home only made me think of my past. It was a place that had my first love written all over it.

Chapter Eight

SARATOGA SPRINGS, NY—CURTIS INSTITUTE OF MUSIC, PA (2022)

By the time I parked my car in Dad's driveway, the sky was as black as ink. Erica sat in my passenger seat, half asleep with drool dripping down her chin. We both smelled of sweat and alcohol. Though I only downed one drink after being made designated driver, the sharp scent was still strong on my breath, and I thanked my lucky stars Dad had gone to Jamie's for the night. A dozen fireflies flickered in the yard, illuminating the path toward the front door. I nudged Erica and she groaned.

"What time is it?"

"Two-thirty I think," I said, desperately wanting to peel out of my sequined dress.

Erica shoved the door open and wobbled around the front end of the car. She leaned against me as we climbed the porch steps.

After graduating this past May, Erica was more than ready to join me on my party runs. Tonight, we'd gone to a party that was hosted by my old high school friend Ella Richmand in her large, vintage-style mansion a few miles north. While it was nice getting to see all of my old friends from high school, I laughed the hardest when Erica grabbed a random boy by the ears and kissed him right on the lips.

Inside the house, I flicked on the lights, and as the darkness vanished, I saw the green look on Erica's face.

"If you're gonna puke, don't do it on my dad's floor. You know where the bathroom is."

She didn't even respond but simply stumbled down the hall and slammed the bathroom door shut. I cringed at the sound of her wrenching.

"I'm *never* getting drunk again!" Erica moaned, flopping down onto the couch.

"You just have to drink responsibly," I reasoned.

She pressed her face into a pillow and waved my comment away. "Whatever, Mom."

I sat down in the opposite armchair and allowed the weight of the night to finally catch up with me. Here in Dad's living room, it was quiet, and yet a thick bass line was still thumping in my ears. I was dizzy with exhaustion; my feet ached from dancing so much. And my throat still burned slightly from the single shot of Fireball Whiskey.

"Did I hook up tonight?" Erica wondered, pressing a hand to her throbbing forehead.

"Actually yes."

Her eyes shot open. "*What?*"

"For like a whole ten minutes, too."

"Shit! I don't even remember that."

I laughed when she grabbed fistfuls of the couch quilt and started thrashing around.

"At *least* tell me he was hot," she whined.

"Oh, he was. No question about it."

"Awesome." Her eyes grew wide as saucers. "I bet he was stunning. You know, he probably wants to marry me. Can you imagine if I married my drunk hook up?" She cackled and a splutter of saliva sprang from her mouth.

"You're a lot more talkative when you're drunk."

"And you're a lot more *ca-ray-ze*!" She howled with laughter again, and I didn't have the energy to tell her I wasn't even intoxicated.

After I helped her settle down, I pushed myself up the stairs and into bed, and it was at that moment that my mind chose to deluge with countless thoughts. One minute, I was contemplating the probability of Erica vomiting on Dad's floor and the severe punishment if he found out we'd been drinking. The next minute, I was thinking about my upcoming trip back to Curtis, and suddenly I wanted nothing more than to play my violin. It was a desperate ache I felt deep in my bones. I'd only been gone from school for a mere three weeks, but it seemed too long. If I didn't play soon, I feared I would develop a nasty rash. Was it possible that music was a stronger addiction than alcohol and dancing?

I tossed and turned all night.

I finally gave up around seven in the morning and wandered downstairs to make some breakfast. Unsurprisingly, Erica was still passed out on the couch. Her mouth was stretched wide open, and her hair resembled the disarray of a chicken coup. Her mascara was smudged all down her cheeks as well.

The eggs crackled in the frying pan, and I poked them with my spatula. I couldn't stop yawning, which annoyed me given the fact that I'd welcomed sleep multiple times last night, but it chose to ignore me. After scrunching my face up with yet another yawn, my eyes fell on a note by the Keurig.

It was a To-Do list, and Dad's near illegible handwriting was scribbled all over the paper in blue ink. Through narrowed eyes, I managed to make out "Remind Gail that Young Artist Summer Program is almost full." Under that, it said "might not be able to find space…"

Anxiety curled its fingers around my neck. I slammed the note down on the counter top and tried to slow my breathing, but it was impossible.

A summer without Professor Autrie's guidance meant a summer without improvement. I wanted this opportunity more than anything else in the world right now, but my chance was slipping away because of *loss of space*?

I spun on my heel and retrieved my cell phone off the table. And without remembering that it was only 7:15 am, I dialed my father's number and impatiently waited for him to answer.

"Hello?" he said, clearly still half-asleep.

"What is this about not being able to enter the Young Artist Summer program?" I demanded.

"What?"

"The note on the counter! When were you gonna tell me that I wasn't gonna be able to go?" I was infuriated, nearly shouting.

"Gail, what are you...Oh, right. No, I saw the other day that spots are filling up and that if we don't enter you soon, you can't do it." He paused. "Don't you normally sleep in on Saturdays?"

"Help me sign up!" I screeched. "Today! As soon as you come home!"

"Okay, I will. Are you feeling alright?"

"I'm fine, I just really need to get into that program."

"And we will take care of it." He enunciated each word.

I blew a few strands of hair out of my face. "Okay. Goodbye."

I ended the call and stood in the stunning silence. My breathing was almost ragged.

It was unlike me to scream at my father. But the thought of not being able to play my violin at the academy this summer felt like I was being stripped of a basic human right.

"What's so important that you have to scream into the phone at this hour?" Erica muttered, stepping into the kitchen with a sick, listless expression on her face.

"I'm sorry. I didn't mean to wake you up."

"Eggs are burning."

A menacing hiss came from the frying pan, and I quickly scooped my breakfast onto a nearby plate. Sure enough, the underside of my scrambled eggs was charred a dark brown. Erica fixed herself a glass of cool water and fell into a seat at the kitchen table. I joined her, almost unwilling to eat the eggs now that they were scorched.

"I have such a headache," she whined, pressing the glass of water to her forehead.

"Here." I got some Advil from the cabinet and handed her two pills, which she swallowed immediately.

"Thanks. So, who was that anyway? What were you going on about?"

"Just my dad." I sighed. "He said I might not be able to do the summer program at Curtis. Apparently spots are filling up really fast."

"Oh, that's it? Geez, I thought he freaking murdered someone and you were calling him out on it."

"I guess I kinda overreacted, yeah."

She took another sip of water and eyed me over the rim of the glass. "You take music a little too seriously sometimes, Gail."

"What do you mean?"

"Well, you basically just cried bloody murder on your dad because you're afraid you aren't gonna get into the summer program, even though you definitely are. I know they love you at that school. There's no way they wouldn't take you."

I stared at her, not seeing the point of confrontation. "I just really wanna play my violin, that's all."

"I understand that. But sometimes you make it seem like that instrument is cocaine and you're an addict. I mean, you play nonstop. In all honesty, I swear you practice more than our entire high school orchestra."

I frowned. "So? That just makes me a good instrumentalist."

"Yes. But...have you ever heard of music therapy?"

"Okay, wait. How did you go from black-out, forget-everything drunk to a therapist?"

She shrugged. "I don't know. Guess this is just me when I'm on the come down." She gestured with her hand. "But that doesn't matter. Music therapy is super helpful. It's been known to cure depression."

"What are you saying?" I was getting tired of her code speak, and my lack of sleep wasn't making my tone any nicer.

"I think that violin is your new source of happiness."

"As opposed to what?"

She gave me a sympathetic look, and I knew what she meant right away. "Don't make me say it."

I threw up my hands in frustration. "*Or* I just really like playing, Erica!"

Despite my acerbic voice, she remained calm, like a therapist would. "You just went hysterical when you found out you might not make it into the school's summer program. Even though if you didn't, you could still play right there in the freaking living room, and it wouldn't matter."

"It *does* matter," I rebuked.

"Why?"

"Because it's the only thing that brings me joy, and Curtis is my home!" My voice echoed off the kitchen cabinets, and the following silence was unbearably awkward.

After a moment, Erica sighed. "Look, I'm not trying to upset you. I think it's great that you're so passionate about the violin. I mean, you're practically Lindsey Stirling on steroids. I'm just saying...I think you rely on the music to *fill* you."

I didn't trust myself to answer now.

"Sorry for bringing it up, but Colton was a huge part of your life. A good part, don't get me wrong. But you *depended* on him for happiness. Like how you *depend* on the violin now. But when you don't get those things, you shut down." She was still rubbing the chilled glass to her forehead. "Why can't you make yourself happy, Gail?"

"I — I...*do* make myself happy." The statement didn't sound convincing. Where had all my temerity gone?

"I know you," Erica continued, wagging her finger at me. "You play and play the violin for hours, but when your dang fingers aren't stuck to that fingerboard, you're distant. To be honest, I think it's a wonder your fingers haven't started bleeding yet."

"I have calluses."

She gave me a look that screamed pity.

"What do you want me to do?" I inquired forlornly. The mention of Colton had sent a cold spike through me, and now it felt like my organs had goosebumps.

"Get to know yourself a little better," Erica said after a sip of water. "You still have two weeks before you go back to the school. And yes, you will go back, I *promise*," she added after my eyes filled with terror. "But use the time to take an actual break from playing. You're not gonna lose all those incredible skills in the span of fourteen days. You deserve a little time off."

"But all I ever do is play. I don't know what else..." I trailed off when I realized my friend had a point. "I-I guess I like parties."

"'M-kay, that's good. But how about something a little less...alcohol-involved?" She massaged her temples wearily.

It was strange. I really had to push myself to think. When I was a child, I liked gardening with my mother and perfecting our flowerbeds, but the effort seemed wasted now that I didn't have her guidance and affection. I also recalled having an interest in art, but that was when I was in kindergarten and could spend the afternoon wrist-deep in paint.

None of these things seemed appealing now. It was like the memories had lost their shine. I didn't dislike gardening or art, but I just couldn't see myself doing them now as a nineteen, almost twenty-year-old.

"What about joining a sports team?" Erica suggested groggily. "Soccer?"

"Not my style."

"Dance?"

"Unless it's at a party where no one is paying attention to me, not a chance."

"I'm not gonna fight your close-mindedness. If music is the only thing you like, I won't go against that. I'm just saying...don't treat it like it's the *only* thing that can foster happiness."

I sighed as her words took effect. I cupped my hand around the back of my neck, lost in thought.

"Now that we've reached an ultimatum, I'm going back to bed." She took her glass of water and trudged toward the living room. "If you want to make me some eggs for later, I like mine sunny-side up, not burnt."

I didn't know what I was doing here, knee deep in classic novels. It seemed a little pointless after the week I'd had. I was sitting on the ground of a library, paging through each book, trying to judge the entirety of the novels through a few words. The book shelves stood looming over me, offering thousands of worlds, themes, and characters.

Ever since Erica had encouraged me to get to know myself outside of music, I'd really taken it in stride. But I was meeting more failures than successes. I tried a kick-boxing class on Monday night, which led to nothing but muscle soreness and a bad headache. Tuesday, I wound up in a pottery class, which I was *told* was set at a beginners level. But when everyone else's clay pot turned out flawless, I was suddenly embarrassed by my own deformed final product. Today, I decided to visit the local library and see if I could find myself in the pages of a novel. So far, I wasn't having any luck.

"That's a good one," someone said.

I looked up to see an old lady with fizzled gray hair that expanded in a sphere around her head. Her glasses were a size too big. I realized then that she was the librarian. With a soft grunt, she knelt down beside me.

"*Little Women* has been around for generations. It follows the lives of four sisters—talks all about their growth from childhood to adulthood."

I smiled politely. "I know. I read it in high school. It's pretty good."

I placed the copy of *Little Women* back into my stack of chosen books, which the librarian eyed curiously.

"Are you in summer school?" she inquired.

"Oh, no, I'm just looking to get back into reading again. I used to read all the time as a kid, but then I got to college, and—"

"Everything changed," she finished for me, chuckling. "Yes, that's usually when kids have better things to do than read. Anything in particular you're looking for?"

I shrugged. "I don't really know what I'm interested in. I just can't seem to find a story that keeps me enticed, you know?"

She shoved her glasses back up her nose and nodded. "Have you ever tried writing?"

My lips broke into a smile and I almost laughed until I saw her solemn expression.

"I mean, I write papers for school, but..." She raised one grizzled gray eyebrow at me. "I'm not very creative like that."

The librarian reached over to collect my stack of books and held them in her arms like they were newborn babies. When her eyes touched mine again, I saw a sparkle of amusement.

"My dear, something tells me you're more creative than you think. Follow me."

She led me to a separate section of the library and we stopped by a bin filled with spiral notebooks.

"Maybe the reason you're not finding the right book is because you're not the one writing it," the librarian murmured.

With her free hand, she reached into the bin and retrieved a thick journal with a sky blue cover. Sunlight leaked in through the massive windows and glinted off the spirals.

"I'm not a good writer," I said. "I could never write a book."

It was funny how this stranger had so much faith in me.

"It doesn't have to be a book." Her laugh was soft like a gentle breeze on a humid day. "It can be whatever you want. Maybe you just use it to relieve stress and write everything you want to say." She shrugged. "A little vent-writing never hurt nobody."

"Now you sound like my old English teacher."

There was that laugh again, and I watched her begin to sort through the stack of classics on a nearby table.

I held the journal in my hands, peering down at it like it was a puzzle I couldn't solve. One word gleamed against the smooth blue cover: *Love*. It was written in stylish calligraphy with gold lettering, which reflected the iridescent lights hanging from the ceiling.

When I was younger, I could spend all afternoon with my nose in a book. I was a sucker for romance. There was just something so dazzling about the sensation of being in love and the stakes one would go to just to protect their significant other.

But the word *love* meant something a little different to me now that I was older. It meant support and encouragement, but it also meant heartbreak. And heartbreak was inevitable. All good things come to an end eventually.

Still, I couldn't tear my eyes away from the word. How could such a small noun mean something so monumental? After a moment I sighed and retrieved my wallet from my purse.

The librarian smiled. "Good choice."

. . .

I didn't write often. When I did, it was for two reasons: either I was bored or I was forcing myself to sit down and consider what Erica had said about finding myself through ways other than music. But I mostly just wrote about people. I wrote about Cara and Erica, my two best friends in the entire world. I wrote about Elijah and how I thought of him every now and then just out of the blue. I wrote about my father and my mother, about Jamie. The pages were filling up with the names of those I felt connected to or had lost.

Every name but one. There was one person I couldn't bring myself to write about for fear of reopening a long-sealed wound, and I knew that if that wound was opened, I could stumble into darkness again.

When I thought of Colton, my body would set on fire. It was like a hundred wires were blazing inside me all at once. The memories were the problem. The memories, as bright and vivid as they were, kept me from the pleasure of indifference. As long as I didn't write them down, the thoughts didn't have to be true.

I ended up securing a spot in the Young Artist Summer Program by the skin of my teeth. I'd gotten the last spot available. I checked back into Curtis on July eleventh, cradling my violin case like it was my child. And later as I plucked my strings, I recalled Erica's analogy of an addict trying to kick his cocaine dependence.

Well, I thought, *at least music is a safe high.*

When I sat down at my first private lesson, Professor Autrie was euphoric.

"*Ma chérie! On va avoir une année super!*" he exclaimed, clapping his wrinkled hands together.

"Professor, I don't speak French," I said sheepishly through a nervous chuckle.

"*Ah, pardonne-moi!* I said it's going to be a great year. I just know that your work ethic will lead to great *success!*" He always emphasized that word, like it was the only word in the English language that meant anything to him.

We didn't waste time either. First, we covered basic conducting techniques as a review from the past year. He would tap his baton on the stand and I would flick my hands this way and that, conducting in either two, three, or four. He handed me piece after piece of music and together we would break it down by measure.

"What about measure forty-two?" he asked, pointing with his baton.

"Well, it's a key change," I answered, and he nodded. "But it also gets slower, so the beats per measure changes." I demonstrated a slow sweeping motion with my hand for emphasis.

Professor Autrie set his baton down and stood. "Excellent."

It went on like this for weeks, and with each session I could tell I was making tremendous progress. My conducting skills were developing overnight. If I kept at it, I could make it as a conductor one day. I would.

The week after my twentieth birthday, Professor Autrie called me to his office.

"A few of our students have been selected to perform at a music festival in Queensbury, New York. I know the head of the festival. He's a very nice man. *Très accueillant.* Each year, he hosts the festival to raise money for the children's hospital. He was wondering if we could send a quartet up to New York to play."

"Queensbury is only a half hour from where my dad lives," I said. "He'd love to come see us play so close to home."

Professor Autrie ran a hand through his thinning silver hair. "Ah, *excellente.* I will let Mark know you are interested. It'll be you on violin, Sheila Baker on viola, Deven Ashwalt on cello, and Christain Santser on bass."

I'd met these people last year when I played with Curtis's orchestra. We weren't the best of friends, but I was happy to travel with them if it meant I could play so close to home.

"Sounds great. What're we playing?"

"Mark says there will be multiple musical acts, so we only have time for one piece."

I watched my instructor dig around in a filing cabinet next to his desk, mumbling unintelligibly when he couldn't find what he was looking for. Finally, he retrieved the sheet music; I took it from him and read the title aloud.

"*The Blue Danube Waltz*...by Johann Strauss II." I looked up at my professor and grinned. "What a shock."

If I'd learned anything about this man, it was that he loved his waltzes.

"Yes, yes, it's going to be great! But Gail, this will be the last time I see you before the start of the school year. I hope you have a great rest of your summer."

I thanked him at least a dozen times before saying, "Don't worry, this summer is already perfect. Nothing could mess it up."

I insisted on driving to Queensbury because I didn't trust Sheila Baker to focus on the road for as much as she ran her mouth. For four and a half hours, I was doomed to listen to her constant babbling. Secretly, I envied the boys for driving separately, but to pass the time, I tried to focus on my surroundings instead of Sheila's shrill, gossip-girl tone.

Queensbury wasn't like Saratoga Springs. It was much smaller, with quaint buildings and tiny roadside diners. It was a nice change of scenery and pace.

We arrived at the festival grounds at one o'clock and met up with Deven and Christain.

"It looks like it's gonna rain," Christain observed.

I peered up at the sky and sure enough, menacing black clouds loomed in the distance.

"Do you think they're gonna cancel?" Sheila asked.

"I sure hope we don't have to," a tall, lanky man responded. He approached us and held out his hand, "I'm Mark Zaniels. I host the festival each year, and I just *love* when Victor sends his students to perform. Your talent really draws a big crowd!"

"Thank you," Sheila answered for us.

"How about this weather situation, sir? Apparently, there's a ninety-percent chance of thunderstorms," Deven murmured, flashing his iPhone toward us so that we could see the forecast as well.

Mark sighed. "That's so unfortunate. I checked the weather all week and it *never* once said rain!" I gave him a sympathetic look. "We'll just have to get through as many acts as we can. But I thank you for coming. Last year, we raised eight-thousand dollars for the children's hospital."

"Well, hopefully we beat that record this year," I said, and Mark's eyes filled with hope.

"God bless you!"

By the time our quartet was called side stage, the wind had picked up and the clouds were shifting ominously. Thankfully, the band playing on the stage now was good enough to distract the audience, who were splayed out on blankets and foldable chairs in the grass.

"How are we supposed to follow these guys?" Deven asked. "We might just lull these people to sleep with the waltz!"

I agreed. The band was covering current day pop songs and adding their own fill of guitar and drum solos. I had to hand it to them; they were incredible, but our waltz was doomed to sound like a lullaby now.

As the band bowed to a roar of cheers, I tightened my grip on my violin and walked steadily up the side stairs. I could hear my dad and Jamie screaming from the audience, but I kept my eyes forward.

The members of the band turned to wish us good luck, and as I shook hands with the drummer a strange expression crossed his face. He'd said hello to me, but that was all he could manage. His eyes narrowed curiously and his lips trembled, like he was trying to say something but the words weren't allowed out. He acted like I was some long lost friend whose name had escaped him. Finally, he forced a smile and jogged to catch up with his other band members. I tried not to let my confusion show on my face. After all, we were in front of a large crowd now.

We each took our seats in a small semi-circle and touched our bows to our strings. Professor Autrie had deemed me the one in charge of counting us off, so I whispered the counts to the others, made a swooping motion with my body, and we were off.

Yes, it was a huge contrast to the rock music of the last performance, but we were just as talented. We moved as one instrument, one person. My fingers danced across the fingerboard like the complicated steps of a ballerina. At one point, I caught Christain's eye, and we both smiled as the crescendo swelled throughout the fairgrounds.

Usually, I kept my eyes trained on my violin as I played, but I risked a glance out into the audience. There were people of all ages scattered across the grass. I was worried I'd spot boredom in their faces, but each and every person looked to be entranced by the movement of our bows. One little girl was even swaying back and forth, twirling around to the soft melodies of Strauss's waltz. I saw the band members standing side stage, their heads bobbing in time with the *bum-bum, bum-bums*. They, too, were affected by the fun, frilliness of the song.

The drummer's eyes stayed trained on my face, and that curious expression found its way into his features again. When he wasn't looking at me, he was searching the crowd for someone else.

All too soon, the waltz came to a lovely end, and people stood out of their seats to applaud for us. Maybe it was the complication of the song, or maybe it was our young age, but they seemed to be in awe.

I found my father and his girlfriend afterward and they gathered me into a tight hug.

"Incredible," Dad exclaimed. "Absolutely incredible. I say we celebrate with some ice cream!"

Just as the suggestion left his mouth, a crack of thunder boomed through the area, causing people to jump out of their seats. I looked up at the sky and felt a single raindrop plop down on my skin.

"On second thought, there's ice cream at home in the freezer," Jamie offered.

Dad sighed. "Are you coming home tonight?"

"Probably. I just have to pack up and say bye to everyone."

"Alright. I'll see you at home then. Hey," he said just as I was about to turn away. He held up a fist and I bumped it with my own. "Awesome job, sweetheart!"

The rain was quickly kicking people out, so after saying goodbye to my friends, I hurried to pack my instrument away before the sprinkling could turn to a downpour. Through the crowd, I spotted Mr. Zaniels and by the look on his face, it was clear he'd already beaten his record for fundraising, which made me smile.

As I zipped my case shut, someone tapped my shoulder. I turned around and froze as a cold fist punched right through my torso.

"Hey, stranger," Colton Reeves said.

He was dressed in dark-wash jeans and a black water-proof jacket. His golden hair was darkened slightly by the rain that was falling more harshly now. And his gold-green eyes were as striking as ever.

"Colton," I said, suddenly breathless. "W — what are you doing here?"

"I know the drummer in the band who played before you guys. He goes to Penn State with me. He said he was playing close to home, and I couldn't pass up that opportunity."

And suddenly it was crystal clear why the drummer had looked at me like he knew me. But then the only way he *would* know of me was if Colton had mentioned me. I felt a blush creep into my cheeks.

For a moment, Colton's face was filled with an emotion I couldn't name. Fear? Desperation? There his jaw went, locking and unlocking. Finally, he cleared his throat.

"You guys were awesome, by the way."

"Thanks," I replied.

You're asleep, my conscience warned. *There's no way this is real.* And yet my heart was lurching forward as if it was being pulled toward Colton by some unseen magnetic force. *This was definitely real.*

Colton shifted his weight and balled his hands into his pockets. "Um...Listen, I don't know if you have plans or something, but I was wondering if you...maybe wanna...grab a coffee or something? Catch up?"

A thousand butterflies flitted around in my stomach; adrenaline leaked through my veins like morphine, and suddenly my heartbreak was all but forgotten...until the memory of that second coffee cup flashed in my mind.

"Aren't you seeing someone?" I felt stupid asking. It made me sound like I cared, which was a satisfaction I didn't want to give Colton, even if it was true.

His face fell ever so slightly. "No. Not anymore."

"I'm sorry. I didn't mean to—"

"It's okay," he answered. "Besides, I don't think she's the one for me anyway."

I nodded and watched the way the rain slid off his jacket. It was starting to downpour, but I hardly noticed. All I was aware of was how clear his voice sounded, how familiar and enchanting it felt to speak to him.

"I'd love to get a coffee with you, Colton," I called over the hiss of the rain.

He blinked the water from his eyes and smiled. What a lovely, familiar smile. It made the rest of the world fade away.

Clutching my violin case in my hand, I stepped up beside him. We weren't touching—we were simply shoulder to shoulder —but the butterflies in my stomach took flight. In my brain, I envisioned us at sixteen. Four years apart had changed us.

We walked up the grassy hill together as the rain swirled furiously around us, washing away the past.

Chapter Nine

JULY 2081

Abigail hadn't seen this many people in her house since the summer of 2066, when her best friends and husband had thrown her that big surprise party for her 65th birthday. Today, she was turning 80. Her closest friends and family sang a painfully off-key rendition of "Happy Birthday," and at the end, Abigail struggled to blow out the candles on her two-tiered cake.

"Happy birthday, Mom!" Aliana shouted excitedly, slicing off a piece.

Abigail's grin was a mile wide as she watched her family and friends crowd in for some cake. They sang and shouted and laughed about random nonsense, but it was the togetherness that made Abigail's heart feel so full.

"Trinity, go get some more plates from the kitchen," Gavin told his daughter, leaning in to help Aliana slice.

Abigail felt someone nudge her shoulder. It was Erica—in all her gray haired and wrinkled beauty.

"This kinda takes me back," Erica said in a wavering, shaky

voice. Her eyes, however, were just as electric and vibrant as they were when she was young.

"I know, right?" Abigail laughed hard, but it soon turned to a wheeze and a violent cough.

The room fell silent as the beloved matriarch of the family coughed harshly into her elbow.

"Grandma, are you okay?" Kota asked.

A dozen echoes followed his question. Abigail straightened, and her hands shook slightly, but that was nothing out of the ordinary. She'd been shaking more and more these days. It was the price of aging.

"I'm okay," Abigail assured everyone.

The talking resumed half a minute later, but Aliana and Gavin glanced at their mother with worried eyes. She had never coughed that hard before.

"Been to the doctor recently?" Gavin inquired subtly as they all sat down with their plates.

"Yep." Abigail took a bite and frosting smeared on her chin. "I went last week to have my back checked."

"And?"

"Well, my skeleton's not twenty years old anymore, but it's all right."

Aliana sighed. "Mom, maybe instead of staying indoors and writing, you should get out some more and go for a walk. I'll even take you to the spa. I have Wednesday off next week—"

"Don't be ridiculous." Abigail laughed, but it sounded like another breathy wheeze. "I'm gonna keep writing."

"That's all you do these days," Gavin said, as if that were something to be afraid of.

"I'm retired." His mother shrugged. "I've got all the time in the world."

"That's what Dad said," Aliana muttered, and the three of them went dead silent.

Pleasant chatter carried on around them, but now Abigail

was remembering a time when she wasn't so much concerned about death as she was about living in the moment. The memories were like magnets; she wanted to return to the desk in her bedroom and continue writing.

"I'll be okay," Abigail insisted, patting her daughter's hand. "It's my birthday today, for Heaven's sake! We shouldn't be talking about those sad things. Let's party instead."

This brought a smile to her children's faces, and they complied. For the rest of the afternoon, Abigail talked, laughed, reminisced, and gossiped with her friends and family. It felt good to have so much positivity in one room, especially since Abigail had really been alone the past couple of months.

Eventually, as the sun became a soft globe on the horizon, Abigail slowly rose to her feet.

"Where're you going, Mom?" Gavin asked.

His wife Hope looked up from the TV. "Yeah, the old *Wonder Woman's* on. Didn't you say this movie came out when you were in high school?"

"Yeah." Abigail watched Gal Gadot flash across the screen and crouch behind her magnificent shield to block the Nazi's bullets. "It's a great movie. But I've got some more writing to do."

"Are you sure? I could make an extra bag of popcorn, and—"

"Shh!" Trinity and Andrea hissed, their eyes glued to the screen.

Abigail smiled. "It's all right," she whispered. "Besides, I can't wait to write the next part of my story."

She headed for the staircase and allowed her excited heartbeat to tow her up the steps and back to her pen and paper.

Chapter Ten

QUEENSBURY, NY—CURTIS INSTITUTE OF MUSIC, PA (2022)

When I sat down with Colton in an old-fashioned diner, my heartbeat was erratic. My palms were sweating, and I couldn't stop gnawing on my lower lip. I had hundreds of questions, but I didn't know how to broach them. I was at war with myself. Was it better to know or not to know?

"So, how's school going?" he asked after we ordered our drinks.

"It's going well. I basically spent the whole summer in private lessons with my orchestra conductor."

Colton chuckled. "Nice."

It was so strange sitting here with him like it was any other day. He was aware of all my secrets, all my good and bad habits. He'd kissed me fiercely on warm summer nights. And here we were, talking about our college experiences like the love we shared never even existed. It was weird.

"How about you?" I asked.

"Good. My classes are going well. I'm really enjoying it."

Neither of us spoke then. An awkward silence filled the quiet, and I felt my rib cage constrict around my lungs.

I didn't want to talk about school, and I knew he didn't either. But school was a safe topic. With school, no personal emotions were exposed. Why did we have to be so stubborn?

We discussed the weather and then ended up on the topic of Colton's acceptance to a volleyball club team.

"I'm really proud of you," I murmured.

He glanced up from his drink, and I found myself lost in his eyes again. Underneath the calm facade, there was a look of wonder on his face. I could see it plain as day, as if looking at myself in the mirror.

"Thanks," he said.

The rain came, cleared, and came again. One moment, there were other people around us, the next moment we were alone. It was amazing how you could waste so much time talking about nothing. But time didn't exist with Colton. Being with him meant being in a separate universe. Maybe we were at a diner in space and the earth was lightyears away. I wouldn't have known...or cared.

Eventually, we found our voices and started joking around like two teenagers again. We'd gotten on the topic of a zombie apocalypse, and I was forced to google methods of survival.

"Have a survival kit ready. Keep weapons handy. Know some good hiding places." I read off the list Google provided me. "Where would your hiding place be, Colton?"

"The mountains," he replied instantly. "Stay on high ground."

"That doesn't mean anything. Zombies have legs — they can climb," I countered.

Colton's laugh was as sweet as the sound of my violin. I'd missed seeing him smile so much. The way his nose crinkled and his eyes squeezed shut. Even how his lips stretched over the gums in his mouth. His laugh made me feel like I was floating.

"We'd be able to see them coming, Gail. The advantage would be in our hands."

"What's this *we* stuff?" I joked. "Isn't it every man for himself?"

"Maybe for everyone else, but you'd come with me."

It was only a simple response, but the way he said it lit a match in my stomach.

When I finally checked my phone again, the screen alerted me that it was ten past six. By now, the rain was gone again, and in its place was a thick, rosy fog that was colored by the setting sun.

"Do you really think there's gonna be a zombie apocalypse?" I asked incredulously.

He leaned back in his chair and cocked his head. "Hard to say. Just watch *The Walking Dead* or *World War Z,* and you'll be set."

"Already seen them," I said, and his beautiful laugh filtered through the air again.

Just like that, the sun was gone, replaced by a clear black sky. Even the clouds had finally disappeared. I was tired after my day of travel, and soon I was yawning repeatedly.

"Am I keeping you from something?" Colton asked. "I'm sorry if—"

"No," I said a bit too quickly. "I don't have anywhere to be."

Colton folded his hands under his chin. "I mean, if you're tired—"

"I don't want to leave."

The words were out before I could stop them. Our eyes touched and something unspoken flowed between us. My heart was galloping again, and something told me his was, too. For a moment, we didn't speak. Neither of us knew what to say after all, for I had finally broken the barrier.

I was suddenly fighting the incredible urge to touch his hand, to feel his skin. *Don't run from this*, my conscience advised me. It was now or never.

"Colton," I said his name very slowly, annunciating it, feeling the weight of it on my tongue. "There are days when I don't think about you, but when I do, it's like...walking through fire. Life's weird without you in it, and I hate it."

Colton watched me as I spoke. His eyes widened slightly, and his mouth was parted like he wanted to say something.

"Abigail—"

"And I know that we should leave the past in the past, but...I think a piece of my heart still belongs to you. I can't fight that...I don't want to."

His eyes skimmed my face, longingly and desperately. The sight sent a heat wave through my body.

"I think I know what you mean," he whispered.

The universe was frozen. Earth at a standstill, waiting to see where this was headed.

"Um, my mom's out of town on a church retreat," Colton murmured. His voice had become husky, rich like velvet. "If you want, we could go back to my house and...talk."

The thought of being alone with him made me dizzy, and I nodded before I could stop myself. At the cash register, he paid the check, and I couldn't take my eyes off of him. If I did, I feared he would disappear, and I would wake up.

Outside, it was hot and muggy. Fireflies glimmered around us, painting our cars in speckles of light.

"Just follow me," Colton said as I unlocked my car.

I turned toward him only to see that his face was inches from mine. My breath hitched in my throat, and my blood boiled inside my body. My heart ached; it wanted its Colton. His breath washed across my face — the sweet fragrance of lemon tea. I knew the look in his eyes well. Desire was burning beneath our skin.

"Okay," I breathed.

My voice broke him from the trance. He stepped back toward his car and waved with a smile.

The drive was neither long enough nor fast enough. My mind was reeling, shifting every which way. Something inside me told me this wasn't a good idea. But as the seconds passed, the logical part of my brain grew quieter and quieter. All I knew was that I was now driving through a painfully familiar neighborhood.

Nothing had changed. His house was still the same red-trimmed, country-style home I'd been to a hundred times. There was the verdant garden split in half by a meandering brick path. We used to sit on that walkway and gaze up into the clouds together. And there was the porch swing where we used to drink fruit punch and talk about our future. My legs were Jell-O as I climbed out of my car.

Colton unlocked the door with a shy smile. "It's been a while since you've been here, I guess."

Never thought I'd be here again. "It's been years."

The living room was a time capsule of its own. Same squishy beige couch, same coffee-stained carpet, same flat screen from 2009. Colton's senior picture sat proudly on the mantel, surrounded by other photos of him at old volleyball tournaments. Movement by the couch caught my eye, and I jumped as a cat sprinted to my feet.

"Lulla!" I cried, reaching down to pet her shiny coat. "I can't believe she's still alive."

Colton set his keys on the hook beside the door. "She's going on fourteen now."

Tears almost stung my eyes. I couldn't believe I was here. I couldn't believe this was real.

Colton flicked some lights on as I stroked Lulla's fur and then after a quick "Be right back," he bounded up the stairs. I heard the squeak of his bedroom door open, and my heart started trembling again. A strong part of me wanted to walk upstairs and walk right into his room, but I didn't know if that would be welcomed. Lulla blinked her brown eyes at me, and I sighed.

My legs started moving before I even knew what I was doing. I reached the top of the stairs all too soon.

"Colton?"

"Just a sec," he called.

His door was slightly ajar, and I watched him pull a softer, more comfortable looking T-shirt over his head. I swallowed nervously. When his door swung open, it took all the strength I had to compose myself. Colton stood there for a minute, searching my eyes with his own.

"You said you wanted to talk?" I asked, hating the way my voice quivered.

Colton nodded slowly and gestured into his room.

It was almost like he never left for college. A collection of sports bags sat outside the closet doors and pictures of volleyball tournaments hung everywhere. He even still had the Juice WRLD poster up on the wall above his desk. Reluctantly, my eyes shifted to his bed and my stomach did cartwheels. Colton offered me the seat at his desk.

"I just figured privacy would serve us better," he said, and I tried very hard not to think about the double meaning of that statement. "But...what you said back there in the diner...I agree. I'd be lying if I said you aren't in my head every now and then. And maybe we're not meant for each other, but I want you to know that you did mean a lot to me."

The silence was killer. I wanted him in my arms, and I wanted him now. He was right — we may not have been meant for each other, but this moment was all that mattered. And I knew what it would take: one of us was going to have to break the barrier again.

I sighed and strode toward him, each step causing my heart to thump harder in my chest. And suddenly, there he was, close enough to touch.

"I'm sick of living with a fake smile," I said, peering up at him. "You need to know what I'm feeling."

He blinked and leaned closer, his nose softly brushing mine. "What're you feeling?"

At his closeness, my lips burned, craving his. I couldn't hear the silence so much now as opposed to my own shallow breathing. "I'm feeling like...I need you."

"I need you," he whispered.

When he pressed his lips to mine, my heart instantly set on fire. It was an explosion of heat. It thawed my stubbornness and my heartbreak. I could feel the wound being sewn shut without a single scar. There was so much familiarity in Colton's lips. This kiss was home.

But it wasn't just a kiss. His hands grazed my shoulders and then pressed against my waist, pulling me closer. The feel of his body against mine sent chills down my heart, and when he touched his lips to my neck, I couldn't help but sigh in pleasure.

Kissing Elijah had felt nothing like this. With Colton I was alive. With Colton, I was home. There was so much passion in his kiss; it was like I was his oxygen, and he hadn't taken a breath in years.

My hands slid down his back, and I froze when my finger grazed what must have been a scar. We broke apart for a moment, and I grimaced.

These scars had been the game changer for us all those years ago, and I was worried they would do the same now. Uncertainty clouded Colton's features. The gears in his mind churned; I could almost see them. But when his eyes touched my lips again, he shook his head and pulled me back to him. He guided my hand along the scars, setting my soul on fire.

The passion was almost too much to take. He was pressed against me, but I wanted him closer still.

We were older now, I realized. There was no risk of our parents finding us; we could let it escalate if we really wanted to.

And we obviously wanted to since I was letting him pull my shirt off over my head. But then my stomach gave a sharp twist.

I pulled away from Colton and glanced down at my feet.

"What's wrong?" he asked. There was a genuine note of concern in his voice.

"Well, I...are we gonna..." I gestured to the bed. "I've never had sex before."

I recalled our small pact as teenagers — that one day we would remove each other's clothing and take things to the next level. But now that that moment was actually here, I was terrified. I didn't want to know who he had lost his virginity to, but the look in his eyes told me he lost it to *someone*.

"You haven't?" Colton's eyebrows shot upward.

"Why're you so surprised?'

"I just thought..." He blinked and then shrugged. "I guess I thought that you'd met someone at college."

"I did," I answered. "But I wasn't ready to give that part of myself to him."

"And you're willing to give it to me?" The hopefulness in his voice made me chuckle.

I'd missed him *so* much.

"Yeah, I am."

A breathtaking, genuine smile played at the corners of his lips. He gathered me into his arms and held me to his chest. The piney scent of his clothing shot me down memory lane, and I could've cried.

It would have been a lie to say that I'd never imagined my first time with him. I *wanted* him to have this part of me. It was almost like it had always been his take.

He sat me down on the bed and removed his shirt, exposing the muscle-toned chest I'd missed so much.

"Are you sure?" he asked. There was fear in his eyes, too. "You can say no at any time if—"

"I'm sure," I whispered.

He kissed the crown of my head and then gently pulled me toward him.

It didn't take long for his nice, made-up sheets to twist and wrinkle.

Pale yellow sunshine seeped in through the curtains, dousing the room in light. It hurt my eyes. It burned like I was staring into the core of the sun. In fact, my entire body ached. There was a knot in my neck, and my muscles protested as I shifted onto my back. Aside from this, my head was clear. I inhaled deeply through my nostrils, filling my belly with oxygen. And then Colton was awake beside me.

I glanced at him, at his lovely angel's face. The sunlight pooled in his gold-green eyes. The sight took my breath away.

"Good morning," he murmured and sat up against the headboard.

He draped an arm around my waist, and I snuggled up to him again, lost in thought over last night's experience.

He'd held me so tightly, kissed me so passionately. It felt like our hearts had merged in some monumental, world-altering collision. All walls had been broken down, and we'd spent the evening lost in each other's embraces. I felt older all of a sudden, like my body was no longer mine. Like I suddenly wasn't me.

I'd heard from multiple people over the years that your first time was the worst time, but I didn't think it was that bad. It was surprising how quickly my body had adapted to the minor pain and moved with his in perfect synchronicity.

"Is all sex like that?" I wondered out loud.

Colton glanced at me, offering a soft smile. "What do you mean?"

I kind of felt embarrassed for even asking. "I mean, I thought first times were supposed to be terrible, but..."

His grin widened, and I buried my face in my hands. His laugh echoed off the walls.

"It's different for everyone, Gail. But for the record," he scooted closer to me. "I enjoyed it, too."

He planted a kiss on my forehead.

It was so strange. How many times had I dreamt of lying with him like this and now here we were. It almost seemed too good to be true, but I was too happy to care.

"What now?"

My question hung in the air, unanswered.

I sat up on my knees to see his face, and something about it made me frown.

"I don't know, to be honest," he replied eventually.

To me, he would always be stunning. A life with him meant a life of perfection. But something still didn't feel right.

How long had it taken me to heal from the bullet wound of heartbreak? Years, and even then, I was still a little fragile. How was it possible that with all that self-work, I'd allowed Colton to lay me down in a heartbeat. Was I truly that weak? Yes, life with Colton meant perfection, but life was far from perfect.

Suddenly self-conscious, I grabbed the sheet and pulled it up over my chest. Colton flashed me a quizzical look and ran a hand through his disheveled hair.

"What's wrong?"

"Just thinking," I muttered.

Now that my head was unclouded by lust, it left room for logic to return. And anxiety.

You shouldn't have done this, a voice in my head nagged incessantly. What exactly did I think would happen? That we would reconnect and then run off and get married? No, Colton and I would go our separate ways just like before. Only now, I would be back at square one again. My heart was already starting to tear. I could feel the tiny fissures like a thousand needle pricks all over my body. How could I have allowed myself to fall once more?

"What're you thinking about?" Colton shifted so that we were face to face.

In my mind, I cursed him for bringing me here. He was impossible to let go of, and that terrified me.

"I'm not staying with you," I muttered. It was meant to be a question, but it came out as a statement.

His soft gaze, which was once sweet, hardened into something like remorse. "What would it do?"

Anger flared inside my chest. "I *could* stay! You could tell me you love me!"

"Gail," he said, hanging his head. "You *know* how I feel about you."

"Then say it!" I shouted.

When he glanced back up at me, he looked wounded. There was such a raw emotion on his face that I almost caved and fell into his arms again. The thought made me despise myself. The cracks in my heart deepened like a claw was physically ripping them apart. My eyes burned; the tears weren't far away. I started to tremble.

"Say it," I whispered.

After a long beat of silence, Colton shook his head. It was a swift motion, filled with regret, but it broke my heart right in half.

"If I do, it'll just make it harder."

And then I was out of the bed, yanking on my clothes and moving on watery legs. He tried to stop me, but I didn't respond. I couldn't think; I couldn't breathe. I just needed to get out of this house.

My phone alerted me that I had eight missed calls and twenty unread messages from my father. I should've felt bad for not telling him where I was, and I knew he'd raise hell as soon as I got home. But a black hole was forming in the pit of my stomach, growing larger by the second. This heartbreak was a tumor, and I had to get away from Colton before it killed me.

"Abigail," he said as I hurried toward the door.

He stepped in front of me just as my hand closed on the knob. I couldn't bring myself to meet his eyes, and when I spoke, my voice shook slightly.

"Please move."

"Abigail, you said it yourself. Living like nothing exists between us is just stupid."

"So, you want to express that how? Through meaningless sex?"

His jaw unhinged. "Gail—"

"Prove me wrong," I dared, glaring up at him with a gaze as sharp as ice.

And there it was, the falter in his expression. He couldn't stay; he wouldn't. Of course, I knew this deep down...it was for the best. But it was getting harder and harder to breathe.

"That's what I thought." I dipped under his arm and escaped through the front door.

I didn't even make it to the car before the dam exploded, and a thunderstorm of emotion erupted inside me.

"Well, what's wrong with her?" someone asked.

Silence followed the question, and I stirred as my mind regained awareness. I was lying on the couch at home with my arms draped over my chest like I was trying to protect myself from something. *The memories*, my conscience whispered. I was trying to protect myself from the memories. But that exact thought was just an invitation for pain. My body ached as I started to cry. Thankfully, the lights were off. Had they been on, I probably would've gotten a migraine.

"It's Colton," my father answered.

And my ears perked like a dog's. I realized he was talking to Jamie in the kitchen, their tones sour and solemn.

"Who is that again?" Jamie asked.

"He was her boyfriend back in high school. The breakup was real bad. Colton's father was an abusive alcoholic...nearly beat the kid to death one night. But Colton blamed Gail."

I could practically hear Jamie's confusion from the living room.

"Don't ask why 'cause I don't know. But ever since then, he has done *nothing* but hurt Gail. The way he acts—I don't know why she would even let herself talk to him. All it does is hurt her. And it hurts *me*! I don't know what to do, and I hate seeing her like this."

Jamie didn't say anything, perhaps pondering the severity of the situation.

"I swear, I will never let that boy back into this house."

"Now hold on," Jamie said, her tone softening. "It sounds like he's had a bad childhood. I mean, physical abuse! I can't imagine a kid going through that! And if he did, it's not in your right to judge."

"It *is* my right to judge after what he's done to my daughter."

For a moment, silence crept back into their conversation, and I sank down against the couch cushions, feeling the room compress around me. The guilt was twice as bad this time. Not only did I let myself down, but I also crushed my father in the process. My heart was beating quickly now, and each pulse stung me like a hornet.

I didn't even remember explaining the story to Dad. Hopefully I'd left out the part about sex, but my brain wasn't fully activated when I was weighed down by heartbreak.

"Colton clearly means a lot to her," Jamie replied.

"I just want her to be happy." Dad sounded on the brink of tears, and I pressed my face into a pillow, hating myself for the way I was hurting him.

I wanted to be mad at Colton. The image of him in my mind brought on a blazing ball of rage, but the fire always subsided eventually. I could never stay mad at him forever. It was absolutely infuriating; I wanted to rip the hair from my scalp. Though I made a deal with myself that this was the last time I would allow Colton Reeves into my life, something deep in my heart told me that wasn't true. Our story was far from over.

To celebrate our first night as sophomores in college, Cara and I went out to a fancy restaurant. This little dinner celebration was the first I'd gone out with a friend in a long time. Ever since my bitter parting with Colton, I'd become hostile. I gave up writing entirely and retreated back to the safety of my violin, which only proved Erica's theory: the music was Colton's replacement. Without my violin, I was a hollow shell of a person.

Cara wanted to know every detail of my life since the end of last year's semester. I talked through my studies with Professor Autrie and about all the parties I'd attended but left out the points of my ex-boyfriend. They were too humiliating to admit.

Cara took a sip of her water and twirled a curl of hair around her finger. "I should tell you that I took your advice with my brother."

"You finally talked to him?"

She nodded, her big brown eyes filling with light. "We talked *everything* out, and then he apologized for being an ass. I guess it's 'cause we're older now, you know? Things change when you get older; you realize what's more important in life."

I munched on my salad without tasting it. "That's great. I'm really happy for you."

"Also," she continued, and there was a change in her tone that made me glance over at her. Her cheeks were pink now, and she stared down at the tabletop with a smile pinching her lips. "I met someone."

I slammed my fork down on the table—the reaction I knew she was expecting. Despite the sinking feeling in my chest, I had to be happy for her. I was as skilled at concealing my emotions as Colton was. "Spill!"

"Okay, okay," she squealed. "I was out at the country club pool with some of my friends, and he was working behind the snack bar. His name's Beau, and...we really hit it off." She couldn't stop smiling. "He gave me his number, and we hung out a lot over the summer. But it gets even better." She paused for dramatic effect. "He goes to Temple!"

I felt my face lift with surprise. Temple University was practically right up from the street from Curtis. "Wow, that is really lucky."

"I know! He said we should hang out a lot this year, and I'm excited because he's so nice...and also really hot."

I'd never seen her so overwhelmed with emotion. She was trapped in the bubble of her thoughts — a bubble this Beau person had taken charge of. My heart swelled at the thought of Cara finding love, but then it deflated when I remembered the state of my own love life.

"That's amazing, Cara."

I tried to swallow my jealousy because this was my best friend. But erasing jealousy was easier said than done.

Instead of staying in a dorm on campus this year, Cara and I had rented an apartment near the school. It wasn't a large apartment —simply a two-bedroom, single bathroom deal, but it sufficed. This thrilled my father because he claimed it was high time I learned to pay for and manage my own place. But I didn't like it at first. The responsibility of furnishing my own space, which cost *real* money, was stressful. It forced me to take two jobs in the area: one at Starbucks and one at a supermarket. Thankfully, they paid well.

It took two months to put the finishing touches on our apartment, but finally by October, it was looking more like home. We added a large plush carpet in the living room, along with an L-shaped, reclining couch, and sprinkled a few plants here and there. I even moved my large desk drawer from home into my room to make things feel more familiar. And the place started to grow on me.

Sophomore year wasn't all that different from freshman year. I was still stuck in some gen ed courses, and I spent most of my nights in the library paging through text books about music history and the origin of song. And except for contracting a terrible stomach bug in late January, it was a monotonous year with little surprises. Professor Autrie was still generous in giving me private lessons on campus, but other than that, I was forced to practice on my own time.

But I didn't mind being alone with my violin; it offered me endless catharsis. Sometimes Cara would even sing along with my music, and we would create a fabulous duet right there in our living room. But I really didn't see much of Cara anyway. She was usually away at Temple visiting her new boyfriend. I didn't get the chance to meet him until Valentine's Day, when Cara invited me to go out to dinner with them.

"That's crazy. No," I said. "I'd be a huge intrusion."

I was standing in the threshold of the bathroom watching Cara swab a shade of red onto her lips.

"It's no trouble! Beau can't wait to meet you, and I don't want you here alone all night!"

It did wonders for my self-esteem: being the third wheel of a happy couple on Valentine's Day. Truthfully, I would've *rather* stayed home alone all night.

Cara turned to me, and her elegant strapless dress swished with the movement. "Please come."

Her eyes were sparkling like a puppy's, and I sighed. "Fine. But I need your help to pick out a dress."

.   .   .

Beau Direns was not the boy I expected him to be. In place of the casual athletic attire I'd originally pictured, he was dressed in a lavish gray suit, unbuttoned to reveal a wrinkleless navy blue shirt. It was the type of clean-cut style that made me question what his occupation was. How much money did he make to own a suit like that? His dark ink-colored hair was gelled and combed back to reveal the entirety of his chiseled, heart-shaped face, where two dimples appeared as he smiled at us. The closer we got to him, the more I noticed the intricacy of his liquid turquoise eyes, which resembled two windows to an ocean. I almost found his beauty unrealistic; he looked as if he had stepped out of a romance novel. In Beau's hand, he held a bouquet of soft red roses.

"Happy Valentine's Day, Cara." With an adoring smile, he extended the roses out toward her.

I had to look away as they embraced. It seemed too private for me to witness.

"Beau, this is Gail," Cara declared.

He turned his attention to me and politely held out his hand. "Nice to meet you. Cara goes on and on about your talent with a violin. You must be awesome."

"Oh, she is the *best*. Hands down!"

Their compliments made me blush, and Beau held the door open for us.

For dinner, we feasted on steamed lobster that was coated in butter and sprinkled with Old Bay. To wash it all down, I had a glass of lemon water, and when Cara announced the punchline to a joke, I almost spit the contents of my drink onto our table.

"Who told you that one?" Beau inquired through a wheeze of laughter.

"My brother," Cara said simply. "Oh, and that reminds me. He's flying out to London tomorrow for that music festival."

"Oh, geez." Beau chuckled one last time and then relaxed back into his seat. "I hope he doesn't catch the Pulmonem Fever." And without saying anything else, he took another bite of his lobster.

Cara and I shared a confused glance.

"The what?" I asked.

Beau wiped his mouth on a napkin. "The Pulmonem Fever. We've been tracking it in school for the past three weeks."

"Well, what is it?" Cara demanded. She sounded worried now, and I knew her mind was centered on her brother.

"From what we've seen, it apparently causes flu-like symptoms and respiratory issues — kind of like pneumonia. The first case was in Moscow, Russia, at the beginning of the month, and the patient died. A few more people have been infected since."

Cara and I inhaled sharply, but Beau waved the matter away. "I wouldn't worry about it. The Russians are working hard to stop the spread. We just have to pray that it doesn't get out of Moscow."

Cara sank in her seat and pushed her plate away. There was a nauseated look on her face, and I was worried she'd get sick right here in the middle of the restaurant.

"Jack," she whispered, nervously wrapping her hands around her torso.

"Hey," Beau said, reaching for her hand and squeezing it lightly. "It's all right. I'm sorry. I shouldn't have brought it up."

"Yeah, I'm sure your brother's gonna be fine, Care," I added.

But truthfully, I didn't know. In all honesty, I wasn't even aware a new virus had sprung up in the world. I'd been so focused on my music that the outside world just seemed nonexistent until this moment.

Our spring concert was now mere weeks away, and Professor Autrie had chosen one of Beethoven's classic compositions — a piece that required a good amount of practice, so, the orchestra met every day to rehearse. Somedays, Professor Autrie was irritated with our lackluster playing, which was always caused by a lack of focus. Besides the Pulmonem Fever, spring break was the hottest topic of conversation.

"*Oh mon Dieu!*" our instructor cried. "Enough about spring break! We have a concert to prepare for that is rapidly approaching. *Monsieur* Wexter," he added, addressing the head of the cello section.

Justin Wexter glanced up from his phone just in time to see Professor Autrie's dark gray eyebrows arch upward.

"I'm going to assume you're contacting someone important and not just browsing Instagram during my rehearsals."

Every eye shifted to Justin's face, which flushed a deep red. His friends beside him began to snicker, and I couldn't help the smile that appeared on my face, too. Justin shook his head.

"No, sir. I was just Googling the latest on the Pulmonem Fever."

There it was *again*. It had such a negative sound to it, bringing an instant cloud cover over the room. All eyes returned to our conductor.

"Ah, *oui*. I heard it is spreading throughout Europe." His tone was suddenly dismal, and I wondered if he was thinking about the rest of his family that lived in France.

"Do you think it's gonna come here?" someone from the second violin section inquired.

This brought on several hushed conversations between everyone, and Professor Autrie had to call our attention back. "If the fever were to spread overseas, we may have to take precautions here at the university."

"It's killed two-thousand people so far, Professor," Justin exclaimed.

And now there was an uproar of terror; however, instead of

fearing for their lives, my peers were scared that spring break would be cancelled.

"Quiet!" Professor Autrie barked and tapped his baton against the stand like a gavel. "I'm sure they are tracking the disease and are doing everything they can to get it under control."

"What if it can't be controlled?" someone else asked.

Needless to say, it was not a very productive rehearsal. But from that point on, the Pulmonem Fever became a worldwide problem. It was on everyone's lips; they talked about it constantly. Some would joke about it — feign a cough and then burst out laughing. Others were already saving up on their hand sanitizer, terrified the fever was coming right for them.

But I didn't understand the hype. It was like one of those things you didn't really believe in until it affected you directly. One morning as I was sipping tea and gazing out into the tall, twisting spires of the city, Cara approached me with a wary look on her face.

"What's wrong?" I asked.

She didn't speak but instead held out her phone for me to read. It was an article from the World Health Organization's website. Big, bolded letters stood out as a title, claiming that the Pumonem Fever had finally reached the United States.

"There's a case in New Jersey," she whimpered.

Unlike me, Cara was keeping up with the rumors about the fever, and what she'd heard had scared her to death. Apparently, this virus had the ability to make you cough so hard your lungs exploded. I thought that was ridiculous, but Cara wouldn't accept my indifference.

"Just relax," I said. "Have you heard from Jack?"

"He's been in London for two weeks, and *so far* he feels fine."

"Well, then there you go. He's fine."

"For *now*." Panic twinkled in her eyes; it put me on edge.

"Did you hear that they might make a travel ban? What if he can't come home?"

I reached for her wrist and reminded her to take deep breaths. Why was she going into hysterics? Diseases spread; it was no big deal. What was one case in New Jersey?

Of course, in no time, the virus gained center spotlight on all news stations. Anchors were either quoting the president's concerns or arguing over just how threatening the virus really was. Cara and I kept the news on for constant coverage, and the increasing apprehension was starting to affect me. The anxiety surfaced like a ghost materializing out of a shadow. It had been there all along, but it was just now tormenting my brain.

A week later as I was writing a paper in the library, my phone buzzed and alerted me that Dad was calling.

"Yes, apparently there are now forty-five cases nationwide. Three of which are in New York City," he answered my question.

My heart gave a dangerous squeeze. Things were different now that the Pulmonem Fever was invading the areas close to home.

Taking a steady breath, I forced myself to ask the question I didn't want to know the answer to. "Is this like a deadly virus, Dad?"

For a second, he didn't answer. "People have died from it, yes. I think they're trying to quarantine the patients — might help stop the spread. I mean, I'd rather they do that than let them roam free, you know?"

"Yeah." My breath was shallow.

"Sweetheart, I wouldn't be surprised if they closed Curtis down. As of right now, the majority of Europe is infected, and if it continues to spread, the president may call for the closing of schools—"

"Wait, wait!" I nearly shouted, which earned a warning glance from the librarian. "They can't close school, that's ridiculous! We have a concert next week."

"I don't think the Pulmonem Fever cares about the concert, Gail. It's better to be safe than sorry."

Anger pulsed inside me. I almost felt betrayed. How dare this virus come and rob me of my concert — the thing I had spent endless hours preparing for. It wasn't right, and it certainly wasn't fair.

Yet my father had a point; the Pulmonem Fever had no intention of holding off for the spring concert. Temple University was the first school to close. It made its announcement that Wednesday, and Beau arrived at our appartement not long after we got the notification.

"I can't believe this is actually happening," I muttered.

Cara, Beau, and I sat in the living room, and I glanced at my violin case resting near the door. I had it all packed up and ready to go for the concert.

"It's gotten worse," Beau said. "Apparently, the stock market's going down like nobody's business. People are afraid to go out and shop. In all honesty, the only company that might benefit from this mess is Amazon."

Cara and I couldn't even snicker.

"I think Westchester's making its announcement tomorrow. And I heard Penn State will be closed by Friday," Beau continued.

Penn State. Colton. I wondered if he was okay and imagined myself shooting him a quick text message just to check. But I knew I wouldn't. Even in the midst of this pandemic, my stubbornness persisted. Vaguely, I thought about how sad that was.

"I heard California is real bad," Cara muttered. "I hope Elijah's okay."

This, I could respond to.

I retrieved my phone from the pocket of my hoodie and FaceTimed Elijah. Cara and Beau crowded in around me to see the screen. Elijah answered on the fourth ring.

It was still bright and sunny in California, and in the background we could see a few palm trees swaying in the wind.

"Elijah!" Cara squealed. "Are you alive?"

Our friend didn't look that much different, save for a tan that made his cinnamon skin tone even darker. He laughed at Cara's question and nodded.

"As of right now, my lungs are healthy, don't worry."

"Did Ashford close?" I asked.

"Yep. Made the announcement this morning. I bought an apartment with a couple of friends, so I guess we'll just lay low and quarantine ourselves till this mess passes."

I suddenly missed him very much. Elijah could make any stressful situation seem like paradise by comparison.

"I heard Curtis is closing," he called over a sudden gust of hot California wind.

"Yeah," Cara answered forlornly. "I just don't understand what's happening. Like, how did we get here?"

"That's a great question that I don't have the answer to, Care."

Just then, Cara's phone chimed and she glanced down at it. "It's my mom, I gotta take this. Nice talking to you, Elijah! Stay healthy!"

"You, too."

Cara answered her phone, and she and Beau disappeared into her bedroom. I watched Elijah through my tiny phone screen and wondered what it would be like to be in California, where the beautiful weather could trick you into thinking everything was fine.

"How are *you*, Gail?" Elijah inquired. His voice had a knowing edge to it, and despite the fact that he was almost three thousand miles away, I somehow felt like this had transformed into private conversation, and he was sitting beside me.

"Do you want the truth or a lie?"

"Truth, of course."

I sighed. "This is crazy. Nothing like this has ever happened, and the scariest part is that anyone could contract it. I don't want to die!"

"You won't die, Gail," he assured me. "The people who are dying have underlying health issues. So long as you don't have any of those, I think you're good."

I wondered why I was fighting off tears until it dawned on me.

"I miss you," I said.

His hazel eyes found mine, sending a weighted message.

Truthfully, I could've ended up with Elijah. He meant the world to me, and wasn't it worth it to be with someone who filled you with such positivity? Elijah was a good man after all— someone who deserved just as much love as he radiated himself. But maybe that's why it wasn't meant to be. Elijah knew where he was headed; he had his future planned out clear as day. I, on the other hand, was still trying to figure out who the hell I was. Nonetheless, I was still just grateful to have him as a friend.

"Promise that when this is all over, and we survive, you'll come home and visit," I murmured.

He smiled, and the sunlight gleamed off his dark hair. "I promise."

Chapter Eleven

PHILADELPHIA, PA (2023)

The Pulmonem Fever was spreading like wildfire, and the president called a national state of emergency. Quarantine was now mandatory in the city of Philadelphia, and I could do nothing but sit on our couch and stare out the window, wondering about how fast things had changed. The previous week felt like a whole year ago.

Cara was a mess. She wasn't allowed to see Beau because he had returned home to be with his family, and he resented the thought of Cara being out in such dire circumstances. As a result, it wasn't uncommon to find her crying her mascara off.

I cried, too, sometimes because it was a lot to take in. When Curtis announced its closure for two weeks, I was forced into the confines of my apartment, although now it felt more like a cage than a home. Spring break was canceled completely, much to our dismay. My violin case sat in the corner, collecting dust. For the first few days, I played it to bring some warmth into our situation, but the notes ended up souring like my mood, and after a while, I gave up. Playing just reminded me of the spring concert that was now canceled, and I was too upset to even tune the instrument.

Philadelphia lost its vigor. Shops and restaurants were closing by the hour, dropping like the people who had contracted the virus. The only places that remained open were grocery stores and pharmacies, although the governor insisted that if our problem wasn't "urgent," we should leave the medicine for people who needed it.

To pass the time, I cleaned, cooked, and tried my best to stay active. Somedays, I did a workout inside; other days, I went out into the world and walked around the block — the only way to get some fresh air. On those days, when the sun was glittering in the sky and the air was sweet, I found it hard to believe a menacing fever could even exist. Nature's beauty was so misleading.

Cara and I went through the cans of Ravioli and chicken soup like they were gourmet meals. We ate together at the table and talked about what life would be like after this mess finally subsided and we could return to school. It was all we could talk about, really. The hope kept us sane as we were forced to stay indoors.

"My dad says that this is the weirdest thing he's ever lived through, and he was in New York City during 9/11!" Cara said one evening as we were bent over a game of checkers.

"Sheesh." I massaged my temples. "Well, how's the rest of your family holding up?"

She moved her checker diagonally behind mine. "I called my parents yesterday, and my mom said she's super depressed. I think she's really spiraling 'cause she can't get out to see her friends and make money at the nail salon. As for Jack," Cara kept her eyes on the checkerboard and inhaled through her nose, "he's stuck quarantining in London, so I don't know."

"I'm sorry." I didn't know what else to say and hugged my knees to my chest.

She sniffled. "At least we bought a year's supply of water bottles and soap before the grocery store turned into a *Hunger Games* cornucopia."

She flipped her black checker upside down to show the crown and gave me a satisfied smirk.

"Jerk," I muttered. There was no way I'd win the game now.

When I wasn't losing at checkers, Cara and I killed time with countless movies, but Cara insisted we save the popcorn for the *best* films, like *The Titanic*.

"That's gonna be me and Beau!" she exclaimed as Jack held Rose at the mast of the ship.

"You mean you're going to let him die in the ocean?"

"Absolutely not! I'm smarter than Rose, Gail. There was room on that stupid door for the both of them."

It went on like this for two weeks—wake up, mindlessly pass time, settle in for a movie, sleep, repeat. Some nights, I spent more than an hour in the shower simply letting the water cascade down my body. It was all I could do not to lose it and become hysterical. Truthfully, I was starting to lose my mind. I drank EmergenC like my life depended on it and tried to change my route of walking in the city, but life had become worse than dull. It was the definition of monotonous. Pure insanity.

Unfortunately though, at the start of April things got worse.

"Gail! Your dad's calling you!" Cara called from the living room.

I'd been absentmindedly doodling in a notebook and rushed out to catch the call.

"Hello?"

"Hey, sweetheart. How are you?"

"Bored and scared."

He sighed. "Most people are these days. Listen, I don't know if you've checked your email recently."

My eyes flickered to the laptop that remained shut on the kitchen table. "No, I haven't."

"All right, well, I just got an email from the president of Curtis. He announced that they will be suspending all in-person learning for the rest of the semester."

My jaw dropped to the ground; it was like getting kicked in the gut. All that talk of returning to school for the rest of our year down the drain. Hope was slipping through the window like a breeze.

"Please tell me you're kidding."

"I'm sorry, sweetheart. I don't know if you want to stay down there in Philly or come home, but you won't be on campus now until August...or until they decide to reopen schools." From the sound of his voice, Dad didn't sound too happy either. "But whatever you're planning, I don't want you out in crowds right now. A few college students went to the beach for spring break and were arrested for breaking quarantine and self-isolation rules."

I was speechless. *What the hell was going on with this world?*

"That's insane."

"No parties, Gail. I don't want to get a call from the cops, do you hear me?"

"Loud and clear."

As soon as I hung up, I turned on the news and held my breath as the screen showed the nearest hospital that was filling by the hour.

" — need more space," the anchor was saying. "But at this point, with the World Health Organization and the front-line workers constantly on the move to develop a cure, the president and his colleagues predict that we may start to see improvement by June. He also reminds American citizens that these shutdowns are necessary to stop the spread of the virus and develop a cure as fast as possible."

Cara touched my shoulder as I shook my head. This was it; I was going to break. I couldn't stay in this apartment one more day. Two weeks was long enough. But at the same time, having the Pulmonem Fever would make it three times worse.

"Get comfortable," I said through clenched teeth. "We're gonna be here for a while."

Masks were everywhere. You couldn't leave the house without one, especially here in the city where Pulmonem Fever cases were skyrocketing by the hour. It got so bad that fashion outlets were starting to advertise *designer* masks online, as if they could make this worldwide quarantine into something stylish and profitable.

Unsurprisingly, the virus was also putting a large divide in our nation. If I had to listen to one more debate between the Democrats and Republicans, I might have just taken a hammer to the TV.

In lieu of in-person classes, Curtis opted for a technological substitution, as was the case with every other school and business in the world. Cara and I had to submit weekly recordings of pre-approved songs to be graded on a pass or fail template. On top of that, I took notes during my online lectures and took quizzes on Google Forms. I never imagined I'd be sitting in my living room and having face-to-screen conversations with Professor Autrie.

Life fell into a cycle again, although no one could call it normalcy. On top of our mandatory social distancing, the economy was still crumbling. The confusion sent people into a frenzy, and I was scared a riot would break out.

I called my father often, desperate to know that he was okay. As a pediatric doctor, he was required to stay and work even with the heightened risk of getting the virus. I pictured him in a hazmat suit every day. He told me how hectic things had gotten at the doctors' office, but that I didn't need to worry because he was taking extra precautions and had it all under control. So, when my thoughts weren't centered on the health of my father, they often strayed into the past.

Where was Colton now? How was he coping with quarantine? Did he ever think of me? I would've expected us to change, to realize that life was too short to hold grudges. After all, this damn virus had stripped all of us of our basic rights. Sometimes, I even considered reaching out to Colton...but I wasn't *that* hysteric. Even with death on the line, my pride was still alive and well.

June first announced itself with a sunrise of dusty rose-gold. The sky was a sparkling ocean of color, brightening a little more with each passing second. The full moon stood its ground — a large, pale sphere against the onslaught of day.

I was lying on the living room floor, mesmerized by the beauty. Anxiety had kept me awake all night and forced me into the living room for a change of scenery from my bedroom. For hours, I had shivered in the darkness, feeling it press all around me, consuming me. Four months inside was just enough time for me to fall victim to the dark recesses of my mind. But there was the gilded light of dawn. A *new* dawn. The soft pink sun rose in the sky, filling me with hope. It was quiet, save for the mind-numbing buzz of the air conditioner, and as dawn's light slowly washed over me, I felt last night's anxiety slipping away. I could have slept then, but I didn't want to miss a moment of nature's masterpiece.

By now, infection numbers were plateauing. There had been talk of quarantine restrictions easing up soon, and even though we were still a long way from normal, I had still never been more grateful in my life.

Cara eventually joined me on the living room floor.

"Did we survive?" I wondered out loud. My eyes never strayed from the sunrise.

"I think so," Cara replied just as distractedly.

When she began to whisper something, I turned toward her. But she wasn't speaking to me; her head was bowed and her hands stayed folded under her chin.

"What're you doing?"

Before answering, she pressed the tip of her finger to her forehead and then down between her heart and shoulders. "Praying. Just thanking God that we *did* survive and that our loved ones did, too."

I cocked my head at her. "I didn't know you were religious."

"Born Christian." She nodded. "Praying just helps me feel better, you know?"

I didn't know. I hardly ever went to church as a child, and though my dad had deepened his relationship with God in the last few years, I'd all but forgotten an afterlife even existed.

"I don't pray very much," I admitted, surprised to find that I felt sheepish to say it.

Cara's eyes bored into mine with a kind of fierce intensity, something like wonder or amazement. "It's worth it, trust me."

My eyes fell to the carpet as I considered the fact. But before I could respond, Cara had the TV remote in her hand.

With a deep inhale, she said, "I think it's time we check the news."

Together, we stood in front of the television, clinging to every word that fell from the anchor's mouth.

"Today, several governors have officially moved the scale from yellow to green in the following places..." We held our breath, watching the cities tick by on the lower half of the screen. "By Friday, several more places will be reopening with precautions as well." Finally, Philadelphia, PA, flashed in big, bolded letters, and Cara and I exploded. "The World Health Organization cautions people to still wear masks in places other than their homes and to maintain social-distancing. The vaccine for the Pulmonem Fever is still being tested."

I turned toward my friend and fell into her arms, the relief so great it took my breath away. We laughed and danced around the living room like two drunk idiots. Cara stopped by the windows and pulled one of them open, sucking in the fresh June air. I did too, and the neighbors did, and the people in the apartment building across from us did. We waved to them and wished them good morning.

It was surreal. It seemed like the entire city was revived at that very moment. People were calling across the streets, waving from different buildings. It was a moment of genuine unity.

"Okay, my turn. If you weren't a singer, what would you be?"

Cara tossed her hair over her shoulder. "Easy. A teacher."

I shrugged. "How come I never knew that?"

"You never asked."

We were spending one of our last days of quarantine at the kitchen table with virgin strawberry daiquiris — a drink Cara claimed she knew the recipe to by heart. Our drinks, though non-alcoholic, made us feel braver somehow, and we'd agreed to engage in a game of Truth.

"Ever stolen anything?"

"Yeah," I said after taking a sip of my drink. "When I was six-years-old, I stole a rainbow slinky from behind the counter at Chuck-E Cheese."

Cara wheezed with laughter. "You must've felt so cool."

"Oh, I was the coolest. Okay, next question. Do you think you're gonna marry Beau?"

It was meant to be a joke, but Cara's expression suddenly mellowed. "Yes."

I chewed on my straw for a moment until her answer registered in my brain. "Oh, shit. You're really into him."

"Well, yeah!" Her giggle was too high-pitched, and her eyes started to sparkle the way they always did when we got on the subject of her boyfriend. "He *genuinely* cares about me, you know? And I feel safe with him, not like I've ever felt before. We've talked about marriage in the past, but I've been thinking, and...I don't want to share my future with anyone else."

And there Colton was, suddenly dancing around my brain like a pesky little fly. I could see him now, clear as day—a vision, a daydream. Just out of reach. My lips burned with the memory of him, and I sank down into my seat. Where was he? What was he doing? What was he planning to do as soon as quarantine was lifted? It was just so second-nature to think about him.

"I'm so happy for you, Cara." It was all I could manage to say.

She stared into her drink, still smiling cheek to cheek. It was a smile that screamed happiness. It was a smile that made others wish they could experience such a feeling.

In my memory, Colton's hands pulled my body to his chest, and I found it funny how a memory could warp your perception of someone. "Cara?"

"Yeah?"

"Do you think loving someone too much is toxic?"

Her face contorted into a grimace, and I could tell she was confused by the question. "I don't know. I think that if you love someone for real, you can't really put a quantity on it. Too much? That's what love is. It's either too much or not at all. But *toxic*?" Her features scrunched up like she'd tasted something sour. "No, that's not toxic. It just means you have a strong heart. Why do you ask?"

I stared at the tabletop, seeing Colton's face stare back. But then I sighed and pushed the image from my mind. "No reason. Just curious."

"You're definitely lying," I squealed, laughing so hard my rib cage felt like it would snap. For as loud as I was laughing though, it was still muffled behind my face mask.

"No, I swear," Elijah said, his voice equally muffled. "I walked right up to her, asked her if she'd take a political survey for The Route, and she slapped me in the face. I think I even still have a bit of swelling."

We were sitting together in the corner of a Chinese restaurant—easily the loudest table in the entire place—and devouring vermicelli noodles with ginger and chicken drenched in soy sauce. It was the best meal I'd eaten in a long time. And it felt so *good* to be out with someone again, especially Elijah.

"Well, thank God she let you live then," I managed through my wheezing laughter. "How is *The Route* doing now anyway since the stock market is coming back up?"

The Route was the Californian journalism unit that Elijah had gotten a job at recently. Though he was stuck with writing political articles, he still loved his job like it was his child. I'd gotten the opportunity to read some of his work, and it was impressive for someone who spent so much time bent over his cello.

"We're getting by. Loui said he wants my final copy on his desk Monday morning, so I'll have to fly back Sunday night to add finishing touches."

"No," I whined. "You're only here for *one* week?"

"It's better than nothing!" His smile was playful, and it almost made me mad. "Besides, I have another friend coming to hang out with us."

I stopped and stared at him. "Wait, who's us?"

"You, me, Cara, Beau, and his name's Evan."

Our friend group had really tightened in the last couple of months over group texting and FaceTime. Elijah and Beau were now like brothers. But I'd never heard of this other boy.

"Ev-an," I said slowly, letting my mouth curve around the syllables. "Interesting. What's happening? What're we all doing?"

Elijah's eyes sparkled mischievously, and a grin split his face in half. "Beau's proposing to Cara."

I choked on a sip of tea. "*What?*"

"It's been so hard not telling you," he replied, leaning back in the booth and folding his arms around his head.

"Wait!" I screamed, and a man at the table next to us asked me to please lower my voice. After a halfhearted apology, I hissed, "When and where is this happening?"

"Friday night. There's a band playing in Franklin Square, and it's supposed to be a really nice night weather-wise."

"Oh, my God." I couldn't breathe—I was so excited. The sugar from the tea went straight to my bloodstream, and I was suddenly bouncing up and down in my seat, which earned yet another judgmental remark from our neighboring table.

But I didn't care. One of my best friends was getting married! The joy was rushing through me so fast I felt faint.

"*Don't* tell her, Gail," Elijah warned. "It's supposed to be a surprise."

"Duh! How does Evan fit into all of this?"

"He doesn't really. He's just a friend of mine who's in town too right now, and Beau said he wanted as many people there as possible."

I shrugged. "It doesn't matter as long as Evan's cool like you."

"You'll love him, trust me."

I was nervous on Friday night, maybe even more nervous than Beau. I'd managed to keep my mouth shut all week, but as my friends and I pulled into the Franklin Square parking lot, my stomach started to twist anxiously. It was hell trying to keep a secret this big.

The sun was already setting, casting rays of gold down on the earth. Our shadows were indigo on the concrete. It was nice seeing so many faces again. Not having to hear the words "Pul-monem Fever" every ten seconds was a major relief. But everyone here was still wearing a face mask.

The band was set up in the center of the square—all men

with a woman as lead singer. They looked classy, and I was pleased to see a bass instrument in the back.

Our group huddled near the back of the crowd, and I watched Cara giggle at something Beau whispered into her ear. This night felt so incredibly right. It was set in my bones. I was like a little kid in a candy shop, nearly shaking with anticipation.

"You need to calm down, or you're gonna give it away," Elijah had to tell me.

I giggled at his tone and resisted the urge to jump up and down. "Hey, where's this friend of yours anyway?"

Elijah checked his watch and then glanced up past my shoulder. "Right there."

Evan jogged toward us, and I watched as he embraced Elijah in a loose hug. He was much taller than Elijah and dressed more casually in black jeans and a fitted black Metallica T-shirt. His skin was pasty like the sun physically tried to avoid him, and his dirty blonde hair stuck out in an unruly fashion.

"Gail, this is Evan," Elijah said, stepping aside.

Evan gazed down at me and gave a simple nod. His posture was relaxed; his hands shoved into his pockets. "Hey."

Closer now, I noticed the hardened sapphire color of his eyes and the fading acne scars adorning his face. Still, there was a grin pinching his lips, and I found it somewhat attractive.

"Hey," I nodded in return.

Though he was handsome in some regard, there was an edge to Evan that piqued my curiosity.

When the band started, I stayed glued to Elijah's side.

"It just occurred to me that I don't remember how to make friends with people. Quarantine was a bitch," I whispered, grateful Evan was distracted and talking to Cara and Beau.

"You've hardly talked to the guy!" Elijah snickered. "He seems like a hardass on the outside, but once you get to know him..." Elijah pressed a hand to his heart. "Great person. Kind of like you."

When I glared at him, he chuckled.

"Real bromance, huh?"

"Without a doubt! I've known him since the fifth grade."

Evan returned to us and smirked. "Thanks for having me out tonight, bro. You've got some pretty cool friends." His eyes swiftly brushed my face.

The band covered modern day songs, and the woman's voice was so deep and rich that it was impossible not to drown in the sweet sound. I kept stealing glances at Cara and Beau, feeling their happiness seep through the air and infect me all the same.

"He tipped the band," Elijah whispered to me and Evan.

"Huh?"

Elijah smiled. "Beau tipped the band to cover 'Perfect' by Ed Sheeran. That's when he's gonna propose."

That was their song; Cara had told me multiple times. And every time she spoke of it, her soul seemed to grow ten feet tall. Love was such a magical thing.

"All right, ladies and gentlemen, we have a special request," the lead singer announced.

I nearly passed out. It took every ounce of my strength not to turn toward my friends already and yell, *Congratulations!*

"This is 'Perfect' by Ed Sheeran."

Cara turned toward Beau, her face glowing. "I love this song!"

Elijah retrieved his phone from his pocket and began recording. Evan and I stood to the side, bodies tense as we waited.

When the final chorus was belted through the park, Beau took a step back from his girlfriend, earning a quizzical look from her.

"Cara, the minute I met you, I knew that you were something special. You understand me in a way others can't, and that's all I've ever wanted in a relationship. You really are perfect."

People were starting to turn toward them, and the singer's voice softened to act as an accompaniment.

"I feel the same." Cara looked around, seeming frightened by other people's interest. I giggled when she turned to me.

"I truly do not think I will ever be able to live without you." Pausing for a moment, as if to steady his heart, Beau retrieved a small velvet box from his back pocket and sank down to one knee.

Cara pressed a hand to her mouth, frozen in shock. All around them, people cheered, and by now the song had ended and even the band members were gazing down at them with heart-shaped eyes.

"I can't escape these feelings I have for you and I don't ever want to. You are my light, and you own my heart now and forever. Cara Draper, will you marry me?"

"YES! YES!" she screamed through her sobs.

The audience roared with applause, and we watched Beau slide a glittering ring onto her finger. After, she fell into his arms, and they embraced in a passionate kiss.

"Can you believe I'm getting married?" Cara screeched in my ear.

It was well past ten o'clock now, but Beau had taken the liberty of putting together a festive celebration after his proposal. His apartment was filled with people I didn't even know, all laughing and drinking.

"I *can't* believe it. I'm so happy for you, Cara!" I called back over the music.

She jumped around gleefully for a moment and then turned to another one of her friends. Elijah stood by the drinks table, chatting with some tall brunette who could have very well been a model from New York City's Fashion Week. She was Cara's friend from home, whom Beau graciously flew out for the celebration.

Someone nudged my arm, and I turned to see Evan with a drink in each of his hands.

"Drinking alone?"

"Not drinking at all, but thanks." I replied.

He copied my stance and leaned up against the wall. For a moment, we watched the party sail around us. The low lights made intimacy easier, and couples took advantage of it. Especially our newly engaged friends who kept twirling through the kitchen, clearly drunk already.

I felt Evan's eyes shift to my face. "It is a party. We should *all* be celebrating."

I smiled as Cara leaned in to kiss Beau. Their passion gave me a bubbly feeling in my chest—something like bravery—and I turned to Evan.

"All right." I took the red solo cup from his hand and downed its contents. Sparkling champagne sizzled as it slid down my throat.

"*Now* it's a party!" Evan hollered.

That made me laugh.

There was something alluring about him. Maybe it was the way he stood—sort of slouched to one side, head tilted slightly, a smirk forever etched into his lips. Maybe it was his persona— very mild, very low-key. The more time I spent with him, the more I felt myself trying to crack his code.

"I'm really happy for them," I said as Cara and Beau waltzed by us, lost in their own world.

"Oh, I know. The wedding's gonna be sick. I only just met them, but I feel like they're really good for each other."

"Definitely." I turned to face Evan. "But they're also really young, you know?"

He shrugged and drank some more. "Love is love. You can't fight it."

I let this sink in, but before it could hit a nerve, I drank some more champagne.

"So, where're you from?"

"I'm from Delaware, but I go to Westchester," he answered.

"Oh, sweet! What's your major?"

"Photography." There was that grin again.

He didn't strike me as the artsy type, but before I could ask, he explained, "I like to travel and take pictures. I'll go to the top of a volcano if I have to just to get the perfect shot."

"Isn't that dangerous?"

He shrugged. "What's life without a little danger?"

I sighed. "Well, I'm a music major. I go to school with Cara."

"Oh, right! You're the violin girl Elijah hooked up with!" I laughed with him, but mortification burned the back of my neck. "He said music is basically your life."

"Yeah, that's me."

Evan stared at me for a moment, amusement fixed on his face. "I'm gonna call you Melody then. It'll fit your musical interest."

I drank more champagne so I could find the courage to laugh.

"Would you ever wanna get married?" he inquired, and I nearly choked. "Just in general," he clarified a moment later, clearly suppressing a laugh.

"Uh," I cleared my throat too loudly like an idiot. "Maybe. I think so, yeah. Way down the road."

"Me, too."

That was when I noticed that Beau's living room had transformed into a make-out haven. Couples were draped over each other, and when clothes started flying, I nodded toward the patio door.

"Wanna take this outside?"

"Good call."

We filled our glasses on the way and then stepped out into the humid night air. Two lounge chairs were set up a few feet away from a rowdy beer pong table.

"I'd win that game in a heartbeat," Evan muttered through another crooked grin.

"You like to play beer pong?"

He glanced at me, two sapphire irises I could easily lose myself in. "For sure. But not tonight. I'd rather chill here."

The reason that statement made my heart quicken was beyond me.

"So why music?" he asked.

I shrugged and swished champagne around in my mouth. "Why photography?"

Another beaming smile. "It gives life purpose, you know? There's nothing like capturing the perfect moment."

"What's a perfect moment to you?"

"It depends. A night like this for sure. The stars, the beer pong. This." His finger pointed back and forth between himself and me.

I downed my champagne. "I'm not perfect."

"You seem cool," he disagreed with a nonchalant shrug.

All I could do was side-eye him, and then a blush painted my cheeks.

We kept our glasses fresh as the hours passed by, and soon my head was swimming. A steady bass was flowing through the closed door, still loud enough to make my bones tremble. I stood up.

"Do you know how to dance?"

Evan tilted his head back and laughed. "If I tell you the truth, you wouldn't like me as much."

"Bullshit."

I pulled him out of his chair and waved my arms around like a banshee. I couldn't dance either, but when you're stoned, the quality of movement doesn't really matter. I swung my arm out and then spun right into him, knocking him backward into his chair with me on top.

He smelled like a mixture of lemon and mint — a fragrance my intoxicated mind only enhanced. And with the addition of alcohol in his breath, it was purely sweet. I raised my head to meet his sapphire eyes and shook my head.

"You know, this never goes well," I said.

"What's that?"

"Drinking with a stranger."

He waved my comment away. "Oh, come on, you've known me for like...eight hours now."

I laughed at this, more than I should have, and took note of how genuinely happy I felt. It might have only been the champagne, but I felt like I was walking on air, and Evan became more and more attractive as the seconds ticked by.

Eventually, someone else stepped out onto the porch, but I was too busy gazing into Evan's eyes that I didn't care to see who it was.

"Hey," Elijah called, snapping his fingers in my ear.

I flinched and moved off of Evan, only to wobble on my own two feet. When I stumbled, Elijah steadied me.

"'Kay, you've *definitely* had enough to drink." He eased the cup out of my grip and laughed. "Geez, I didn't realize you guys were so close already."

I found that I wanted to return to Evan's arms and smell the heavenly aroma that clung to his clothing.

"Ev, Beau said we can crash here for the night," Elijah said.

Evan rose to his feet and swayed slightly. "Sweet." When his eyes fell to my face again, my heart galloped away to rejoin his. "See you later, Melody."

Elijah was pulling me back through the glass door before I could respond.

"Come on," he said. "I'll drive you home."

He towed me toward the door, and we passed Cara and Beau who were making out on the couch.

"Oh, *congratulations!*" I shrieked before I could stop myself.

My shrill voice made Elijah flinch, and he stuck a finger in his ear. "Ouch, Gail."

· · ·

My eyes fluttered open, burning as the white light of day spilled in through the curtains of my bedroom. Not one second had passed and already my head was spinning like a ferris wheel. My stomach reacted, churning violently, and before I knew it, I was leaning over the bed and vomiting onto the floor. The sharp, acrid taste lingered on my tongue, and I nearly emptied my stomach again. But instead, I fell back down onto my pillows.

I had never been this hungover in my life. Everything hurt: my back, my neck, even my left foot was sore for some reason. Annoyingly, my eye kept twitching, and it only made me dizzier.

I hardly left my bed at all, and when I did it was only to clean the puddle of vomit from earlier and to take a cold shower. It wasn't until I trudged into the kitchen for some tea that I remembered. Remembered the proposal, the extreme joy that Cara is getting married, and Evan.

Evan.

Chagrin set my cheeks on fire.

Would he even want to talk to me now that I'd embarrassed myself by getting drunk? Although surprisingly, I found that my memories of him still filled me with joy. It wasn't just a drunk connection. Thinking about him suddenly had my heart racing.

I stopped pouring the tea and turned my mind inward. Yes, that was correct. He excited me. Aside from my sickened stomach, I was giddy and light on my feet.

But something stopped me. It pulsed beneath my bones, snaked up my spine, and invaded the recesses of my heart. It was the fear of uncertainty.

Why fall in love again just to watch it crumble? Because surely it would. This was life, not some enchanting fairytale. And what did falling love again even mean? If *I* was doing it, then Colton undoubtedly was. But why did Colton matter? He had already fallen in love again — twice! And probably more times than I was even aware of. Wasn't it time I let myself fall again? Didn't I owe it to myself after all this time?

Besides, Evan was handsome and intriguing. And he gave me that bubbly feeling in my chest that had become foreign over the years. I wanted to fall for someone again, even if it was doomed to end.

You don't know that for sure! my conscience argued. *That's just the pain talking.* I pictured Colton for a moment, and my heart swelled at his beauty. But that beauty was no longer mine...when would that fact penetrate through my thick skull?

I stood in the kitchen, the teapot still poised in one hand and a cup in the other, arguing with myself. It was a tough debate, both sides presenting very accurate claims. All I knew for certain was that I wanted to see Evan again, and when my phone buzzed, it made up my mind for me.

An unidentified number sat in the inbox.

```
Hey Gail. It's Evan. Elijah gave me your
number. That was a crazy party last
night lol but we should totally hang out
again sometime.
```

Chapter Twelve

PHILADELPHIA, PA (2023)

Instead of spending my twenty-first birthday in a bar or at some big blowout party, I spent the day in Evan's bed. We were pressed against each other, his lips teasing the crook of my neck, his hands curving around my body. Had I been single, I would've opted for the loud, chaotic vibe of a club. But this was much better.

"By the way," Evan whispered in his husky tone, "happy birthday, Melody."

It was the third time he'd told me that. Now, he was gazing into my eyes with a brooding look that could've stopped my heart. And the nickname was starting to fit. The way he said it sent shivers through my bones.

"Thank you," I said and closed my eyes when his lips found mine again.

I had nothing but time on my hands this summer, and I spent most hours with Evan. Our relationship began slowly, like all flames do. First, we went out to small restaurants, then it escalated to late-night conversations on park benches. Eventually, I walked into his apartment and his bedroom for the first time, and it seemed I never left. It was a very small, very private piece of heaven that only we had access to.

Evan had a way of pulling me out of my emotional torrents and making me forget all the heartbreak I'd faced in the past. When I was with him, Colton abandoned his home in my head, and at long last, I found peace.

"It's crazy," I murmured eventually, snuggled up to Evan's chest. "I don't feel twenty-one."

"What can I do to make you feel more special then?"

"Oh, you've done enough, thank you."

He shifted beside me. "Hmm. Too bad I'm not a one surprise kind of guy."

"You don't have to do anything else."

He got out of bed.

"Evan."

He crossed his room and retrieved something from his desk drawer. "I thought it would make the night even better."

I sat for a moment, staring at the velvet box he was holding out to me.

"Evan, having you is enough of a birthday—"

"Just open it," he said with his trademark smirk.

I flipped it open with a sigh. Inside was a silver necklace with two charms: one large oval with tiny stars engraved in it and hanging to the side was a crescent moon. I recognized the stars to be in the pattern of the Leo zodiac constellation, which fit my birthday, July 24.

"Had it custom made," he said.

I was breathless. It made it even better how the necklace matched Erica's bracelet, which hung from my wrist. Now, I could have two special people close to me at all times.

"Evan, I don't even know what to say." He took the piece of jewelry from me and moved my long, wavy hair to the side.

Slowly, he secured it to my neck. The moon and the oval sat right on my beating heart.

"Don't say anything." Evan took a step back to admire me. His eyes were glowing, which brought a smile to my face. "God, you're gorgeous."

I wanted to kiss him again, but he ducked away from my wandering hands.

"There is just one more thing I want to do tonight."

Whenever he spoke like that, with an amused tone, I got slightly nervous. In the span of a month, I'd gathered that Evan was a bit of a daredevil. What that meant for me, I wasn't sure, but as long as we were together, anything would've been great.

"What's that?"

He threw a mischievous look in the direction of his bedroom door. "Why don't we go for a ride?"

I wasn't sure what I expected, but when I followed him into the garage and spotted the bright yellow motorbike, my heart flipped upside down.

"Absolutely not."

"Come on!"

"No! That's a death trap!" But even as I said it, butterflies were already crowding into my stomach, and my voice was high-pitched with adrenaline.

"Abigail." Evan pulled me into his arms. "Do you really think I'd let you on the bike if I thought you'd get hurt? You've got to trust me a little!"

I scoffed at his words, but if I was being honest, I did want to experience the rush I was always told about.

"Fine."

"Yes!" Evan exclaimed. He pulled a helmet from one of the shelves and held it up to my face.

"I'm gonna look like a weirdo in that."

"Shh. Safety first." He slid the bulky thing onto my head, and

I stared back at him through the glass, trying not to think about my claustrophobia.

"Okay, you in my helmet...hottest thing ever."

I giggled. Evan paused for a moment and held up his index finger, signaling me to wait. He disappeared into the apartment again and returned with a camera.

"No!" I tried to shield my face with my hands, but the helmet was too large to be covered.

With a wide grin, Evan snapped the picture.

"*This* is a perfect moment. There, see? You're beautiful," he said, showing me the photo.

I just rolled my eyes at him.

It had been such a long time since I felt like this — nervous and jittery but in a good way. Feeling like I was sneaking around, even though no one was looking for us anyway. I was already exhilarated, and I hadn't even gotten on the bike yet.

When Evan ignited the engine, I locked my arms around him so tightly that he may have struggled to breathe. The sound roared off the garage walls, and I trembled. Evan opened the garage door, revealing a dark, starry night sky.

"You'll be fine, Melody, I promise," he assured me over the guttural sound of his bike. "Besides, you're twenty-one now! Time to live a little!"

When we started to move, my arms tightened around him even more. The sound of the bike scared me; it was too loud against the quiet of the night. But as we continued to glide and zoom down the streets, my heart eased into the adrenaline, and I soon felt like I was flying. I didn't dare let go of him though. I was content just the way I was.

Evan took me down the roads of Philadelphia, some still loud and awake, and others asleep. I laid my head against Evan's back and watched the glowing street lamps swish by with my heart jumping wildly in my ribcage.

. . .

Cara and I spent the last week of summer cleaning, washing, and organizing our apartment. Because we missed out on spring cleaning due to the misery of mandatory quarantine, we had to make up for it now. When we were *finally* finished, we collapsed onto the couch. Outside, Philadelphia was alive. Cars honked, people talked, the streets were filled. I listened to all the commotion until Cara started talking.

"Can I just say something?"

"Go for it."

She turned to face me, and I knew whatever it was she had to say, it was important. She always resituated herself whenever she had something critical to say.

"This summer started off *terribly*. I don't know about you, but social distancing was the hardest thing I've ever had to do. And to be honest, I really thought I wouldn't make it. Either I'd contract the stupid fever or lose my mind."

"Trust me. I was right there with you." The memory of quarantine made me want to gag.

"But...something terrible turned into something beautiful. I mean, all the fever did was just remind us what's important, you know? I got to know you better, Gail, and I'm so thankful for that. And of course, I'm engaged now."

I cocked my head, letting her words sink in. She was right. When I really thought about it, the Pulmonem Fever was a blessing in disguise. After all, I was with Evan now. Cara was happy. My father was safe and healthy. What more could I have wanted?

"I just have to thank God for everything because...he really does work in mysterious ways." Now, she was blinking back tears.

When the memories rolled through my mind, they were overwhelming. My first day of college, meeting Cara for the first time. Professor Autrie's guidance and support. The times Cara sang while I played my violin. Sleeping with Colton. Being forced into quarantine. Meeting Evan...Tears pricked my eyes, too.

"Life is weird, Gail," Cara muttered. Her gaze was distant. "We really are growing up."

As was the truth since we were now entering our junior year at Curtis. Despite the opening of some stores and dine-in restaurants, many schools were still forcing students into a hybrid situation: on campus two days a week and online for three. Our professors had the option to continue in-person lectures if they wanted to, but only if they promised to abide by CDC guidelines. Much to my luck, Professor Autrie decided he would teach us in person.

Junior year meant diving head-first into my major without the stress of gen ed classes, so I was extremely excited to return to campus, even though it looked drastically different under the circumstances of the pandemic. Social-distancing was still mandatory; all seating areas were closed off. And of course, masks were required everywhere.

Evan texted me every day, explaining how much he longed for the comfort of my arms, and I said I felt the same. Being away from him was painful. But it wasn't until I entered the orchestra hall that I realized I'd never played my violin for him. During quarantine, I took a break from playing, and Evan was such an amazing distraction that I'd forgotten my violin almost entirely during those long summer weeks.

`You'll have to hear me play some time,` I texted him after my morning conducting class.

`Can't wait.`

"Ah, *bonjour*, Abigail!"

For a moment, relief swelled inside of me. It was so great to see my favorite professor alive and well after such a scary period of time. But the closer I got to him, the more I noticed that there was something off about his appearance. His face, though just as wrinkled and weathered as before, seemed hollower in some places. Indigo shadows underlined his eyes, and his skin was terribly sallow.

"How are you doing, Professor?"

"I'm excellent! Thrilled to be back here teaching!" My smile faltered as he coughed harshly into his elbow.

Attempting to keep my voice light, I said, "That doesn't sound excellent."

"Just a cough, ma chérie. Don't worry. I'm perfectly healthy!"

And apparently a good liar, but I could see that he had no intention of answering anymore questions. I promised myself that I would check up on him later.

Our orchestra had doubled in number this year, except half of the students were off-campus and enduring their online courses, which made the auditorium feel abnormally large. Those of us who were here settled into our chairs, and instinctively, I began tuning my instrument.

Professor Autrie tapped his baton on the stand. "I am so happy to see your shining faces again...even if it's just half of you. This year, juniors and seniors will have the chance to sign up for the ensemble, and soloist auditions for our first concert will be held the first week of September! Sign-up sheets are outside my office."

"Are we going to *have* a fall concert?" Christain Sanster called from behind his colossal bass.

Professor Autrie coughed harshly into his elbow and then glanced at Christain. "One can only hope, right? Now, please open your song books to page 213."

That afternoon, I went home for lunch and called my father.

"Hey, sweetheart!" he said after the third ring.

I held the phone with one hand and forked through a salad with the other. "Hey, Dad."

"How's junior year?"

"Well, as good as it's gonna get with the fever restrictions."

"And Cara's not married yet?"

"No."

When I explained the big news of my friend's wedding to my father, he hadn't reacted the way I expected, but rather exploded from an anxiety attack. He claimed she was too young and that love wasn't something to be rushed. I had to repeatedly tell him that it wasn't his decision, but in the end, he seemed happy enough having voiced his opinion anyway.

There was just one problem though. I hadn't told my father about Evan yet, and that was sure to cause him a heart attack considering what happened with my last boyfriend. But I didn't want to sneak around with Evan forever. As I speared a piece of cauliflower and munched down on it, I felt my heart give a nervous flutter. It was now or never.

"Oh, well, that's a relief! I'm glad to hear they're not just running off into each other's arms."

"Dad, there actually is something I wanted to tell you."

"What's that?"

I scrunched my face, trying to find the courage. "I met someone."

Silence.

"His name's Evan, and he's been friends with Elijah since like, the fifth grade." I wasn't sure why this mattered, but I felt the need to explain it. "He's really nice."

The silence continued.

"He goes to Westchester, so he's close by." Now I was just mumbling out of wariness.

"What's he going to school for?"

"Photography," I answered. "Look, Dad. He's really cool and sweet, and—"

"And?"

"And I like him. A lot."

That was all that needed to be said; it was simple after all. My dad didn't need to know every detail, like how I'd gotten on Evan's motorbike and rode close to fifteen miles with him.

"Well...as long as he treats you with respect." My father's voice was guarded. I could tell he was considering the probability of having to retrieve a gun from his safe.

"He really does, Dad. There's no need to worry."

"All right. When am I going to meet him?"

"We have a Friday off coming up. I'll come home that weekend and bring him with me."

"Can't wait." His voice was drenched in sarcasm.

"You're stunning, Melody," Evan whispered in my ear as I waited outside one of Curtis's main auditoriums. I had my soloist audition tonight and had donned a floor-length black gown that protruded slightly from my hips.

Because it was Friday, Evan had left Westchester as soon as his last class was over, just in time to wish me luck before I was called in. Though I was nervous to perform for Professor Autrie and his colleagues, I was even more nervous that Evan would be able to hear me from the hall. The auditorium's acoustics were incredible, and this was the first time he would hear me play.

"You're going to be amazing," he assured me. "No sweat. A piece of cake!"

"You don't even know if I'm good," I pointed out.

He shrugged. "You're good at everything."

Before I could argue, Wendy Cheng exited the auditorium and regarded me with a slight nod. Professor Autrie called my name.

"Real quick before you go—for good luck!" Evan pulled me to his lips and kissed me with so much fervor that I felt faint for a second afterwards.

As if moving on air, I glided down the aisles as quickly as my dress would allow and scurried up the side-stage steps.

"Good afternoon," I greeted them.

I recognized Professor Autrie, of course, and Miss Atlas who was the dean of students, but the two other men remained nameless in my brain. This brought on flashbacks of my first audition to get into this school, and I drew a deep breath. Evan was waiting.

"Today I will be performing an excerpt from *The Four Seasons* by Antonio Vivaldi."

With that, I raised my violin and allowed the music to course out into the audience like a waterfall. The fast parts made my fingers burn and ache, but I powered through, never missing a beat. Though Evan wasn't allowed to be in here while I was performing, I made sure to play to the back of the auditorium, even at the quietest parts. When I met my last crescendo, I let my bow saw away on the strings and ended with a spine-tingling vibrato.

My judges rose to their feet, applauding and hollering for me.

"*Bravo!*" Professor Autrie called.

I bowed and exited the stage, trying not to run. But I had to see Evan's expression before it killed me. He was sitting on the bench, right where I left him. But when he glanced up at me, he looked stunned. So much so that his eyes flicked between the violin and my face multiple times before he spoke.

"Holy sh..." He rose to his feet, mouth agape. "Okay, I knew you were good, but I didn't know you were *that* good."

I giggled. "Told you."

At a loss for words, he simply shook his head and pulled me into a tight hug.

"Damn, Melody. You're incredible!"

As we broke from our embrace, a group of friends moved past us down the hall. Evan turned toward them.

"Did you just hear her play?" he demanded.

"Oh, my God. Evan, stop." I turned into him again, trying to hide my embarrassment. But even though I was mortified, I still felt bubbly inside.

I was starting to fall for Evan harder and harder with each passing second. How could my father *not* like this funny, supportive person that I'd come to know? Evan was everything that I wanted in a man: sentimental, honest, loving, and encouraging. If my family and friends loved me, they would try to see Evan for who he was. And speaking of friends, I couldn't wait to see what Erica would say when she met him. We had FaceTimed so much recently, and she was bouncing off the walls when I described him. Unfortunately, with her college schedule, the first possible date we could meet up was in March. I wished she could come home this weekend to see Evan, but that wouldn't work, much to my dismay. So, this trip was strictly father-meeting-boyfriend.

Saturday afternoon, Evan held my hand as I pulled the car into my childhood neighborhood. Even though it felt like I hadn't been here in a lifetime, things hadn't changed a bit. There was the bakery and the Brook Tavern. The flower shop and the hair salon I went to as a teenager.

"Cool place," Evan commented, gazing out at the passing stores and restaurants.

"Oh, yeah. Home's the best."

Eventually, I rounded the small bend at the end of the street and pulled into the driveway. Evan peered up at the house, gouging it through narrowed eyes.

"How do I look?" he asked.

Roguishly handsome. I slid my fingers into his hair, which had been combed into a more presentable style. The stickiness of gel coated my fingers, but I didn't pull away. Whenever I did this, his eyes clouded with longing, and he turned toward me to steal a kiss.

"You look amazing," I murmured, inhaling his rich cologne. "My dad's gonna love you."

The door opened even before I could get my key out of the car's ignition. My father and Jamie stood in the doorway—Jamie smiling politely, and Dad staging a grimace.

"Hey, guys. This is Evan."

Evan held out a hand, which Jamie shook first, and thankfully, my father was nice enough not to break my boyfriend's hand.

"Come on in," he said somewhat stiffly. "Gail, let me help carry something."

To my surprise, the living room no longer had a polished wood floor but a plush white carpet instead. I turned back to my father.

"Renovations," he clarified. "I just needed a change."

"It looks great." So perfect in fact that I felt the need to remove my shoes before venturing further.

"Gail, I'm making spaghetti for dinner. I know you like that." Jamie grinned.

"Yes, thank you!"

"We're gonna eat around five-thirty, so..." Dad trailed off when his eyes touched Evan's face.

"'Kay. Evan, let me show you around."

Grateful to be out of my father's watchful eye, Evan followed me willingly into the foyer.

"I used to ride my scooter around here when I was little," I said, gesturing to the faded tire marks that were stubborn enough to withstand every mopping.

Evan laughed. "I can see that."

I guided him in through the dining room and through the kitchen that held a disarray of sorted vegetables, sauces, and a pot of boiling noodles. Jamie glanced up from her half-chopped carrot and smiled as we passed. I led him into the basement, which contained nothing more than piles of boxes and holiday storage. Upstairs, I pulled him into my bedroom with a smirk. He chuckled and gazed around at my bookshelves and posters of male actors, at the armchair in the corner and the music stand beside it.

"So, *this* is where you grew up."

"Yeah. As you can tell, I like blue." Hence the color of the walls and my old bedspread.

"I love it," he said. "It's you."

My lips pulled upward into a smile as I watched him move around the space. He stopped in front of my bulletin board, which was still aglow under a string of lights.

"These your high school buds?"

"Oh, yeah," I answered, stepping closer.

Truthfully, I'd forgotten all about the pictures I had hanging up there. There were even still pictures of me and Katy from freshman year. There was me and Erica after my last concert as a senior, and there was—

"Whoa, who's this?" Evan asked, pointing to a picture of homecoming from sophomore year.

Me in a powdery lavender gown, Coltan looking dapper in a suit and matching bowtie. We were turned toward each other, locked in a passionate kiss.

Evan glanced at me. "Ex-boyfriend?"

Guilt twisted painfully in my gut, but I tried my best to keep my voice even. "Uh, yeah. Sorry, I completely forgot I even had those up there."

Evan didn't seem offended at all; in fact, he looked like he was trying to conceal his laughter. "Hmm...should I be jealous?"

"Definitely *not*." It was a sharper answer than I'd intended.

His grin faltered and morphed into confusion. All signs of joking were erased. I sighed and pressed a hand to my forehead.

"Sorry. It's just...that guy's an asshole. So, you really don't have reason to be jealous, trust me."

Evan's eyes locked on the photo again. "If he's such a bad guy, why did you keep his picture up?"

"Because..." I stopped, at a loss for words. What excuse could I share that wouldn't make me sound insane? "Look, I've been away at college. That was a long time ago. I simply *forgot* to take it down—"

"Melody," Evan said, turning to face me, his voice calm and mellow. "I'm not putting you on trial. Relax."

I exhaled and sank down onto the foot of my bed. "I'm sorry. This wasn't how I wanted to start things out. Just know that *you're* the one I want to be with. One hundred percent."

"I feel the same. Besides, I'm kind of excited to spend the night in your old bedroom." The smirk was back; I didn't have to look at him; I could hear it in his tone.

Grateful to be out of the past, I closed my hand around the fabric of Evan's shirt and pulled him to my lips.

Dinner was successful. Now that Dad had met Evan, and the awkward introductions were out of the way, he was more tranquil and open to asking questions. We discussed college and career choices, but I was thankful when Evan mentioned the Tampa Bay Buccaneers. The way to Dad's heart was always to compliment the skills of Tom Brady. In the end, my father patted Evan on the shoulder, his face red from laughing and hollering so much. I caught Jamie's eye as the boys loudly expressed their football opinions. She gave me a subtle wink, and my heart smiled.

Once we were full and satisfied, Evan and I wandered out onto the back patio and collapsed into the porch swing. The evening was cool and fragrant with the smell of autumn—all the more reason to snuggle up together.

"Okay, so you got to know my family. Tell me about yours."

Evan scratched his chin. "Uh...they're kinda crazy."

"Crazy's cool."

He hesitated, taking a moment to gaze over at me. "All right. Well, my mom's a baker. She owns her own shop near my house in Delaware. And Dad's a cop. Has been for like fifty-five years."

"Dang."

"I have two sisters and one brother. My sisters are younger than me, but my brother graduated college last year. We're tight, I guess, but they can be annoying sometimes. Especially Gracy— ugh! My youngest sister...she's insane. Won't shut up at all, goes on and on about anything that comes to her mind."

I giggled at Evan's hostility because despite his words, there was still a sparkle in his eye.

"She's in fifth grade, too, so she's still pretty young. But...I don't know. I kinda miss them. Like, college is dope, but there really is no place like home."

I watched him speak, watched the forlorn expression cross his face. He was distant now, miles away, probably surrounded by his family.

"They sound awesome," I said.

He chuckled. "Yeah. But my mom laughs like a hyena. It is the most annoying, high-pitched laugh you will ever hear."

I was really laughing now, feeling the sensation tickle my stomach. Evan laughed, too, and for a few minutes, our hilarity echoed off the trees in the backyard.

"I can't wait to meet them," I said when I recovered from my guffaws.

"They're gonna love *you*." He was serious again, eyes wide with the realization.

I shifted and laid my head down in his lap so I could stare up at him from a new angle. "I mean, I hope so. But why do you say it like that?"

"Just because I usually bring home—" he shrugged. "—girls who aren't as...put-together as you."

"Is that a compliment?"

"Definitely." He glanced down at me, sapphire eyes glowing in the moonlight. "You're better than every other girl I've ever dated."

"How so?"

He scoffed. "For starters, you don't spend every night getting high in a back alley somewhere. I swear my first girlfriend was part of a gang or something. The shit that she did..." He shook his head, disgust distorting his features.

"That sounds awful."

"Oh, it was. Especially because she lied about her name, too. I thought I was dating Alex. No, turns out her real name was Jemma."

"What the heck?"

He shrugged. "She was insane."

"My first boyfriend was almost beaten to death by his alcoholic dad." It slipped out before I even knew it was on the tip of my tongue.

Evan shot out of his reverie and looked down at me, lips parted in shock.

Something cold slivered through my lungs, making it hard to breathe for a moment. But now that it was said, I needed to explain myself to ease Evan's disbelief.

"Yeah," I nodded, "his dad was abused a lot when *he* was young, so he had terrible PTSD all his life. That was why his wife eventually divorced him, 'cause she couldn't take it. But, you know, time goes on, and my ex wanted to make things right with his dad, so he went to spend Easter weekend with him and came back bloodied and scarred. My ex didn't even *tell* me about it, and when I finally found out, he dumped me." I realized I was fuming, so I drew a deep breath to steady my thinking.

"How does that work?"

I stared out into the yard. Above the looming shapes of trees, stars twinkled like jewels in the dark sky.

"I don't know. Still to this day, I'm not sure why we broke up."

Evan was silent for a moment, and I realized my mistake. Turning my eyes back to his, I reached a hand up to touch his cheek.

"But if he never would've left, I never would've met you."

A small smile lifted Evan's features, but it didn't reach his eyes. "Was that the boy in the picture?"

"Yeah. Listen, I really am sorry about that. I'll take it down—"

"It's all right. I can't imagine what he went through...But that's no excuse to dump *you*. I guess I should thank him though because you're mine now, and I'm so thankful."

"Me, too."

"I never had to deal with a parental abuse situation, but I've dated my fair share of lunatics, which is exactly why my family's gonna love you. You're real, Gail. Like, you don't smoke and lie. You don't play people for your own benefit. You're a really good person."

"Go on," I joked.

"Oh, I will. You're driven and determined. Talk about an independent woman."

I sat up, recognizing the change in his tone. Slowly, I straddled his waist and cocked my head, grinning. "Go on."

"You're also drop-dead gorgeous and an incredible kisser," he whispered.

I nodded, repressing a laugh. I leaned in and pressed my lips to his, basking in the pleasurable heat that his touch always sent throughout my body. Then suddenly remembering where we were, I pulled back and sat beside him once more.

"Gosh, I feel like I'm in high school again. Having to steal kisses when my dad isn't watching, it's ridiculous."

Evan sighed. "I know what you mean, but it's not all that bad.

Being in high school means we're young and don't have to worry about anything. It's fun to pretend sometimes."

A chilly breeze kissed my bare arms, and I shivered. "I guess you're right."

I'd never really thought about it in that way, but the feeling of being younger simply made me want to kiss him even more.

The sliding glass door squeaked open, and Jamie poked her head outside.

"We're about to have dessert if you guys want any." Behind her, you could hear my father ranting about how good Jamie's baking was.

"Yeah, we'll be right in," I assured her.

"Jamie really is an awesome baker," I told Evan when the door was shut.

He pursed his lips. "She should have a bake-off with my mom. I wonder who'd win."

Chapter Thirteen

PHILADELPHIA, PA (2023)

I spent nearly every evening in the orchestra room, working one-on-one with Professor Autrie. Thankfully, I'd been awarded the soloist position for our first concert, assuming it was still happening. Pulmonem Fever cases were falling and rising like a seesaw, so all I could do was practice and hope the university stayed open.

"I would recommend shifting to third position in measure sixty," my instructor advised me.

I shoved a strand of hair behind my ear and huffed as I wrote these notes into my sheet music. I was rehearsing so much that my arms were starting to feel like Jell-O, and my neck had a terrible knot in it.

"No, no, no. Stop. That G sharp in measure twenty-one—it's not high enough."

I stole a glance at the clock and felt dizzy when I saw that it was fifteen minutes after six. We'd been at this for two hours now, and my stomach was growling so loudly it was competing against the volume of my instrument. I couldn't work well on an empty stomach.

"These are long nights, I know," Professor Autrie said, "but you are a soloist now, which means we've got to step it up." He turned away to cough into his elbow.

It was a gurgling, spine-pinching cough, and I winced. He had been doing that all evening.

"Are you sure you're okay?"

After recovering from his coughing spell, he pressed his lips together, and the wounded look in his eyes nearly broke my heart. But he covered it quickly. "Of course. Now, again from the adagio."

"No, hold on." I set my violin on a nearby chair and raised my eyebrows at him. "I'm really worried about you, Professor. You've been coughing like this for weeks now. Have you been to a doctor?"

He slouched in his seat and released a long held sigh, which came out more as a wheeze. "Of course, I've been to a doctor."

I waited for him to continue with my jaw locked into place. Whatever this was, it couldn't be good.

He glanced up at me with an apology already shining in his eyes. "They say I have emphysema."

Fear, cold as ice, slid its scaly finger down my spine. I felt sick. Worse than that, I was terrified. Professor Autrie watched my reaction and hung his head.

"W—So are you...How—?"

"I smoked a lot as a boy and continued through my adulthood," he admitted. "*C'est triste, oui.* I tried to quit a hundred times, and I did eventually. But that was only four years ago."

My hands were quivering in my lap; my mind filled with questions. All the while, grief stood near me like an unseen ghost. I felt it watching and waiting to bite.

"They can help you, right?" I demanded.

"*Oui.* They prescribed me some antibiotics, but that's just temporary until they find a new solution." Despite his words, he didn't sound all that confident.

I shook my head, trying to process this information. "Professor, if you get the Pulmonem Fever, it could—" I couldn't even finish my sentence.

"Hey, *écoute, ma chérie*. I'm gonna be just fine. Don't you worry about me one bit. You've got a solo to prepare for after all." There was that smile, that brilliant smile that made you feel all warm. He was strong. A trooper. And if that was the case, I would be one for him.

"You will keep me informed though, right?" It was more of a demand than a question.

The sad look in his eyes deepened. "Of course."

It took me a moment to let his words sink in, but then I nodded. As long as he kept his promise, I could help in some way. I reached for my violin again. "From the adagio, then?"

Weeks passed, and *thankfully*, with the cases of Pulmonem Fever down again, Curtis was able to host its annual fall concert. The auditorium was packed every other seat with a bunch of masked faces. People rushed all around me, plucking the strings of their instruments, murmuring excitedly to one another. I stood in the curtains with Professor Autrie, quietly humming the tune of my solo. Beside me, my instructor coughed violently into his elbow even though he was wearing a mask. His condition had only worsened.

"Listen, if you're not well enough—"

"Hush, Abigail," he murmured. "I can get through this."

He had made me keep his illness a secret in an attempt to keep peace and order alive in the orchestra. If there was one thing he absolutely hated, it was people fussing over him. If they didn't worry about him in Vietnam as a young immigrant who got drafted, then they sure as hell weren't going to worry about him now. And that was what he had firmly stated, even though I loudly disagreed.

He straightened his tie and rolled his shoulders. "Now then...break a leg, Miss Ferr." He patted my shoulder just as the curtains split open.

Nerves alive and humming, I sashayed out onto the stage and bowed to an upsurge of cheers, then turned to tune the orchestra. The real applause erupted when Professor Autrie followed me out. He waved and even though his mouth was covered, his eyes reflected the beaming smile under his mask. Once his back was to the crowd, he faced us with a look of assurance. This was a very difficult piece after all. Once he had the orchestra's undivided attention, he glanced down at me and nodded.

I felt like I was moving through water. This was my first time as a soloist and with every eye trained on my face, my stomach was a mess of knots. Somehow, I got up and stood apart from my fellow instrumentalists, violin poised and ready.

Professor Autrie didn't waste a moment. His baton flicked into motion, and we were off. I was sure my face was a stone, locked in some look of concentration. My fingers, skipping gleefully across the fingerboard, stretched so far apart that it was a wonder they didn't break off.

It was boiling up here on stage. With the stress of the song and the heat of the lights, I could feel sweat trickling down the back of my neck. I kept perfect posture even though my aching arms begged for a rest.

And here it was — my part. The sound of my violin wafted out into the crowd, an elegant sound that could charm anyone just by the eerie tone of it. I shifted into third position and climbed the scale like steps, ending on that high F sharp that sent people to the edge of their seats. I lingered on the note, varying my vibrato, and faded out when Professor Autrie queued the rest of the orchestra back in. We raced to the end of the piece, bows flying in unison. The audience held their breath.

But something was wrong. I should have noticed it when Professor Autrie didn't que my last note; thank goodness I was counting or I wouldn't have come in on time. I risked a glance over at our conductor just in time to see his eyes close. And then it all happened so fast. He tumbled backward, and I reached out to catch him. I collapsed under his limp weight. The orchestra came to a screeching stop, and the audience took a sharp collective inhale.

Professor Autrie had passed out. He wasn't moving...or breathing.

"Help!" I shrieked. For a moment, nobody moved, and the silence screamed at us. I looked out into the crowd, meeting a few terrified faces. "HELP!" I yelled again, and this time a frenzy broke out.

A couple professors whom I vaguely recognized rushed out onstage. One checked Professor Autrie's pulse, the other shouted into a phone, presumably speaking with the 911 operator. When they heaved his body off of me, I searched the crowd for Evan. He came rushing down the aisle, hand outstretched for me. Behind him, my father and Jamie looked mystified. As I stared at Evan's hand, it was then that I realized my own hands were empty.

A sick feeling squeezed my stomach. As everyone else hurried this way and that, I slowly turned to see my violin, which I had dropped in order to catch Professor Autrie. It lay on the ground, cracked and damaged beyond repair.

The sky was angry. Black clouds hovered over the streets of Philadelphia, menacing and threatening to unleash a downpour at any moment. Thunder even groaned in the distance. The living room of our apartment was filled. Every seat was occupied, yet no one spoke. Evan's hand covered my own, and he squeezed it every few minutes.

"So," my father began, and every head turned to look at him, "this guy has emphysema?"

I could only nod.

"And you knew this?"

Evan squeezed my hand.

"Yes," I managed, "but he told me not to tell anyone because he didn't want to scare—"

"No one's blaming you, Gail," Cara said gently.

"You actually broke his fall," Evan added. "If anything, you saved him from an even bigger injury."

My cheeks were still wet from the tears that were coming and going. The only thing I could think about was Professor Autrie's face when he coughed into his elbow backstage.

"I don't think he'll be leaving the hospital anytime soon," Jamie muttered.

"We should go and see him," I insisted. "Wish him well."

"No, Gail. I don't think that's a good idea right now," Dad rebuked. "He needs to rest, heal. Plus, there are patients there with the Pulmonem Fever. It's not safe."

"You don't heal from emphysema!" I snapped. "And I don't care, I can wear a mask."

My statement drowned the room in silence.

"He doesn't have long," I said, feeling tears slip down my cheeks again. "And he helped me through so much! The least I could do is thank him...I never got to thank him."

Evan pulled me to him, and I sobbed into his shirt. For a while, my cries were the only thing you could hear.

"Is there anything we can do?" Evan whispered eventually.

But I didn't hear a reply.

I raced down the hospital hallways, trying to locate room 126. It was like a maze; I couldn't get there fast enough, and every twist and turn just made me more anxious. I'd asked if Cara wanted to come with me today, but she had choir rehearsal almost all day, so I was on my own to navigate the hospital.

"Can I help you, miss?" a nurse asked.

I must have looked frantic because she regarded me with stiff vigilance.

"Room 126," I said, my words slightly muffled by my face mask.

"Straight down this hallway and to the right. First door on the right, can't miss it."

"Thank you!" I shouted as I sprinted the rest of the way.

The door was ajar just to the point where I could see the foot of his bed. There was a slight buzzing noise coming from inside. Perhaps the sound of a ventilator, I realized. Slowly, I pushed the door open the rest of the way and entered.

Seeing my professor in a hospital bed made something inside me wince. Though his face was fairly peaceful, the image was all wrong. He looked sickly pale now, his skin the color of white paste. His cheek-bones were high and defined, leaving purplish hollow spaces in his cheeks. Only his head was visible under the mountain of blankets, and a string of tubes protruded from his nostrils. As he slept, his heartbeat was a slow beep on the machine beside him.

It wasn't until I took another step inside that I noticed the woman sitting in the corner. Her gray corkscrew curls bounced as she rose to greet me.

"What can I do for you?" she inquired quietly, securing a mask to her face before approaching me.

My eyes flickered between her face and the hospital bed. "I'm here to see my professor. I was first chair in his orchestra."

Some of the tension disappeared from her face, and she nodded. "Ah, Victor is quite popular today. Many students have come to wish him well."

I could see that. The room was already decorated with colorful balloons and cards of all different sizes.

"Are you—?"

"His wife." She glanced back at me with hard emerald eyes.

"Right. Nice to meet you."

"I was there, you know. At the concert. You were the soloist, the one who saved him from his fall."

"Yeah."

Her eyes became misty. "Thank you, truly."

Before I could respond, the sheets on the hospital bed shifted and demanded my attention. Professor Autrie was awake now, though when he saw me, his gleeful expression was weakened by his condition.

"Abigail," he said. His voice rasped, and he wheezed into his elbow. His arm was just a bone with sagging skin. "What a surprise."

"Professor," I breathed.

He struggled to sit up, but his wife stopped him with a steady hand. "Oh, no, no. You're resting right now," she chastised gently.

"I just came to see you," I said. "How have you gone this long without listening to one of your waltzes?" It was sweet relief to see his face light up.

"Oh, he doesn't," his wife answered with a small smile. "Makes me play one every two hours."

He laughed a ragged laugh that ended in a coughing spell so harsh it made my own lungs hurt just to witness.

"Thank you for coming, Abigail." I had to come closer just to hear his words. Eventually, I just sank down to my knees right by the bed. He stared up at the ceiling, breath heavy and shallow. Ever so slowly, his heart rate returned to normal, and when it did, he turned his head to face me.

"I have a request," he whispered.

"Of course, Professor. Anything."

A weak smile pinched his lips. "Play."

"What?"

"At my funeral, play."

Though it was a request of compassion, it felt as if I'd been slapped in the face. Hearing him say such a thing — like death was even a *possibility* for him...my eyes drowned in tears.

"You want me to play my violin?"

"Mhm."

I recalled the broken shards of my instrument and struggled to keep a composed face.

"Any particular piece?"

"Something cheery," he mused. "Something that will make people — " Another coughing attack struck him, and his wife closed her eyes. "Th-that will make people want to dance."

I nodded. "A waltz?"

He pursed his lips. "Surprise me."

"Why me though?"

"There's something about you, *ma chérie*. You remind me a lot of myself at that age." He cleared his throat and flinched at the pain. "You feel the music. It comes from your heart...and you don't find people like that every day."

Though I was on my knees, my legs quivered. My core was liquid. Grief sat in the corner, watching our conversation with sad, tear-filled eyes.

"I'll do it."

The corners of his lips tilted upward. "*Merci*."

I glanced up at his wife, who offered a polite smile in return.

"Abigail," Professor Autrie said as I stood up.

"Yes?"

He reached out to take my hand, and I nearly jumped at the coldness of his grip. "You are so young. You've got your whole life ahead of you yet...never say never."

I stared down at him, trying to make sense of the words. He'd said them in such a personal, gut-wrenching way that I couldn't decipher what he meant exactly. His hand slipped from mine, and he stared back up at the ceiling, as if already forgetting my presence.

Hesitantly, I turned toward the door, but something in his distant expression made me want to stay. I could feel the window of togetherness slowly closing.

"Thank you for coming," his wife said. "It really cheers him up."

"Of course." I stole another glance at him. "I'm gonna try to find a piece that I can play."

"Oh, dear, I can give you money to fix your violin. The whole auditorium saw you drop it." She went to grab her purse from the seat.

"No way! Absolutely not. I can pay for it."

Her emerald eyes met mine, uncertain. "Are you sure?"

"Of course." Professor Autrie had fallen asleep again, looking just as peaceful as when I entered. "Besides, his life is more important than my violin."

"How do I look?"

"Gorgeous," my father and Evan replied in unison.

I stared at my reflection in the mirror once more and tried to fluff my curls. But they just fell back into place. I heaved a frustrated sigh.

Today, I was set to play at Professor Autrie's funeral, but I was painfully jittery, and my body shook as I moved around. I hadn't slept well anyway, sick from the grief. It weighed on my shoulders, irritated and provoked my anxiety. I was nothing but a bundle of nerves. I trudged toward the door, my dark velvet gown swishing around my legs.

"My violin's in the trunk, right?" I called to Dad.

"Yes."

The moment I'd left the hospital that day a few weeks ago, Dad had called to order me a new instrument. It was bright and shiny but lacking the dust of rosin and the weariness of practice. It made me miss my old one, the one I'd had since high school. But if I was going to honor Professor Autrie's request, my pesky memories had to be set aside.

Evan helped me to the car by keeping a steady arm around my waist. I was grateful for this, seeing as it felt like I may pass out at any second. I knew as soon as I saw my professor laying in a coffin that I would lose it. I already felt weak and on the verge of tears.

"How does he think I can do this?" I shook my head, trying to clear it.

The grief choked me like a boa constrictor. I didn't want to go to the funeral; I didn't want to *know* he was truly gone.

"I can't do it." My voice was hoarse.

"Hey, hey," Evan whispered, pressing his lips to ear. "You *can* do this. He wouldn't have picked you if he thought you couldn't."

"How am I supposed to perform when his corpse is feet away?"

"Shh. Don't think of it like that, Abigail. You're *honoring* him. Of course, it'll be tough. If you mess up, start to cry—who cares? You're human. It's to be expected."

I shook my head again as the anxiety closed off my airways. My hand shot out in search of Evan's, and I gasped for air. How was I supposed to spend the remainder of my junior year and all of senior year without my professor's unmatchable guidance? He deepened my love for music. He was my mentor. I idolized him.

The sight of Dad exiting the apartment building steadied me a little bit. I climbed into the backseat with Evan and rested my head on his shoulder. We didn't speak on the way to the funeral home, just watched the dreary day cruise by. It hadn't stopped raining in weeks, but I was glad. It made it seem like the earth was mourning, too, and Professor Autrie deserved nothing less. Though the funeral home was only a few blocks away, the car ride felt like years. By the time we finally arrived, I'd managed to let the grief drown me into exhaustion, which I decided was better than non-stop fidgeting. Raindrops kissed our skin as we walked to the entrance; my new violin case felt cold and strange in my hand.

Inside, the fragrance of lilacs was almost too sweet to bear. There was an easel in the corner that held a collage of pictures, all of Professor Autrie smiling and living his life. Some photos showed him conducting with an angelic smile on his face. Others were taken of his time with family members. One photo in particular drew my eye: a standstill of him blowing a kiss to the Eiffel Tower.

His wife and who were presumably his other family members stood at the entrance to the parlor. Seeing them, I was suddenly nervous again. There was a line leading into the parlor that stretched down the hall and wrapped around the corner. It mostly consisted of elderly people, but there were a few middle-aged adults who had to hold their kids in place and explain that this was not a playground. Dad, Evan, and I made our way to the back of the line.

Unsurprisingly, one of Johann Strauss' waltzes was floating from the speakers. It was a delightful piece, one that sounded too lively for the circumstances. But that had been Professor Autrie's wish after all.

The line moved steadily, and all too soon, his wife stepped forward to greet us. Her eyes fell upon my violin case, and a sad smile crept onto her lips.

"He's going to love this," she said.

She turned to the others beside her and murmured something in French. The women nodded in agreement.

"*Bonjour*," they said quietly as we passed.

The parlor was lovely of course, with soft coral-colored walls and elegant gilded chairs set up for the public. At the head of the room stood a dark podium, and in the corner—

No. I couldn't look. I looked down at my black heels instead.

They clicked on the marble floors with each step I took. Evan glanced down at me and kissed my cheek for reassurance, but it didn't help as much as it should have.

"Abigail," a familiar voice hollered.

I looked down one of the aisles and spotted Christain Sanster and Sheila Baker. Behind them, a handful of freshmen and sophomores occupied the last few seats of the row. I waved at them half-heartedly, grateful to see some of my peers here for Professor Autrie.

"You playing today?" Christain eyed my case.

"Yeah."

Sheila tossed her hair over her shoulder. "You're brave."

I shrugged. "Where's Deven? We could've been a quartet. Autrie would've loved it."

Christain eyed the casket over my shoulder and grimaced. "I doubt Deven would be up for it," he muttered.

Fear turned my spine into an icicle, and I turned to go.

Cara and Beau appeared through the crowd, offering me a thumbs-up and two grief-stricken smiles. It was all I could do to keep my breathing normal.

Evan was a solid force, warm and comforting. Once we found our own seats, I retreated into the peace of his arms, and it was there that I finally willed myself to look into the corner.

It was a beautiful casket, I had to admit. It was pale blue like the shade of his eyes and adorned with tiny markings of the Eiffel Tower, which were hand carved into the wood. He looked like he was sleeping. With his eyes gently closed, he could've been lost in some exciting dream. Even at this distance, it looked like he was smiling, like this was a joke, and he would sit up soon and we would all laugh. There was a small, green book perched in his folded hands, and I raised my head to get a better look at it. His composition book, of course. He'd written hundreds of melodies in there and jotted notes from his favorite composers. It was only fitting that he be buried with it.

I drew in a shaky breath. Seeing him look so content was almost closure for me. It was a sure sign that even though his life had to end, he had accepted it and was resting peacefully.

A minister approached the podium, and the room quieted.

"We are gathered here today to commemorate the life of Victor Autrie, who was not just a husband or a brother or a conductor...but a kind, compassionate human being who made the world a little brighter with each passing day."

His family, who was seated in the front row, hunched over and sobbed into their tissues. I tried to keep the tears away, but it was like putting up a fire cone to stop a tsunami.

"Victor was admired for many things in his lifetime, one of which was music. His wife Charlotte will be the first to claim that Victor was happiest when onstage, conducting an orchestra."

Charlotte looked up from her folded hands and nodded with a quivering smile.

"He had quite the reputation at the Curtis Institute of Music," the minister continued. "Teaching young pupils to accept music into their hearts. In fact, one of his students is here to perform today. Please give a warm welcome to Victor's first-chair and friend, Miss Abigail Ferr."

People clapped, but I couldn't really hear them. I moved in slow motion, the new violin resting in my grip. The closer I got to the casket, the more my emotions overwhelmed me. But it wasn't out of fear; I was simply remembering all of the good times I'd had with my professor.

Turning to face the crowd, I inhaled, felt the air pulse in my lungs.

"Professor Autrie wanted me to play something cheerful, but he also gave me the liberty of choice." My voice cracked as I met Charlotte's gaze. "Instead of playing one of his beloved waltzes, I instead chose Francesco Sartori's *Con te Partiró*...which means 'time to say goodbye.'"

The audience did not react; they just craned their necks to see as I pressed my bow to the strings. I steadied my breathing and drew my bow down.

It was a song that had you in tears from the first note. It was such an endearing, heart-felt tune. I swayed as my bow connected each note. It was a fairly easy piece, and my eyes drifted shut as the music filled the parlor. With each repeated part, more and more people hung their heads to empty their tears. Even Evan's eyes started to glisten.

I could feel my professor watching with that dazzling smile. He was happy; I felt it in my bones. There was no better send off than *Con te* and if he were alive, he would've fully agreed.

It wasn't long before my own eyes started to burn, and I blinked a few times. But this song was infamous for wrapping you up in its sweet melodies, and soon I was crying, too. But it didn't affect my playing; in fact, I played with more emotion than before. And when the song finally ended, I turned to the casket and gave Professor Autrie my best smile.

"Thank you for everything you've done for me," I whispered and went to return to my seat.

"Haven't you learned other ways to deal with your grief?" Evan asked.

Before answering, I tilted my head back and downed the contents of my drink.

"What're you talking about? I'm celebrating his life, like he would've wanted."

We were at a bar downtown because I'd refused to return to the confines of my apartment. I was too riled up to sit inside and stare into the gloomy night.

"I agree, we *should* be celebrating his life," Evan answered, taking a sip of beer. "But I've seen you drunk, and it's quite a show."

"Don't be ridiculous." I finished my raspberry Svedka in one sip. "I'm not getting drunk. I'm just...not acknowledging my feelings yet."

"Uh huh," he replied.

The bar was tacky with TVs hanging all around, showcasing different sports games. Strings of lights lined the walls, which were already covered with retro photographs from the '60s. Country music blared from hidden speakers, and bottles of beer stood behind the counter, glowing different colors in time with the song.

"Another flavored vodka?" the bartender asked.

"Yes, thank you."

"*One* more," Evan clarified, and I glared at him. "Look, you may think I'm a daredevil, but even I can see that you're just drinking to soothe the pain."

"Why stop me?" I accepted the glass that was handed to me and sipped from it slowly.

"Because this isn't right, and if I were the type of boyfriend who *let* you drink pain away, then your dad would personally chop my head off."

I let myself smile, but it faded too quickly. "Is my professor really gone, Evan?"

He sighed, like telling the truth was a wound in his side. "Yes."

I sipped my drink until my brain really started to buzz, and then I slid my car keys into Evan's hand.

"Beau's staying over tonight, so can we go to your place?" I asked.

"Of course." His smile was soft and sweet.

Outside, the cold November air smacked me in the face, but I wouldn't let Evan roll up the car windows. Despite its bite, the fresh air felt good in my raw lungs, and I closed my eyes as the wind tangled my hair. I must've fallen asleep, too, because the next thing I knew I was in Evan's bed with a quilt wrapped snugly around me. Evan laid next to me, his breathing smooth and even.

The moonlight poured in through the blinds, showering every object in pale light. It made Evan seem younger, more innocent—no longer a daredevil with a dangerous motorbike and a yearning to live life on the edge just to capture that perfect moment. His bare chest rose and fell in time with his breaths.

Loss was funny. It triggered the harshest pain imaginable, but it also reminded you to be grateful for what you already had. I scooted closer to Evan, and he sleepily wrapped an arm around me.

"You okay?" he whispered.

Professor Autrie was resting peacefully; I could let him go knowing that.

"Yeah. I'm all right."

And with that, I closed my eyes and fell into a deep, dreamless sleep.

Chapter Fourteen

PHILADELPHIA, PA—SEAFORD, DE (2023--2024)

Curtis' orchestra didn't have a conductor for the final weeks of November. Our meetings were bleak because the elephant in the room refused to go unnoticed. We all missed Professor Autrie terribly. The administration eventually found someone, a well-dressed, stocky man from Virginia, who was dedicated but lacked Professor Autrie's effortless shine. I ended up disliking him simply because of that.

Before we knew it, the streets of Philadelphia were dusted over with snow. It snowed the first day of December, as if Mother Nature was happily welcoming us into the Christmas season. I was on my way home from work when the fat flurries began to fall again, and when I climbed out of my car, they stuck in my hair like giant cotton balls. I shivered vehemently.

I found Cara inside our apartment, scrolling through Pinterest on her phone and gazing at several pictures of wedding cakes. As I scrubbed my boots across the door mat, she excitedly announced that *her* cake would be red velvet with buttercream icing.

Cara ran a hand through her honey curls. "I can't wait to get out of Philly for holiday break. Beau and I are going up to the mountains for a few days. My parents are letting us stay in their cabin for two weeks, which means we're gonna be alone." Her eyebrows did a mischievous dance.

I laughed. "Hey, first comes marriage *then* the baby carriage."

"Oh, you don't have to tell me twice."

Ever the conservative, Cara would never *dream* of something as preposterous as having a baby before marriage. It simply wasn't in her blood.

"What are you doing for break?" she inquired.

I shrugged. "Spending Christmas with my dad and Jamie, and then Evan wants to take me to Delaware to meet his family."

"Oh, that'll be fun," Cara said.

"I'm just worried they won't like me, you know?"

Cara grunted and shook her head disapprovingly. "Can we *not* do the whole aw-geez-what-if-I'm-a-loser-and-they-find-out spiel?" She whined that last part like a little kid. "Gail, come on. I know you're great, you know you're great. *Evan* knows you're great." Her eyebrows shot up. "That's 'cause you are. His parents are gonna adore you. So, don't even go there."

I laughed. "Okay, sure. But I'm still nervous. I need to make a good impression. Any outfit ideas?"

"I do have that red gown with the dipping neck-line. It's modest enough that his parents will think you're classy, but sexy enough that Evan won't be able to take his eyes off you."

"That sounds great. Yeah, I'm only friends with you because of your taste in fashion."

She rolled her eyes and stood up off the couch. "Good one. Don't worry, Gail. You are gonna be hard to forget."

When I spun around in front of Evan a couple weeks later, his jaw dropped. I giggled and reached up on my tiptoes to kiss him.

The snow held off for our long drive, but what had already fallen was shoveled to the sides of the roads, forming large white hills. Evan was driving this time, so I had the opportunity to gaze out at the shimmering landscape as it passed. Aside from two rest stops and a quick gas refill, we made pretty decent time, and the road started to thin out, revealing the Nanticoke River, which now looked like a giant ice skating rink.

As we passed the sign welcoming us to Seaford, Evan's hand rested on my knee and slowly slid upward.

"Can I help you?" I laughed.

He massaged the fabric of my borrowed red dress between his pointer finger and thumb. "You are absolutely gorgeous."

I took his hand away and held it in my own. "Thank you. Now keep your eyes on the road."

He chuckled as the car chugged along. Soon enough, we were gliding down a neighborhood street that was lined with the skeletons of tall trees.

"Welcome to the Caldwell residence," Evan declared.

I glanced up at the house. It was a fairly sizable structure with extensions branching off in all directions. Sand-colored stucco made up the house's decor, complete with a swatch of ivy that stretched up the west end wall. It looked like something out of *American Dream Magazine*— the type of home that screamed perfect yet slightly dysfunctional family.

"I'm sure Mom will have dinner ready," Evan said as he opened my car door for me.

As he rang the doorbell, a loud bark sounded from inside the house.

"Great Dane," Evan clarified. "He likes to act tough, but he's really sweet. His name's Otis."

I heard feet pounding against the floor and then suddenly the door flew open, revealing a young girl with beady eyes and cherry-colored cheeks. She had the same dirty blonde locks as Evan, except hers looked velvety and fell to her shoulders in golden waves. She leaned against the door frame and grinned up at her older brother.

"So, *this* is Abigail?"

"Yes, Gracy," Evan sighed, "let us in. It's freezing!"

And she did, but not before flashing me a wide grin. I smiled down at her and hoped I didn't look as nervous as I felt.

Otis attacked Evan with kisses, jumping up into his arms once he'd dropped our bags. I grimaced as he allowed the dog to lick his cheek.

"Hey, boy. How are you?"

"Evan?" A woman appeared from the hall.

She was a full head shorter than me with eyes like dazzling diamonds. She was dressed in an apron, smeared over with various, unidentifiable stains; she quickly removed it and hung it on the banister leading upstairs.

"Hi, I'm Beth," she said, sticking out her hand. Her smile was the kind that made you feel like you were already part of the family.

I shook her hand. "Gail, nice to meet you."

"Oh, you too! We've been dying to meet you. Grant! Get down here! They're here!"

Beth pulled Otis off of her son and fell into Evan's arms, mumbling how much she'd missed him. Grant, Evan's father, clomped downstairs and clapped his hands together. He offered me a shy smile and greeted his son. All the while, Gracy smirked at me.

"Well, please come in and stay awhile!" Beth announced. "Dinner will be ready in five."

Evan stored my jacket in a nearby closet and led me up the staircase, which led up to an overlook. Down the hall, there was a master bathroom and three doors, one of which was shut.

"That's my brother Lain's room," he said. "Fair warning: his girlfriend's here, and they're *very* physically affectionate."

"Noted."

"This is my other sister's room—Danielle. We call her Dani." Evan paused in the threshold, and I peered in to see a young blonde hunched over her desk, writing in a journal.

"Yo, Dani," Evan said.

Dani turned. "Hey, bro." When her eyes fell on me, her face went blank for a moment.

"This is Gail."

The recognition showed in her expression, and she nodded. "Oh, right. Hi, how are you?"

"I'm great, thank you," I replied.

She smiled politely and returned to her notebook.

"How old is she?" I inquired as Evan towed me down the hall.

"Seventeen, a junior in high school."

"Seems pretty mellow for a teenager."

"Yeah, Dani's the best. I'm probably closer with her than any of my other siblings."

He froze outside of the final door and grinned. "This is my room."

It certainly reflected his personality. Four navy blue walls covered in posters of famous football stars, a collection of assorted beanies, and a desk that held a closed laptop, several fidget spinners, and a gaming console. A few wrinkled shirts were strewn across his bedspread, and a Nike bag lay unzipped at the foot of the bed, exposing neon green cleats.

I gave Evan a look.

"I ran track in high school," he explained, clearing the shirts off his bed.

"Were you any good?"

"Best long-distance runner on the team," he answered pridefully. "I was unstoppable."

As if to prove his point, the top of his dresser was cluttered with several first-place trophies. Above them, a framed picture hung on the wall, showing Evan posing with two other boys. They all held up their medals.

"I had no idea I was dating a star athlete."

Evan scoffed. "Ex-star athlete. Busted my Achilles tendon senior year, three weeks before the start of the season."

"Ouch," I grimaced.

He tossed the Nike bag into the closet. "Had to get surgery and everything, so I couldn't run at all. It sucked."

"Why don't you do track now that you've healed?"

"I don't know." He shrugged. "That was high school, and as much as I loved it, it wasn't really something I wanted to pursue. But enough about me."

He pulled me into his arms, and we stumbled backward onto the bed. I giggled and let myself melt when his lips touched mine. It was different now that we were in *his* old bedroom; it made the kiss that much more intimate. His hands slid up the back of my dress, nearly removing it completely.

"Hey," I murmured against his lips, "your door's open, so don't go crazy."

"Dammit," he sighed, "how am I gonna keep my hands off you until after dinner?"

I climbed off of him and fixed my dress, feeling a smile pinch my lips. "I'm sure you'll figure it out."

He laid there, gazing up at me with such adoration. It twinkled in his sapphire eyes and softened his features. My heart galloped at the sight, almost bursting from my chest.

"Hey," Dani said from the doorway, causing both of us to jump, "dinner's ready."

The table was full of dishes: steamed broccoli coated in butter, a mountain of bread rolls, golden sweet potato soup (made tastier by the addition of burrata and sage pesto), and the tender turkey, which Otis eyed longingly from a distance. As soon as Evan and I sat down, his parents eyed me curiously.

"So, you're a violinist?" Beth inquired.

"Yes, I am," I replied.

"Did you hear, Grant? She goes to the Curtis Institute of Music."

Grant looked up from his spoonful of soup. "Wow, that's a great school. Tough to get into."

"You should play for us after dinner!" Gracy cried.

I laughed when Beth agreed. "I didn't bring my violin with me, but I would love to play for you all sometime."

Lain reached for the salt and cleared his throat. "Taryn played the cello in high school, didn't you, babe?"

His girlfriend, Taryn, blushed profusely. "I did, but my instructor was a pain in the butt. He made me hate music." She rolled her eyes and took a sip of water.

"That's terrible," I said. "I could never live without music."

Taryn simply shrugged.

"Well, that's all right, honey," Beth said, "some other time. Actually, I was thinking we could all play a round of Uno after supper—"

All four of Beth's children whined in unison. It was funny actually, seeing Evan and Dani make large gestures at their mother. I'd always wanted siblings to complain with.

"Oh, hush!" Beth said over the ruckus. "You're all playing!" She bit her lip for a second and then glanced over at me. "Gail, honey, do you like Uno?"

"So, *she* gets a choice?" Gracy yelled.

The uproar started again, and this time, I burst out laughing. Even Grant was whining now.

When we finished eating, Evan and I helped to clear the table. His sisters wandered into the living room, chatting among themselves, and Lain and Taryn tried to escape upstairs once more—perhaps to have a few more moments of privacy before Uno began.

"I baked at least a hundred cookies," Beth said as she scrubbed her plate over the sink. "There's chocolate-chip, raisin, oatmeal—just help yourself, honey."

"Thank you. Evan always talks about your baking. He says you're amazing."

Beth set the plate on a mat to dry and turned toward us. "Evan was always my taste-tester when he was little. Weren't you, son?"

"Mhm."

I smiled. "Well, I can't wait to try one."

There certainly was a buffet in the separate dining room. I ended up choosing a sugar cookie, which had always been my favorite growing up. The taste was exquisite, and the sweetness sent me right back to my childhood. I stood there for a moment, mind blank as I munched on the treat. But Beth's voice broke me from my reverie. She was speaking to Evan in the kitchen.

"She's a very nice girl, Ev. I like her a lot."

"Yeah, she's a special one." There was a smile in Evan's voice.

"She's so poised! And I think your father likes her, too. I've never seen him so impressed with one of your girlfriends. Looks like you found a keeper."

Evan's hands were tangled in my hair, and his lips were setting my body ablaze. The rest of the house had fallen asleep hours ago. And now that Evan's door was shut, Cara's lovely red dress was a crumpled puddle on the floor.

"See, look. You made it through dinner," I whispered.

This comment earned me a quiet chortle, but he didn't respond with his usual wit. Instead, he stared into my eyes with enough intimacy that his gaze could've been another loving caress.

"What?" I asked finally.

His lips twitched a few times, and his jaw slackened before he said, "I love you."

The sentence stopped my heart.

We'd been together now for seven months. And though it

may have just been a series of hookups in the beginning, our relationship had clearly escalated. Realizing that now, my breath started to sprint. Love was scary. It had crushed me in the past and was very capable of doing the same now. But staring into Evan's eyes, I never felt more alive. I could see the universe in those sapphire irises, our universe and the ones beyond. I belonged in this bedroom, in this atmosphere. I belonged with him.

"I love you, too."

The words tasted sweet in my mouth, like medicine after years of isolation.

His face lit up, and when he kissed me again, we were no longer two bodies, but one soul.

"I wish I would've known you in high school," I said and giggled as I considered something. "I could've come to support you at your track meets."

"I'm happy you didn't know me then," he disagreed. "I was an asshole in high school, and you definitely wouldn't have liked me at all. But you came into my life at a perfect time. I need someone like you."

He climbed off of me and pulled me against his chest.

A thought occurred to me. "Let's make a pact."

"A what?"

"A pact," I repeated. "Let's vow to always have each other's back — no matter what. Even if we fight or God forbid, break up."

A genuine smile slid across his face. "Okay."

I sat up and raised my right hand. "Repeat after me. I, Evan Caldwell."

He laughed now and raised his own right hand. "I, Evan Caldwell."

"Solemnly swear."

"Solemnly swear."

"To protect this love with everything I have forever."

"Forever," he agreed with a nod of certainty.

"And I pledge the same," I whispered.

Eventually, we fell asleep hand-in-hand.

"Come on, Otis. You'd look so cute if you would just sit still!" Gracy was trying to put a stocking hat on Otis' head. She was all bundled up herself, ready to go play in the snow that had been falling all night.

"Stop tormenting the dog," Lain called from the kitchen.

Evan rolled his eyes and nodded for Gracy to continue. My boyfriend was on his knees, camera poised to capture the moment their Great Dane would give in and wear the pink floral stocking hat without protest. But Otis simply pawed the piece of fabric away, uninterested.

After a while, Gracy gave up and turned to me. "So, did Evan show you his trophy collection from track?"

"Yeah."

"Did he tell you he used to—?"

"Gracy." Evan narrowed his eyes at her, but she only smirked.

"Did he tell you he used to pose in the mirror with them every morning and pretend to give speeches?"

"Hey!" Evan dove at her, and the two rolled across the carpet, forcing Otis to move. The poor dog retreated to the corner and laid back down with a groan.

Gracy was giggling uncontrollably as Evan attacked her with tickling fingers. I brought my knees to my chest, laughing at their guffaws. When Grant entered the living room, he stepped over the wrestling siblings and collapsed into the recliner. He eyed me over the rim of his coffee mug.

"Don't worry," he said. "This is a normal sight."

Out of the corner of my eye, I spotted Dani as she emerged from the basement door. Her arms were filled with boxes, piled high on top of each other and towering above her head.

I sprang to my feet. "Here, let me help you."

"Thank you," she huffed.

I took a few boxes off the top and followed her upstairs.

"If you don't mind me asking, what's in these things?" I put the boxes on her bed and shoved a few strands of hair back behind my ears.

"Journals," she replied with a grunt.

I stared at her in disbelief.

"Yeah, I write a lot." She opened one of the packages, and sure enough, it was filled with spiral notebooks.

They had gorgeous covers, ranging from heart-felt quotes to pictures of rainbows, to solid colors of velvet and leather.

"These are all filled."

"Dani, there are like, six boxes in here!" I exclaimed, my mouth hanging open in astonishment.

She only smiled. "I wasn't kidding."

"What do you write about?"

"Well..." She retrieved a lavender-colored notebook from the open box and flipped to a random page. "This box has my diaries. I've kept diaries since the first grade, and I didn't want to give them up because they're remnants of life, you know?" She read the page, and a grin split her face in half. "In fact, you'd find some pretty funny stuff about Evan in these things."

She put the book back and went to another box. "These are my description journals."

I held a question in my gaze.

"If I go to a new place, I write down what I see," she explained. "Where we go, what I eat, what I feel. It helps when I sit down to *actually* write."

Now, I was generally confused, and she laughed.

"I want to be an author one day, Abigail. I'm writing a book, and all these journals help me to organize my thoughts and dreams. Like, I've never been to New York City, but I can imagine what it's like."

"Oh, I can help you there," I said. "I grew up just a few hours from the city, so I've been there more times than I can count."

Her eyes twinkled as I said this, but she kept her smile soft and polite as she moved to the next box. "Well, *these* are story ideas."

She pried open the biggest box of all. It was full of all sorts of journals: thick, slim, spiral, and bound. All different colors and sizes. I shook my head.

"And they're all *filled?*"

"Yep." Dani stared into the box. "Every time I get an idea, it goes in one of these journals."

"Like what?"

She shrugged. "Apocalypse stories, supernatural stories, romances — if you think of something, I've probably got it in here."

These journals were direct windows into Dani's powerful imagination. I suddenly felt like I was speaking to a scholar; she had a mind unlike anyone I'd ever met before.

"That's incredible," I murmured.

She laughed. "It's nothing really, just my creative outlet. Kind of like you with music."

"Wait, you said you were writing a book. What's it about?"

Her cheeks flushed with color. "It's about a group of aliens who are sent back in time to evacuate the earth before their mothership lands and takes over."

I blinked a couple of times. "Wow. Sounds intense."

"It is, but there's a great twist at the end." Her grin was back, and I laughed.

"This is amazing, Dani. Evan didn't mention you were so into writing."

"That's 'cause Evan's brainless sometimes."

"Well, you should teach me how to write like you. I got a journal a few months ago, but I've hardly written in it. And anything I *have* written is below amateur."

Dani flipped through another notebook for a moment before answering. "You just have to let it come to you naturally. The more you write, the better you'll get." She glanced up at me. "And everyone has a story, so don't think yours isn't worth writing."

Her words sparked something inside me. It was a small flame of thought, flickering in my mind. But it didn't have time to grow before Evan appeared in the doorway.

"Whoa, you movin' out?" he asked.

"Ha, ha," his sister replied without looking up from her journal.

"Hey, watch that tone," I teased him. "You're talking to the world's best upcoming author."

Dani flashed me a brilliant smile.

"Need some inspiration again, huh?" Evan inquired, coming to sit beside me on the bed.

"Always." Dani sighed, her piercing blue eyes shifting left to right as she read her own writing.

Evan looked over at me, and my heart fluttered as it always did when he stared at me like that.

"We'll leave you to it," he said.

"Thanks for your help, Gail," Dani said as we went to leave.

"Anytime! And for the record, I think it's amazing that you're a writer. You'll have to send me a copy of that book someday!"

Excitement blossomed into her features.

Evan and I stayed busy. We spent our mornings helping Beth cook breakfast (which was always a big feast) and some days, Dani would read her work to me while I sat with a glass of orange juice, listening intently. We spent our afternoons lounging around the table engaged in some family card game, which Lain and his girlfriend always managed to win. And in the evenings, we all gathered in front of the large flat screen to watch a Christmas movie, even though Christmas was already a week past. I felt more and more ingrained into the family, like I was part of their silly chaos now.

But the weeks passed quickly, and all too soon, Evan and I were standing in the foyer with our bags again. Otis, who had finally warmed up to me, offered a big, sloppy kiss on my arm. Gracy stood by the banister as she had the first night, and though I could tell she wouldn't admit it, she was going to miss me a lot. Beth was almost in tears.

"You're welcome here anytime, Abigail. *Anytime!*" she exclaimed, throwing her arms around me.

Grant nodded, no longer shy. "Yes, I'm glad our son has someone like you."

"Thank you."

Even Lain and Taryn seemed to appreciate me. They both shook my hand, and Lain clapped Evan on the back.

"Wait!" Dani called as she bounded down the stairs.

She practically jumped on me, and I dropped my bag to hug her back. I'd never seen her so forward or emotional, but it made my heart stutter.

"I'll see you again, right?" she asked before going to embrace her brother.

"Of course you'll see her again," Evan insisted.

It was a bittersweet parting. As we pulled out of the driveway waving, I found that I missed them already. As crazy as they were, I felt right at home with them. I vocalized this to Evan as we turned onto the highway, and he replied with a sigh of relief.

"Yeah, I've never seen Dani that happy about one of my girlfriends. I mean, she actually read her writing to you. That *never* happens."

"Well, I'm flattered."

Dani had successfully awakened my inspiration. I pictured the sky-blue journal in my drawer, just waiting to be opened. I would write about Evan and his family, all the memories that made me happy. My mind was racing just thinking about it.

The sun remained in the sky until we hit the Pennsylvania state line, which welcomed us into a gray fortress of snowflakes. Philadelphia was a winter wonderland with snow covered streets, icicle-adorned lamps, and thick skeletal trees. When we finally arrived back at my apartment, I spotted Beau's car parked next to Cara's.

"Uh oh, wedding planners—dead-ahead," Evan said.

But that was an understatement. The living room was covered in tiny pieces of paper, cut from magazines. Some lay in piles, others were scattered, and in the center of it all, the happy couple was deep in conversation.

"I think the bouquet toss should go before the garter toss—that's more traditional," Cara was saying.

"What is all of this?" I asked, setting my suitcase against the wall.

Cara and Beau glanced up and gave us a cheerful greeting.

"How was the trip?" Beau inquired.

"Incredible," Evan answered.

I tiptoed through the maze of paper scraps and sat down beside Cara. She was beaming, and Beau took her hand.

"We have a surprise," she said.

Evan and I raised our eyebrows.

"We finally chose a date!"

"That's amazing!" I exclaimed and pulled Cara into a hug. "When?"

"July 16, 2024."

"Right after senior year," Evan mused.

"We don't want to wait," Cara explained. "This is the man I want to spend the rest of my life with."

As they embraced, I looked around at all the cut-outs. Closest to me were photos of grand ballrooms, each one different in style. "Do you have a location yet?"

"Well..." Cara started and then gestured for Beau to deliver the happy news.

"Have you ever seen this girl's house?" He laughed. "Her backyard is big enough to host five parties at once."

"You're making me sound like a rich snob, stop it." Cara smiled, then she turned to me. "Hey, can I talk to you for a minute?" Her eyes flickered toward the kitchen.

"Sure."

Once we were away from our boyfriends, she threw her arms around me again. The action startled me, and I almost stumbled backward into the table.

"Sorry," she whispered, trying to repress a laugh, "but I just have to thank you for being an amazing person. Gail, I really feel like you're my best friend. We've been through a lot together. I mean, that quarantine was hell."

I rolled my eyes. "Yeah, that sucked. But I'm glad we got to suffer together."

"Exactly. So, I have something huge to ask you." Her brown, doughy eyes were shimmering with elation. "Will you be my maid of honor?"

I stared at her.

Four years ago, I was a junior in high school. It was a time when my friends and I only *daydreamed* about wedding dresses and bridesmaids and pretty cakes. But we were children then. Cara stood before me now, her hand folded around mine, a loving smile on her lips.

Holy crap, my conscience shouted. *We're not little kids anymore.*

"Yes!" I shouted.

We squealed in each other's arms, and the girly-girl in me took over.

"What should I wear? What shoes? My hair—"

"Don't worry," Cara giggled, "I'll take care of all of that. But I'll give you the numbers of my other bridesmaids, and you guys can plan the bachelorette party."

My mind started buzzing with ideas — all things from a spa

day to nightclub drinking. I wasn't about to put a price on Cara's happiness.

"Thank you, Cara," I said breathlessly. "It's an honor."

She did a little dance of victory after my *yes*. "Of course, I'm so excited. Oh hey, how'd meeting Evan's family go?"

"I really like them. They're so sweet and funny." It was hard to miss the passion in my voice. "And Evan is just...incredible."

Cara smirked. "My little red dress do the trick?"

"You have no idea."

She shook her head. "Works like a charm every single time."

We returned to the living room in a fit of giggles, linked arm-in-arm.

"Maid of honor? That's awesome! Tell Cara and Beau I'm really happy for them," Erica gushed.

We were on FaceTime, catching up on each other's lives from the past month. I felt my pulse jumping at how much I had to tell her. I explained all of it in a rush: the fact that I adored Evan's family and that I now had to learn the names of thirteen other girls, who were Cara's bridesmaids. Erica shook her head at these things.

"At least you don't have *my* problem. I went on *one* date with this guy and now he won't leave me alone."

I laughed. "We'll have to get together soon, Erica. I miss you like crazy."

"Ditto. Who knew college would take up so much of our lives?"

"I hope you're drinking responsibly."

"I have a little fun every now and then." She winked.

I looked out the big windows and into the frost covered streets of the city. The sun was just beginning to set, painting the sky a soft pastel orange. It reflected off the spires in the distance, making them glow.

"Also, hey, I just want to let you know that you were right."

"About college? I know! It's like, who *cares* about going to every single morning class—"

"No. About Evan."

When I first told her about him, Erica had accused me of already having huge feelings for Evan, but I'd just brushed her comment off with an annoyed eye roll and a rosy blush.

Now, Erica went quiet, staring at me with two large gray-blue eyes. The words stayed on the tip of my tongue for a moment, but they caused something in my chest to swirl.

"I love him."

She blinked, looking me up and down through the screen. Then she screamed, and I jumped out of my skin.

"You two are soulmates, I *know* it! When am I going to meet him?"

"This summer for sure. I'll come back home and bring him with me."

Erica shoved her face into the camera so that only her lips were visible. "You better." She backed away again. "Does he have a cute brother?"

I pictured Lain with his mop of floppy blond hair, the hint of a mustache, the arrow shape of his nose. And Taryn, of course, who found all of these things attractive.

"His brother's taken."

Chapter Fifteen

PHILADELPHIA, PA—SARATOGA SPRINGS, NY (2024)

I had never been so stressed in my life. The remainder of junior year consisted of tests and graded performances. The new conductor, Professor Burffow, offered me generous feedback on my conducting skills. But conducting wasn't my biggest issue. It was the written exams I was worried about. But instead of studying, I spent my time talking with Cara's other bridesmaids.

Each girl proudly mentioned her idea for the bachelorette party: a night on the town, an old-fashion sleepover, binge-drinking, and watching rom-coms. One girl even suggested hiring a male stripper. The ideas were as diverse as Cara's friends, each from different backgrounds, housing several different opinions. I quickly became overwhelmed with my choices and was forced to put the bridesmaids on hold for a few days.

On top of everything, I also had to prepare for a concert commemorating those who had perished during the Pulmonem Fever outbreak one year ago. Looking back on the past year made me dizzy and emotional. So much had happened, and so much had *yet* to happen. It seemed like I was temporarily stuck in a time warp, where nothing was certain. Would there be another fever outbreak? Would one of Cara's bridesmaids drop out? What if something terrible happened in the next few weeks, and this small piece of happiness was taken from me?

Needless to say, my anxiety was red-hot and seething.

On the day of the concert, I stood in the bathroom, putting on diamond earrings and trying not to panic with all the thoughts in my mind. Cara passed by, her dress chic and black. She was going to be singing this afternoon and had to look her best.

"Cara," I called, grateful to have a spare moment.

She reappeared. "Yeah?"

I fluffed my chestnut curls once in the mirror and turned to her. "How do you feel about male strippers?"

"That's hilarious." But she wasn't laughing. "I don't feel comfortable with Beau going to a strip club, and I doubt he'd be cool with me around one," she said matter-of-factly, but then horror struck her eyes. "You didn't hire someone, did you?"

Obviously more stressed than the maid of honor was the bride. I quickly shook my head.

"No, it was just one of the suggestions."

She exhaled. "It was Angel, wasn't it?"

"Yeah."

Cara was all smiles again, back to her usual, bubbly self. "That is so like her."

We carpooled to the concert, and Cara sang scales the entire way, sitting up in her seat like it didn't have a backrest. I was lucky to be accompanying her today. Playing along with Cara was like starring next to Angelina Jolie in a movie.

Naturally, the concert was a success. People came from all over to admire the memorial of those who had died from the virus, mostly professors from Curtis, students, and family members. And even though Professor Autrie's killer was emphysema, he too was pictured on the marble monument. Cara's voice was angelic. She had a solo in the choir, and as I played the melody on my violin, I felt tears sting my eyes. The audience was already bawling.

Afterwards, I cut through the crowd to the monument and stood there gazing up at my old professor. He was pictured in a suit and tie with a baton in hand and with that wide, warm smile on his face. My heart ached, and I almost thought he would come up beside me and say, "Don't cry, *ma chérie*." All my success here at Curtis was because of him. Hopefully I would find a decent conducting job in the future and continue his legacy. He would be proud of that.

"He was a brilliant man, so I'm told."

I turned to see Professor Burffow, and my mood soured.

He simply could not replace Professor Autrie, and I pitied him for trying. Over the last few weeks, I couldn't bring myself to like him, much less respect him. But truthfully, I only hated Burffow because he wasn't an old French man with thinning gray hair and words of wisdom.

"He was the best," I answered curtly.

My new instructor glanced over at me. "Listen, Abigail—"

"Gail."

"Listen, Gail. You being the first chair of our orchestra, that's huge. That means you're one of the most talented instrumentalists in this school, and that's saying a *lot*."

Did he think flattery would win him acceptance? My eyes stayed trained on the memorial.

"But you and I have to be on the same page. The conductor and the first chairman are like oil and vinegar." Finally, I turned my eyes toward his. "I know I'm not your favorite person in the world, probably nowhere near Victor."

It was hard not to scoff.

"But you're never going to get anywhere in life if you just disregard new people because you miss the old."

Something pinched my stomach then.

For a second, I was lost in the past, and when I pictured Colton, my heart cracked the tiniest bit. Where was he now? What was he doing? Why did it matter? The thoughts overwhelmed me, and I pictured Evan instead. Sweet, loving Evan.

Burffow was right. I glanced back at Professor Autrie's picture for a moment longer and then sighed.

"Okay," I said.

Professor Burffow clasped his hands together. "Excellent. Now that that's settled, we can discuss your solo piece to play for the seniors at graduation."

I walked with him, listening to his music and composer suggestions, trying my absolute hardest not to compare him to Autrie anymore.

Thankfully, with the exception of Juliet who was stuck at work, most of the bridesmaids were able to meet me for breakfast the Saturday after the concert. I thanked the hostess and sat down in a booth, trying to calm my nerves. This was the first time I would be meeting them in person. One thing that made me nervous was the fact that all of these girls had known each other since they were teenagers, yet Cara entrusted *me* to be maid of honor. I had to prove that I was cut out for this job.

I sat anxiously twirling my hair until a stream of young women crowded in from outside. They all had the catalogue look: designer shoes, professionally styled hair, expensive handbags. Even their face masks were from big-name designer brands. Sometimes, I forgot that Cara had a place in this crowd because she never flaunted her riches.

I waved with a polite smile, and they all scurried over to meet me.

"Hi, Angel." I laughed when she yanked me into a hug.

She stepped back, nearly glowing in a yellow sundress that

contrasted beautifully against her dark skin. "Girl, you look amazing! I'm so happy we get to do this today."

She stepped aside so that Jasmine, Gwen, Izzy, and Stella could hug me as well.

After we all gushed over the fact that Cara was getting married, the next fifteen minutes were spent on ordering. The girls were overly concerned about the amount of carbs they should consume to have the perfect swimsuit body by summer. How much fruit should they get on top of their pancakes? Was a side of sausage a sin? Eventually, they told the poor waitress what they wanted, and she rushed off toward the kitchen.

"Okay," Jasmine said, "let's get down to business."

"Well, you all had great ideas," I began, "but I've been thinking, and maybe we should combine some of them. Gwen, your sleepover idea was awesome, but I know Cara loves to drink every once in a while."

"Oh, don't we know it?" Izzy laughed, tossing a tendril of red hair over her shoulder.

"How about an old-fashion sleepover-slash-spa night where we get drunk and watch rom-coms?"

They all squealed and the praise showered over me like roses after a performance. I could finally breathe a sigh of relief. Impressing them had been one big challenge, but I surpassed it.

Our food came and disappeared, and the conversation unsurprisingly shifted from dresses to boys.

"Guys, Jake and I are going to look so cute at the wedding," Gwen said, sighing. "We'll all have to get pictures together."

"Of course," I chimed in.

"Gail, you have a date, right?"

"Yeah." Thinking of Evan always made me blush, but to imagine him in a suit and tie, my heart was already galloping.

Stella groaned and speared a strawberry with her fork. "Am I the only one who doesn't have a date?"

We all looked over at her, and Angel shook her head.

"Wait, I thought you were going with someone from Penn State."

I blinked. "You go to Penn State?"

Stella smiled shyly. "Yeah. And I *was* going to invite him, but that's not happening anymore."

"We're talking about the blond guy, right?"

I felt so out of the loop, but a deep pressure was mounting in my torso. Something didn't feel right in my bones.

"Yeah." Stella looked so forlorn I could have hugged her, but instead, I felt myself shrinking.

Don't say it. Don't ask, my conscience warned. But my lips were already moving. "What's his name?"

Stella waved her hand dismissively. "You wouldn't know him. His name's Colton."

"I thought you guys were super close," Izzy said.

"Apparently, he thinks of me more as a friend. But it doesn't even matter because he's back with his ex now."

"Whoa, Gail," Angel said. "You okay? You look like you're gonna be sick."

The pancakes spun in my stomach, building back up my throat.

What were the odds? And why did this small bit of information throw me off a cliff? Suddenly, Stella wasn't so pretty anymore. Her designer clothes were too flashy. What did she have that I didn't?

It was like hitting the concrete after a fall of fifty-thousand feet. My emotions were blazing, inundating my mind with questions and above all, guilt. Self-loathing. Had I not gotten over this by now? Jealousy sprinted through my body, and I hated it. I didn't hate Colton; he was living his life. I hated *myself* because the past could suck me back in whenever it wanted to.

All the girls were facing me now with concerned expressions. I drew a deep, shaky breath.

"Yeah, I'm fine." It was a lie. But I wasn't about to explain my past to them.

Izzy turned back to Stella. "So, Colton's back with his ex?"

Stella rolled her eyes. "Yeah, he's with Beverly Andrews." She stuck her tongue out but then frowned and forked another strawberry. "She's absolutely gorgeous though. An actual model. I'm *so* not as pretty as her."

"No!" the girls cried in unison. They gushed over Stella's effortless beauty — her soft round cheeks with a sprinkling of freckles, her bulbous blue eyes that were agonizingly gorgeous, and her lush copper-colored hair.

I swallowed some water to cool my raging fever.

So, *Beverly* was the one he'd met at Starbucks that day...*Beverly* turned out to be his type even after he told me she wasn't. And what was I? A perfectly convenient ghost from the past. It wasn't Stella's fault she felt excluded. *Beverly* was the one he'd wanted in the end.

"Yeah, Stella, you're beautiful," I said breathlessly. I could almost hear my heart crack.

"He's such an asshole," Jasmine exclaimed.

"A hot asshole." Stella sighed.

Anger pulsed inside me. When would I be free of this boy? It seemed no matter where I went, there he was, popping up at the worst times. Times of weakness. Was the universe punishing me for something? But even as I writhed in my self-loathing, their talk of Colton upset me even more. They didn't know him at all. They didn't know his father was an abusive alcoholic who suffered from PTSD or that *I* was the one Colton said he would love forever. Not *Beverly*.

"To Colton Reeves," Izzy raised her glass, "the boy who doesn't deserve a second chance."

I hesitated when all the glasses rose, but if I didn't partici-pate they would suspect something.

"To Colton Reeves," I muttered and took a drink.

When the girls finally left, I drove all the way to Evan's apartment. He had invited me over for the weekend. I thought driving would take my mind off things, but as I got on the highway, I realized I was still frowning.

I tried to tell myself it wasn't Colton. It was the amount of stress I was under; I had a whole sleepover to plan now. But instead of focusing on decorations and activities, my mind constantly returned to the past.

This worried me. I was with Evan now, and he had such a strong-hold on my heart. Why did I still picture the sweet blond boy from my past? And with a fluttering heart, too. I recalled our last interaction—the intimacy of the night, the fierce wildfire of passion. My cheeks reddened immediately, though not from regret.

I had to let it go.

I turned up the music until the bass shook the glass, loud enough so that my pesky thoughts wouldn't be acknowledged. But Colton had a way of shoving his memory to the front of my brain.

Why *had* we broken up? Colton had just been beaten by his father. He was young and confused and seriously hurt. That didn't make our split a regular case, did it? And even though it destroyed my heart when he left, I knew that he needed space to heal.

Thinking back through these things, a burning hatred effloresced inside me. I cursed Mr. Reeves out loud and banged a hand on the steering wheel. How could he hurt his own child? How could he be so *sick-minded?* No...not sick-minded, just lost in his disorder. Still, that wasn't an excuse. Colton already faced enough trauma to last two lifetimes.

Maybe our relationship was lost by accident.

Then again, people changed. People developed. Who we were in high school was definitely *not* who we were today as juniors in college. Opinions morphed; individuality was formed. Surely, those old connections meant nothing now?

These thoughts bombarded my brain all the way to Westchester University, and when I finally arrived, my mood had worsened. I hauled my duffel up the porch steps to Evan's apartment.

"Hey, Gail," Evan said, his voice deep and rich.

"Hi."

It wasn't fair of me to speak to Evan in a bitter tone; he was innocent in all of this. But I had a bad habit of pulling people into my problems.

"Let me guess, the bridesmaids were too much for you?"

I dropped my duffel bag by the door and kicked off my shoes. "No, they were fine."

Evan gave me a strange look as I passed him on my way to the living room. I fell onto the couch and pretended to scroll through my already read emails, desperately in need of something to do as a distraction. Evan appeared beside me, and I felt him trying to catch my gaze.

"What's wrong?"

"Nothing."

How could I explain that the recent news of my first love had completely taken over my mind? Or that any news of Colton was powerful enough to stop me dead in my tracks?

Evan tried for humor. "You're a terrible liar."

"I don't want to talk about it."

"Geez, I've never seen you so...irritated. Are the bridesmaids really that bad?"

"It's not them!" I shouted impatiently.

It wasn't Stella's fault she ran into Colton one day at Penn State and ended up falling for him. That happened all the time. And it wasn't Colton's fault for retreating back to an ex-girlfriend although she, whoever this *Beverly* was, would never love him like I did.

"Then what is it?" Evan ventured. "Did I do something to piss you off?"

"No," I sighed, "never."

The look in his eyes made me feel a hundred times worse. It was like staring at a fork in the road, either confessing or risking damaging our communication. Wasn't that what all the TV psychologists said? That communication was crucial to keeping a relationship afloat?

I swallowed the lump in my throat. "You remember my ex-boyfriend? The one with the abusive dad?"

Evan's expression was suddenly guarded. "Yeah."

"Well, one of the bridesmaids knows him and said that she was going to invite him to Cara and Beau's wedding, but she said he thinks of her more as a friend."

"And?"

"And it kind of...upset me."

"What, the part that she knows him or the part that he's not coming?" Evan sat ramrod straight with a face carved of stone.

"Neither. Just that they were friends at all, I guess."

As I said the words, I felt like a jerk. Maybe communication should've been avoided for this one.

Evan didn't answer for a minute. He stared at the ground, arms crossed, nostrils flared. "Do you...still love him?"

"No, absolutely not!" I answered quickly.

Evan shook his head like he was confused. "Then why be upset over nothing?"

I pressed my clammy hands together. "Because the girls started talking about him like he's a jerk, but they don't understand."

"Understand what? I thought you said he broke your heart! That doesn't *bother* you?"

"Of course, it does, but he'd just been beaten by his own father!"

"Who gives a shit? That was *his* problem, not yours! It's his fault he broke up with you!"

The words were a slap across my face. They stung so bad the room started spinning.

"Do you really not care about what he went through?"

"I don't understand why you still do!" Evan yelled. "It's in the past! There's nothing you can do to change it, and I'm sure he's seen justice by now! What is with you and this guy?"

The lump formed in my throat again as large as a golf ball this time.

I'd expected Evan to understand, to have a heart and agree that Colton should never be judged for his character given what he went through. But this was my own fault. I felt sick about the fact that my first fight with Evan had to be over something so serious.

"Do you even love me?" Evan asked.

"Of course, I do," I whispered.

He didn't look convinced. "Maybe if you got your head out of the past, you'd show it a little more."

With that, he stood up from the couch and retreated to his bedroom.

My body instantly turned to ice. My lungs contracted, and I hiccupped once or twice, but I was too shocked to even cry. My mouth hung open; my bones turned to liquid.

Every mistake I'd ever made came crashing down on me then, and it stole the oxygen right out of my windpipe. When would I learn that other people have feelings, too? What was it about Colton Reeves that had me so caught?

This was it: the ultimate low, a crushing realization that you will never amount to anything because you are so plagued by your own mistakes. Maybe I was already at rock bottom, and the tidal wave of emotion had yet to hit me like it was now.

It was here, in this dreadful, terrifying state of mind, that my anxiety gladly raised its voice.

Well, Gail, here you are, it whispered in its raspy tone. *Stuck. And you deserve to be for hurting Evan, for hurting your father, for leading Colton into the lion's den. You are nothing but a mistake. And you know you'll never get past what happened with Colton. You'll die with a broken heart. Evan's better off without you.*

"No," I said firmly.

But I felt the inner demon nod its head. *You'll never admit it to yourself, but you're broken beyond repair. And there is no hope.*

The world stopped then, and all was quiet. A sick, morbid feeling clawed its way into my conscience, filling my mind with blood-curdling ideas: a one-way ticket...out. It was a single thought. A very dark, selfish, frightening thought. The demon had its hands around my neck, snickering at my despair. The images persisted in my mind until I was shaking. And for one moment, I considered it. But for some reason, I chose not to move.

Reality faded into my awareness again, and I greedily gasped for air. Several deep breaths later, I realized that my anxiety had nothing more to say. It was just gone, like it decided to crawl back into a hole that led to the darkest part of my mind. I glanced wildly around the room, half expecting some monster to crash through the wall and slit my throat. Chills skipped up and down my arms; my cheeks flushed bright red. *What the hell had gotten into me?*

"Evan," I whispered, suddenly needing his arms. They were a castle that could protect me from the monsters.

I stood up from the couch and stumbled toward his bedroom, choking back a sob. I found him splayed out on his bed, clicking through photos on his professional camera. His face was still rigid and upset. I approached him slowly.

"Evan, I'm sorry," I murmured. "It's just been a crazy time recently, and there's so much on my mind." I took a shaky breath to steady myself. "I love *you* more than anything. I'm sorry."

He glanced up at me, and the way his sapphire eyes glowed

with remorse, my stomach sank to my feet. But after a moment, the look on his face softened, and he reached for me.

"I'm sorry too. I shouldn't have said what I did."

I swallowed loudly and blinked the tears from my eyes. "I love you so much. Seriously."

"I love you more," he whispered with the soft touch of a smile.

I pinned myself against his chest and tried to fight off the gut-wrenching terror of those scary thoughts.

"Whoa. Gail, are you okay? You're shaking." Evan anxiously peered down at me.

My stomach gave a sharp twist, like a warning that the anxiety would return at any moment if I snitched about what it had said, so I swallowed my initial response.

"Yeah, I'm fine." A lie straight through my teeth.

Over the next couple of weeks, I never put down my violin. The music thawed the coldness that had taken my heart hostage. I needed the sweet notes like therapy.

Ever since that moment in Evan's living room, I'd felt strange on my feet, like I was suddenly walking in a stranger's shoes. I even looked different. There were bags under my eyes, and my skin looked sallow as if all the joy and happiness had been sucked right out of me. Talking with other people wasn't the problem. In fact, being social even made me feel somewhat better. But it was when I was alone that the coldness grew, and something about that frightened me. When I was alone, I became a terrifying cynic toward myself and others. And that wasn't like me at all.

My violin was a tangible reminder of who I was. It did a nice job of combating the new hollowness in my heart.

And on top of my heightening paranoia, junior year finally ended, bringing on a whole new list of stressful tasks.

Cara's bridesmaids became my main priority again. They had important questions: what champagne should we order? Which movies would have us all crying? What nail polish would complement our individual skin tones? According to them, these minute details couldn't be overlooked if we wanted to throw a *memorable* bachelorette party. And the wedding was now one year away.

I ran myself ragged trying to find the perfect decorations. The bachelorette party itself would be held in *our* apartment, meaning Cara had to be distracted the day of, which was just one more thing to coordinate.

In fact, the hardest part was trying to keep Cara in the dark.

"So, my party," she said as we sat down to dinner.

This was the fourth time she'd asked all week, and now it was really trying my patience.

"I'm not telling you," I answered a bit too harshly.

When she glanced back at me, a cold fist squeezed my heart. I knew she didn't mean any harm with the question, but I didn't seem to understand that anymore.

She set her fork down and pressed her lips into a hard line. "Stupid question, but...are you okay?"

I swallowed another hurtful reply and conjured a calmer tone. "Not really. I just have a lot going on, and..." My voice trailed off as I remembered that moment in Evan's living room.

How could I explain that I now felt weak and strange in my own skin? And how could I explain that I'd actually considered something so dark and sinister?

"It's the stress." Cara nodded. "I totally understand. You need a break."

"But the girls are—"

"I'll tell them to lay off for a few days. Besides, the party planning can be put on hold. Your mental health is way more important than some bachelorette get-together."

The phrase *mental health* caught me by surprise, and I froze with a mouthful of chicken.

Maybe I *was* mentally unhealthy all of a sudden. Sure, I'd faced some challenging times in my life, but in Evan's living room, I had just felt so low, so depressed...that I was considering suicide.

Ice cold fear licked my spine.

What a scary thing it was to realize...that someone like me could be suicidal. But was that even the right word? Was I even mentally unwell? Or was it just a fleeting moment of terror?

Heat crept up my neck and scorched my cheeks. I felt my palms moisten as the words walked to the tip of my tongue. Why was I getting so anxious to confide in Cara?

"Also," she was saying, "I think I'm gonna have you guys in gold dresses. Wouldn't that be pretty?"

"Cara?"

Her exhilarated expression quickly sobered. The horror must've been visible on my face. "Gail, what's wrong?"

I stared at her. My mouth had gone bone dry, and the shame coursed through my bloodstream.

Maybe I was just overreacting, and the self-harm thought wasn't real. But when I recalled that terrible vision, I suddenly felt like I was going to vomit.

"Cara, I think I might be—"

I was interrupted by the loud wailing of her cell phone. She groaned and reached for it, apologizing as she clicked the answer button.

"I gotta take this. Hey, Mom."

I started to panic as I watched her leave the room. Since when was I afraid to be alone? I placed my head in my hands and felt the tears trickle down onto my wrists. *What was wrong with me?* I had a great life, great friends, a loving boyfriend. But then I started to think about our fight and how the past never seemed to leave me. And now my tears came faster.

There was no way I could tell my father about this; I'd

already hurt him too many times. And what about Cara? She didn't need to worry about me. I wasn't worth the fret.

I quickly brushed my tears away as Cara came back into the room. She plopped down into her chair and grunted.

"Sorry, I've missed my mom's call like the past eight times, and I couldn't leave her hanging again. Anyway, what were you gonna say?"

Not worth the worry.

"Nothing. Don't worry about it."

I excused myself from the table, grabbed my violin, and trudged toward my bedroom.

On June 3rd, Evan and I traveled back to New York just as planned. We decided to take the more scenic route and lose ourselves in the beauty of nature, which I was in desperate need of.

Being with Evan made things easier. When I was with him, my lungs didn't feel so tight in my chest. He made me laugh, kept me talking. He was the perfect distraction — almost as perfect as my instrument, which was in its case in the trunk.

I hadn't told Evan about the recent discovery of my mental health, but I could tell he suspected something. Whenever I felt the cold fist around my heart, I tended to become distant. And Evan gave me strange looks, though he never broached the subject. We had plenty of opportunities to talk. Plenty of times I could've come clean, admitted that I was unwell. But at the end of the day, I just didn't *want* to talk about it. And I didn't think Evan wanted to engage in another fight.

And so, we simply acted like nothing was wrong.

Dad, of course, was thrilled to see us. He gave me a tight hug, shook Evan's hand, and then helped to haul our suitcases into the house. Jamie had gotten a haircut, making her pixie-like face seem even more precious and dainty. As the boys greeted each other, I followed her into the kitchen.

"I really can't believe you're officially a senior in college now," she said as she retrieved a gallon of lemonade from the fridge.

"Whoa, it's still summer. Don't jump ahead yet."

I sat at the table and accepted the glass she handed to me. Jamie grinned.

"I know. But to think you were just a freshman yesterday."

"It is crazy." I took a sip of lemonade and stared into space. "Now look at me, trying to apply for actual jobs."

"Have you found any yet?"

My anxiety flared. There were so many choices, so many decisions. "Not yet."

She leaned against the counter and stared out the kitchen windows. "You know, you could always be a high school orchestra conductor. My one friend teaches at a school in Maryland, and she loves it. She said getting to influence young kids is so rewarding." Jamie's eyes sparkled. "You could do the same."

The idea sounded very appealing all of a sudden, and the cold fist slightly loosened its grip. I exhaled and smiled up at Jamie.

"Thanks. I'll look into it."

The next day, Evan and I were set to meet Erica at the Brook Tavern for lunch. I hadn't seen her in a year and a half, and the thought of finally being in her physical company again filled me with unimaginable excitement. She was right in some regard; college did suck because we didn't have all the time in the world to see each other anymore.

Evan opted for his classic black jeans and Red Hot Chili Peppers T-shirt. As he stood in my bedroom mirror, smoothing his hair to one side, I shook my head.

"Did I ever tell you how hot you are?"

His reflection grinned, and he turned and started strutting, which had me giggling uncontrollably in seconds.

"And did anyone ever tell *you* how drop-dead gorgeous you are, Gail?"

I barely nodded before his lips found mine. The kiss was soft and innocent at first. But it quickly grew into a feverish embrace. I liked when he kissed me this way; it chased the coldness away with pulsing waves of heat. It was all I could do not to let it escalate, for I'd already braided my hair and didn't feel like smoothing away any wrinkles in my shirt. I gently pushed him away and rose to my feet. He frowned and started to pout.

I laughed. "Later. But we've gotta go. Erica hates waiting."

The minute I spotted Erica sitting alone in a booth at the restaurant, I broke into a sprint. She shot up out of her seat, and we fell into each other's arms, twirling and screaming.

Her wavy hair was pulled into two low buns on either side of her head, and she was wearing a red sundress with blue flowers embroidered into the fabric. She was shining brighter than the dimmed lights above. As soon as we parted, her eyes flickered to Evan's face.

"Erica, this is Evan."

She stared at him for a moment as she peeled off her face mask. Her eyes scrutinized his face. And after a moment, she smiled cheek to cheek. "It's so nice to finally meet you! I'm Gail's best friend."

Evan nodded. "This is the ultimate test then."

Erica seemed pleased at his response and invited us to sit down. "So, I hear you're a photographer."

"Yep. Have been since I was eight years old."

"That's awesome. What kinds of stuff do you like to take pictures of?"

Evan shrugged. "Well, I love nature. I've climbed a dozen

mountain ranges, went out into the middle of the Pacific Ocean. I've taken pictures with sharks and blue whales. Oh, and this one time, my partner and I went to the mouth of a volcano and got some *amazing* shots. It was dormant, don't worry, but the way the rocks were aligned, it was awesome."

Erica's eyes widened. "I'd love to see some of the pictures sometime."

"Sure thing."

The waiter came with our drink orders. Erica chewed her straw and eyed Evan's shirt.

"Favorite Red Hot Chili Peppers song, go."

Evan exhaled and sat back in the booth. "Oh man. 'Dani California.' Maybe 'Otherside.' 'Dark Necessities' is great, too. I mean, that's not really a fair question. I can't give you an answer."

"'Dark Necessities,'" Erica said, grinning and chewing her straw. "There is no other answer."

I loved how well they were getting along. It eased some more of my anxiety.

Erica blinked her gray-blue eyes at Evan curiously. "So, how long have you guys been together?"

I glanced at Evan. "I guess it's almost been a year."

"Aw," Erica gushed, "what're you gonna do for the big anniversary?"

Evan laughed. "How about another motorbike ride?"

I laughed, too, because I hadn't been on the bike since my twenty-first birthday, but I would go again.

Erica chuckled, except this time it seemed forced. "Wait. Gail, I thought you hated motorcycles."

"Motor*bike*," Evan corrected patiently. "I'm not some Harley-loving grandpa."

I turned to Erica and smiled. "Well, I didn't like them until Evan showed me how fun they are."

Erica cocked her head, a single line creasing the skin between her eyebrows. But the expression was swiftly replaced by another friendly smile.

"Oh, I'm sure they're loads of fun. Anyway, you guys should go out on a super romantic date."

"I'll think of something," Evan said, linking an arm around my waist, making me blush.

"Must be nice to be in love right now." Erica sighed. "That guy I told you about, Gail? *Complete* weirdo. Won't leave me alone. I actually considered getting a restraining order."

"Sheesh. Is it that bad?"

Her eyes bored into mine with a look of disgust. "The dude clearly has a warped perception of love. Not like you guys though." She smiled at Evan tentatively.

"I don't really think you can fully understand love," I said. "It's a complicated thing. You feel it, but you can't really define it."

"I've *never* felt it," Erica muttered. She chewed her straw again.

"Hey, it can happen to anyone," Evan chimed in. "If a guy like me can end up with Gail, then you'll definitely find someone amazing."

"What are you talking about?" I laughed, staring at Evan's profile. "You're an amazing guy."

He shrugged. "I am now, but I have you to thank for that."

Later, after we paid our bill, Evan jogged outside into the sheeting rain to pull the car around. Erica and I stood under the restaurant's threshold.

Erica cleared her throat. "Can I be honest?"

"Don't tell me you hate him."

"No," she said quickly. "He seems to really like you a lot, which is great. You deserve that connection."

"Thanks, Erica."

"Plus," she squinted into the rain and wind, "he has good taste in music, which is *always* a good sign. But just be careful. If he's some photographer-adrenaline-junkie, you might become one, too."

"I don't even own a professional camera."

"No, I mean he's gonna turn you into a daredevil. People like that do stupid shit. Just be careful."

"I will. It's just that...he's making life a hell of a lot better right now."

Erica's expression faltered. "What do you mean? Are you okay?"

The usual occurred: my heart took off; my palms grew slick. I wondered when I would be able to confess something in confidence again. Erica was one of my closest friends. I could trust her with my fears.

"Erica, I think I might be—"

Evan's car zipped through the parking lot, squealing on the wet pavement. He stopped in front of the threshold and unlocked the doors for us to climb in. But before I could move, Erica nudged my arm.

"Gail, what is it?"

I shook my head. "Nothing. I'll tell you later."

I hoped that was true.

Chapter Sixteen

SARATOGA SPRINGS, NY—PHILADELPHIA, PA (2024)

The first thing I did when I got back home was Google symptoms for depression. I sat in the corner of the living room, isolated off from my father and Jamie, who were snuggled up on the couch and absorbed in some comedian's opening monologue.

As I typed the words into the search bar, I tried to swallow the lump in my throat. I couldn't believe I was even researching this.

The results were not a surprise: *The persistent feelings of sadness or loss of interests...can lead to a range of behavioral and physical symptoms.* A list followed this brief description, including anything from guilt to agitation to hopelessness. My eyes scanned the words quickly, my chest growing tighter by the second. *Depression can also be associated with thoughts of suicide.*

I had to look away then.

The comedian on the TV had said something to make my dad howl with laughter, and he glanced over at me.

"You hear that?" he asked, his eyes crinkling the way they always did when he laughed.

I faked a smile and nodded. But the moment he turned away, my nerves came back to life. They were sharp, blazing, basically sawing my insides open.

Pressing my lips into a firm line, I typed a new question into the search bar: *What causes depression?* For this, there were no clear, concise answers. Only theories. But a few of them managed to strike a nerve. Death or loss, conflict with friends or a loved one.

I felt it all: the memory of how angry I'd been at my mother when she left. The helpless grief I felt when Professor Autrie passed away. And of course, the searing pain of getting my young heart broken for the first time. I had to blink back tears. *Depression may also cause excessive crying.*

I turned my phone off and slammed it down on the coffee table, catching my father and Jamie's attention immediately.

"You okay?"

I met Dad's questioning gaze, and somewhere inside my bones, my anxiety snickered.

"Yeah," I answered as smoothly as I could and rose to go upstairs.

I would need to find a way to keep this under wraps. My father and Jamie didn't need to worry. No one did. I could handle this on my own.

A massive walnut tree stood as a soldier outside my bedroom window, its dark green leaves shivering in the summer wind. I stared at it for a moment until an idea popped into my head.

How to cure depression, I Googled. Scrolling past the suggestions of medication and therapy, I found other treatments, ones that didn't involve other people. Practice self-love and gratitude, set individual goals, journal.

Journal.

My eyes flicked to the top drawer of my desk, and I recalled

Dani's words: "Everyone has a story, so don't think yours isn't worth writing."

The sky-blue notebook had lost some of its shine, but the word *Love* appeared to be just as bright. I opened it and reread my entries about Evan and his family. About Professor Autrie. About my parents. I fell into the seat at my desk and retrieved a pencil.

How long I sat there writing, I wasn't sure, but I finished with a six-page description of my fear of depression. It was raw and dark, but it was the truth. And it helped a *little* bit, but writing was only a temporary painkiller.

The symptoms I'd Googled were becoming more apparent as the weeks passed. I was losing my appetite, my temper was shortening, and sleep chose to avoid me. I tossed and turned all night while my mind paced around the room.

I did have the option to return to my own apartment back in Pennsylvania, but I wasn't ready to rejoin that part of my life yet. Here in my childhood home, I felt safer somehow. Cara was busy with the wedding anyway; my absence didn't affect her.

But my father had the eyes of a hawk.

"Alright, we need to talk," he said one night as we sat down to dinner.

I glanced up at him. "Huh?"

"Something's up with you." He narrowed his eyes. "All your little excuses, they aren't working anymore, Gail. Why don't you tell me what's really going on." His face suddenly drained of color. "Did Evan do something?"

"No."

"Then what is happening with you?"

"What makes you think something's up?" It was a stupid question, and I could've kicked myself.

He stared at me. "Honey, you're almost twenty-two years old, you have your own life and a boyfriend. Friends who love you.

You know I miss you like crazy, and I love having you here, but...being home this long isn't like you."

I swallowed. "I just needed some time away from the city."

He bit into his corn on the cob and spoke through the mouthful. "Still playing your violin?"

I discreetly rolled my eyes. We'd had this conversation once before—a lifetime ago when my heart was tattered and broken.

"Yes."

We were quiet for a few moments, and then he said, "Sweetheart, you *would* tell me if something was wrong, right?"

Good question. Here we were, alone in the kitchen. Jamie had gone back to her place for the night, probably sensing we needed some father-daughter time. There were no distractions; nothing could cut me off. Perfect time to confess. Yet I plastered a smile on my face and buried the coldness instead.

"Of course."

We stared at each other for another moment, but luckily he caved before my facade could fall.

The one thing that remained solid in my life was Evan. He managed to keep me whole, which was a gift considering my own anxiety chose to chew away at my self-esteem these days. But he was stuck back in Delaware for the month of July, shadowing his uncle who was a professional photographer. Our contact was subjected to FaceTime only for several weeks.

The following Saturday, I was contemplating all that we would do when Evan got back when my dad entered the living room and pulled me from my thoughts.

"Hey, I was talking to Tony yesterday, and he said there's gonna be an end-of-summer carnival this year!"

Tony was our neighbor, and he was more into the town gossip than any woman on the block.

My eyebrows arched. "When's that?"

"August..." Dad pinched the bridge of his nose. "Ugh, shoot. I'll have to check the calendar. I know it's the week before you go back to school, but I can't remember the exact day. Well anyway, I thought maybe you could have everyone come back for a few days and go to it."

"You mean have Erica and Evan drive all the way here for a carnival?"

"Hey! Tony said they're gonna be roller coasters and all sorts of fun rides and games. I wouldn't underestimate it. Besides, Gail," he said when I started to shake my head. "This is your last summer as a student. After this, it's off to the real world. Why not have one last go as a kid?"

I wasn't a kid anymore, but his mention of the real world brought the coldness back at a stinging force.

I deserved to have a little fun, right? There was no harm in that. So I nodded, and after dinner, I went to call my friends.

Being lost in my head managed to kill so much time. When Evan texted me to say that he was finally on his way to Saratoga Springs, my jaw practically fell off.

"Please don't tell me it's the end of August already," I said as I entered the kitchen that morning.

Jamie smiled politely. "Yeah."

Dad peeked up at me from his phone. "Thought you would've been counting down the days. Evan hasn't been around all summer, and now you finally get to see him again."

It was true. On top of shadowing his uncle, Evan had gotten a job as an assistant at a photography shop near Westchester. He was really diving into his interests, and I was happy for him, even slightly jealous that he was already so far ahead of me.

But I was finally going to see him tonight for the carnival. And for the first time in months, my heart shot gleefully out of my chest. Erica was coming, too, which made the sunny day outside that much brighter.

I suddenly had a purpose, and I raced upstairs to invade my

closet in search of the perfect outfit. After what felt like hours of tossing clothes all over the place, I settled on a dandelion-colored tank top and ripped jeans. And after brushing the count-less knots out of my reddish-brown hair, I slicked it back into a pretty braid. It felt good, suddenly having a reason to get dressed. The sense of accomplishment almost diminished my anxiety entirely.

At five o'clock, there was a knock on the door.

Erica threw her arms around me before I could even open the door the whole way. She smelled sweet, like strawberries, and even under the sunglasses, I could tell her eyes were shining.

"I passed the carnival on my way here. It's already packed. Like, we might have to park a mile away!" she exclaimed. "Plus, I can't tell you how happy I am to not have to wear *this* anymore." She held up the pastel pink face mask.

"Oh, right."

Ever since the Pulmonem Fever vaccine had been distributed, masks weren't required anymore. I'd been too lost in my mental trance to even remember.

"It's gonna be weird seeing people without masks on now," I said.

Erica shoved her own mask into her purse. "Tell me about it."

The sound of tires squelching on gravel drew our attention to the end of the street, where a black Mercedes Benz was cruising toward the house.

Erica laughed. "Here comes the daredevil."

My smile felt a mile wide. I rushed down the porch steps, nearly tripping over my own two feet. And there he was, climbing out of the driver's side, barely shutting the door before I crashed into his arms.

"Hey, Gail," he laughed, "long time, no see."

I pressed my lips to his. There was no other world outside of this moment. His kiss sent a tsunami of warmth through my body, chasing down the coldness and demolishing my depression. For the first time in months, I felt alive.

"Save it for *after* the carnival when I'm gone," Erica called.

Evan pulled away first and plastered the famous smirk on his face. "Hey, Erica."

Erica smiled and waved.

"I'll see you later, Dad!" I called as the three of us crowded into Evan's car.

"Be careful, sweetheart," Dad called from the porch. "I love you!"

"Love you!"

Erica was right. We had to park at least a mile away. Cars were parked bumper to bumper on both sides of the street, and the nearest parking garage was full except for a few spaces on the top level. Even from here, you could hear the whirring of amusement rides and distant screams.

"If I don't eat cotton candy right now, I'll go into sugar withdrawal," Erica whined as she skipped along the sidewalk next to us.

"Shouldn't you wait until after we ride rides?"

She laughed. "Gail, haven't you known me long enough to know that my stomach is made of steel? I'll be fine."

"Let's get on the Claw," Evan cooed, eyeing the rotating structure as it swung through the air in the distance.

"I'm down." Erica nodded.

Naturally, the ticket line stretched as long as a fresh bundle of tickets. By the time we made it to the ticket booth, Erica had managed to convince Evan that the Space Turner was a far better ride than the Zipper. I slid my twenty dollar bill under the glass slit, and the man gave me a wrist band in exchange.

"To the cotton candy stand!" Erica shouted, towing us in the direction of the pink and blue sign.

It felt like Evan and I were supervising a little kid, and the thought made me chuckle.

"I bet I can win you one of those giant teddy bears," Evan said, gesturing to the dunk tank, where a very angry looking clown sat with his arms crossed.

"I don't need a teddy bear, I have you. I've been waiting for some alone time with you anyway." I squeezed Evan's hand, and his eyebrows quirked.

"What do you have in mind?"

"You'll see." I winked, and his smile stretched to the corners of his face.

The three of us navigated the carnival grounds, rushing toward every blinking light in sight. After exiting the Claw, my vision seesawed slightly, and my stomach was only just turning back into solid matter.

"Last stop," Erica said, eyeing the massive tangle of bright green tracks.

It was dark now, and so when the roller coaster cart shot above my head, I shrieked. This line was twice as long as any of the others. The tracks sailed all around the perimeter of the festival grounds, and a few massive hills gleamed impishly in the moonlight.

The ten-minute wait felt more like ten years, but finally, I climbed into the cart next to Evan. Erica was in the cart behind us with a dark-haired stranger who she apparently found attractive because she wiggled her eyebrows at me mischievously.

I reached for Evan's hand, but when the roller coaster took off, I was pinned against the back of the cart. At the speed of light, we zipped around the carnival, nearly blinded by the flashing lights and disoriented from the scattered laughing and screaming. I howled on the first drop, feeling my entire skeleton momentarily disconnect. For those few minutes while I was being jolted around on a rickety track, I wasn't worrying about anything. It was the endorphin rush I'd needed. At the end of the ride, I was dizzy with excitement.

"That was awesome," I exclaimed, still shaking from that last monumental drop.

Erica pulled her ponytail out and flipped her head upside down to regather her hair.

"Thanks for inviting us to this," Evan said, glancing around at the aisles of games, which were still crowded with people. "I feel like a kid again."

"Me too," Erica agreed. She flipped her head up again, but then her eyes locked on something behind me, and all the happiness vanished from her face. In fact, she looked disgusted. "*Speaking* of feeling like a kid again." She grimaced and pointed over my shoulder.

Three things happened in the short span of a minute. One, anxiety flooded my body again, only this time, it was stronger than any adrenaline rush. Two, I heard Evan curse under his breath. And three, Colton Reeves met my gaze from at least six feet away.

He wasn't alone.

A tall brunette was secured to his arm. Her tight, floral shorts exposed long, tanned legs, and her top was past the definition of risqué. But she was gorgeous. Even from here, her sharp hazel eyes gleamed like a cat's. Her skin was beautifully clear, and her lips were large and plump. Stella was right. She could have very well been a model. Even as the usual wave of jealousy whirled through me, I had to admit it. I swallowed loudly then, suddenly feeling self-conscious in my lame tank top and jeans.

But as flawless as she was, Colton far surpassed her. He looked like an angel in the moonlight. Realizing I was staring, I blinked a few times and redirected my vision elsewhere.

Erica stiffened. "Oh, God, they're coming over here."

Confirming her observation, Colton waved with a smile. I felt sick and leaned into Evan, who wrapped a protective arm around my waist. This made Colton's smile fade, though only slightly. If I didn't know him so well, I wouldn't have noticed. Before they could reach us, I gave Erica a warning look.

"Be nice."

This didn't need to turn into a bloodbath.

"Hey, Abigail," Colton said, his painfully familiar voice ricocheting in my brain.

For a moment, I could do nothing but stare. Did he think a cheery greeting would make me forget our last encounter? AKA the time he removed my clothes but then failed to accept his feelings for me? I wanted to scream at him, but the last thing I wanted was to cause a scene here in public. Instead, I forced a smile. "Hey."

The girl, who had to be Beverly Andrews, suddenly looked shocked. "*This* is Abigail?"

Colton's ears went pink in response, and Beverly turned her now cold gaze back to me. I didn't know why I felt so criticized by her; I was nothing but an old ex-girlfriend. Maybe her envy was worse than mine. I took note of this, happy that I'd found one flaw in her.

"It's good to see you again," Colton said, undeterred by his girlfriend's silent rage.

"Yeah." It was all I could bring myself to say. It still hurt to see him because I knew that underneath all of my resentment...my heart still yearned for him. That was the curse of first loves.

Colton glanced up at Evan. Tall as Colton was, Evan had a whole inch on him.

"Hey, man."

Evan barely nodded in response.

"Colton, this is my boyfriend Evan." The words suddenly felt strange in my mouth, like the sentence was a puzzle and the pieces didn't fit right.

I knew Colton well enough to know he was forcing a smile now, too. "Nice to meet you."

Evan's head bobbed stiffly. My eyes flickered back to Beverly, and something inside me snapped when I realized she was twirling her hair at *my* boyfriend. Colton didn't seem to notice; his eyes never left my face. *What kind of relationship were they running?* I turned back to Erica, now deeply uncomfortable and praying for an escape route.

"Well, we were just leaving."

Erica nodded. "Yeah, there's too much cheap perfume here, so—"

I clenched my jaw and flashed her a glare. Beverly, whose sweet perfume *was* a little on the strong side, narrowed her eyes at Erica. Colton only laughed, missing the tension entirely.

"Small world seeing you guys again. I was home anyway—"

"So that I could meet his parents," Beverly cut in with a prideful little smirk.

I took note of the plural noun, and a match struck in my chest. "Parents?"

Something in Colton's expression twitched as he met my eyes. "My mom married again."

The five of us were quiet, but over the hum of distant laughter and carnival music, Colton and I were locked in a weighted glance. So much...there was so much that nobody else knew. Only him and I. Had he even told Beverly where his scars had come from?

Evan touched my arm, making me jump. "Gail, we should go."

Talk about awkward: poor Evan. I nodded and turned to go but not before taking one last look at Colton. A miniscule part of me wanted to feel his hands in mine. But that had been Erica's warning. I would always have those feelings around Colton.

"Bye," I murmured.

Beverly didn't feel the need to respond, but Colton's eyes lingered on my face. "See you later."

None of us spoke on the way home, and as strange as my friends must have been feeling, I was sure I felt worse. Erica hugged me before departing and gave me an encouraging smile. She had been with me through thick and thin; she knew how much an impact Colton had on me. Evan waited by my front door, hands balled into his pockets.

Erica leaned closer to whisper something in my ear. "Head high. The past is in the past, you'll be okay."

I swallowed, allowing her words to melt over me. They were strangely calming, and I wished Erica could stay the night, too. Having her around made it easier to hold on to my sanity. But she had a life to return to.

"Thank you," I said.

She squeezed my arm and disappeared into her car.

It was starting to rain now, but as I returned to Evan, not a single drop hit me. I was walking in a daze.

When I approached him, Evan simply looked at me. His eyes weren't angry or happy. I reached up on my tiptoes to kiss him. It wasn't our best kiss, but at least I could tell him I was happy he was here with me.

After a moment, a ghost of a smile appeared on his lips, and some of my heartbreak was mended.

Senior year of college went by even faster than my senior year of high school. It made me nervous knowing that in just a few months I would be entering the real world. No more ridiculous theory tests, no more worrying if I had studied enough, no more carrying around a backpack full of textbooks. It felt like I was saying goodbye to so much; it was terribly bittersweet. My depression never allowed me to let it go.

I ran for president of the orchestra that year and gained the position by a landslide of votes. I figured there was value in being president. If I couldn't gain control over my own life and feelings, having control of the orchestra was the next best thing. Professor Burrfow, whom I'd grudgingly come to appreciate, happily applauded me when I won. He even let me pick our music for the concerts, and I conducted two of the five performances.

There was a certain joy in conducting. It was the joy Professor Autrie had spoken so passionately about, like the music was filling you to the brim. I was happiest in the moments when my baton was raised; depression and anxiety simply didn't exist.

But with every enjoyable moment came an equally stressful moment. Miss Atlas, the dean of students, spoke endlessly about the importance of finding a job right out of college. Jamie's suggestion of a high school conductor remained front and center in my brain, so I finally decided to do some shadowing.

I spent hours in the dean's office with endless questions and mountains of paperwork. She ended up submitting me to shadow a conductor from the High School for Creative and Performing Arts, which was a short five-minute drive from Curtis.

"This is a great opportunity for you," Miss Atlas said once I'd finished signing my name a hundred times. "And I've seen you conduct. You're good, one of the best students we've seen."

I thanked her at least thirty times over before she kicked me out of her office with a proud-mom kind of smirk.

And shadowing turned out to be a blast.

Most of the teenagers were uninterested in me, too busy gossiping to acknowledge my presence. Some of them had AirPods in and didn't even notice I was there. While most people would find this behavior entirely disrespectful, it actually amused me. I was a teenager once, too. I knew what was going through these kids' minds, and it sure as hell wasn't *I have to find a good job right now, or my life will be over!* What a thing to be young.

The months passed by. I was working double time in my classes at Curtis and hightailing it to the high school every afternoon. On the weekends, I slept in Evan's arms, and we talked about what life would be like after college was a thing of the past.

Cara and Beau were like chatterboxes hyped up on sugar because we were only five short months away from the wedding now. And after hours of shopping, I'd finally gotten all of the decorations for Cara's bachelorette party.

Everything was in line again...everything except my own mental health.

One night in March, I stood in the bathroom staring at my reflection. I couldn't remember the last time I did this — put everything on pause to take inventory of myself.

I'd changed over the years. My eyes, blue as they were, seemed distant and aged, if that was even possible. And there were actual worry lines creasing my forehead. I stood back from the mirror, feeling my heart beat sideways in my chest.

No, I was okay. Sure, life forced me to grow up a little bit, but that was life's job.

"I think I've aged at least a decade in the last year," I murmured that same evening.

His TV droned on about something neither of us were listening to, yet we were on his couch staring at the screen. Evan turned toward me.

"What do you mean?"

I pointed to my forehead, where the worry lines cut across my skin. He shook his head like he didn't know what to look at.

"We are weeks away from college graduation. How did we get here? Just yesterday I was riding my scooter through the house."

Living with endless nostalgia was no picnic. It clouded my brain with anxiety.

Evan chuckled. "You're still the same girl deep down."

I shook my head. "I don't feel like it."

The TV filtered the thick silence between us. I knew that look on his face well. Something was bothering him.

"What's wrong?"

Two heart beats passed before he met my eyes. "I guess now's the best time to tell you. One of my uncle's friends lives in Ohio, and he owns his own photography company. Well...he offered me a job right out of college."

"Ohio?" The word slipped past my teeth like a breath.

I swallowed as the cold fist wrap its chilling fingers around my heart. This was it. The beginning of the end. After graduation, he would tell me he no longer needed me, and then he would disappear to Ohio, and I'd never see him again. Besides, nothing was for forever.

"Why didn't you tell—"

"I wasn't sure I was gonna take the offer at first," Evan explained. "And you didn't need to know until I made the decision."

And he'd chosen Ohio.

I bit my lip, dreading graduation even more now. Evan sighed and gathered me into his arms. We sat like that for so long that I almost convinced myself everything would be okay, but then Evan spoke again.

"Gail, why are you always so scared for the future?" His voice wasn't judgmental, simply curious. Maybe even worried.

I frowned. "I don't know. Maybe I'm just scared that what I have now is all I'll ever have." I was just thinking out loud, not really hearing myself. "So, I guess I'm scared the future won't be so happy."

"What happened to focusing on the now?" Evan asked gently.

I couldn't answer that.

"Look, Gail," he continued, taking my face in his hands. "You don't have to worry about the future. Life has a funny way of working itself out." He paused and then adapted an amused expression. "What's your biggest fear?"

I pursed my lips. "Silly or legit?"

"I didn't know there was a specific type."

"My biggest fear is that...I'm never going to amount to anything. Like this is it — forever struggling, forever confused, forever lost."

It took a moment for him to respond. "Well if you think that's a legit fear, I disagree. It belongs in the other category — it's silly." He was shaking his head. "You have so many talents that are going to take you far in life."

"Evan," I said before I could stop myself, "I think I have depression or something close to it. I'm not sure. Sometimes...it seems like my life isn't going anywhere and —" The words were coming in a rush now, like they'd been waiting to be spoken for centuries. "I'm scared that I'll black out and do something terrible."

"Like what?"

I swallowed loudly. "Like...hurt myself. I don't know! That's why I've been so distant lately. I have good moments, but even in those moments, I wish something would change, though I don't know what. And in the bad moments, well..."

He stared at me with a soft, glistening gaze. One line of worry pinched the skin between his eyebrows. Then he leaned forward and pressed his lips to mine. It was a whisper of a kiss, but it stopped my heart all the same.

"Abigail Ferr, you are not stuck. And you're not going to disappear on me — not that easily." His arms tightened around my waist. "And you're not alone either. My aunt has depression and so do like a million other people. You have no *idea* how much you're loved."

I swallowed the burning lump in my throat and blinked back my tears.

"Yeah, we graduate in a few weeks. And yeah, we'll have to go out and find real jobs, and a bunch of other shit is gonna happen. But that's life. It's okay to feel stuck every once in a while. You don't have to walk through it alone."

When he laced his fingers through mine, the cold fist loosened its grip entirely, which left me breathless. Was this the moment I would finally wake up?

No, my anxiety decided to take one last jab.

"What about Ohio?" I asked.

Evan looked down at our intertwined hands. "We'll figure it out. All I know is that I love having you by my side."

I'd heard the words before in another lifetime. This time, I hoped it was true. I laid my head against his chest and tried to focus on the TV, praying it would occupy my mind for a little while.

Before I knew it, it was my last day shadowing in the high school orchestra. Though it took a few weeks for the students to warm up to me, they all lined up now to give me hugs and wish me luck for after graduation. The conductor thanked me, and I told the seniors to appreciate every moment because it would all be over in the blink of an eye.

The week of college graduation, Cara could not stop singing. Not that I was complaining; I would miss her angelic voice more than anything. Thank goodness we still had the party and the wedding before she moved out. I didn't want to think about this apartment without her in it.

Curtis' orchestra had a rehearsal-free week to celebrate our success. Professor Burrfow brought in cupcakes for everyone, and we laughed as we listened to all of our recorded performances throughout the year. Sitting in the music room one last time, I felt goosebumps cover my arms. I was going to miss this place *so* much.

On Thursday morning, I woke up with butterflies in my stomach. Compared to high school graduation, this felt more prestigious, more formal. For one thing, Colton Reeves wasn't going to be sitting a few rows behind me.

My father texted me and said that he and Jamie had arrived in Philly a couple of hours ago and were getting breakfast in a restaurant a few blocks away. Erica texted me, wishing me congratulations and constantly repeating how much she wished she could trade her vacation to Aruba to see me walk across the stage. I took her word for it. And of course, Evan, who had graduated last week, alerted me that he was speeding down the highway and would make it just in time. He also told me he was bringing a surprise, and I hoped it wasn't a sparkling red motorbike that said *Just graduated!* on the side.

In the meantime, Cara and I shared the bathroom to get ready one last time.

"Remember freshman orientation?" she mused, pulling a straight iron down her honey-colored hair.

"Of course. And the Pulmonem Fever lockdown?"

"Ugh, don't even bring that up." She rolled her eyes and turned to show off her glittering white gown. "What do you think?"

I was thinking how I'd come to love her like a sister. As an answer, I threw my arms around her.

"I'm really gonna miss you."

"Aw, me, too. But hey, you'll be there for my wedding." She pulled back so I could see her dazzling smile. "And I'll be there for yours when you get married. This isn't goodbye forever."

I bit my lip to keep from crying, but it was a wasted effort. Today emotions were running higher than high.

She sighed and held out her hand. "Come on. Let's go graduate college."

When I walked across the stage to receive my degree, a tremendous pressure lifted off my chest. When I inhaled, a full breath entered my lungs and left. I shook Miss Atlas' hand, then Professor Burrfow's, and I even directed a *thank you* up at the sky, telling Professor Autrie just how grateful I was for him. I returned to my seat and exhaled. It was finally over...and the sense of accomplishment was unreal.

Afterward, I was bombarded by my father and Jamie. They each hugged me, and Dad handed me a bouquet of red roses. Evan was there, too, dressed in a handsome navy-blue shirt and khakis. His sapphire eyes were electrified with joy, and I accepted his bouquet of flowers as well. But it wasn't until he moved to the side that a sharp spike of emotion hit me. I'd forgotten about the surprise.

Elijah stood there with a crooked smile etched in his lips and with his hands in the pockets of his dress pants. I nearly dropped my flowers and fell into his arms. He laughed such a stunning, familiar laugh, and I nearly cried.

"Ashford graduated last week, so I thought I'd fly in early before the wedding and catch *your* graduation."

Evan clapped Elijah on the back. "I told you I could keep it a secret, bro."

"Yes," I said breathlessly. "Everything's perfect now."

Chapter Seventeen

PHILADELPHIA, PA—DETROIT, MI (2024)

SURPRISE!" we all screamed as I removed my hands from Cara's eyes.

She took in the sight of our apartment, which was all but spray painted the color pink. Rose-colored streamers hung from the ceiling, and there was a bar set up in the corner with assorted champagne and fancy wine glasses. A rainbow of food was sorted on the table — all of Cara's favorites: flaming hot Cheetos, Twizzlers, Toasted Cheez Its, pretty much a kid's dream diet. Each of us wore a glittering tiara with our names on them. That had been Izzy's idea. I placed the largest tiara on Cara's head and wrapped her in a fluffy pink boa. The other bridesmaids hopped out of their hiding places and sprinted to give her a hug.

"Oh, my gosh," Cara gushed. "This is amazing!"

"Nothing like an old school sleepover, huh?" Angel said as she took Cara in her arms.

After all that hard work, the bachelorette party was even more fun than I anticipated. There was something about crowding around a flat screen and watching *Letters to Juliet* while braiding each other's hair that made me feel all bubbly inside. Young again. We could never go wrong with a girls' night, and as the champagne stole my nerves, I found it easier to relax. During a game of Truth or Drink, I was borderlining on being flat out drunk, but I didn't care.

It was my turn, and Stella turned to me. "Gail, have you and Evan ever done it in his car with his windows rolled down?"

"Tell the truth or drink!" Jasmine shouted.

"The truth," I managed, "is no, we have—not. Though that's an i-interesting technique. I'll have to try it sometime."

Everyone's laughing was intensified by the alcohol, so much so that when the doorbell rang, I thought I just imagined it at first.

"You *did* get a male stripper!" Angel exclaimed, and Cara's eyes grew wide despite her intoxication.

"No, I didn't," I said, rising and stumbling to the door.

I wondered who it could be, especially since all of the boys were away with Beau for his bachelor party. I opened the door and was shocked to see Elijah standing there. He gave me a quick once-over, and his eyes paused on the tiara sitting on my head. He pressed his lips into a thin line, trying not to laugh.

"What're you doing here?" I asked groggily, happy to see him nonetheless.

"Hey, your highness. Can we talk for a minute?"

I hooked my tiara on the closet handle. When Cara asked who it was, I told her and stepped out into the hall.

"What're you doing here?" I asked again. "Aren't you and the guys supposed t-to be like...partying?"

He gave me a funny look. "Are you drunk?"

I blinked and forced my tongue to work. "May-maybe. It's a *party*! What do you expect?"

I said this loud enough for our neighbors to hear, and Elijah actually howled this time.

"Well," he said when he'd recovered, "I'm on my way to Beau's now, but I was in the neighborhood and decided to stop by and pick up the schedule for Saturday. Didn't you print extra copies?"

"I got some extra, sure."

Cara had created a detailed itinerary for us for the day of her wedding—everything from what time our flight left to the time the reception party was set to end.

Elijah's eyes flickered from my face to the door and back again. "Gail?"

"Oh," I said, realizing I hadn't moved. "Yeah, I'll—I'm gonna go grab the papers, yeah."

Inside, the girls were laughing so hard that no sound was exiting their mouths. But when they all inhaled and laughed again, they sounded like a bunch of banshees, nearly crying over something Jasmine had said. I wasn't even there for the joke, but I started to crack up, too. I snatched an extra itinerary off the printer and returned to Elijah.

"Here's your special copy, Eli!" I shoved the paper into his hand.

He quirked an eyebrow. "Did you just call me Eli?"

"Yeah, I like—I think it suits you." I hiccupped and leaned back against the wall.

"Okay, well I was gonna ask you something else, but maybe I should wait until you're sober." He raked a hand through his hair with a lopsided grin.

"Oh, come on! I — I'm not *that* drunk!" I shrieked, loud enough to wake the whole apartment building.

Elijah just shook his head. "Right. So, Evan's treating you well?"

"Worships me like a princess," I answered, pointing to myself obnoxiously.

Elijah sighed and rested his head back against the wall.

"Good. If he ever hurt you, I'd personally disown him as a friend."

As out of it as I was, that made me frown. "You're not gonna —gonna have to worry about that."

In the silence that followed, something actually clicked in my brain. "Wait, wait, wait." Elijah glanced at me, eyebrows raised. "The night Beau proposed to Cara, b—before I had even met Evan, y—you said I was gonna like him. Were you trying to—"

"Hook you two up?" One corner of his mouth slid up into a smile. "Maybe. I knew you'd hit it off. Plus, he needed to date someone *good* for once."

"Me," I deadpanned.

"Exactly. I figured you were ready to date someone new, too. It was just a hunch, but when I saw you after the quarantine, you just seemed so much more alive. Almost like you had a new appreciation for life. Kinda like you had finally...healed."

The thought of trying to heal almost sobered me completely.

His eyes touched mine. "How's that going, by the way? Healing."

I felt the muscles in my neck tense like the fine strings of my violin. Why would he even ask me that question? I searched his eyes before answering, but when the champagne threatened my skull with the first tremor of a headache, I sighed. Overthinking was too difficult right now.

"Sometimes, I'm okay, a-and sometimes I'm not." It was the best response I could give.

Elijah looked down at my feet, at the banana ankle socks I was wearing. Something about the sight brought his smile back.

"You're not alone. Just remember that."

I smiled then, too. I was so grateful to have Elijah as a friend, even if he did live in perfect, sunny California. He was here now, and he was real and as kind as ever.

"I'll see you at the airport. Hopefully by then, you'll be sober." He chuckled and dodged my swinging punch.

. . .

Our plane landed in Detroit bright and early on July fifteenth. I was more than happy to finally be out from in between Elijah and Evan, who were like two toddlers, giggling over the stupidest things.

I had never been to Michigan, but the city was dazzling with towering skyscrapers. It was a stage of steel, glowing in a spotlight of golden sun rays.

The boys and I didn't waste time. Cara and Beau had come early, and the bridesmaids were all on scattered flights. I couldn't speak for the groomsmen. But as long as everyone was here before two o'clock tomorrow, I didn't care.

I pulled Cara's address up on my phone as our Uber driver appeared in a silver Volvo. The three of us squished into the backseat, and I found myself between the boys again.

"This is a nice part of town," the driver commented. "Lots of big houses."

The three of us squeezed to one side, peering out at the upscale, clearly expensive homes. One of them could have easily been mistaken for a castle, as it was large enough to swallow my dad's house whole, let alone my own apartment.

Eventually, we pulled into a circular driveway, the tires stirring the gravel as we gasped at the sight of Cara's house, which was more like a palace. After a few seconds of gaping, wide-eyed expressions, the driver nicely told us to get out.

Massive white columns stretched up the front exterior, leading to perfectly symmetrical arches. The marble was stark against the red brick foundation, and every windowsill glimmered in the afternoon sunlight. Parked to our right were four spotless Audis, each a different color, and the walkway leading to the stairs was lined with perfectly kept roses. I felt bad for whoever had to cut this massive lawn.

We climbed the steps with our suitcases, and Evan knocked

on the large eighteenth-century oak door. It wasn't Cara who appeared, but an older woman with frizzing gray hair. She was wearing an apron.

"I'm guessing you're Abigail?" she asked.

I stepped forward. "Yes."

She opened the door wider and gave us a welcoming smile. "Please come in. I'll take your bags up to your rooms, and you can just store your shoes in the closet right here. I believe Cara and her mother are on the deck."

We stared at her like three clueless children.

"Right this way," she said with a kind, patient smile.

"Okay, I might move to Michigan," Elijah murmured as we navigated our way through this gorgeous monster of a house.

"Yeah right," Evan said distractedly, ogling the shimmering chandelier in the living room. "Like you could afford to move into a place like this."

Sure enough, we found Cara and her Nicole Kidman look-alike mother on the deck. They were holding mugs and lounging on the beach chairs. The deck, like the rest of the house, was massive. A whole furniture collection surrounded a built-in firepit, and in the corner was a sparkling steel grill. The stairs leading off the deck stretched down to a large in-ground pool and tiki bar, and beyond that was a field of freshly cut grass. People were already out there setting up white chairs.

Cara looked up from her mug and squealed when she saw us. "You finally made it!"

"Hi, Mrs. Draper," I said to her mother.

"Oh, please, Gail, sweetheart. Call me Jen."

"Nice place, Cara," Evan said, peering over at the mini garden that lined the left side of the deck.

"Thanks," Cara replied. "It's nothing really. Just home."

Cara Draper — never one to brag about her riches. I shook my head and laughed.

Cara left the boys to do their exploring and then sat down to review the plan with me. I recognized the nervous expression in her eyes to be pre-marriage jitters, which was completely understandable. I gave her my best smile of encouragement.

She sighed and stared into the ashes of the firepit. "By this time tomorrow, I'm gonna be married."

It was still baffling.

"Oh, hey," she said, calling my attention back. "Thanks again for my bachelorette party." Her warm brown eyes twinkled. "It really was perfect."

I spun in front of the mirror, examining myself from every accessible angle. The dress Cara picked out for me was *gorgeous*. The material was light gold, almost nude-colored, and soft like satin. The train stretched down to my feet. There was a slit up my right leg, leaving a way to see the matching pumps that were already hurting my feet. Complete with the braided bun in my hair, I really did look pretty. I twirled once more, enjoying the excitement that skipped through my veins. But when Cara called for me in an unusually distressed voice, I ran out of the master bathroom and met her at the foot of her bed.

She was stunning. Her Cinderella-like dress made my jaw drop every time I saw it. In her trembling hands was a bouquet of white roses.

"What's wrong, Care? You look great!"

I gave her shoulder a reassuring squeeze, and she smiled nervously.

"I just...don't want to be alone right now," she managed through quivering lips.

"You're not alone," I said. "As the maid of honor, it's my job to keep you calm." She giggled at my authoritative tone, so I continued. "There is an *incredibly* lucky man out there waiting by that altar. And as soon as he sees you, he's gonna be in tears because you're beautiful. Today is your day, Care. It doesn't matter where you two go in life, you're never gonna lose sight of who you are. I can guarantee that."

She wrapped her arms around me, and I hugged her back, trying to blink away my tears. I would be strong for her. At least until she was married; then, I would cry until my eyes were sore.

"Thank you for everything," she whispered and stepped anxiously toward the door. I immediately helped to straighten the train of her dress.

I met with the other bridesmaids, who were dressed in matching gowns, and we struggled to control our laughter before the music began. I took my spot at the front of the pack and led them down the stairs, through the courtyard, and out into the field. I didn't recognize many people, but when I met Evan's eyes, an electric current shot through me.

He was so handsome in his tuxedo that my heart was suddenly beating in double time. The sun gleamed off his gelled blond hair and pooled in his sapphire eyes.

And the way he was looking at me. Like I was the only other person on earth, the one he wanted to get lost in forever. I briefly considered dropping my own bouquet and just sprinting to him, but I had to stay professional for Cara's sake.

People gasped when the bride appeared, escorted by her very emotional-looking father. Cara, the girl who I once met by chance and was now my best friend, smiled at me as she stepped down the makeshift aisle of grass and rose petals.

The ceremony was full of laughs and *awws* ringing out from the crowd. But instead of basking in the moment for my friend, my eyes kept shifting to Evan's. Elijah sat beside him, looking just as content as ever.

I love you, Evan mouthed at me.

And for a second, I felt like I was flying because I loved him, too. More than he would ever know.

"Well then," the minister concluded. "I now pronounce you husband and wife. You may kiss the bride."

I almost dropped my bouquet as I clapped and shouted for the beautiful union. The happy couple even got a standing ovation, and behind me, all the bridesmaids squealed.

Immediately following the ceremony, Cara's gigantic backyard transformed into an outdoor night club, complete with a marked off dance floor, a DJ, and countless tables of food. I ate so much I feared my bloated stomach would burst through the satin of my gown. But I managed to keep that from happening.

Evan, Elijah, and I laughed the night away. And for once, there was no such thing as a job after college, or anxiety, or depression, or Colton Reeves, or even a past at all. Just for this moment at least, I was free.

A couple times throughout the night, Evan swept me toward the dance floor and held me close to him as we swayed. His eyes were so curious, wandering over my body like it was a van Gogh painting.

"Why would a wonderful, gorgeous girl like you ever walk into my orbit?" he whispered.

I was already lost in his mesmerizing eyes. "Technically, you walked into mine."

He flashed his signature smile, and it took all my energy to resist the urge to kiss him.

"But seriously," he said. "I don't know how I ever got so lucky."

There was no one but him on that dance floor. No one but us. I could see the better part of myself in him, the way *he* saw me. And I didn't want to look away.

"It's time for the bouquet toss!" Cara called, and all the women came rushing forward.

Evan had to practically push me away. "Go win those flowers, Abigail."

With a grin, he returned to Elijah and accepted a glass of champagne.

I stood with my fellow bridesmaids and the other ladies who

I didn't recognize. Cara turned around and tossed the flowers over her head. I wasn't really thinking. Lost in the excitement of the moment, I leapt for the bouquet and collided with Jasmine before we both stumbled backward. It was then that I noticed I was the one who'd caught the flowers. I stared at them numbly, unsure of what to do.

Cara screamed. "Looks like I'll be going to another wedding when I get back from my honeymoon!"

Both Evan and Elijah were howling with laughter when I returned to my seat. I set the bouquet down on the table and smoothed my dress.

"What's so funny?" I demanded.

"Nothing," Evan answered, gazing up at me with heart-shaped eyes. "You just really took a fall for those flowers."

"And?"

"*And*," Elijah cut in. "It was awesome. I wish I'd been recording."

The party raged long into the evening. When I wasn't dancing, I was drinking and taking photos with the other bridesmaids. Evan brought his professional camera, so he captured a few solo pictures of me as well.

"Where's Elijah?" I asked as we walked back from the west side of the house.

"Congratulating the bride and groom."

Evan unexpectedly steered me in another direction, toward a quiet bench that sat in the midst of Miss Jennifer's rose garden. There was a full moon, which was tinged with orange. We stared at it for a few minutes. Or, I stared at it, until I realized Evan's eyes never left my face.

"Don't look at me like that," I sighed.

"Why?"

"Because all it does is just make me want you." I finally kissed him.

He kissed me back.

"I will look at my beautiful girlfriend whenever I want," he answered in a tone that made me laugh.

I took his hand in mine, noting how warm and right it felt. If there was such a thing as a perfect night, this was it. I tried to take in every little detail: the roses at our feet that were washed in the light of the moon, the warmth of the bench that was seeping through my dress. But all I could concentrate on was Evan's body next to mine.

"Marriage is a crazy thing," he said, drawing my attention back to more appropriate thoughts.

"Why's that?"

He shrugged, seeming lost in a daze. "Because you never really know if you're ready for it. Being in love is bliss, and it's something people would kill for, but to know that you've finally found the person you want to be with forever..." He met my gaze. "That's the best thing you'll ever experience."

"I agree."

"Listen, Gail. I know you struggle with depression."

The forward statement took me aback, nearly knocking the breath from my lungs. Where was this coming from? Where was it going?

"I know that I can't be the one to help you — at least not fully," he mended. "But I want to *try*. I want to be the one you turn to when things get rough. I want you to cry and scream and kick and come back knowing that I still love you despite all of that."

"Evan..." My voice caught in my throat.

"I want to be the one, Gail. I want you to choose me."

"I do choose you," I said firmly. "Always."

A smile touched his lips, but then he swallowed, and the smile was replaced by a nervous look I couldn't understand. I wanted to ask what the hell was going on because this conversation seemed too deep to be having while people were getting drunk sixty feet away.

Evan stood from the bench, his hair glowing in the moonlight. A shadow fell across his face, yet his eyes were as vibrant as
ever. "I want you to come to Ohio with me."

"What?" I tried to wrap my head around the request. "But
you—"

"I've made up my mind. I'm not living without you."

And with that, he dropped to one knee and retrieved a velvet
box from his pocket. Words came to a screeching halt on my
tongue, and I covered my mouth with my hand.

"Abigail Ferr," he murmured, "I didn't know what joy there
was to life until I met you. And I'd be the biggest asshole alive if
I were to give that up. So please—" he asked breathlessly, closing
his eyes for just a moment before reopening them — "will you
marry me?"

Of all the times in my life that I'd felt alone and scared and
confused, they all faded into nothing now. I wanted to cry, run
until my lungs burst, scream until my throat was sore, shout for
glee until the whole world turned to look at me. But instead, I
managed, "Yes."

Chapter Eighteen

PHILADELPHIA, PA—ROCKY, RIVER, OH (2024—2025)

My mind finally woke up when I realized I was in the middle of a wedding dress boutique completely surrounded by white gowns. Claustrophobia attacked me, and I pressed a hand against my chest. Marriage was something that happened to everyone else, but it was just a fairytale to me. And yet here I was, scanning the racks of huge, poofy dresses. I wondered how my father even let me get away with this...probably because he'd already come to love Evan as a member of the family.

And I guess I'd said yes because I loved Evan, too. So much so that it burned.

Jamie stood beside me, dragging her finger down a velvet cream-colored dress. I realized why she was with me all of a sudden—because I had once dreamed of shopping for a wedding dress with my mother, and Jamie was the next best person.

A girl appeared through the maze of dresses, holding a gown

in her hand. "I grabbed this one from the back." She had a permanent, perfect smile fixed on her lips.

The dress' neckline swooped way too low, covered in the middle with a thin see-through netting. The bodice was beaded, but the gems reflected the fluorescent lights above and nearly blinded me.

"I don't think so."

"Wait, hold on," Jamie said, laying a gentle hand on my shoulder. "The thing about wedding dresses is that you have to try them on."

"She's right." The girl nodded. "You never know which dress will work until you try it on."

I pressed my lips together, suddenly feeling a little short-tempered. There were too many options staring me in the face, and the whole idea of marrying just seemed outlandish. But I'd said yes, and I had meant it.

Instead of snapping at them both, I said, "I have a budget."

"Of course," the girl said, draping the gown over her arm and pulling out a notebook. "What's your limit?"

"No more than a thousand." I sighed. "But preferably nowhere near a thousand."

She copied this into her tablet and then she tapped the pen against her chin. "I'll look through the back again, but in the meantime..." She handed me the dress.

It was terribly itchy, and I stood in front of the mirror with my arms stuck out from my sides like the lace was cutting into my skin. Jamie, oblivious and happy, stood to the side smiling. The girl came back, offering several more dresses, which were all either too big, too tight, or too showy for my taste.

"I do have one last item I think you'd look great in," the girl said, expertly staying calm.

She disappeared for about the twelfth time and returned with a simple chic gown.

"This is silk," she explained. "Therefore, not too itchy. The skirt pans out from the waist, therefore not too tight. And unless you consider a backless dress to be risqué..." She held the dress up and turned it around to show her point. "Not too showy." The smile fixed itself onto her lips like a period at the end of a statement.

I scrutinized the dress, not finding any visible problems with it and then agreed to try it on. Jamie and the tailor stood side-by-side as I gazed into the mirror. The dress fit so perfectly I almost didn't want to change back into my regular clothes.

"I love it," I heard myself say.

Jamie clasped her hands together and gave a little shout of joy.

The girl exhaled, probably relieved that she wouldn't have to deal with me anymore. "Well, that's fantastic because here's the best part." We both stared at her. "It's only two hundred dollars."

Unlike Cara, who was actively engaged in her own wedding planning, I felt like I was drifting through a dream the whole time. Decisions stared me in the face: what flavor is the cake? What's the location? What about the guest list? Cocktails or classy champagne...or both? Somehow I chose, and the wedding day drew closer with each sunset.

I wasn't really aware of what was going on. I just felt like I was floating a million miles above ground, lost in a castle in the clouds—a kingdom Evan and I built ourselves, where we slow-danced each night and got lost in each other's eyes.

When October finally arrived, my lovely daze was broken by an influx of emotion. It finally hit me that in just fourteen short days, I would be a married woman. The thought was frightening, and I was grateful to have Cara and Erica there to calm me down and assure me that this was the right decision.

And I knew deep down that it was. Evan was my true love. Destiny had brought us together; I was finally going to get my happy ending. But I was also painfully aware of an old voice in the back of my mind that wondered what Colton would say if he were here.

In a perfect world, if we had remained friends after our breakup, maybe he still could've seen me walk down the aisle. Would it have been awkward? Would he have been jealous? I liked to think the answer would have been no because we were adults now. And a sixteen-year-old romance was nothing compared to the kind of love you donned a wedding dress for...even if that was the future Colton and I had once dreamt about.

The night before our wedding, I lay cocooned in Evan's side, his hand lightly caressing my shoulder. Comfortable as I was, my mind was chaotic.

"You're quiet," Evan observed.

"Just gathering my thoughts."

"Mhm." His lips found my neck, and I wished he would kiss me forever and make me forget my nerves and anxiety and Colton like he often did. But something kept nagging in the pit of my stomach.

"Tomorrow, I'll be able to call you Mrs. Caldwell," Evan said, gazing into my eyes.

"That's crazy." I shook my head. "Hey, I was thinking we could spend our honeymoon in Venice."

He cocked his head. "As in Italy?"

"Yeah." I gave him a *duh* look. "It's always been my dream to go honeymooning there. You know, it's one of the most romantic cities in the world."

Evan rolled over onto his back and shoved a hand through his matted hair.

"What's the matter?"

"Gail, we can't go on a real honeymoon, remember?"

I did remember then. He was starting his job as a National Geographic photographer in just two weeks, leaving no time for a romantic getaway. After the wedding, we had to move straight into the new house in Ohio. I frowned, feeling a little defeated. What was a wedding without a proper honeymoon? Even though this upset me, I didn't say so. Evan was going to be working his dream job; there was nothing to be but happy for him.

"Right," I said in the most chipper voice I could manage.

"We can't go on a honeymoon *yet*," he backpedaled, "but after we settle down, we'll go to Venice." He took my hand in his. "That's a promise."

I feigned a smile, and then his lips were tracing my body again. I let him explore, but my mind drifted to the future. I imagined us walking the cobbled streets of Venice and listening to the romantic music of guitar players and Italian singers.

I would kiss him there for sure, and it would be perfect.

The next day arrived all too quickly. I spent the morning in Cara and Erica's care as they curled my hair and painted blush over my cheeks and silver over my eyes. And after I had a mini panic attack, they helped me into my dress and assured me that everything was going to be perfect.

"Come on, Dad. Stop crying," I giggled later as he approached me before the ceremony started.

He pinched the bridge of his nose and shook his head. We were standing in the narthex of my childhood church, waiting for the music to shift so that he could guide me into the sanctuary to my soon-to-be husband.

"Who are you getting all emotional for? Me or Evan?" I laughed when he shot me a glare.

"I can't believe my little girl is getting married."

I glanced down at my dress and managed a smile. "It's been a fun twenty-some years."

"Don't even start," he muttered.

And I was laughing again, though this time, it was a nervous chortle. Evan was waiting just beyond the door. My *future* was waiting just beyond the door, saying ready or not, here you come.

The music shifted, and I tightened my grip on Dad's arm. He led me forward, through the glass doorway and into the large, shimmering sanctuary. There was Cara, Erica, Ella, and Brie, standing close in their matching gowns. There was Elijah, dressed in a lavish gray suit, standing out from the other grooms-men. And right beside Elijah was Beau, who smiled as I met his eyes. There was Jamie, and Beth and Grant, and their three chil-dren. Even Taryn, Lain's girlfriend, seemed misty-eyed.

And then there was Evan.

My heart lurched out of my chest, and all of a sudden, it wasn't my own feet moving me down the aisle but a potent gravity that belonged to the boy at the altar. His sapphire eyes gleamed, drawing me closer and closer. I couldn't move fast enough. My father and I walked in slow motion, and I felt like I was falling from some extravagant height.

At the altar, my father froze as Evan extended his hand. For as close as they were, Dad was suddenly reluctant. I gave him an encouraging smile, trying not to let it falter. I would miss him more than words could express. He kissed my forehead and with a sort of begrudging sigh, he placed my hand in Evan's.

The touch of Evan's skin was tangible electricity. The minister said something I didn't hear because I was too busy gazing into Evan's eyes. And I suddenly wished we'd written our own vows. There was so much I wanted to say to him, more than the minister could ever repeat.

Evan slid the diamond ring onto my finger. My skin burned under it, like the diamond was constructed of fire. I could barely wait for the moment to say I do, and after I did, my lips crashed into Evan's. Applause erupted from our friends and family.

Breathless, I broke our kiss and scanned the crowd, my face starting to ache from all the smiling. But I couldn't stop. I was walking on air.

Ever since I had met him, Evan was the person who helped me through all the battles in my mind. From our first conversation, when he intrigued me with his strange, nonchalant demeanor, to our kiss here at the altar, this boy was the boy I was destined to marry.

It felt so right.

And even after dancing with my father at the reception and having Evan slip under my dress to find the garter, it still felt right. We sliced into the large, elegant cake and toasted with sparkling champagne. Everyone was in great spirits. And deep down, I wondered when my anxiety would return; it had to be any minute now. How much happiness was a person capable of feeling before it was washed away?

"Don't you dare be a stranger," Erica warned before pulling me into a hug.

"Yeah," Cara agreed. "I wanna hear about Ohio."

"Trust me, you guys will be the first to know."

I took deep, calculating breaths. If I let the reality of the moment hit me, I might break down and never get on the plane. I would miss my friends too much. In fact, one look at Elijah, and I was almost in tears.

"Erica has a point," he murmured as I ducked under his arm. "It's my fault we didn't keep in touch while I was in California, but that stops now. My best friend just married my other best friend for crying out loud!" His grin had me giggling until my lungs burned. "I mean, that's huge. I'm gonna miss you guys so much."

There was that feeling—the slow burn in my chest and the threatening bite of tears. I held my breath, forcing the sensation away.

"I'm gonna miss you, too."

I could hear Brie talking a mile a minute somewhere behind me, and the sound caught Elijah's ears. He glanced up past my shoulder, and something changed in his expression. His eyes were wistful, filled with longing. It took me a minute to put the puzzle together, and then a laugh burst from my lips.

"Brie's a great girl. You guys would really hit it off."

Elijah shifted on his feet and cleared his throat, though the pinkish color in his cheeks spoke enough words.

I shrugged. "Go introduce yourself. I'm *almost* positive she'll fall for you."

"Good one. Thanks, Gail." He shot me a wink and then sauntered off toward Brie.

It was kind of funny watching him approach her. Once upon a time, I thought I would've ended up with Elijah, but time had a funny way of putting things in perspective. Maybe I was meant to meet Elijah so I could eventually meet Evan.

On our way out, Beth was ecstatic. Her tears glistened on her round face, and she hauled me into the tightest hug of my life.

"Thank God he has you," she whispered through her sobs.

"I'm glad I can call you my sister-in-law," Dani added. "It's cool to have someone to look up to."

Evan cast her down with an offended look. "What about me?"

"Don't ask the question you don't want the answer to," she responded, rolling her eyes with a lazy grin.

Evan yanked her into a hug.

Moments later, I spotted my father in the corner. Jamie was talking about something, though he was staring off into space, hands balled into the pockets of his dress pants. Here was the hardest goodbye, waiting just a few steps away.

"Hey," I said, pressing my lips together.

"Hey."

"Wonderful ceremony, Gail," Jamie gushed. "I know you two will be very happy together."

"Yeah, and you know...call if you ever need anything," Dad said. It was clear he was choking back tears. "And I'm not going anywhere. You know Saratoga Springs is always your home."

I realized he wanted an answer. "Yeah, of course."

Before the emotion could hit me, I wrapped my arms around him, thanking him for everything and telling him not to worry. I had this life thing pretty much figured out. It might have been a small lie, but he never would've let me go if I told him otherwise.

"I love you, Dad."

He huffed and slouched and nodded, trying to be the man. "I love you too, sweetheart."

Evan touched my shoulder. It was a light beckoning touch, urging me toward the future. "We'd better get going."

I smiled at him. He looked so handsome even changed into a polo T-shirt and khaki shorts. "Right."

Evan shook hands with my father, and the two exchanged goodbyes. I swore I saw a tear roll down Dad's cheek after Evan turned away.

With Ella's and Brie's help, I changed out of my dress and into something more comfortable. And then Evan was pulling the passenger door open for me. We waved as he maneuvered the car out of the parking lot, and I took one last look at all my friends and family. Saying goodbye was a strange thing, but I still wasn't anxious. Even now as we zoomed down the highway, it still felt right. Using one hand to steer, Evan used his other hand to draw soothing circles into the skin of my palm.

Rocky River, Ohio, was a charming town right outside of Cleveland. Staring out at the quaint little shops and some cavernous, Corinthian-like homes, I suddenly felt like I was passing through a place like Amsterdam. Rocky River was its own little world.

Months before the wedding, Evan and I combined our funds and rented a place here. It was like half a cottage, complete with gray hardiplank and cream-colored shutters — a nice place to settle down. It was well past midnight by the time we arrived, thanks to Evan's idea of leaving right after the wedding. But I wasn't tired. In fact, my heart was pounding.

I took the key from Evan's hand and unlocked the door. He came up behind me and swept me off my feet, shooting a shock through my veins, and I actually screamed.

"It's tradition," he explained smoothly and carried me inside.

I looked around at the space that would be our living room and the kitchen down a small stretch of hallway.

"A work in progress," Evan said, setting me down. "But good enough for now."

"It's perfect," I replied.

I would've thought that by standing in the apartment I was now paying for as a married woman, my anxiety would be red-hot. This was my new life; this was the epitome of change. Shouldn't these thoughts have sent me spiraling? No, because now Evan was kissing my neck and his hands were starting to wander, and it was distorting my train of thought. I eagerly welcomed the distraction. I waited impatiently as he unrolled the blow up bed and began to fill it with air. Once it was full, we collapsed onto it in a mess of tangled limbs.

When I woke up the next morning, the sky was only a light gray; dawn had yet to make its full appearance. Moving quietly so as not to disturb Evan, I got dressed and left to go look for a grocery store.

The more I drove through this town, the more I fell in love with it. It had its own atmosphere, which seemed so welcoming and endearing. There was a pizza shop and an ice cream parlor, a whole park to jog in. And as luck would have it, there was a market right on the corner just opening its doors.

I gathered our essentials: cereal, boxes of mac 'n' cheese, frozen chicken, cans of ravioli and assorted vegetables, a fruit tray, potato chips, water bottles, and for the heck of it, a pack of

Twizzlers. By the time I was finished, the sun had materialized in the sky.

Evan kissed me when I walked through the door again. "What're your plans today?"

He was already dressed in a wrinkless T-shirt and cargo shorts, moving his prized camera into a protective case.

"Job hunting," I answered.

As I placed our new groceries into the cupboards, I recited the information from my resume — all very musical achievements.

"I think there's a Menchies Music somewhere around here," Evan said, pulling on his shoes. "You should go there. They'd be lucky to have you. Also, after I get off work, we should go into town and find a furniture store."

He approached me and took both my hands in his. I stared into those gorgeous sapphire eyes and smiled.

"By the way," he murmured after kissing me. "Last night was incredible. We should do it again sometime."

"How tempting." I grinned.

He winked and disappeared out the door.

Job hunting was not as easy as Miss Atlas described it to be. Even though I was an alumni from the Curtis Institute of Music, businesses weren't breaking down their doors to have me. I was feeling defeated now, run-down after my day of disappointing interactions with managers. There was one place left on my list: a high school which had an opening for a musical conductor. I went into the office, showed the woman my resume, and offered my best smile.

"We'll be in touch," she said absentmindedly.

It was the best news I'd heard all day.

In the weeks that followed, I managed to stay busy. The apartment was starting to look more like home with new furniture and a few framed pictures on the walls and actual kitchen appliances, so that when Evan came home, I had *cooked* dinners waiting for him. We slept tangled together on our new bed and woke to another day of monotony. But was this not the real world?

On the third Friday after we moved in, my cell phone chimed. I was in the middle of a book and immediately reached for it. It was Rocky River High School, calling to tell me that they were impressed with my resume and wanted to interview me as soon as possible.

"Me!" I exclaimed that night during dinner. "An actual conductor!" I squeezed my hands into fists and squealed.

Evan's smile beamed. "That's incredible. You're gonna be amazing! But hey, eat your soup before it gets cold."

But my mouth continued to run.

My anxiety was nowhere to be found. Despite the few normal jitters I had before walking into the interview, I was well-prepared. How long had it been? Three weeks since our wedding...all anxiety-free. I actually felt reborn, like I was dipped in confidence and wrapped in a towel of tranquility.

"Welcome to the team, Mrs. Caldwell. We're honored to have you on board."

I shook the principal's hand, basking in the excitement that was shooting off inside me like fireworks.

"Good luck today," Evan said on the morning of my first day. "I love you."

Just like every morning, he planted a kiss on my forehead and then slipped out the door, camera bag dangling at his side.

I wasn't sure what I expected when the students started to file into the room, though it was a little unnerving to think that I was sitting in their seats only a few years ago. Now I was the one in charge. There were a few minutes to spare before the bell rang, so I pretended to click through my laptop and not notice the whispered questions: Who is she? Where'd she come from?

"Good morning," I said after the piercing ring of the bell.

The teenagers only nodded in response. It was easy to pick out the stereotypes. There were the chatty girls who always chewed gum despite being told to spit it out. There were the nerds who set their instruments down to work on next week's homework. There were the athletes in their Nike shorts and Asics sneakers, who were clearly only here for an A to boost their grades. And then there was the girl in first chair with the glasses and wavy black hair. She sat back in her seat, staring off into space, her fingers plucking the strings softly. Something about her was painfully familiar.

I explained how I graduated from Curtis and that I'd been in love with music since the fourth grade. But I forgot I was speaking to adolescents, some of which were wearing AirPods the whole time. I broke off mid-sentence, feeling their judgmental eyes bore into my skull.

My conscience rolled its eyes. *Enough of this.*

"Can I see your violin?" I asked the girl in first chair.

Her cheeks pinkened but she nodded.

"You're gonna want to take those out," I told the boys in the cello section, gesturing to their AirPods.

They did so reluctantly.

I didn't hold back. The thing about teenagers was that you had to command their respect from the beginning. Otherwise, they would never listen to a word you said. I knew this because I thought I was too cool as a sixteen-year-old as well.

I ripped the bow across the strings, allowing my fingers to dance at the speed of light. A strange melody formed from my on-the-spot concoction, and the bow moved so quickly, a piece of hair came unattached. All the while, my audience drew a collective gasp. When I finished, their faces were frozen in shock.

"Thank you," I whispered to the girl in first chair.

And then there was an eruption of praise. I laughed,

accepting their applause with a polite smile and small bow. The students spent all period asking me questions about my musical skill, and I was happy to answer. The girl in first chair, whose name I discovered was Naomi, gazed up at me with sparkling pale green eyes.

Life fell into a pattern. I got to pursue my passion and teach music, then come home to my loving husband, who always found a way to keep me captive in his kiss for a few hours every night. I called Dad often, just so I could assure him that I was all right and that Ohio was starting to feel more and more like home.

A part of me missed Saratoga Springs and Philadelphia, but I knew that there was nothing wrong with that. Those places had been my life for over twenty years. It was normal to feel a little nostalgic every once in a while. But it never dragged me down like it used to. It was like my depression had vanished completely.

One night, I snuggled up next to Evan, who was far warmer than the thin blanket I had over my shoulders.

"Hey, you," he whispered.

I smiled in the darkness. "Hey."

"Today, they had me out on Lake Erie, taking pictures in a speedboat."

"Sounds exhilarating."

"It was. You had the sun in the background, it was a perfectly cloudless day." His arms were stretched up toward the ceiling like he was trying to paint the picture for me. "*Great* shot for the speed boat company."

We laughed together.

"But it got me thinking." He dropped his arms back to his chest. "Nature is unbelievably beautiful. It's a work of art."

"Mhm." I snuggled closer to him, lost in the fervor in his voice.

"But it's how I feel about you, Gail," he whispered. "*You're like a work of art.*"

"Stop making me blush," I joked.

His voice remained serious. "Marrying you was the best decision of my life."

I sighed. "And we still have our pact."

"Our what?"

I sat up and squinted at him through the darkness. "Remember? To protect each other and fight forever no matter what?"

He chuckled softly. "Oh right, how could I forget?"

"You better not forget."

"No, Abigail. You'll never have to worry about that. I promised to love and protect you the moment you agreed to be my girlfriend."

We chuckled together, and I twirled my fingers in his hair.

"Forever then?" I asked.

He nodded once with a determined sparkle in his eye. "Forever."

The year was moving too quickly. I conducted the spring concert in March, more than happy with my students' performance. They were incredibly talented for young teenagers who "didn't care about anything." Or so they said. Naomi in particular was phenomenal. As the months passed by, she and I developed a friendship.

She came to me with her dreams of becoming a famous violinist; I told her the dream was achievable. She came to me with friend issues, and I told her to keep her head high. She came to me after her boyfriend dumped her in the middle of the cafeteria; I told her, "The pain won't last forever."

High school was a place of broken hearts and change. I'd learned that better than anyone. But maybe that was why I loved my job so much—so that I could lift these teenagers' spirits and remind them that there was more to life than the drama between two friends. There was more to life than that one person you thought you would be with forever.

In June, I wished all of the seniors good luck and told the rest of the students I was looking forward to another great year. We were all sort of intertwined now, a family, more or less. This orchestra room was a safe place.

The summer that followed my first year of teaching, Evan took me on some of his photography adventures. By July, I had witnessed several parasailing and surfing competitions. I had spent the night in a forest, and I came nose-to-nose with a beluga whale when Evan took pictures at an aquatic animal resort.

It turned out to be one of the best summers of my life, and spending it with Evan just made it all the more exciting. We often cooked outside on the grill, which had been a Christmas gift from Beth and Grant. A summer wasn't summer without burgers and hot dogs.

"We're out of ketchup and mustard," I realized one evening as I was combing through the fridge.

"I'll run out and get some," Evan offered.

"No, it's okay. You stay and grill. I'll be back by the time you finish."

Evan kissed the tip of my nose and slipped through the sliding glass door, holding a plate of uncooked hamburgers.

The weather was perfect for the last night of July. The air was sweet and warm, offering a gentle breeze. The sunset was a masterpiece, complete with striking pastel colors that turned the trees into daunting silhouettes. I entered the market and walked right to the condiment aisle. My eyes flickered across the labels, trying to locate the ketchup and mustard.

"Mommy, can we get some candy?" I looked up to see a mother pushing a cart down the aisle. A small child sat in the cart, and even from here, it was easy to see that she was a spitting image of the woman.

"No, sweetheart. You'll spoil your dinner."

"But I don't want dinner." The little girl sighed and crossed her arms in disappointment. It actually made me laugh.

The mother was amused, too. "Don't give me that look. Veggies are better than candy."

"But I don't *like* veggies."

The mother laughed, a silvery, joyful sound, and leaned down to kiss her daughter. Something inside me twitched when the little girl finally giggled. I watched the way her mom hugged her and the tiny arms that hugged back.

Was there anything better than the love a mother gave her child? It was something I only experienced for a small amount of time before my own mother grew distant and callous. I shook my head. I would never leave my own child like she did. I would love it and care for it like there was no tomorrow. I would push her around the store in a grocery cart and have her ask *me* for candy. I would risk my life for her.

The mother noticed me watching and glanced in my direction. I quickly offered a kind smile and returned my eyes to the condiment labels. Only now, there was just one thing on my mind.

Longing burned inside me. It circulated my organs, tugged on my bones. My heartbeat quickened at the thought. It was almost painful how much I wanted this. I turned my head to glance at the mother and daughter again, but they were gone. I exhaled, grabbed a bottle of ketchup and mustard, and hurried to the checkout line.

My mind was lost in a fantasy world that was full of devotion and love. Nothing but love. I would do it. I would go through all of it. Not a single shadow of doubt clouded my mind.

"Ma'am?" the cashier asked.

I blinked. "Sorry?"

"Do you have a bonus card?"

"No."

I drove home in a daze, my eyes not really resting on the road in front of me.

The fantasy was so clear, so amazing. I was breathless just considering it. Even now as I daydreamed about this life-altering decision, my anxiety didn't raise its voice.

I smelled the burgers as soon as I got out of my car. Evan was in and out of the kitchen, grabbing plates. I set the condiments down on the table and felt a rush of emotion bubble up in my chest, like what happens to a soda can after you shake it.

"Dinner's ready," Evan announced with a grin that made my heart stutter.

I watched him fill our plates.

He was so handsome. So perfect. I was meant to be with Evan. He was my other half. The last piece to complete life's puzzle, which was why he was the perfect one to do it.

"What's up? You're quiet," Evan said as we sat down at the table. He looked like a bloodhound ready to tear into its last meal.

"Well..."

What was the easiest way to say this? I loved Evan more than life itself, and he loved me, possibly even more. So, I shouldn't have been frightened to tell him. In fact, I didn't think frightened was the right word at all. Giddy sounded better.

Evan glanced up at me, suddenly concerned that I hadn't answered yet. But I softened his worry with a smile. Placing my hands on top of his, I took a deep breath.

"I've been thinking."

He returned my smile, though it seemed a little guarded. "About?"

The desire burned my throat, pushing the words up and out. "I want to have a baby."

Chapter Nineteen

ROCKY RIVER, OH (2025—2026)

To my complete surprise, Evan shot the idea down. He offered excuses like how we didn't have enough money for a baby right now or that he just wasn't ready to be a father. I took all of this to heart and tried to keep my voice calm.

"It doesn't have to be now," I said gently. "If we work for another six months or so, we'll have enough—"

"It's not that simple, Abigail! We'd have to set up a nursery and buy diapers and a bunch of other stuff. The baby would keep us up all night, we'd never get any sleep. And I *need* sleep for the job I have."

"That part doesn't last forever."

"Then we'd have to raise it and be willing to risk anything."

I shrugged. "That's what love is."

"You're not hearing me," Evan said, shaking his head. He set down his burger and pinned me with an intense gaze. "Having a baby is more than just some physical activity. It's something you have to *mentally* prepare for. 'Cause once you're pregnant, there's no turning back."

Though it was the truth, something in his tone stung. I'd only seen him this livid one other time, and I refused to revisit that memory of us in his living room. The night my inner demons nearly took advantage of me. I pictured the little girl in the shopping cart instead — her white-blonde hair, that perfect little giggle. Her smile when she stared up at her mother.

"I'm well aware of all of those things," I said after a moment, "but having a baby may also be life's greatest adventure. Yeah, we both have incredible achievements under our belts, but a child?" Evan leaned back in his chair and crossed his arms grudgingly. "Imagine a little you running around. Or a little me. Would that not be incredible?"

For a fraction of a second, a smile slipped across his face, but it disappeared too quickly, and he pinched the bridge of his nose.

"I'm not ready to be a dad, Gail."

The statement echoed off the cupboards, making it seem deafening. For what felt like an eternity, neither of us said anything. I stared at my hamburger, suddenly not hungry.

I knew in my mind that I would give anything to have a child. Maybe it was because my own mother left me, and I felt the need to be a *better* mother. Or maybe it was because I wanted something that was permanently mine that I could love forever. But Evan's hesitancy finally brought back a spark of anxiety.

What if I was going crazy, wanting a child like this?

"Look, I'm sorry," Evan sighed, "it's just...that's a crazy thing to ask me."

I couldn't help it, so I asked, "Why?"

He met my eyes again. "You can't have a baby if you're still a kid. And...I feel like I'm still a kid."

There it was: the cold acceptance back into reality. It was actually painful to close the door on such a future, and I pushed my plate away. Evan sighed and shrugged.

"I'll give you permission to convince me." His voice was weary. "But I can't promise anything."

After a moment, I nodded. At least this way, he would consider it. But I didn't push it any more that night. I simply took his hand and tried my best to smile. And after a moment, he smiled, too.

Over the next few months, I became painfully aware of parents and their kids. I would see them out sitting on park benches with ice cream cones. Or a young couple happily walking through the neighborhood with their baby in a stroller. Or a young father teaching his son how to ride a bike. It also didn't help that I was a high school teacher. I found myself asking Naomi, who was a junior this year, how she was doing and if any of her past troubles were still bothering her. I took care of her like she was my own.

I worked my butt off for my students. Together, Evan and I made good money. In a couple of months time, he wouldn't have the excuse of limited funds anymore.

Every once in a while, I would drop hints: little notes or pauses in our conversations to remind him of my extreme desire. He was well aware of what I wanted, yet convincing him was like trying to force a cat into the bath. But I didn't give up hope. I knew deep down that this was the right decision, and Evan was going to be a great father.

We celebrated our one year anniversary in October with a wonderful night out to Jesabell's, a gorgeous Italian restaurant downtown. I was wearing my favorite strapless teal dress, the one that made Evan give me heart eyes, and I was determined to convince him that night. I even ordered us martinis instead of our typical wine and gin.

"You look...*amazing*," he said, clinking his glass against mine.

I tossed a curled lock of hair over my shoulder. "Well, this day is certainly something to commemorate."

We sipped our drinks and got to talking about the good old

days: when we first met and our first kiss, the first time I'd slept with him and how we ate pancakes afterward. The day he told me he loved me.

Once we were full and satisfied from our shared fettuccini alfredo, I decided it was time to make my move.

"You know I love you, right?" My heart burned just by saying it.

Evan took my hand. "Of course. And I love you."

"That's why I know we can do it."

It took him a moment to realize what I meant, and then he sighed and dropped my hand. He leaned back in his seat like he always did. But I wasn't giving up this time.

"Evan, we are amazing people. We are strong and smart and worthy of bringing someone into this world. I know you're scared because I'm scared, too, but think about it." When he started to protest, I said more forcefully, "*Think* about it."

He gave me a look but then closed his eyes.

"Picture me," I said. "My little baby bump. *Our* baby. The day it's born and the joy we'd be feeling...We have the power to raise someone who's going to better this world."

There was a change in my husband's expression. Instead of the skeptical expression he *was* wearing, there was nothing but serenity now. It melted into his features. And then his eyes were open and staring into mine again.

"You really think we can do this?"

"I know we can," I said firmly. "There's no question. Besides..." I dragged my foot up the side of his leg. "There's something else we have to do before the baby arrives."

He only laughed and took my hand once more. "We're just so young, Gail."

"I know." I sighed. "My mom left when I was young. And thank goodness for Jamie, but I just want to prove that I'm the woman my mother wasn't."

"Well, from what you've said about her, I don't think you're anything like her."

A small smile pinched the corners of my lips. "I just want to know what it's like."

Evan exhaled through his nose. He looked around at the tables close by, especially at the one with the family of three in the back corner. When he finally glanced back at me, his eyes had a sharp edge to them. It looked something like caution.

"If you're sure about this, then...I trust you."

We rode home in silence. The sky darkened to welcome a downpour, and the clouds were a combination of magenta and violet, passing slowly over the small town of Rocky River. The rain came quickly, as if in excitement, and then slowed to gentle drops that plopped onto the pavement. Something about the whole storm was mystical and romantic.

Evan led me inside and closed the door. I faced him, feeling somewhat vulnerable. This time would be different. He approached me and slowly kissed my lips. I allowed the feeling to wash over me, to cleanse me of my blazing nerves. When my hands moved to the buttons of his shirt, he tensed.

"It's okay," I whispered. "We can do this."

He glanced back at my lips and nodded slowly.

I pulled him back to me and kissed him more fiercely. "We only have one life. Let's live fearlessly."

I took his hand and led him toward our bedroom.

Each day for an entire week, I looked into the mirror and oscillated my body, trying to detect any changes in my appearance. But there were none.

I pictured a tiny bundle of happiness asleep in my arms. I pictured us laughing together, learning together. I imagined my father's reaction when I would tell him. And what Cara and Erica and Elijah would say. It consumed me with happiness.

But waiting was the hardest part.

"No bump yet," I said, folding down my night shirt and going to crawl in bed with Evan.

"That doesn't happen for a while, Gail."

I flopped down next to him and rested my hands on my stomach. "I know, but I just can't wait. What should we name it?"

When Evan didn't answer, I glanced over at him. He was clicking through his camera, reviewing the day's work. He noticed my attention and met my eyes.

"Huh? Oh, I'm not sure."

He resumed clicking and something about it offended me. But I kept my voice light. "What about Willow? I've always loved that name. Or Griffin?"

The clicking continued, and I rolled my eyes.

"Evan."

He looked over at me. "What?"

"You know, if you love that thing so much, you should've married *it* and not me. Are you really gonna cheat on me with a camera?" It was meant to be a joke, but Evan missed the punchline.

"Would you just *relax*?"

I sat up, taken aback by his unexpected outburst. "What is wrong with you?"

"What's wrong with *you*?"

I was having that strange, out-of-body experience you get when you fight with someone you love, and it feels off like it might be a dream. But this was no dream. I didn't understand what was more important than the name of our child, and for a split second, I felt like we were enemies instead of allies.

This must have been showing on my face because Evan laid his head in his hands and said, "I'm sorry, Gail. It was a rough day." His sapphire eyes were piercing blue.

He fell back onto the pillows and ran a hand through his

shaggy hair. I stared at him, not sure what to make of the situation. Because now, something really didn't feel right. I wanted to touch him, to hold his hand, but the action seemed unwelcomed. Instead, I pressed a hand against my still flat belly.

"Evan," I said gently.

He looked at me and smiled though it was clearly forced.

"Ev, we communicate with each other. Always. You can tell me if something's wrong."

His jaw had a habit of clenching just like Colton's did. It flexed crazily against his skin like it might pop out. And there was an odd emotion that crossed his face, but whatever it was, I couldn't name it. His false smile returned. "Of course."

I nodded. Even though I knew something was wrong, I didn't broach it...maybe for my own sake. Instead, I let his fib trick me like it was the truth, and I laid down beside him. What I didn't know couldn't kill me.

"So Willow?"

A small beat of silence passed. "How do you know it's gonna be a girl?" I was relieved to hear amusement in his tone.

"Just a guess."

"Well then sure. But if it's a boy...I kind of like Gavin."

"Gavin?"

The name echoed in my ears, ringing a clear bell of approval. "I like it."

"Good, then it's settled."

Evan turned out the light and drew me against him.

Nearly a month later, I had the misfortune of grading forty individual playing tests from my students. Evan had gone to work, so I was alone in the kitchen, typing away on my laptop and listening to all of the recordings. They were actually pretty good. I was more than impressed with my students' progress. But it was raining outside, and I felt sluggish and irritated, which made the task of grading way more difficult. Eventually, I couldn't sit still any longer and went to fix myself some tea.

I tapped my foot impatiently as I dipped the tea bag into the water because it was taking forever to seep in, and I was extremely thirsty for some reason. Finally, I drew the cup to my lips and nearly choked. The tea scorched my tongue, and I winced. My mouth felt like it had been incinerated.

This tiny incident made me want to punch right through the wall. I ground my teeth and clenched my fists until my nails dug into the skin of my palm. *What was my problem today?* Heaving a frustrated sigh, I returned to my laptop. But as I sat down, a thought occurred to me.

I pulled a tracker app up on my phone and waited for it to load. Finally, at the top of the screen were the words Good morning, Gail. You are EIGHT DAYS LATE for your period.

My brain twisted around this information, but nothing clicked. Eight days couldn't be right. I was supposed to have gotten my period last—

I froze. The world froze. And ever so slightly, understanding curled and stretched inside me. I inhaled, feeling the pulsating sensation of shock, and placed my hand against my stomach. Goosebumps pricked my skin. I tried to gather my thoughts.

Yeah, okay, it all made sense now. My irritability, my tender breasts, the *missed period.*

"Oh my God, oh my God," I chanted as I slammed my laptop shut and grabbed my car keys.

My knees were rubber as I walked into the drug store and grabbed a pregnancy test from one of the shelves. The lady at the cash register rang the item through and then gave me a genuine smile. I didn't miss it when her eyes swept over my abdomen.

Back at home, I followed the instructions on the box and then collapsed against the wall of the bathroom. My breathing was shallow as if I'd just run a marathon, and I pulled my knees up to my chest, holding the pregnancy test away from me like it was some type of weapon. To distract myself, I envisioned that perfect future: me and Evan pushing a stroller down the sidewalk. Hearing my daughter laugh for the first time. Hearing her say she loved me.

Not able to resist it any longer, I squeezed my eyes shut and then cautiously opened one eye to examine the test. Two lines for pregnant, one line for not. And sure enough, two pink lines stretched down the screen.

An indescribable feeling burst through me. I suddenly felt too cramped there in the tiny bathroom; I needed to run outside and scream and dance and jump into the sky. On top of this intoxicating enthusiasm, there was also a tsunami of fear. Fear of the unknown, fear of protection, fear of the pain of childbirth. But the positive overwhelmed the negative, and I sprung up from the ground to go call everyone I knew.

My phone conversations lasted well into the afternoon as Cara and Erica couldn't stop crying. Elijah was speechless. He stumbled through a congratulatory speech, but it was clear he was too overcome with emotion to speak. After hanging up with him, I considered dialing my father's number but thought better of it. I would tell him in person.

Evan came home around seven o'clock. I made his favorite meal for dinner: chicken cacciatore with steamed, buttered broccoli.

"How was work?" I asked, surprised I could conceal my excitement at all.

"Great. Xander had me out taking pictures of the trees today for some Autumn festival they advertise for."

I nodded. "Nice."

I watched him eat for a moment, and then I was out of my seat. He looked up at me, alarmed by my sudden movement, but it was all I could do to stand still.

"Evan...I'm pregnant."

He dropped his fork, and it collided against his glass plate, which made both of us jump. But then he was on his feet, too.

"Wow," was all he could say as his face drained of color.

"Isn't this *incredible?*" I threw my arms around him and screamed into his shirt.

He held me loosely. "It's something."

"I guess my emotions are gonna be pretty whack for a little while," I said, stepping back to face him with a wide grin. "I'm sorry in advance...you know, for being a bitch or whining or whatever's gonna happen. But just know that I love you with all my heart."

His smile was strained. "Of course."

A lot of little things went into being pregnant. I had to start taking prenatal vitamins and call to make an appointment with the doctor. I had to check the labels of my makeup to make sure they didn't contain chemicals that could harm my baby. I had to say goodbye to some of my favorite fried foods and force myself to spend some extra time in the gym. My throat was always parched; no amount of water could satiate me, and then of course, I was always using the bathroom.

Evan and I went shopping to purchase the healthiest, most organic foods possible and to search for a crib. By the end of November, we'd sectioned off the back corner of our bedroom with a rocking chair and crib, and things were starting to feel official.

My students' reactions were priceless. Some of them jumped all around me, nearly dropping their instruments in the process. Others congratulated me in passing, and some just lifted their eyebrows as if to say, "Wow. Cool."

Evan and I finally returned to Saratoga Springs the Tuesday before Thanksgiving. Evan sat behind the wheel so that I could contemplate the best way to tell my father. It had to come out of nowhere and shock him. This had to be one for the books.

"I think I have an idea," Evan said as we crossed the New York state line.

It was genius, of course, so I was a jittery mess by the time we finally arrived.

Ever the gracious cook, Jamie had Thanksgiving dinner ready for us when we walked through the door. Dad shook Evan's hand —best friends reuniting—and then came to give me a hug.

"Help yourself," Jamie said, welcoming us to the table.

Before we could dig in though, Dad grunted and stood up from his chair. "To love, friendship, and health," he said, holding up his soda can.

We all held up a glass and then took a drink. My father lowered his eyes and turned his can around in his hands. He was never great at speeches, and the pink color flushing his cheeks spoke for itself. I giggled.

"Uh, I'm grateful that my daughter has found someone so loving," he muttered, staring down at the table. "You guys are great for each other. And I'm grateful for Jamie here, who has...pretty much kept me sane over the years."

Jamie flashed her kind smile.

Evan squeezed my hand under the table—a signal.

"Dad, we should take a family picture on Evan's professional camera this year," I suggested.

"That's a great idea," Jamie said, beaming.

My father, having always detested the idea of being in photos, grimaced.

"Oh, come on, Dad!" I urged.

He looked at Jamie who raised her eyebrows in hope. And he couldn't say no to that.

"All right, fine."

So, as we crowded into the living room after our delicious

meal, I felt my heart skip a beat. I leaned into Evan for support, and he squeezed my shoulders reassuringly.

"No fear, right?" he whispered.

Evan set his camera on the mantle and set it to count down from five. He positioned us accordingly and then clicked a button and rushed to take his place. I counted the beeps in my head, though they were hard to hear over the blood rushing in my ears. Finally, at one, I said, "Oh, by the way, I'm pregnant."

The picture had to be one of the greatest photos of all time. I was staring at my father, grinning cheek to cheek. Jamie was a raging ball of energy, her mouth hanging open mid-shriek. And my father simply stared at the camera, his face stark white and frozen in disbelief.

"Surprise," I said.

Jamie screamed and wrapped her arms around me. Dad dragged a hand down his face as his eyes flicked between me and Evan. Eventually, he exhaled and shook his head.

"Congratulations. But I'm too young to be a grandpa. D-do I look like a—?" He gestured to Jamie, running a hand through his graying hair.

Evan laughed and then passed his camera around for everyone to see. "That's a keeper."

"So," Dad swallowed loudly, something he did when he was nervous, "h-how are things? How's the...baby doing? Do you know?"

"She's fine," I assured him with a gentle smile.

"She?" Jamie repeated hopefully.

"We obviously don't know yet," Evan answered before I could. "Gail just really wants a daughter."

"Well, what if I want a grandson?" Dad joked.

"You'll have to wait and see," I said.

We had quite the Thanksgiving outing. After celebrating with my dad and Jamie, we traveled all the way to Delaware to be with Evan's family. And when we pulled the same trick on them,

Beth actually started crying. Gracy and Dani were over the moon, and Lain clapped Evan on the back.

"What's it gonna be, Gail?" he asked. "Am I gonna have a niece or a nephew?"

"Can't say for sure, Lain," I answered.

"Well, I'm hoping for a girl!" Gracy cried. "Then we can play Barbies together."

After wiping her eyes on the edge of her apron, Beth pulled me into her arms. "If you need *anything*, give us a call. We'll always be here for you, honey."

And then I thanked her profusely because she had always been so sweet and welcoming to me. Almost like the mother I'd lost. Like the mother I wanted to be.

At dinner that night while the rest of them debated over which football teams were going to make the Super Bowl, I caught Dani's eye.

"How's the book going?" I asked.

She shrugged and plopped a piece of ham into her mouth. "It's hard to say. I'm having awful writer's block right now, so I'm taking a break to see if I can gain some inspiration."

"Makes sense."

She kept eyeing my stomach and then looking away.

"It's okay," I said. "Is there something you want to know?"

Her lips twitched, and then she leaned forward so as to make our conversation more private. "What's it like?"

I set my fork down and glanced over at Evan, who was in a heated debate about some quarterback with his brother and parents.

"To be honest, it's a little scary," I answered. "But it also feels right, like it's meant to happen. Does that make sense?"

She nodded, seeming lost in thought. "It's just that one of my characters is gonna be pregnant in a few chapters, so I guess this is perfect timing."

I laughed. "Well, then I'm glad I can be your inspiration."

Her face instantly lit up like an actual light bulb, and then she asked to be excused.

"Wait, where're you going?" I asked.

"To get my planning journal. You gave me an idea." She balked mid-sprint up the hall and then turned back to me. "You really are the best, Gail."

A few weeks after Christmas, Cara flew in to visit while Evan was away on a business trip. Today, she was accompanying me to my next check up.

I watched the shops and restaurants cruise by as we drove past. "What about you, Cara, no baby yet?"

Cara maneuvered the car through the neighborhood and shrugged. "Not yet. We're both still undecided. But it's better to talk it out than to just assume, you know?"

I recalled Evan's hesitancy and placed a protective hand on my abdomen. "Yeah."

"Speaking of babies, is Evan shaping up to be the best dad ever?"

"Yeah. Well...maybe."

We approached a stoplight, and she tapped her brakes. "What does that mean?"

"Nothing. He's just distant sometimes. Like one minute, he's present, and we're talking about our baby, but the next minute he's—"

"Different?" Cara offered.

"You could say that."

We began moving again. "Well, that's stupid! Have you talked to him about it?"

I went to answer, but closed my mouth as I realized, no. I hadn't.

"Communication is everything, Gail. Without that and trust, relationships can't be stable."

"I know that."

I glanced down at my belly and envisioned a tiny, precious face staring back. That always cheered me up.

"Hey, it'll be okay," Cara said after a moment. "It'll work itself out."

But she had me thinking now. Was it rude of Evan to not take off work to accompany me to this appointment? Or was I just overthinking like usual?

"Mrs. Caldwell, hello! How are you?" Doctor Bellinx exclaimed as she entered the room.

She then asked me the usual questions: was I sleeping? What was I eating? Was I staying active? We ran through the whole thing and she pressed on my belly and explained that the baby could start kicking as soon as eighteen weeks. At the end of the appointment, Dr. Bellinx copied all of this into a computer and saved it.

"So, where's the hubby today?" she inquired conversationally.

"Working," I answered.

I watched Cara roll her eyes from where she was standing in the corner.

"Well, that's too bad," my doctor said. She clicked out of her document and turned back to me. "Every woman's different, but you'll start to show around twelve to sixteen weeks, so...middle of January. And then I'll see you in February for your next ultrasound. That's when we'll be able to determine the gender of your baby."

"Can't wait." I flashed her a smile. "And my husband will definitely be here for that appointment."

But just to be sure, I decided to broach the issue that night. Communicate, as Cara had put it.

"Evan, do you think it's possible that you...work too much?"

He was folding laundry and storing the clothes in a drawer. "No. Why?"

I shrugged and went to help him. "I don't know. I just kinda wanted you there with me today."

"It was just a checkup. I bet they asked you the same questions they do every time. And have you had any changes?" He turned to face me, and I shook my head. "Exactly."

Cara was out in the living room, asleep on the couch, yet I wished she could be in here to back me up.

"Well...still. Next time, you're coming with me."

"All right." It didn't sound very convincing.

"You're being a jerk."

He dropped his folded shirt on the bed and turned his cold gaze back to me. "How am I being a jerk?"

"You act like you want nothing to do with this baby!"

"You know that's not true."

"How should I know? You always disappear when I need you. Or when *she* needs you."

"You don't even know if it's a girl yet!"

"Does it matter?" I screamed.

And all went quiet. I hoped I didn't disturb Cara, though with my rising anger that was probably inevitable.

"I'm only gonna ask this once," I said through a hushed voice. Still, there was acid dripping from my tone. "Do you love me?"

It was the typical reaction: clenched jaw, running a hand through his soft, blond hair. Hesitancy. And then, "Of course I do."

"Then you should love her."

I threw his stupid shirt in the drawer and then crawled into bed, trying to stay as far to the edge as possible so that I wouldn't be near him. A part of me felt pride for putting him in his place, but another part of me was breaking that we even had to have that conversation. Something between us was changing, and for the first time in my life, I fell asleep truly despising Evan Caldwell.

The next morning, Cara and I sat down to breakfast together. Evan had already left for work.

"So," Cara said after sipping her coffee. I already knew what she was gonna say, and I pressed a hand against my forehead. "It's not my place to judge, Gail. And I really am over the moon happy for you and Evan, but...I just want to make sure things between the two of you are cool."

"You heard, didn't you?"

She shrugged and took a bite of her omelet.

"Everything's fine." It sounded like I was trying harder to convince myself. "Evan just loses perspective sometimes, I think."

"Maybe you do, too," Cara offered, and I gave her a sharp look. "I'm not saying this—" she gestured to my abdomen, "—is a mistake, so put that out of your head. I'm simply suggesting you and Evan try to hear each other out a little more. There's nothing wrong with arguing. All couples do it. But you two have a kid on the way now. Shouldn't that bring you closer together?"

I stared into the depths of my cup, feeling determined to change something. "You're right."

As Dr. Bellinx had predicted, my abdomen started to swell in January. I once again found myself staring into the mirror, turning this way and that, obsessing over the growing bump. It amazed me that there was another human being growing inside of me. But while that simple fact blew my mind, I was also starting to feel heavy and misshapen. I'd read stories about other women's pregnancies and knew that soon, I wouldn't be able to wear tight jeans or bend to tie my own shoes. It was a self-esteem killer to say the least.

And carrying was not as easy as the movies and TV shows

made it seem. February was the worst. No one told me that morning sickness could last into the second trimester. Most days, I awoke to a stunning dizziness and came to with my head lodged in the toilet, puking up whatever was in my stomach. I became crabby and impatient, and if I didn't eat something salty *this* second, I would rip someone's head off. No one told me my husband would become my terrified servant either. It would've been funny to see him scrambling around for me if I didn't feel unbearably bloated and short-tempered all the time. He went everywhere for me, that was, when he wasn't working, which was pretty much never. But no one told me that my sense of smell would become bionic either. If I was even in a five-mile radius of fish, I would vomit profusely.

But through all the stress and alterations, I felt my heart changing as well. I had loved and lost people in my life, yet this...*baby* growing inside me was mine to love and keep forever. I would protect her with my life, and I would *give* her a life worth living.

In the moments when I was me and not a stone-cold bitch, I felt like I was sharing this intimate, private connection with my baby. A connection that no one else could ever understand or interpret. We spoke to each other without words, in a language only we knew. It was one of the most surreal things I'd ever experienced.

The end of February arrived before we knew it, and I insisted that Evan drive me to my appointment. We were silent in the car and in the waiting room, which made me want to cry. I'd been crying a lot recently.

"Welcome back, Mrs. Caldwell. Mr. Caldwell, how are you?" Doctor Bellinx greeted us.

She led us into a separate room where a woman waited by a large screen.

"Gail, this is Krissy Treajen. She will be your ultrasound technician."

The girl smiled at us and gestured for me to lie down on the table. We ran through the usual questions, and this time, I happily explained that I'd felt kicking the previous week. I was alone to witness the incredible event; Evan had been working.

"You're right on track then, Mrs. Caldwell," Krissy said.

I jumped under her touch as she smeared a cold, clear paste on my stomach and pelvis. I instinctively reached for Evan's hand. We both glanced at our intertwined fingers and then at each other, and he smiled the smile I'd been missing for days.

"Okay, let's see what we have here," Krissy murmured, pressing a probe against my skin.

My heart was pounding out of my chest, and I squeezed Evan's hand as images of darkness flashed across the screen. It seemed we were all holding our breaths and then...

"Ah, here we go."

I stared at the footage, feeling tears well up in my eyes. Krissy guided the probe over my belly, and there was the head. And the body. And the tiny legs. And the beauty of it nearly stunned me to death.

"It appears that the baby's heartbeat is 139 beats per minute," the technician announced, squinting at the screen. She muttered something about a cranial notch, which went straight over my head, and then she grinned. "Congratulations Mr. and Mrs. Caldwell. You're having a baby boy."

Evan squeezed my hand. "That's incredible."

I stared at the screen, in awe over the sight. *Blue, not pink,* my conscience chastised. But what did it matter? The image on the screen revealed the small bundle of joy that was huddled up in my stomach, waiting to enter this world and be loved and accepted. I didn't want to look away.

"Have we thought of any names yet?" Krissy asked.

Evan and I glanced at each other, and all remaining arguments fell through the floorboards. We were on the same team again, now and forever.

"Gavin," we answered in unison.

The technician smiled politely and copied the information on the screen into a separate computer. She printed a small piece of paper along with a photograph of the ultrasound and handed it to me before congratulating us again and slipping out the door.

Doctor Bellinx reentered the room with a file under her arm. She pulled the rolling stool away from the wall and took a seat. "First of all, congratulations on your baby boy. I have a son at home, just getting into those teenage years." She rolled her eyes and smiled. "But let's talk about delivery."

The word sent a spike of fear down my spine, and I swallowed nervously. In all my excitement to *meet* the baby, I'd forgotten that the scariest part was yet to come.

"According to your charts, you're set to deliver on July fifteenth. That's your predicted date. Anything earlier would be around July tenth or as late as July twenty-fifth."

"Ooh, right around your birthday," Evan chirped happily.

The doctor grinned. "It'd be one heck of a birthday present."

I tried to smile, but now I was thinking about the pain I'd have to endure, and a cold sweat broke out over my forehead.

"Well, you have a few options, Abigail," the doctor continued. "Obviously, the most common option is hospitalized, assisted delivery. With that, either I would be in with you or another obstetrician." She continued through several other options, most of which I forgot the name of as soon as she moved on.

I told her that I was terrified of the pain, so she suggested an epidural and listed all the pros and cons of such a method. It actually made me a little angry, the fact that there was no clear-cut way to do this.

"It's up to you," she said with a nonchalant shrug. "It's your child. In the meantime, practice calmness and continue what you're doing."

There was a lot to think about on the way home, and I was starting to get a headache, so I tried to focus on the gorgeous spring trees outside the car window.

The future was so close now; it brushed my fingertips. And pregnancy, special as it was, was getting extremely old. I wanted to meet my baby, hold him, hug him, hear his laugh. It was all I could think about.

Something changed after that appointment because Evan suddenly became my own personal superman. For the next four months, he distracted me with card games, fabulously cooked meals, and small walks around the block. He held my spirits high when I had to announce to my students that I would be leaving on maternity soon. They all wished me luck and promised to practice as much as possible. Naomi even gave me a card, saying how happy she was for me. Evan clipped it to the fridge so that I could see it and be reminded. He held me close in the evenings and kept his distance when my crabbiness returned. He sat and listened as I played my violin for our son.

At the start of July, Evan's boss Xander forced him on a weekend-long trip to Columbus so he could take pictures of a national tennis match. I didn't understand the excitement around the trip until Evan claimed his photos would be featured in a sports catalogue and that this was a huge opportunity.

"It's only one weekend, and you're not due for another week and a half."

"Or a couple days," I reminded him with a shiver.

He pulled me in for a hug and kissed my forehead. "If you feel anything at all, call me, and I'll be home as fast as I can."

I sighed. "Have a good time."

"Hey," he said before disappearing out the door. I glanced back at him. "I love you."

"I love you, too."

The house felt so empty without my husband here. It almost made me nervous, like something was going to happen. Either I'd slip into an early labor or I'd pass out or something equally terrifying would occur. But I did as my doctor instructed and focused on my breathing instead.

It was a long weekend. I completed my exercises, cooked myself meals and found work around the house. I also spent a few hours with a book and watched plenty of mind-numbing television.

Sometimes, I would just sit in our bedroom in the new rocking chair and let my imagination run wild. *Soon,* I told myself. *Soon, you'll be able to hold him here.* It was quiet and peaceful. I rocked gently back and forth, nearly crying when I felt him kick.

"This is your home, Gavin," I whispered. "This is where we're gonna raise you. And I can't wait." The truth in the words overwhelmed me. "I can't wait to watch you grow up and laugh and fall in love..."

Without even realizing it, I was picturing Colton Reeves. His handsome face, those gold-green eyes. It was the first I'd thought of him in two years, and it brought on a whirlwind of emotion. I told myself it was just the hormones, the pregnancy itself, the major changes that were coming. But in my mind, I was sixteen again, holding hands with the loving boy from my past.

In that moment, I felt old and fragile. It had been ten years since Colton kissed me in his backyard by the crackling fire. Ten years since we lounged in the summer sun, laughing until we cried. Ten years and it still felt like yesterday. What would life be like if we'd remained friends? What would he say if he knew I was nine months pregnant, when...once upon a time, I'd dreamed of carrying *his* child?

Gavin's kick was harsh this time, and I grunted at the pain. It was enough to bring me back to the present, and I swiped at the runaway tear that was trickling down my cheek. I glanced down at my swollen belly and shook my head at how strange life could be.

On the morning of July fifteenth, I was a nervous wreck. For days my lower back had been killing me, and I spent more time using the bathroom than normal. Most obvious of all, I found it easier to breathe these days, meaning my baby was dropping lower, a sure sign Gavin was sick of waiting around. He wanted to be a part of this world, and today he would be.

My body couldn't stop quivering as if it was bracing for impact. Bracing for the pain. Evan was glued to my side, and at first I thought it was because today was delivery day, but then I realized he hadn't left my side since he returned home from Columbus.

"Are you okay?" It was the twelfth time he'd asked me in the span of forty-five minutes. His eyes glinted with an emotion I couldn't name. His constant questioning nearly suffocated me. I needed room to breathe, to collect myself, to brace for impact.

"I'm fine right now," I assured him again. "Geez, you're worse than me."

Normally, he would've chuckled in response, but he didn't even meet my eyes.

We sat down for lunch, and I watched him eat his turkey sandwich with trembling hands. It just seemed uncharacteristic...even for today. In all my hard times, Evan was the calm one, so why was he glancing all around like a bomb was about to go off?

"I think it's time I ask you," I said after a bite of salad. "Are *you* okay?"

He stared at me for a moment, and that was when I realized the difference. The tiniest bit of guilt was hiding in his eyes, and if I didn't know him so well, it would've gone undetected.

"I'm all right."

I waited, but it was clear he wasn't going to elaborate. My lips moved to speak, but I was quickly cut off by an unexpected sensation. I twisted in my seat, suddenly uncomfortable. I set my fork down and watched Evan devour his sandwich for a few seconds longer, trying to decipher what my body was telling me. It had been the slightest feeling. I wasn't sure if I'd only imagined it.

"Uh..." I stared at the table like the answer was plastered there. All of my muscles and organs were frozen; my body was on high alert.

Evan stared at me, his mouth full and eyes wide.

After a moment, I just shook my head. "I don't know. I thought—"

A second gush made me clench my jaw so hard it could've popped.

"Gail?" Evan asked in an alarmed tone.

I took a breath once the sensation faded and glanced at the clock. 12:09 p.m.

"I think my water just broke."

Evan threw his chair back and lunged for his car keys on the counter. I watched him toss water bottles into a backpack cooler and snatch the pamphlet on breathing techniques off the fridge door.

All the while, he was chanting, "Oh my God, oh my God, oh my—"

"Evan, relax." I grabbed a paperback book off the couch and met him at the door. "It's gonna be all right."

On the way to the hospital, Evan called my father, who was already on his way from Saratoga Springs. Beth and Grant were also not far away, having left very early that morning. Steering with one hand, Evan tried to rub soothing circles into the skin of my palm, but I hardly felt it. Gavin was becoming impatient; I knew it in my soul.

"Keep breathing," Evan instructed.

I rolled my eyes. "What did you think I was gonna do? Hold my breath?"

"Sorry."

Once I was examined and Evan filled out some paperwork, I was admitted to the hospital, and a nurse led us down the hall. She got me situated into a gown and then helped me into a bed. Doctor Bellinx was quick to show up, wearing her usual smile.

"Right on track," she assured me in a light voice.

I appreciated that a nurse was always present so that when another round of contractions attacked my body, she coached me through it in a sweet, polite manner. As time passed, the contractions got more painful, and I was getting more angsty. Evan never left, of course, writhing in his own pain as I squeezed his hand.

Dad and Jamie arrived around one o'clock, and my father collapsed in the blue recliner in the corner.

"I remember the day *you* were born," he said. Jamie placed her hand on his shoulder because now, his eyes were shimmering.

I wasn't in the mood for an *I remember when* speech from my father, especially when my pelvis felt like it was on fire, and I wanted nothing more than to scream at everyone. When the pain subsided once more, I drew a deep breath and tried to be kind.

"You don't have to worry about me," I told Dad. "You raised me well, and I'm gonna do the same for my son."

It was an infuriatingly slow afternoon. Beth and Grant got to the hospital at three, and Beth recounted each of her children's births, which only made Evan groan and made me want to rip the hair from my scalp. The contractions continued to worsen. I was relieved when the pain faded, if only slightly.

Doctor Bellinx came back at a quarter to four, and at the sight of her, terror shot through me like a bullet. Having her there meant it was getting close to delivery time. She spent a few minutes chatting and laughing with my family. A part of me felt like this was some kind of calming technique. Her airy conversations were meant to distract from the fact that she was now donning a mask and rubber gloves. Another contraction seared my abdomen in half, and I threw my head back in agony.

"I'm right here," Evan insisted for the third time, rubbing my arm for comfort.

But if he kept saying that, I was going to bite his head off.

Doctor Bellinx pulled a rolling stool to the foot of my bed, where she examined me and murmured, "Ten centimeters." Her eyes flicked between her watch and a monitor above my head. It was time. My father and Grant went to stand just outside the door, and Dad gave me a thumbs-up like this was gonna be as simple as a violin solo on stage. Beth and Jamie came to either side of the bed.

"Okay, Abigail," Dr. Bellinx said, "you've got a big contraction coming. We're gonna push on this one, okay?"

I grabbed Evan's hand and braced for impact.

The pain was like a knife slowly being dragged across the lower half of my body. It hurt so bad that a scream escaped my trembling lips, but that felt way better than keeping it pent up. Evan, who had promised to be emotionally supportive, was screaming, too, probably because my grip was cutting off the circulation in his hand. Not to mention he looked like a deer frozen in the headlights.

"Push," Doctor Bellinx ordered.

Her face was tranquil, like this was an everyday sight to her. It probably was.

Flames crawled their way up my body, and I squeezed my eyes shut with all the effort to get my baby out.

"I see a head," Doctor Bellinx announced happily.

"Come on, honey, you've got this," Jamie coached.

"One more big push, Abigail."

I gritted my teeth, nearly passing out as the torturous pain bit into my flesh. But then someone else was screaming. I laid my head back against the pillows, unsure if I was just imagining it, but I wasn't. A baby's cries echoed off the walls. My eyes, wet from crying, stared up at the ceiling as I felt my body slip into a sort of welcomed numbness.

"Oh, he's beautiful," Beth gushed.

And then Evan was wiping his own tears.

"Congratulations, Mr. and Mrs. Caldwell," Doctor Bellinx said.

I forced my head up to peer down to the foot of the bed. And there in the doctor's arms was my perfect bundle of joy.

Chapter Twenty

NOVEMBER 2081

Abigail blinked and lifted her eyes from the paper. It was snowing today, and fluffy, little crystals cascaded toward the ground. It was mesmerizing to watch, and Abigail lost herself in the beauty for a few minutes.

The house was cold and empty these days, like a brittle ghost town of memories. Chilling gray light spilled in through the windows, and Abigail shivered in her cardigan. What she would give to have her husband here with her on these dank, isolating afternoons. What she would give to sit with him one more time, to sip hot chocolate and watch a nice movie.

Abigail had been feeling this way for some time—gloomy and dejected. She'd spent this whole week with her old friends Elijah and Brie, Christmas shopping and going out for lunch. But it was as if Abigail's inner light was growing dimmer and dimmer. Not because she was weakening, but because she simply missed the man she loved. Missed his arms and his lovely smell, his radiant smile, and his glowing eyes. She would give anything to have that back.

But this was why she wrote as much as she did. The writing was her ticket back in time. With this pen and this piece of paper, Abigail could feel him again and remember what it was like to be young and in love. It was the only way she knew how to cope; otherwise, the doctor would put her on more Cymbalta to combat the depression. And that was the *last* thing Abigail wanted.

She reread the sentence she'd just finished and laughed breathlessly. What a day that had been, Gavin's birth. She remembered the anger and the fear and the exhaustion. She remembered nearly punching the lights out of Evan if he didn't stop whispering to her. The memory made Abigail chuckle harder. Flash forward to today, as her son was the lead manager of his company.

It was crazy how fast time flew by.

Sometimes, writing was hard for the very reason it was enjoyable. Writing about all of these events in her life was like walking through a garden of memories before heading straight to her death. As much as she hated to admit it, Abigail wasn't young and sturdy anymore. She was simply an old woman recalling her life story. But maybe that was why she did it. She needed her children to have a piece of her forever, even after the Lord above decided to call her home.

Abigail sighed and took a sip of her drink. It was chamomile tea, her husband's favorite. It burned her windpipe on the way down, but it was a soothing warmth, hot enough to chase away the chill that was always in her bones these days. She pictured her husband's face one more time and then returned her attention to the story.

Chapter Twenty-One

ROCKY RIVER, OH (2026—2027)

Gavin was beautiful. I sat in the rocking chair and held him close in my arms. His blue-gray eyes peered into mine and then drooped closed as he fell asleep. I slowed my rocking, unable to look away.

I must have been dreaming. All that waiting and preparing led to this moment, and it was beyond anything I could have ever imagined. From the tiny cap on top of his small head to his button nose, my baby was stunning. The purity in his sleeping angel's face made my heart squeeze, and I pressed my lips together to try to hold back the tears.

Nothing felt better than this. I contemplated whispering just how much I loved him but thought better of it because I didn't want to wake him and face a crying fit. Besides, this was the first time in a week that I'd had a peaceful silence.

I gently lowered Gavin into his crib, as careful as someone trying not to set off a bomb, and then sighed in relief when I didn't wake him. Then I tiptoed out and closed the door behind me.

Evan was sitting at the table, typing away on his laptop.

"Oh, Gail, come here!"

"Shh!" I hissed at him, holding a finger to my lips.

"Sorry," he whispered. "But come here. They finally posted the sports article with my pictures of the tennis match."

I sat down beside him and laid my head on his shoulder as he scrolled through a sports webpage. The site displayed several courtside photos that were snapped at perfect intervals. The last one portrayed a man in yellow holding his racket up in the air triumphantly.

"Evan, these are amazing. No wonder your boss recommended you. How much did you make again?"

"Eight-hundred, but that doesn't include all the extra time I put in to capture their interviews afterward."

"Holy crap."

"I'm kinda bummed though," he admitted forlornly. "They didn't use my favorites. There are a whole lot more on my camera, some better than these. But oh well. It's the money that counts, I guess."

"Wait, there are pictures *better* than these?" I exclaimed, gesturing to the computer screen in shock. "Let me see them."

Evan's eyes darkened. "Nah, don't worry about it."

I stared at him. "Is that a joke?"

"No," he said, forcing a smile. "I'm just glad they picked me at all, like you said. That was an awesome opportunity, and hopefully now that they've seen my work, Xander will be able to book me for more public events."

"I'm sure he will."

Something about the way Evan glanced at his camera didn't sit right in the pit of my stomach, but I didn't ask. I didn't like the way my muscles tensed like something could be wrong. I'd felt that same sensation before, and it made my palms clammy. Besides, Evan was the love of my life. He could do no wrong. I repeated this in my mind until I was convinced and laid my head back against Evan's shoulder.

"Are you ready for dinner?" I asked. "I think we have some chicken left over from—"

"Oh, don't worry about that. What are you hungry for? Let me cook you something."

I glanced up at him, surprised by the unexpected offer, especially after seven sleepless nights. But he flashed his handsome smile that I couldn't say no to.

"Well...I have been kind of in the mood for fajitas. You know, like you made when we first moved in."

"Coming right up." He kissed the crown of my head and moved into the kitchen.

I sat at the table and watched him work, happy to be cooked *for* for a change. As he tossed some ground meat into a pan, my eyes fell back to his camera, and that nagging feeling swirled through me again. I couldn't name the emotion; I could only describe it: a desire to know something that was probably better left unknown. But it had to have just been my anxiety making its impending return.

Evan turned back to face me. "You know, later we should—"

He was cut off by the sharp, piercing cry of our newborn baby, and I rubbed my eyes. So much for a peaceful silence. Still, it was a joy to hear.

"Hold that thought," I said and rose to go tend to Gavin.

Evan was suddenly superhuman. He held Gavin and made him giggle. He changed diapers, entertained the baby while I showered and cooked, and he read to Gavin each night. I even got to live out my dream of walking arm in arm with my husband as we strolled through the park with our son in a stroller. It made it even better that Gavin was a fairly easy baby. Having read countless blogs about colic babies, I'd been worried Gavin would struggle. But my son surprised me. As the weeks turned into months, he cried less and less.

When my father and Jamie came to visit in early September, Gavin reacted harmlessly, almost as if he'd known my father his whole life. Dad, once opposed to being a grandfather, now fit right into the role as he held my son and chuckled with him.

"Wow, Dad, your hair's getting really gray," I said, squinting at his head.

He turned his attention to me, clearly offended. "You don't stay young forever, sweetheart."

"Ain't that the truth." Evan nodded.

I finally returned to work in October, which was tremendously difficult. But it helped, for once, that my students were a bunch of nosy teenagers, wanting to know every detail. So, I got to talk about my baby for some time before I forced them to sit down and rehearse for the fall concert.

For Gavin's first Halloween, we dressed him up in a skeleton suit. Evan sat him on the porch steps next to the pumpkins we carved and snapped a few dozen pictures. I was frozen, gushing over how adorable Gavin was. He stared up at us, his chubby face devoid of emotion. He didn't know what was going on, and here we were torturing him with flashes of bright light.

"All right, I guess that's enough," Evan said, sighing.

"Let me see!" I squealed.

Evan set his camera down and scooped up Gavin instead. "I'll print them and show them to you. Don't worry, they're all great," he assured me when I started to protest.

It went on like this for some time. Evan photographed Gavin's first Thanksgiving, Christmas, even his first Valentine's Day. And each time I tugged on Evan's arm to see the photos, he would claim they were all amazing and that I'd see them in due time. They *were* amazing, once Evan printed them and I could finally see them. Some I framed, some I clipped to the fridge alongside Evan's lovely photos of nature.

Life became a kind of wonderful monotony, the kind you're grateful for, even if you days were replicas of each other. Everything was perfect.

Until the following March.

Evan didn't have to be into work until noon one day, which was a rare occurrence, so while he and the baby slept, I tiptoed into the kitchen to whip up some pancakes. The sun was just beginning to peak over the horizon, smearing streaks of orange through the sky. While the pancake batter sizzled on the skillet, I stared out into the clouds, losing myself in their beauty. It was when I looked away that I noticed Evan's camera sitting alone and unattended on the kitchen table.

A tingle curled down my spine.

Why wouldn't Evan ever let me look through his photos? Was there something he was hiding? Was it bad? I swallowed nervously. It was one of those situations you saw on TV, where the devil was on your left shoulder and an angel was perched on the right, each whispering highly logical things. Evan had never given me reason to mistrust him before, so I didn't understand why I now felt the need to invade his privacy.

The camera sat innocently staring up at me.

"Morning, gorgeous," Evan said, startling me out of my skin. He hugged me to his chest and then kissed my cheek. "Something smells good."

"Just making pancakes."

He kissed me again. "Thank you."

I watched him snatch the camera up from the table and plop down into a chair. If there was something on that device that he was keeping a secret, his nonchalant expression didn't betray him. I allowed this to restore my faith. *Nothing is wrong. You're just being paranoid, Gail.* Still, as I flipped the pancakes and listened to the batter sizzle, something inside me didn't feel right.

Evan and I spent the rest of the morning watching the news. It was the usual information: updated vaccines for the

Pulmonem Fever were being distributed to fight the variant, homeless people were still roaming Venice Beach in California, and gas prices were still climbing. Evan and I watched in stern silence until Gavin's cries rang out, and I retreated into the bedroom to pick him up.

He had just started drinking milk from a bottle, and I was grateful that he drank without complaining. More than anything, I was happy to have finished breast-feeding. I sat in the rocking chair, holding the bottle to my baby's lips when Evan popped his head through the door.

"I'm heading out, Gail," he whispered.

"Okay, I love you." The words felt heavy on my tongue, which had never happened before.

"Love you more."

"Love you most."

"Gavin, you'll listen to me, right?" I asked when I heard the front door shut. "For some reason, I have this weird feeling that I can't trust—" I stopped when I glanced down and met Gavin's blue-gray eyes. He was just an infant and could hardly make sense of my words yet.

I sighed and held him against me, gently patting his back until he burped. And then, because I adored the feeling of holding my child, I rocked him back and forth for what felt like hours. This was my place of solace, the place where I could regain control of my breath.

I stared absentmindedly across the room as I rocked, and that was when the vibrant flash of yellow caught my eye. It was a crumpled piece of paper on my husband's nightstand. I gave it a questioning look and lowered Gavin into his crib to play with his toys while I went to investigate.

I picked up the piece of paper and slowly smoothed it out on the nightstand. It was just a phone number: an Ohio area code followed by seven random digits, and below that was the name Ken.

Ken.

To my knowledge, Evan didn't work with a Ken. Or if he did, he never mentioned him. Panic constricted my chest, and I forced a breath into my lungs. *Relax,* I commanded myself. *Ken is a guy's name.* But even then, I was still reaching for my phone.

I dialed the number slowly, trying to talk myself out of it with each passing digit. But when that desire to know kicked in, there was just no stopping it. I glanced over at Gavin as I held the phone to my ear. It rang a few times, and I expected to hear a man's voice answer, but what I actually heard stopped my heart.

"Hey, this is Kennedy. Sorry I missed your call but leave a message, and I'll try to get back to you as fast as possible."

I was frozen until the beep sounded in my ear, and I was forced to hang up. Gavin sat happily toying with his multicolored rings, completely oblivious to the horror that was heaving through my body.

I was stunned beyond words; a million scenarios flashed through my mind in the span of one second. My anxiety made its long-awaited return at full blast, and it almost knocked me to my knees. It slinked through my body, cut off my airways, and made my head feel so foggy I could've passed out.

Who was Kennedy? And why was this piece of paper crumpled up on Evan's nightstand? Why wouldn't he ever let me see his camera?

I gasped for breath, startling Gavin, who looked over at me with wide, worried eyes. I turned away from him immediately and scrambled to the bathroom. I couldn't let my son see me like this.

Standing in front of the mirror, I bent my head over the sink while my entire body shook to the point of pain. I squeezed my eyes shut, feeling the tears quiver their way from my eyes and drop into the sink. It was all I could do not to scream—not to scare Gavin again. So, I pressed my lips together and swallowed a shriek.

Betrayal is an odd thing. How was it that such a simple, easy task could murder somebody else's heart?

I collapsed against the wall, holding a towel against my lips to muffle my horrified sobs.

How could Evan do this to me — abuse my trust and take advantage of my love? It made no sense. In fact, I was almost sure it was a complete lie and that I was dreaming. But when I pinched myself hard enough to bruise the skin, I realized with a sickening wave of nausea that I was very much awake.

I didn't know how long I sat there, at least long enough for my poor legs to cramp. But moving was impossible. The entire world seemed to be pressing down on my shoulders at that very moment, and I was bound to shatter if I moved even one muscle.

The only thing that brought me back to life, if only temporarily, was Gavin's frustrated whining. He wanted out of his crib, no doubt already bored with his toys. I carried him out into the living room, each step sending needles through my legs, and placed him on the floor with a new set of toys.

Something else was coursing through my veins now: anger. Disbelief. Downright fury. I wouldn't let Evan get away with this. I would confront him as soon as he walked through that door. I just hoped my brief bravery wouldn't flee when I needed it most.

That night, Evan cooked spaghetti for dinner, seemingly as carefree as ever. He even whistled while dousing our noodles in sauce. I glared at the back of his head, feeling the anger heat my skin like a vicious fever.

"Here you go," he said, setting a bowl down in front of me.

I thanked him curtly and felt his eyes shift to my face as he sat down.

"Something wrong?" he inquired with a note of concern in his voice.

I drew a deep breath. It was now or never. *Just do it, just rip the Band-Aid off, just—* "Who's Kennedy?"

His weary face went blank as he chewed a forkful of noodles. "Who?"

"Kennedy, Evan," I said impatiently, not wanting him to play the dumb card. "There was a note on your nightstand, and it had her number on it. Who is she?"

Evan set his fork down, all traces of concern gone from his face. Instead, his expression was a stone. There his jaw went, slacking and stretching against his skin. "Why did you call her?"

I stared at him in shock. "Why wouldn't I?"

"Because it's really none of your business," he grumbled.

"Excuse me? What would you do if you found some random guy's number on *my* nightst—"

"All right, Gail!" he roared, and I shrank back in my seat, frightened by his outburst. He shook his head at me and held his hands up. "I cheated on you."

Hearing the words out loud sent a serrated knife straight through my chest.

He shrugged. "It's true."

"Is that what you're hiding on your camera?" I shrieked.

His nostrils flared. "What I have on my camera is none of your business."

White hot fury nearly blinded me. *Where was this coming from?!*

"Who is she?" I demanded.

"I met her in Columbus the weekend of the tennis match." My stomach clawed its way up my throat as I realized I was nine months pregnant with our child at that time. "Was it my intention to get with her? No. Was I drunk? Yes. Do I regret it? I did...until now."

My eyes flashed to him in utter disbelief.

"See, I did so much for you. I picked you up when you were down, I was there when you were depressed. I even married you and asked you to live in Ohio with me, for God's sake! I did all of this with a loving heart, but you just took all of that for granted. How dumb do you think I am?"

"What are you talking about?" I whispered, hot tears blurring my vision.

"Oh, don't give me that shit!" he yelled, his face glowing pink with all his anger. "I was just your toy. You wanted a son? You got one. You wanted to sleep with someone? You got it. You wanted space? You pushed me away. You wanted to get over heartbreak? You used me. I mean, who was that prick we saw at the fair? Colton something? You never stopped loving him. Ever. And after a while, I think we both knew I was never gonna compare to him."

I shook my head in protest, but he cut me off.

"The way you looked at him at the carnival..." Evan's eyes shimmered with sadness. "You've never looked at me like that."

"How can you say I don't love you?" I cried. "That's *such* a lie!"

"Oh, is it? Let me just ask your selfishness then. How all you do is want and want and want for *yourself* and no one else!"

His booming voice caused Gavin to cry from the other room, and the knife in my chest twisted.

Evan jerked his thumb over his shoulder. "Like the baby. I didn't want to have one, yet you refused to listen to me. You pushed me."

I pressed a trembling hand to my mouth as tears streamed down my cheeks.

"But Gavin makes *you* happy, so I went along with it because unlike you, I actually put *respect* into this relationship. But then you started describing a future I never wanted, and I had to get out. That's why I took the job to go to Columbus. Was it to meet Kennedy? No. But she happened to be there at the bar. And I made a mistake, but at least I own up to it. Not like you and your silent yearning for that other asshole—"

It happened so fast. I slapped him hard across the face. It was simply a reflex out of blind rage, but it shocked Evan into silence. The only other sound besides Gavin's raucous sobbing was my ragged breathing. Evan blinked a couple of times, and I watched as a handprint slowly formed on the skin of his reddened cheek. When he looked back at me, his eyes were blazing. They were dangerous, and it took all of my strength not to cower away.

"Get out," he ordered in a low, menacing tone.

"Gladly," I spit back and shot up from the table.

In my haste to get to the bathroom, I heard him call me an immature bitch under his breath. I bent myself over the toilet and heaved until the vomit left my stomach.

How could Evan have turned *his* cheating scandal into an attack on me? Not only did I feel betrayed, but now I felt worthless and incompetent. I wanted to scratch my wrists open, take a shower in boiling water, shut my hand in the door. More than anything, I wanted to leave this detrimental, toxic hell hole where my heart was breaking for the second time.

I shivered over the toilet, nausea rolling through me like a tsunami.

I pictured everything I was giving up by leaving: Evan's loving family, who were actually good people, my connection to Dani and her amazing book, my dream of living happily ever after with a husband who loved me, my students at the school—Naomi! But I couldn't...I couldn't stay here. Not with what had happened, and being in the same state as Kennedy made me want to rip every hair from my head.

What would my father say? I felt pathetic and weak, like I would *never* be the strong woman I was so sure he'd raised. What about Erica and Cara and Beau? Elijah! I placed my hands on my head. The shock was too overwhelming to bear.

I wished I would die right here on the pale bathroom tiles.

But then a sound registered in my mind. Gavin was still crying. My body instantly overflowed with adrenaline.

I rushed out of the bathroom and locked myself in the bedroom, where Gavin sat in his crib, convulsing with sobs. I picked him up and tried desperately to calm him down, and I thanked the stars he was such an easy baby.

I packed in a complete daze, just tossing everything into my suitcase, not stopping to fold. My limbs tingled with numbness, like at any moment, I would black out. But I had to get out of here right now, and I was taking Gavin with me.

Gathering every ounce of strength I had left and holding my child in one arm, I walked out of the bedroom and to the door. Evan hadn't moved from his place at the table; he was even finishing his plate of spaghetti.

"Bye," I said with as much acid on my tongue as I could muster.

He didn't even respond, and my heart cracked into a million pieces.

It was late; the sky was already a vast inky canvas, but no stars were twinkling. I secured Gavin into his car seat, threw my suitcase into the trunk of my car, and climbed into the driver's seat.

I struggled to breathe. My lungs were sandpaper. They were on fire, and it burned when I gasped. A very small part of me reasoned that if I went back inside and tried to talk this out, all would be okay. I wouldn't lose the man I loved, and that happily ever after could still exist.

But the idea crumbled. What was a relationship without communication?

"Dead," I said out loud to myself.

It made the whole situation feel as final as death itself, and a few more tears trickled from my eyes.

Evan's and my communication had been dead for months. I just hadn't wanted to deal with it; I didn't want to lose him. I didn't want to be broken again. But life had a funny way of turning someone's happiness into their own poison.

As I merged onto the highway, I dialed the number of the only person I felt comfortable enough to call.

"Hey, Gail," Cara answered on the third ring. "What's up?"

Tears blurred the taillights ahead of me. "I need your help."

Chapter Twenty-Two

LAKE ERIE, MI (2027)

I woke up in a strange room. It was cold. I shivered under the blankets, feeling the emptiness take its hold on my body as the memories returned. The fear, the regret — it was all there, gnawing on my organs, enjoying the sweet taste of my agony. The darkness compressed down on top of me, pinning me to this unfamiliar bed. I lay motionless...The once sealed wound was now a wide reopened gash. *And it hurt so bad.*

Beside the bed, Gavin was fast asleep in a new crib. He slept on his back with his arms and legs spread and his head rolled to one side. The pacifier was still gripped between his teeth. I could do nothing but stare at my son as dozens of emotions thrashed around inside of me.

He wasn't just *my* son. He had a father, but would I ever let Evan back into Gavin's life? The decision was mine alone, but gazing at my perfect bundle of joy, I suddenly didn't think Evan was worth the effort. Still, the choice wrenched its way to the front of my brain. I'd lost my mother due to her callous, unfeeling behavior...but at least I knew her for a little while. I *dreaded* the moment I would have to come clean to Gavin about his father because one day he would ask. And what would I tell him? *Evan cheated on me because he was tired of my supposed egotism, so I slapped him and ran out, meaning I gave up on providing you a perfect life and running from my problems at the same time.*

How could any child bear to hear such a thing?

I took every ounce of the blame on my shoulders. It sawed through my bones, mincing me into tiny, useless pieces.

My body grew stiffer as the hours crawled by, but I still couldn't move. It was like everything was frozen in time, except for my brain, which was pacing frantically across the room.

When I thought of Colton, my spine became an icicle.

I really did try to keep him out of my relationship with Evan because I didn't want to drag Evan into that drama. But I couldn't help broaching the subject every once in a while, and of course I paid for it by having too many conversations with that demon in my head. But seeing Colton and Beverly at the fair was completely out of my control. I had no clue he would be there. What Evan didn't understand was that Colton would always make my heart beat sideways. It was the long-term effect of first love.

Colton was my innocence. And I was craving that now more than ever.

But Evan had no right to bring my ex into this. It was *our* fight, and he'd cheated in the end. The thought made me grit my teeth so hard they might've snapped. How dare he treat me like this? After I supported his achievements and gave him nothing but love.

I loved him...more than he would ever know. He brought me *out* of the dark place. But I guess love was capable of sending you straight back through the wringer.

I hated him...more than he would ever know.

The fury was enough to help my stiff muscles work again.

Slowly, I pushed myself up, ignoring my body's protests. Gavin slept on, lost in some beautiful little dream. I envied him.

I had driven the near hour car ride all the way to Lake Erie, Michigan, last night. This was Cara's lake house, and she and Beau were spending the week here for a nice getaway. Of course, I had to ruin it by barging in on them, but my friends kindly welcomed me with open arms and helped me get situated in one of the several master bedrooms. The lake house was smaller than Cara's holy mansion in Detroit, but it was still larger than any house I'd ever seen. Still, it was strange...not waking up beside Evan.

A quiet knock at the door startled me.

"Gail?" Cara asked before peeking her head in. "Hey. How're you doing?"

I shrugged as she sat down beside me. "It doesn't feel real. Like, I'm sure if I just pinch myself hard enough—"

"Stop, Gail." Cara pushed my hand away from my arm. The skin there was covered in blooming bruises from all my attempts to wake up. "I'm really, really sorry. I can't imagine what you must be feeling, but I'm here. You can talk to me, always."

"Thank you," I whispered.

But there was *too much* to talk about. My mind was screaming; I didn't know where to start.

"Breakfast?" Cara offered after a moment.

"I don't think I can eat." Courtesy of my queasy stomach. "But Gavin will need to."

"Of course. Soon as he wakes up, I'll feed him if you wanna grab a shower or something."

I blinked at her. "Cara, I'm so sorry for just...crashing here. It —it's pathetic, I know. I just didn't want to go home and face my dad, and—"

"Don't even say it," she muttered. "Gail, we *all* go through bad times. Every single one of us. It's just a part of life. This is when friends stick together, and I'm not gonna let you drown. I know the truth is like a bullet to the heart, and that's why I let you stay here 'cause, well, because no one deserves to go through that kind of pain alone."

I gave her my strongest smile.

"I think you should call your dad," she added.

"My phone's been blowing up ever since I texted him last night." I sniffled. "You're probably right."

"He'll be on your side, trust me. And I know this may sound crazy, but try not to worry about Evan anymore. God knows everything that's gonna happen. He has it all under control."

I kept forgetting that Cara and Beau were die-hard Christians and that they put more faith into a questionable being than into reality and science. But I didn't have the energy to argue with her right now, so I just feigned a smile. She squeezed my hand and then left the room.

Gavin's wails cut into the quiet, and I was at his side in a moment.

"Hey, sweetheart," I whispered, reaching into the crib. "I know these aren't the best circumstances, but I promise I'll make it better, okay?"

He stared at me unknowingly, the pacifier bouncing up and down between his tiny lips.

"I love you so much, you know that?"

Cara came to retrieve him, and not a minute after she was gone, my phone started ringing, which made me freeze in place. If it was Evan, I wasn't sure I could handle talking to him. But my father's picture blinked on the screen.

"Hello?" My attempt to sound cheerful was wasted.

There was a beat of silence before he said, "Well, thank God you answered" in an uncharacteristically furious voice.

I squeezed my eyes shut. "Dad, I'm sorry."

"What the hell are *you* apologizing for?" he demanded. "It's that asshole's fault, and I think I need to come pay him a visit."

"Stop," I insisted. "I'm not with Evan anymore. I took Gavin and left."

"Where to?"

"Cara has a house here in Lake Erie. She and Beau are letting me stay."

"Gail, they don't need to be dragged into this mess. Come home."

"I can't." I shook my head though he couldn't see. "One of my favorite students is graduating this year, and I've gotta be there to see her off...even if it means crashing here for a few months."

"That's too long. You're gonna overstay your welcome," he chastised, and all of my strength withered away.

"Listen, sweetheart, I know you may not want to, but you've gotta get back on your feet. If you won't come home, then at least consider buying a new house there. I — I'll pull from my emergency funds to help you."

The emptiness was a black hole that slowly consumed my body. I felt numb again.

"Gail? You there?"

"Do not waste your money on me," I forced through clenched teeth.

"I'm your father, Abigail," he snapped. "I *help* you. It's my *job*."

"No, that just makes me feel worse. Suddenly, my marriage fails, and I'm a single mother who can't even support her own son? That makes me sound like such a *loser*."

He didn't answer for so long that I almost thought he had hung up.

"It happens to the best of us," he said at last. "And you're not a loser, you're a human being. A human being who's *allowed* to feel sad."

I exhaled, forcing every ounce of air from my lungs. "Fine."

"So, you'll look for a house?"

I thought of Gavin and how he deserved a fulfilling life. He was mine to raise and mine to raise alone. Evan had made that choice when he slept with Kennedy in the back of some bar.

"I'll keep an eye open," I answered.

"I love you, sweetheart. Keep your head up. Everything's gonna be okay."

I took a shower after hanging up. It felt good to just let the water pour over me like rain. I tried very hard not to think of Evan, but he wouldn't go away. The more I thought of him, the more my mind changed my perception of him. He wasn't the man I fell in love with; he was a lying, cheating bastard now. And even though my heart yearned to see his good side, those traits stood up like a blockade. Evan wasn't a good person at all. What had I ever seen in him? The question made me look inward. What *had* I ever seen in him?

"There are some blueberry muffins in the fridge if you'd like one," Beau offered once I trudged into the kitchen an hour later.

He was scrubbing down the granite countertops.

"Thanks," I answered. "How are things at the pharmacy?"

"Good. I should be working on that stack of paperwork, but..." He turned to me and shrugged. "I'm technically on vacation. I'll do it later."

Something in his tone brought an actual smile to my face. He set his cloth on the counter and stood up. "What about you? How are...how are things?"

There was the typical sinking feeling in my chest. "I feel like I just...lost a huge part of me."

Beau nodded, his expression grim. "Breakups do that."

I stared at him for a moment, trying to consider what his and Cara's lives had been like since *their* wedding. He was a highly-regarded pharmacist technician, probably the best in the business. And she was a musical therapist who used her angelic voice to soothe the tantrums of little children. They were both successful in their own way, independent yet linked. Their marriage had been full of communication and trust. They were smart. And here I was, bombarding in on their perfect little world with my stupidity. Heat kissed my neck, and I took a few wary steps backward.

"This is crazy, I shouldn't be here. I'm sorry for wasting your—"

"What?" Beau stepped toward me, concern wrinkling the skin around his eyebrows. "Of course, you should be here."

"He's right," Cara said from behind me, making me jump. She held Gavin in her arms, ignoring the fact that he was yanking on a few locks of her hair. "Don't even think about walking out that door."

"But you guys have stuff to do, and I'm just intruding—"

"Are you kidding? Gail, we're always here for you," Beau insisted.

"Yeah." Cara walked over to stand next to her husband, and with my son in her arms, they could've been a happy little family. "It's *okay* to ask for help, Gail. You have nothing to prove. We know you're strong, but life happens sometimes."

Her doughy eyes filled with compassion, and she placed Gavin back in my arms. As a substitute for Cara's hair, he reached instead for the necklace I was wearing. It was the necklace Evan had gotten me for my twenty-first birthday. I'd forgotten I even had it on, but now it stung my skin.

"You can stay here as long as you need," Cara continued. "We don't judge."

As I stared at my friends, at their linked arms, a very small bit of tension eased off my shoulders.

Over the next few days, I stayed wrapped in the silk sheets of a solitary queen-sized bed. I only got up to tend to my baby. But not even the violin case that was sitting in the corner and collecting dust appealed to me now. I spent hours contemplating what would happen if I called Evan. I had several theories and several plans, but they all crumbled when reality set back in. Evan was not a person I knew anymore. He wouldn't react the way I wanted him to.

Cara checked on me occasionally, just to try to convince me to eat or go for a walk along the water. I declined and tried to come up with an excuse. She never pushed me of course, but the look in her eyes told me everything she wouldn't say.

"I was thinking the other day that I haven't heard you play the violin in forever," she exclaimed one evening. "Don't tell me you've lost all those incredible skills." There was a kind of warning in her voice

"I haven't."

"Well then, what do you say to a little concert tonight?"

I stared at her, confused.

"I don't think Beau's *ever* heard you play, which is an actual crime now that I think about it. So why don't we put on a show tonight? You on violin, me singing. Like the good old days."

The good old days, meaning our college lives back in Philadelphia. When life was still full of opportunities, and Professor Autrie was still alive to be my impeccable mentor. *The good old days...*

Gavin squealed in Cara's arms and started clapping his tiny hands together. The excitement that flashed in his petite features was beautiful enough to stop my heart.

"And don't worry, Gavin and I already discussed it. He'll have a front row seat," Cara said in the high-pitched tone you reserve for children. She reached out to tickle his stomach, and he squealed again.

A smile tugged on the corners of my lips, and I let it blossom fully. How could I have ever gotten so lucky to have a friend like Cara?

We didn't waste time. After handing Gavin to Beau, my friend and I scurried up the stairs to prepare. She did her usual vocal warm-ups while I tuned my instrument and rosined my bow. I had to admit, it did feel good to have my violin in my arms again; it felt like returning home after a long trip. I practiced a few scales and then turned to face Cara.

"What songs do you know by heart?" she asked.

For as many songs as I did know, my brain was suddenly empty.

"We could do a pop song," she suggested.

I shrugged. "Pop music is overrated."

"Opera?"

That just made me laugh.

As she rambled on about all the songs she knew, a sudden feeling of hope wrapped its arms around me. My pain was subsiding, and it was easy, for the time being at least, to pretend that it didn't even exist. I'd felt like this one other time in my life —when I was *young* and heartbroken. My fingers were already plucking the tune on my violin.

"Hallelujah," I murmured, cutting Cara off mid-sentence

She turned her gaze to me. "Oh, I love that song! That's a good one. Do you know it?"

"By heart."

"Okay." She gave me a genuine smile, took my hand, and led me back down the stairs.

Beau and Gavin were sitting on the couch, waiting for their performance. They each clapped as we entered the living room, and my lips curled into a smile. Before we started, Cara squeezed my shoulder.

Just like the good old days...

Cara began singing of David's secret chord in a voice richer than velvet. No time had made me immune to her gift. The beauty of her tone stunned, me and I almost missed my cue near the end of the first verse. Together, we soared toward the first hallelujah, earning a gasp from Beau, whose eyes sparkled into the dim lighting. But it was Gavin's expression that made my heart skip a beat.

My son sat in Beau's lap, his blue-gray eyes flickering between my violin and Cara as we continued the serenade. His miniature lips were parted like he wanted to shout, but the shock on his face kept him from doing so. He was mesmerized by the music, just as I had been at such a young age. We had captured his full attention.

I dragged my bow to a halt, providing Cara the full spotlight as she sang of an utterly cold and broken hallelujah, her high note enveloping our bodies in goosebumps. She offered a brief smile before continuing with me, and we slowly moved to a diminuendo, growing softer and softer until my bow brushed the last chord.

Silence clung to the air for a fraction of a second before Beau erupted with cheers. He clapped wildly, gushing over how talented we both were. Gavin simply sat in Beau's lap, still stunned. I had to laugh at the sight before I collapsed into Cara's arms.

Accompanying her was much better than playing alone; it sparked something in me that wasn't there before, and I willingly accepted Beau's offer of ice cream and a movie before bed.

The next morning, a sneaky ray of sunshine slinked in through the curtains and rested right on my eyes, bright enough to force me awake. My phone was full of messages from my father, from Erica, even from Jamie, though not from Evan. I tried hard not to take offense to that; besides, I now understood that boys *needed* to harvest their pride for a few weeks after a breakup. Texting me would only make him weak.

Asshole.

I fed Gavin and then carried him downstairs to play with his toys while I ate breakfast. And thankfully, my stomach took the eggs and bacon without a hint of protest.

"How are you this morning?" Cara inquired, sitting across from me.

"Okay, for now." I didn't want to jinx myself and then have the pain return at full-force later.

Because I knew that was as likely as the sun setting.

Cara nodded and gave me a polite smile. "Beau and I were originally planning to go hiking today. You're welcome to come, of course, but don't feel like you have to. I mean, if you're *really* not feeling well, I can tell Beau to—"

"No way are you skipping a hike just to stay with me. I'll be fine."

Her face twisted with hesitance. "All right, well, call me if you need anything. You won't be alone though, so that's good."

I looked up from my empty plate. "What do you mean?"

"Someone's stopping by to see you," she said simply and then walked into the living room before I could ask more questions.

Elijah stood in the doorway. His cinnamon-colored skin looked tanner than the last time I'd seen him, which was at my own wedding. He ran a hand through his charcoal hair before meeting my eyes, and I glanced at Cara for an explanation.

"He needs to talk to you," she said, zipping her jacket. "Elijah, you should stay for dinner. We all need to catch up."

"Definitely," he responded and looked at me again.

"Have fun, guys," Cara said as she squeezed past us and out the door. She winked at me before climbing into Beau's truck.

"Good to see you, man," Beau murmured before stepping out.

And then the door was shut, and it was just me and my old friend.

"What're you doing here?" I asked.

I loved having Elijah around; he was one of my closest friends, but this meeting felt strange. Forced. Like he was a therapist who intended to trick me into a session. But I beckoned him into the living room anyway. If this *was* a therapy session, and I was forced to bite, at least I had him of all people. Gavin was still lost in his own little world, playing with a shape separator. Elijah smiled at him, but then his expression sobered, and he turned back to me.

"He's disowned."

"Huh?" I asked.

"Evan and I aren't friends anymore."

I pressed a hand to my forehead, feeling weak at the sound of his name. I didn't want to be the reason for drama between two friends. That was too high school, and we were supposed to be older now.

"Why, Elijah? You've known him way longer than you've known me, and—"

"So, you're *defending* his cheating ass now?" he demanded.

"No!" I retorted harshly. "And can you please not curse in front of my son?"

Elijah hung his head and adopted a softer tone. "I'm sorry. It's just that I've had to watch you go through some dark stuff over the years, and you don't deserve any of it."

I shook my head. "Stop making me sound like I play the victim."

"You don't, you do the opposite. You *bury* your feelings, which as far as I'm concerned is worse."

We listened to Gavin's unintelligible babbling for a moment, and the pain returned. If heartbreak was an untamed wild animal, it would have been gouging my heart out with its razor claws at this very moment.

"I guess I just don't understand why you aren't angrier," Elijah murmured. "If someone did that to me, I'd be livid."

"Of course, I'm angry, but...when we broke up, he said things to me. Awful things...but they were true."

Elijah's eyebrows pulled together. "What kinds of things?"

I swallowed, but the lump in my throat was too large, and it hurt. "H-he called me selfish for not listening to his input about Gavin. He didn't want a baby, but I did, and I totally disregarded his fear. And he...called me out for other things, too, l-like my past, which is something I would *very* much like to forget."

"The thing you were healing from." Elijah nodded.

"Yeah." I drew a shaky breath. "Every once in a while, I think about...someone. An old boyfriend — my *first* boyfriend. H-he meant a lot to me." The words made my tongue as dry as the Sahara. "I've always been self-conscious about the fact that I still miss him, so I tried to bury the feelings like you said. You know, play my violin until my fingers bleed or...kiss Evan. But sometimes my ex...just pops into my head, and I can't resist thinking about him."

"And Evan..."

I shook my head, feeling chagrin paint my cheeks. "Evan had every right to call me out over that. It was my fault that he felt neglected sometimes—even when I was suicidal."

Elijah's eyes widened, and I realized I'd never told him. But I didn't feel like recalling my horrific encounter with the demons that lived in my head, so I waved the matter away with my hand.

"Our communication just died after a while, but I still feel like...his cheating is my fault."

"Gail—"

"No, it is. I *always* do this. I pushed Evan to cheat. I pushed Colton to go see his dad, who quite literally could've killed him..." I trailed off as Elijah inhaled sharply.

And it seemed that I was also an expert at running my mouth.

"God, I suck." I dropped my head into my hands.

"Wait, hold on! You do *not* suck! And this isn't all your fault.

You can't take the blame for every little thing, Gail. That's gonna kill *you*."

I could feel him now, the demon making his return. I felt him grin at the idea of my anguish; he enjoyed it.

"Look, I don't — I don't know who this Colton is, but that probably wasn't all your fault either."

I wondered why I wasn't crying. The amount of emotion that was coursing through me should have sent tears rolling down my cheeks. But I just sat curled up in a ball beside Elijah, allowing the emptiness to spread.

"I just wish I could make something work for *once*." I stared at Gavin as I spoke. "How am I supposed to give him a life without a father?"

"You need to take a deep breath for one thing. You look like you're about to pass out," Elijah replied. He draped an arm around my shoulder to steady me. "And you'll figure it out, you always do."

I wanted to swat at him for lying. I never knew what to do; even now as a twenty-five-year-old, I still had no clue what life had in store for me. It was a very unnerving thought.

"I'm just scared he's gonna grow up to be like me, and I don't want that."

Elijah whipped his head to the side, glancing at me like I was crazy. "Why *wouldn't* you want him to be like you? You are an incredible person."

"I meant my situation," I clarified through a hollow voice.

Gavin placed a red square into the square slot and then squealed with delight when all the shapes were in place. Elijah sighed and drew me against him; he smelled faintly of lavender, and I closed my eyes.

"You are going to be okay," he said firmly, enunciating each word clearly. "Gavin will be okay. This isn't gonna be the death of you."

I shifted my head to look up at him. "I've heard that one before."

"And you're still here, aren't you? It's the truth."

I didn't want to talk about me anymore; it was a sore subject that only made me feel worse.

"How are things with you and Brie?"

He failed to conceal his smile. I knew that look: he was in love. Good for him.

"We're moving in together. Oh, and you'll never believe this. She got a job as a psychiatrist at Four Winds Saratoga."

My mouth fell open. "Wait, so you're gonna live in—"

"Saratoga Springs." Elijah nodded, grinning cheek to cheek now.

"That's amazing!"

"Yeah, well here's the best part. There's a house about a block away that's for sale, and it's only $1,200 a month. Nice place, manageable lawn. I think you'd really like it. Plus, it's—"

"I can't go back. There are students I need to see graduate. I have a relationship with these kids. I can't turn my back on them now."

Elijah sighed. "Gail, why are you really choosing to stay?"

I stared at him, feeling my defenses rise. "I just told you. Besides, Ohio is home now. It's where—"

"It's where Evan lives," he cut in, and my mouth snapped shut. "I know you, Gail, sometimes better than I think you know yourself. Your students, they're gonna be fine. They're all gonna graduate and have good lives. Wanna know how I know that?"

I blinked, trying to stop my emotions from escalating.

"I know because *you* were their teacher. You have a way with people, you connect with them. Sure, it'll be hard to say good-bye, but you need to start doing what's right for *you*. I just don't see how continuing to teach at a school near your ex's house is healthy at all. Plus, I know you can't look me dead in the eye and insist you never wanna come home."

Sometimes, I hated Elijah for how right he was about every-thing. Naturally, I tried to prove him wrong; I tried to look him in the eye and say that home was behind me. But of course, he was right. And now that he'd said it, Evan's close proximity with the school was too convenient for my liking.

"Home," I breathed. I did miss it terribly.

Elijah chuckled. "At *least* come back with me and check out the house. Brie's been dying to see you anyway. And you can raise Gavin in a nice, familiar neighborhood."

"What do I say to my students?" I asked, picturing Naomi and her beaming smile.

"Send a nice email. They're not kids, Gail. They're high school students. They're gonna understand. Nothing really lasts forever anyway."

I let my eyes drop to the ground in thought. Gavin wriggled the shape separator, and that was what brought me back.

"Okay. I'll go back to Saratoga Springs."

Elijah's lips curled into a genuine smile. "You just have to promise me something though. Please don't let other people's mistakes bring you down anymore. If they want to screw up their own life, let them. You just stay focused on you. Can you promise me that?"

I opened my mouth and then closed it because that was what I was best at: taking responsibility for other people's actions. I didn't know how to *not* do that.

Elijah sighed. "I stopped at your house before I came here. Your dad sent me his address," Elijah explained when I blinked a question at him. "He wanted me to give this to you."

He reached into his plastic bag and retrieved a sky-blue journal with the word *Love* scrawled across the cover. I snatched it from him, feeling my face grow hot again.

"Don't worry, I didn't read it." He held up his hands. "I swear. But your dad said maybe you can write down how you're feeling."

I nodded, gazing down at my notebook. I didn't realize how

much I missed it until now, and I pressed it against my heart. "Thank you."

"How about that promise?" he inquired gently.

Gavin looked up at us, his chubby face glowing with delight, and I scooped him up into my arms. "Okay. I promise."

"I'm gonna miss having you here," Cara said as I shoved my clothes into the open suitcase.

I was actually folding them this time, and she stepped closer to help me.

"I owe you big time," I responded. "For opening your lake house up, for feeding me, for—"

"Shh," she shook her head and neatly placed one of my shirts in the corner of the suitcase. "You owe me nothing, not after all the times you were there for me."

We packed in silence for a few minutes, and I wanted to argue that I did owe her, that I would probably never stop owing her. But she didn't seem in the mood to bicker like that.

"Gail, I just want you to know that Beau and I have been praying for you every night."

I glanced over at her; she'd stopped packing and was facing me with a look I had never seen her wear before. Was it desperation? I couldn't tell.

"We pray for you and Gavin and even Evan, just so that he may admit his mistakes and find the light one day," she explained when I drew back at the mention of his name.

"Why would you pray for him?" I demanded. It offended me.

Cara's face fell slightly. "Some people hurt others when they're lost, but no one *deserves* to be lost."

A bitter response tensed on the tip of my tongue, but I swallowed it. "What's your point?"

Her dark chocolate eyes touched mine. "I know it's not your

thing, and I'm not trying to push you in any sort of direction, but...have you ever tried praying?"

"I am *not* praying for Evan's revival!" I said tersely.

Cara didn't flinch. "Not for Evan. But for yourself? Or your baby?"

My eyes flickered to Gavin, who was unsuccessfully attempting to climb out of his crib. He was trying to escape the four built-up walls that trapped him...just like I was trying to escape my past mistakes.

"God can help you," Cara said, as if hearing my thoughts.

I turned back to her. "If God really cared about us, he wouldn't let any of this stuff happen. Like heartbreak." My voice cracked on the word.

My hands worked faster now, folding the clothes and tossing them into the suitcase.

"God's plan is different for everyone," Cara answered. "Maybe you should ask him about yours."

That stopped me.

I remembered the evening when I came home after Colton had just asked me out. I was exhilarated, but then my father announced he and my mother were getting divorced. What was the book he was reading? *God—The Giver of All.*

"All right," I said at last. "What if I did pray? What would it change?"

"Probably nothing immediately, but over time, you'd see that there's more to life than loss. There's *so* much more. And you would start to see that you are loved more than you could ever know." Her voice was full of wonder, encouragement.

"Cara, I don't even know *how* to pray. I don't know what to say, I don't know how to act. I mean, how do I know I'm not just talking to the ceiling?"

"I'll leave that one up to you to figure out. But just be yourself. God loves you regardless of who you are and what you've been through..." She trailed off at my raised eyebrows. "I just think it would really be worth your while, Gail."

It was a soft nudge in the right direction. Or so she claimed. She kissed Gavin goodnight and then gave me one of her kindest smiles. "See you in the morning."

I just stared at the closed door.

Praying wouldn't solve anything; it was a stupid way to trick people into having hope. Well, when your beloved husband cheated on you and called you a selfish bitch, your hope tended to fade pretty quickly.

Gavin called my attention again as he tried his absolute hardest to climb out of that crib. I couldn't take it.

"Here, buddy. Let me help you."

Once I had him out, he wrapped his little arms around my neck and started chewing on my hair. It made me happy that I could get him out of his prison and keep him in my loving embrace. And I'm sure he was grateful, too. The hair chewing was a way to thank me.

As I rocked him back and forth, my eyes fixated on the white carpet at my feet. The house was quiet; Elijah was asleep downstairs on the couch, and Cara and Beau were probably already in bed, too. Gavin yawned in my arms.

I didn't notice the feeling at first. It was the faintest tugging on my bones. As the seconds ticked by, the sensation grew. It moved from my heart and entered my veins like a steady stream, bubbling, pulling, coaxing. I was frozen as it flowed through me.

What was it?

A hazy image materialized in my mind: nothing but bright, hot, glittering light. Shivers licked my arms and legs as I visualized this, and before I knew what I was doing, I set Gavin down on the bed and had my hands folded.

It was an understatement to say that I felt silly. My face burned in embarrassment as I lowered my head, but that steadily flowing stream was too prevalent to ignore.

My hands shook slightly as I whispered, "God...if you're there, if you even exist, I—I'd like to talk with you."

There was no answer except for a deafening silence and Gavin's occasional coos.

I bit my lip. "Cara seems to think that you can help me. I-I know that I've made some mistakes in life, but they are eating me alive. And I don't want to keep running. I get it if you don't want to help, but please just...*listen*."

As I said this, something unexpected happened: my eyes actually started to sting. I hadn't felt this pin-prick sensation in days, not since I walked out of Evan's house. For the longest time, I thought maybe I was just incapable of crying. Of feeling too much to react. But suddenly there was a steady stream of tears leaking from my eyes, almost like the river inside me had finally found an escape route.

I gasped at the emotion that overtook me. It kicked my legs out from under me, and I collapsed onto my knees. My hands remained folded, except now my forehead was touching them.

"I don't...want to feel like this anymore," I sobbed into my hands. "I just want to be happy and give my child a life worth living."

There was still no answer, yet my mouth hung open, allowing the tears to spill in. My eyes were squeezed shut, and I struggled to breathe as the sadness overwhelmed me. All the while, that river in my veins pulsed with energy.

"Please help me," I begged.

I must've looked so stupid slouched over with my hands folded like that. But for a brief second, I didn't care.

"I lost my mother and Colton and Katy and Evan and his family, and all these people that I loved with all my heart! It hurts, God. I don't understand w—I just d-don't understand..."

My body quivered with this overdue confession. It burned like fire, but every breath I drew eased the pain. There came a point when the river sang to me. It vibrated deep in my bones and kissed my forehead.

"I'm sorry for everything I've done. I know I don't deserve it, but please just help me turn things around. Please!"

It was all I could do not to burst out of myself. But with this last plea, the river vanished. I looked up from my hands and tried to see through the blurriness of my tears. The room was the same; Gavin lay on the bed behind me, fiddling with his feet. The silence was even stronger now.

I laid my head back against the foot of the bed, taking deep breaths to calm my heart. Whatever had just happened, I'd never experienced it before. As Gavin playfully tugged on my hair, I sat there in wonder.

Maybe I really had just talked to God.

Chapter Twenty-Three

SARATOGA SPRINGS, NY—HANOVER, PA (2027)

It was on the long car ride home that Gavin finally said his first full word: Momma.

I clenched the steering wheel and glanced in the rearview mirror at my son, whose eyes were sparkling in the afternoon sunlight.

"Momma," I cooed. "That's right, baby. Momma." My eyes flickered between the mirror and the road, and I tried relentlessly for the next forty-five minutes to get him to repeat it. But Gavin just continued to smile at me.

My father and Jamie were nice enough to babysit Gavin while Elijah and I went to look at the house that was for sale. We met Brie there, and I gave her a big hug, happy to see another loving, familiar face.

The house really was perfect. It was a home characterized by color and geometric architecture, like the picket fence type only much less rigid. A long sandstone walkway stretched to the oak-colored front door, and the wrap around porch promised endless evenings on a porch swing with a glass of lemonade. I could maybe even put a tire swing on the giant sycamore tree for Gavin when he was older. It all came together in my mind — a puzzle finally completed.

Elijah and Brie helped me move in at the end of May. I took the desk that had been with me my whole life and stored it in my new bedroom, locking the sky-blue journal in the top drawer. Gavin finally had his own room, complete with a new rocking chair, crib, and cubby holes to store his many toys. I was in love with the place. It seemed I was meant to live and die in Saratoga Springs, but I was perfectly okay with that.

Until I could find an actual job, I handed out private violin lessons. Lucky for me, there were two twins on the corner of the street who each played the violin and whose parents were looking for a way to get the twins out of the house. Dad eventually emailed me a flyer announcing the commencement of the Saratoga Strings, a new touring symphony who was accepting new and experienced players by the end of summer. The best part though was that a spot in this orchestra was a paying job. I saved the email and booked the date of my audition on the calendar.

Music made its return to the household, and my fingers ached from playing so much. Gavin enjoyed it though; he clapped along and bounced in his high chair. I liked having someone to play for all the time. He was my biggest fan, and I often found myself wishing he wouldn't grow up. *Please don't become a teenager who thinks I'm irrelevant.*

I spent as much time with my son as possible until I had to retreat to my violin and rehearse for my upcoming audition. It was the Friday before when my phone started ringing.

I'd been running scales and looked down at my phone only to have my heart stop. Beth Caldwell's picture illuminated the screen, her smile bright and beautiful in the photo. But I couldn't imagine she would be as happy now.

I swallowed my fear and set my instrument down.

"Hello?"

"Abigail!" Beth exclaimed. She sounded breathless. "I wasn't sure I'd be able to reach you. Evan told us everything."

A boy openly admitting his mistakes to his family? That couldn't be right. I waited for her to list all the senseless accusations and call me out for being a bad wife. But she remained quiet.

"Oh," was all I could say.

"Sweetheart, I can't believe this is happening; I feel sick over it. I'd love to meet and talk through it, maybe...find some closure."

Even though she couldn't see, my face was stony. "I'm sorry, but I'd rather not talk to Evan."

"He wouldn't have to know."

That was surprising. Could it be possible that this woman didn't think of me as the selfish bitch her son claimed I was? Then again, it could all be a trick, something to guilt-trip me back into the family. Maybe Evan was behind this, though as I recalled our cruel parting, I doubted it.

"Mrs. Caldwell, I'm all the way in Saratoga Springs. That's a long drive just to meet and talk."

She didn't respond for a second, and the longer the silence filled the air, the more I wished this conversation would end. It was stirring an emotion inside me that I wanted gone. It was like standing in an ice cold shower.

"I could meet you halfway," she offered, and I massaged my temples. "It's no trouble. If you really don't want to, I completely understand."

Of course, I wanted to. She was the mother of the man I had loved. And as much as I'd recently trained my brain to despise Evan, that nagging part of me still sought a connection to him. Still, was it worth tearing open the wound? I guess I did want a little closure, like she'd said. I guess I deserved it after being treated so badly. And Beth deserved it, too. She deserved to know things from my point of view, and I would admit my faults to her because she needed to know the *full* story...no matter how bad it made me look.

"Where should I meet you?" I asked.

I sat down in the corner of a Chick-Fil-A and munched on my chicken nuggets with one eye glued to the door. Dad was babysitting Gavin while I was away, and I was grateful. It would have been worse if I'd brought the baby because I'd gotten to know Beth, and I knew she would cry if her grandson was present.

I didn't want anyone to cry today.

At a quarter to five, she walked through the door — alone, thank goodness. Even though I trusted her word, a part of me had worried that she would drag Evan along just to settle our war. If that would've happened, this could've been a bloodbath.

"Hi, honey, thanks so much for meeting me," she said sweetly, setting her tray down on the table.

It made me uncomfortable when she reached for my hand, but I tried to ignore the feeling. This woman was my mother-in-law and despite myself, I still loved her very much. Missed her even.

"No problem," I said. "So, Evan told you?"

"Well not the extent of it, but he never tells us about his breakups, so I figured this one was ugly."

"Cheating scandals often are."

She froze, fork tensed in her hand, her diamond eyes as wide as saucers.

I sighed.

So, Evan *hadn't* told them the whole truth...now *that* sounded more like it. But now I felt like my hands were tied because if I explained everything, I would sound like I was playing snitch, and that was the last thing I wanted. But Beth was waiting.

"Evan cheated on me," I muttered, "but our relationship wasn't perfect either."

She shook her head and blinked several times before answering. "What are you talking about? You just had a son—"

"Evan never wanted the baby," I interrupted and then bit my tongue.

You might as well have just written *snitch* and *victim-player* across my forehead in permanent sharpie.

"Y—you two were both sobbing in the hospital when Gavin was born," Beth argued.

I shook my head. "He was only happy because Gavin made *me* happy. I disregarded his fear when I should've listened."

My ex-mother-in-law frowned at her salad. I knew this must have been hard to hear. After all, we'd all formed connections. She might've missed me as much as I missed her. So, it was the least I could do to give her an honest explanation.

"There were things we left undiscussed, either because we didn't want to face them or because we just didn't have the heart to anymore. And there were moments when I would snap and not...credit him enough. I regret that, I really do. But when he cheated, I just...I didn't want to stick around." It felt lame, but it was the truth.

Beth didn't speak for a while. Her cheek continued to twitch like she was trying hard not to overreact.

At last, she said, "I guess cheating isn't something you bounce back from, huh?" She tried to smile, but it faltered, and she hung her head again.

I didn't know what to say to that. Part of me wanted to comfort her, to tell her it would all be okay. But I didn't know.

"That doesn't sound like my Evan."

I'd wanted to believe the same thing.

I shrugged. "People change over time. I'm certainly not the same person I was when Evan met me."

She nodded with that watery smile again. "I'm so sorry."

A happy family was in the booth next to us, and the little girl was an incessant chatterbox. She squealed wildly when her father set a tray of fries in front of her. That could've been us.

"Where is Gavin anyway?" Beth wondered.

And here was the one subject I had hoped to avoid. But he was such a prominent part of this ordeal that I should've felt stupid for hoping she wouldn't mention him.

"My father is taking care of him in New York while I'm here."

A realization dawned on her face, and she set her fork down. "Will I ever get to see my grandson again?"

My mouth went bone dry in an instant. She couldn't ask me this question; it was too overwhelming. She *shouldn't* have asked it...yet she had every right to.

"Gail," her eyes were shattered crystals, "will Evan not see his son?"

I almost said that I didn't think Evan wanted anything to do with our baby, but instead, I muttered, "That has yet to be decided."

Normally, I would've offered a generous response, something to ease her despair. But I was an adult now, too—old enough and strong enough to make my own decisions regardless of her input.

She sat back in her seat, looking like she'd just been punched in the gut. She tossed a smoky topaz curl over her shoulder and shook her head. "If you don't mind me saying...I think that's a little immature."

And so it began.

"When you file for divorce, there will be a decision for custody. My son deserves to see the boy he helped raise."

Your son who lied through his teeth and cheated on me, was what I wanted to throw at her. But I'd had lots of practice with self-control. Honesty was best, even if it stung.

"Mrs. Caldwell, a part of me doesn't feel comfortable having Gavin around Evan, especially after what happened."

She pressed her lips together. "Is there nothing I can do? It's not just the baby, Gail. We all miss you. Dani's a mess."

My heart cracked at the mention of her name. "Tell her that I miss her, too."

Beth's smile was slight. "I will. And I'm sorry," she said again, "for everything."

"Thank you." I bit my lip, hating the way these words were cutting into my skin.

It was all I could do not to plead with her to let me talk to Evan. To tell him to contact me. To ask him if he regretted his decision even the tiniest bit. But I doubted she even knew where Evan was. He seemed like the type who would disappear and go visit a random bar in the next state over. I would know.

Just like before, I was in the middle of a tug-of-war game. One side wanted Evan back, to forget the problems and move on. But the more logical part of my brain said no. That was dangerous. *Get out now while you can; otherwise, it'll just get uglier.*

For a moment, I considered the fact that I might never hear from Evan again. It slashed my heart into several pieces, and I blinked furiously, trying to push the thought away. But perhaps that was better. Maybe it was healthier to let it go. To let him go.

I drew a deep breath, and Beth searched my face.

"Can I ask you a question?" I ventured.

"Of course."

"Do you think...we moved too fast?"

Evan and I had made the pact to love each other forever. But what was forever? And how could we have known? I felt stupid now for doing that, but I'd made that mistake once before as well. Forever, it seemed, was an unreachable thing. When would I get that through my thick skull?

Beth pondered my question. "It's not really my place to judge. I gave birth to Lain when I was sixteen." Her face pinkened, and she smiled tightly. "My parents threw me out and everything. So, by my standards, no, you didn't move fast at all. But...that's a question you need to ask yourself."

I pictured our son and tried to consider what life would've been like if we'd waited, if our communication had remained strong. It was then that I figured...yes, we did move too fast. But I couldn't bring myself to regret my beloved baby. He was far too precious; I loved him too much to even feel guilty. And if I loved him this much, it would only stand to reason that I provide him a fresh start, one that didn't involve stupid family drama. I would tell him one day; I had to. He would start asking questions, and I had to be there to answer them, whether I was ready or not. He deserved to know...but he didn't deserve to deal with it.

"Beth, I'm going to keep my son." My voice was calm, decisive. "I don't see a way around this and quite frankly, I'm ready to leave it in the past. Maybe Evan and I weren't meant to be together, but he did give me Gavin, and for that, I will always be grateful. So, you have to understand that I'm doing this for Gavin's own good."

I watched the muscles in her neck tense like wires. She was biting back an argument; I could tell by the way her lips twitched. But she surprised me yet again by exhaling and saying, "I understand."

"I won't keep him in the dark," I promised. "Someday, I'll tell Gavin about his beautiful, courageous grandmother and how she loved him with all her heart."

This earned a breathless laugh from Beth and a single tear trailed down her cheek. I swallowed, willing myself not to fall apart, but she needed to hear this. I reached out and took her hand.

"Thank you for everything. Please tell your family, especially Dani, that I wish them all the best. And that I'm...sorry I couldn't make it work."

She squeezed my hand. "Take care of yourself and my grandson."

"Always."

With one last smile, I pushed myself up from the table, tossed my garbage in the trash, and moved toward the door on popsicle stick legs. I wasn't sad though; I was almost...overjoyed. Our conversation had gone very well, and it was the perfect ending to a tragic story. But that was exactly what this was—an ending. The final chapter. I would learn to forget Evan because forgetting meant moving on. And I was more than ready to leave this mess in the past where it belonged.

I had never really felt this way before, and I wondered why it seemed easier to let Evan go than it was to let Colton go. Maybe it was a sign that things weren't meant to work between us and for *once in my life*...I was okay with that. It wouldn't be simple. I was sure I'd spend some nights downing a carton of chocolate ice cream and crying my eyes out—typical breakup stuff. But I had to remember this feeling: the odd sensation that things would be okay.

It might've been a sign from God.

My hands locked on the steering wheel.

The last time I thanked God for something, I was six and in Vacation Bible School, too young to even comprehend what I was saying. But this was real. As I drove an hour back to Saratoga Springs, I let my mind begin to wander. Ever since I prayed that one evening, I couldn't shake the desire to learn more about God. About Heaven. If there was such a thing as an afterlife, I wanted all the details.

A sign on the side of the road caught my eye. It was a white cross with the words *Come into the light of God* scrawled across a purple garland that was intricately tied around the wooden posts. And behind it sat a square brick building with painted glass and a steeple that seemed to glow.

Before I knew what I was doing, I turned into the near empty church parking lot and walked hesitantly up to the doors. I couldn't see much of what was inside since it was mostly dark, but a thin spill of light from a room told me someone was here. I tried the door, but it was locked, and I realized that it was Tuesday evening. As far as I knew, churches were only open for worship on Sunday. Sighing, I turned around and trotted back to the car. Just as I placed a foot into the vehicle, the church door squeaked open.

A tall, oval-faced man stepped outside. He extended a hand to wave, and I felt slightly embarrassed as I returned the gesture.

"I'm sorry, I didn't know the church was closed tonight," I explained as I approached him.

"That's quite allr ight. I was just finishing some paperwork."

Now that I was closer to him, I could see the aging lines that weaved through his tan waxy skin. Though he couldn't be over fifty, they made him look way older.

"I'm David. Head pastor here," he said chipperly. I wouldn't have been able to tell by his casual khaki shorts and navy blue polo shirt, but he had a certain air about him that was immediately respectable.

"Abigail, nice to meet you."

"I haven't seen you around here," he said after shaking my hand. "Are you new in town?"

"Not technically. I grew up here. I recently lived in Ohio, but I moved back. Personal reasons."

He nodded politely. "Well, we'd love to have you here for worship sometime."

I forced myself to smile. "Actually, that's why I came. I was wondering if there's a spot for me and my son in the congregation."

He laughed a big, hearty laugh that shook my bones.

"Of course, there is! The house of God welcomes everyone. Services are Wednesday, Friday, Saturday, and Sunday. We also have weekly prayer programs to encourage faith in the congregation."

I blinked. "What's the program this week?"

"Forgiveness."

If anything, his answer just creeped me out. Talk about incredible timing.

"I think I'm in need of a lesson on that," I admitted, and he smiled.

"We would love to have you."

I thanked him for his kindness and promised that I'd see him this Sunday for worship. Cara would be so proud of me. For once in my life, I felt like there was a higher power gazing down on me, protecting me. It felt good.

Church was more packed than I thought. I had to sit in the back, in a nearly empty pew except for an elderly couple at the other end. I felt slightly out of place, like a whale among dolphins, and I glanced around to see what other people were doing. Some already had their heads bowed in prayer, and others were reading what I assumed to be the daily scripture, so I picked up the book that was perched in the cubby hole in front of me and started to flip through the pages. Gavin sat impatiently in my lap, reaching this way and that, and I had to restrain him multiple times.

When the service finally did start, Pastor David took his spot at the podium. He greeted the congregation sweetly, and as his eyes touched mine, a welcoming smile formed on his lips.

"Forgiveness is not easy," he declared. "It is a winding road full of barriers and excuses and heartache. Driving this road of forgiveness is not a one-night trip, but you will reach the end some day, a changed and happier person. By grace through faith, you let yourself wander the twists and turns, face the excuses and the disinterest. But through it all, if you give your heart up to God and ask for nothing but hope and strength, you will come out triumphant."

I lost myself in Pastor David's message. The more he spoke,

the more I pictured Evan. Navigating life without him wasn't really all that difficult, and I wondered sometimes if that was because I loved him for the wrong reasons. I had wanted a connection to someone—there he was. I wanted to feel loved—there he was. I wanted a kid—there he was. All like he said. Could it have been possible that I *was* with Evan just to fill a void? I waited for the typical wave of guilt, but it never came. Maybe I was learning to forgive myself, too.

"Abigail!" Pastor David called after the service. He waved and maneuvered his way through the crowd. "What did you think of the message today?"

"It was powerful," I admitted. "You're very good at what you do."

"It's the word of the Lord, I simply deliver it. But I'm glad you enjoyed it." He smiled when Gavin waved at him. "You're welcome to join us for a Bible study this afternoon here in the narthex."

I shifted Gavin in my arms. "Thank you, but I have another meeting today."

I explained that I'd made first chair in the Saratoga Strings Orchestra and had my first orchestral meeting this afternoon.

"Wow, you must be a very talented musician."

I smiled politely. "I just practice a lot."

I said the exact same thing to my conductor, Tod Niles, when he asked me later that evening. We were seated in an arch, and he stood at the center, gesturing with his baton. He was very witty and had us all laughing within minutes, which I appreciated. There was nothing more nerve-wracking than starting in a new group where you didn't know anyone.

Most of the players looked to be my age or older, and when I scanned the cello section, I spotted a man that had to be a hundred years old.

"That's Lester," the girl to my left said. She nodded toward the elderly man. "He's been playing since he was four."

"Do you know him well?"

She nodded. "Might as well. He's been my neighbor for years. Taught me how to play." She tossed her gleaming black braid over her shoulder. "I'm Veronica."

"Gail," I said amiably.

"And I'm Seth."

I glanced behind me to see a man with the face of a model. Stark green eyes, warm golden skin, and silky bronze hair. I blinked a few times, stunned by his appearance. But Veronica only laughed.

"Don't get any ideas. Seth's gay."

"Born and raised in New York City," he explained jovially. "Until little miss plays-a-lot dragged me here to Saratoga Springs."

"We met on the subway!" Veronica howled with laughter. "Can you believe that?"

"Been friends ever since," Seth finished with a wiggle of his eyebrows.

"That's awesome," I said.

Tod Niles called our attention back and explained that our first performance was at a festival in Pennsylvania at the end of July. We would be playing selections from several scores, which I was excited about. Scores were my favorite pieces to play.

"Think I'll find a hot Pennsylvania boy while we're there?" Seth whispered.

Veronica scoffed. "In your dreams, lover boy."

That actually made me laugh, and I joined in on their hushed snickers. I could see myself being friends with them, and something told me they would be just as accepting of me.

. . .

Time was passing quickly. Life fell into a routine again: I met with the Saratoga Strings every other week day and went to church on Sunday. I was getting more comfortable in the congregation, and I even stayed afterwards for a Bible study some days. I was finding it easier and easier to talk to God, even in my weakest moments when I missed Evan and stayed in bed to cry. But I was healing. My dark episodes were becoming less frequent, and I let Veronica and Seth talk me into going out for drinks one evening while Gavin was at my dad's.

Days became weeks. Weeks turned into a month, and on my twenty-sixth birthday, I came home to a house full of my friends and family. It was a surprise party. Cara and Beau set a bottle of sparkling champagne down on the island, which was already crammed full of fruit and veggie trays, grilled hot dogs, and a gorgeous two tiered marble cake.

Cara giggled at my amazed expression. "I know a baker in Michigan. He baked the cake for my wedding, and I figured you deserve the best, too."

I hugged her until someone tapped me on the shoulder. It was Erica and her boyfriend Spencer. Having all of my favorite people in one room was celebration enough.

Erica shoved a glass of champagne into my hand. "How long have we been friends, Gail?"

I glanced at Spencer, who was staring affectionately at Erica.

"Since I was a sophomore in high school," I said, suddenly amazed at such a thing.

How incredible was it that our relationship had stood the test of time? That was rare. People came and went, but Erica was my constant.

"That's right," she continued. "So don't freak out when I show you *this*."

She stuck her hand out so that the enormous engagement ring on her finger glittered in the light.

"Holy cow!" I shouted. "Congratulations, guys!"

Spencer Wade was, as Erica gushed many times, her prince charming. They were meant for each other. But even if things someday went down-hill and God forbid they separated, I knew Erica would be okay. She was a firecracker. I didn't need to worry about her.

While everyone took turns holding Gavin, we ate until our stomachs were incapable of taking more. We sipped our drinks and talked of how the times had changed.

"Remember that sixteen-year-old girl with the dream of being a violinist?" Erica announced. "Well, look at her now!"

I laughed as I watched my father play peek-a-boo with Gavin, and my heart grew ten sizes.

Some time during the festivities, I pulled Elijah into the foyer. He was slightly tipsy and swayed as I threw my arms around him.

"Whoa! What's the occasion?"

I pulled away to stare intently into his hazel eyes. "Thank you. For everything. Not just the party, but for being my rock and bringing me back to life."

His smile was like home to me. "You're my best friend. It's what friends do."

I was living in a perfect bubble. My son was growing up, happy and healthy; my musical skills were improving ten-fold. Nothing could bring me down. Nothing could throw me for a loop. I was ready to take on the world, and nothing would pull me back.

Until the following Thursday.

I was in the grocery store, grazing the aisles for my weekend trip to Pennsylvania for the festival we were performing at. Gavin, who had just recently turned two, sat in the cart and frantically tried to reach for extra items.

"Mommy!" he screamed. "Choes!"

It took me a few days to realize this was his way of saying

Cheerios. I grabbed a box as we passed and said, "Cheer-ios, honey."

I steered the cart toward checkout. When I reached the front of the line, I began placing each item on the moving surface, hardly noticing the woman who stood behind the counter until I looked up.

And just like that, I was flung into the past. My jaw dropped to the floor.

"*Katy?*"

She planted a hand on the counter and leaned forward, offering a wide smile that exposed too much gum. "Abigail. It's been so long."

I stared at her sickly pale skin. At the dark circles under her eyes, the frizzy curls of blonde hair, and the grotesque yellow tinge to her teeth. Realizing I was staring, I quickly dropped my eyes and fumbled with my wallet.

Katy turned to stare at my son. "I see you've been busy. Sheesh, aren't you a little young?"

I didn't want to talk to Katy Marsh. She'd left me in the midst of my heartbreak, left me to navigate it alone. She'd become a liar and a terrible person over the years, and I suddenly felt the need to protect Gavin from her corrupted mind. But if Pastor David had taught me anything it was that forgiveness was the key to happiness. This must have just been one of my barriers.

"I have been busy," I replied as politely as possible. "What about you?"

She shrugged. "Oh, you know, dropped out of college. It wasn't for me."

"Why?"

"I wanted to get high instead." Something changed in her voice, and when she glanced back at me, I saw something like regret flash in her eyes. "Been to rehab three times already. That's a weird place, Gail. A scary place."

"I'm sorry."

"Nah." She waved her hand and punched a key to open the cash register. "I've been clean for six months."

You were a good person, I wanted to say. *You had your whole life made out for you, and you threw it away for drugs. Why would you do that?* I managed to swallow my anger.

"That's great."

"It *would've* been great had I not gotten into drugs in the first place. Now, I'm a fucking cashier at twenty-seven." She shoved a clump of matted hair over her shoulder and rolled her eyes when I glanced nervously at my son. "Five dollars is your change."

I accepted the money and bored my eyes into hers, fighting to keep my voice at an even level. "Why *did* you start using?"

Her amused expression turned cold. "You were only cool if you used."

"But that stuff hurts you, Katy!"

"You don't think I don't know that?" she hissed. "And honestly, I'm surprised you never started using. Colton messed you up pretty bad."

That was it. I couldn't take anymore. I tossed the bags into the cart and walked away. Except it wasn't that simple because now the past was wrapping itself around me like a shroud. It stuck with me the entire drive home, and my mood soured as the seconds ticked by.

Damn Katy and her addiction. Why did she have to leave me? I could've helped her! I could've saved her. Of course, I knew deep down that was a lie. People only changed unless they themselves wanted to change.

Still, something didn't feel right. Katy was my warning. Something was going to happen now. I could feel it in my bones like a steadily increasing fever. I could feel it in the heat of the sunset. Something was going to pop my perfect little bubble.

. . .

When I dropped Gavin off at my father's for the weekend, and he asked if I was all right, I told him I was. No sense in trying to explain things to him. I would face this battle when it came — whatever it was.

I expected a text from Evan or maybe his mother again, a text saying they wanted to talk and patch things up. The entire ride to Hanover, Pennsylvania, I tried to give myself a pep talk about forgiveness and trusting God in whatever he had planned for me.

On Friday night, I met Veronica and Seth for dinner. Our performance was the next morning, so we had tonight to relax. They ordered wine and demanded that the refills keep coming. All the while, I sat with my phone clenched tightly in my hands. I was waiting for Evan. I knew he was going to call, and I would be ready.

"What's the matter, Gail?" Veronica wondered. "Aren't you gonna drink?"

"Not tonight," I said, faking a smile. "I don't drink before performances."

"Oh, you know, I used to be like that before I tried a Mojito for the first time," Seth admitted. "Veronica, do you remember the time—"

I stopped listening and checked my messages for the twentieth time in a half hour. Nothing.

It was kind of tortuous, not knowing when he would reach out. But it had to be him. Why else would I have this sinking feeling in my stomach? He would call and wonder how Gavin was, and I would tell him because I could be mature. And then we would discuss the divorce and custody. Even though it was bound to be a sad conversation, I just wanted to hear his voice.

But he never called. By nine p.m. I was practically hysterical. I sat on the bed in my hotel room and nervously bounced my leg, waiting for my phone to light up.

Why was I doing this? Why was I waiting up for a guy who

really hurt me? The thoughts seemed to spark me to life, and I shook my head.

To distract myself, I took a shower and then called my father to see how Gavin was holding up. And when it was clear that my son was perfectly fine, I ate an apple and watched reruns of *Friends* until midnight. And though I told myself I wasn't waiting, I knew I was.

Sighing, I turned the TV off and bowed my head.

"God, whatever this is, please just give me strength to get through it."

Praying always made me feel better now, like a dose of medicine to fight off a virus. I settled down into the sheets and forced deep breaths into my lungs. I only slept for a few hours before my alarm shrieked, and I pushed myself up and into the bathroom. Unfortunately, the pit in my stomach had only grown deeper.

The Saratoga Strings' first performance was a massive hit. Tod Niles, it seemed, was born to be onstage. His quick wit and humor was a delight to the audience, and we had them on the edge of their seats as we played the works of John Williams' score for *Star Wars*. I wished I could've enjoyed it more, but I was too busy being stuck in my own head.

Afterwards, Tod called me over and happily shook my hand. "Amazing, Abigail. Simply amazing."

"Thank you, sir."

"I have to be honest. You are one of the best violinists I've ever met."

I explained that I went to Curtis for college, and he gasped, clearly impressed. But I liked talking with him anyway. It made me feel like Professor Autrie was standing close by with a loving smile on his face. That helped to calm the bundle of nerves in my stomach.

"Wanna grab lunch?" Veronica suggested later on.

"You said we could check out that new bookstore first," Seth whined.

"I'll catch up with you," I told them.

I didn't want to sit down in a restaurant or go plowing through several aisles of books. What I really needed was to sit down and write out my feelings. My anxiety was slowly turning to anger. Evan wasn't calling me, and as much as I secretly wanted to, I sure as hell wasn't going to call him. So, it was a good thing that I'd packed my favorite sky-blue journal.

The concert hall was still packed, but I pushed my way through the crowd to a nice sitting area with large plush chairs. I set my instrument down, took a seat, and opened my notebook.

My heart was pounding now, and I drew deep breaths as I glanced at my phone. There were no new messages. But it wasn't until I looked up that I realized Evan wasn't the source of my feelings at all.

My heart leapt into my throat as Colton Reeves emerged from the crowd and walked toward me.

Chapter Twenty-Four

HANOVER, PA (2027)

What are you doing here?" It came out harsher than I intended.

"Nice to see you, too."

I shifted uncomfortably as Colton sat in the chair next to me. It was impossible not to stare at him; he was older but somehow just as handsome.

Except I didn't want to talk to him.

My life was good now. Simple. I didn't need Colton to magically appear and cause me a stress-related heart attack. I had healed from his absence. I didn't want to face it again, nor did I want him to try to influence me in any way.

"What are you doing here?" I asked again, clenching my notebook in my hands.

He blinked those gold-green eyes at me. "I needed to talk to you."

"What, have you forgotten how to text?"

"This conversation couldn't be texted," he answered simply and my stomach coiled. "Plus, I doubt you would've answered."

"You're right, I wouldn't have. Where's Beverly anyway? Does she know you're talking to me?"

"I dumped her." The bite in his tone caused me to look back at him. His face was serious, carved from marble. His jaw flexed against the barrier of skin.

"Why?"

I could think of a hundred reasons why, but it wasn't my place to pass judgment given my recent parting from Evan.

"I didn't want to be with *her*."

And there it was, the usual pounding of my heart. It was actually funny. After all these years, my heart still stuttered for Colton Reeves. I wanted to rip it from my chest and stomp on it because I couldn't go down this path. Not again.

"How did you even know where to find me?" I threw at him. "Are you stalking me?"

"I live in Clifton Park, Gail. That's only a half hour from Saratoga Springs, and the announcement of a new orchestra group wasn't hard to miss since they're advertised everywhere. And your face is literally on the pamphlet."

I glared at him.

"Abigail, I just need to talk to you. Would you mind if we went somewhere—"

"Hold on," I cut in, instantly fuming. "I know this story. You come here and flash your charm because you know it used to work on me every time. You take me out, and the next thing I know, I'm in bed with you until I come to my senses and realize you never even wanted anything to do with *me*! You just want my body!"

A woman sitting close by gave me a wary, crazed look and then hurriedly excused herself from the area.

Colton's ears went pink. "That was years ago, Gail."

"What does it matter?" I hissed. "'Cause the *next* time I saw you, Beverly was wrapped around your waist. Wasn't she the girl you were waiting for at Starbucks all those years ago on

Christmas break? And the girl you went back to after we had sex? I won't be caught up in this game, Colton." I shook my head, finalizing the statement. "I'm not that girl anymore."

"And I'm not that *guy* anymore," he fired back. "I was an asshole. Hell, I was in college, for crying out loud. I didn't know who I was or what I wanted. And I made some mistakes, but *you*...you were *not* a mistake."

And now it was time for my ears to redden.

"I regret a lot of things, but I have never regretted our relationship. I just wish—" He dragged a hand down his face, and I noticed the exhaustion shining in his eyes, "—I wish I would've handled things differently. Or maybe met you later rather than sooner because no one has ever compared to you."

The room was suddenly too loud, too crowded. The colorful, ugly carpet under our feet spun. I felt faint.

It was like putting a newly cleaned addict in front of fresh cocaine. Of course, I had feelings for Colton. Burning, passionate feelings. But I'd gotten so good at burying them that now I wasn't sure I could face them.

Taking a breath, I returned my eyes to his. "I can't give you the answer you want. So much has changed, Colton. I have a kid now!"

His eyes bulged open, practically popping out of their sockets. "So then... where's—"

"Evan's not here," I answered tersely. "He cheated on me and we're getting a divorce."

His jaw fell to the floor, and I didn't miss it when his eyes brushed over my abdomen. What was that look in his eyes? Rage? Jealousy? I looked away before I could overthink it.

"Gail, I think we have some catching up to do."

I sighed, forcing every ounce of air from my lungs.

Perhaps the reason I was being so hostile was because I still loved him and hated myself for it. But that constant hatred was getting very, very tiring. I didn't want to hate anymore; I wanted to find peace. Pastor David's voice spoke to my thoughts: "Forgiveness heals, Gail." So why couldn't I learn to forgive the man who had meant so much to me?

I glanced back at Colton. "Fine. Maybe we do."

For the dozenth time in my life, I sat down at a restaurant with Colton Reeves, except this time, the waitress wasn't looking at us with heart-shaped eyes, and no one cared because we weren't sixteen. We were in our upper twenties, and young love didn't exist anymore.

"Tell me everything," he urged gently.

That soft, curious tone almost made me want to itch my skin off because it was so familiar and beautiful. But I told him anyway and started from the beginning: how if it weren't for Cara, I would've lost my mind during the Pulmonem Fever outbreak, and how I was the maid of honor at her wedding. How I met Evan on the night of the proposal and how we danced drunkenly around the patio of Beau's apartment. I mentioned my first ride on a motorbike and confessed to drinking profusely after Professor Autrie's funeral. I told Colton about my marriage, every part of it. The good and the bad and how the birth of my son was the best day of my life. I talked about how I found out Evan had cheated and the immense heartbreak that followed. Through it all, Colton took in every word. I'd forgotten how easy it was to converse with him, and getting this stuff off my chest, especially to an old...friend was actually making me feel better.

"Looking back though, I really don't think I was with Evan for the right reasons," I continued.

"Was he not your type?" Colton asked.

I shrugged. "I think we were just...two kids who loved the idea of not being alone."

Colton took a sip of his water and nodded. "I've been there."

I watched him while he considered all of this, watched how a crease formed between his eyebrows and then cleared and how he looked like he might want to ask a question but thought better of it. After a while, he just offered an amiable grin.

"What about you?" I wondered out loud. "Fill me in."

He cleared his throat and set his elbows on the table. "During the Pulmonem Fever outbreak, Penn State kicked us all out, so I was home for the pandemic. It was terrible. My mom actually broke her wrist, and we had to go to the hospital, which turned out to be a three hour wait. Everything that could go wrong went wrong. That's a year I would love to forget if I could. But anyway, I went back in the fall and started hanging out with some of my friends again, and that's how I got back with Beverly. She and I have mutual friends, so it was hard to ignore her.

"But like you said, I don't think I was with her for the right reasons. She was very...controlling, wanted everything to be perfect. I didn't feel accepted with her. I couldn't be myself."

"So why did you go back to her then?" I bit my lip at how the question was posed. I sounded too interested.

He opened his mouth and then closed it, pressing a palm to the back of his neck.

"What?" I pressed.

When his eyes met mine, they sent a streak of warmth through me. "You know how sometimes you settle for less because you can't have what you actually want?"

I looked away then, trying very hard not to overthink his words. "Yeah."

I felt his eyes on me, and my heart ached eagerly, so I downed a glass of ice cold water to clear my head before saying, "You said your mom got remarried. Tell me about that."

Colton smiled. "Oh, Sean's awesome. He's an amazing home remodeler. Taught me everything I know."

"Are you a remodeler now?"

"Nah." Another dazzling smile. "I'm an architectural engineer, but Sean's a genius in his field. We get along really well."

"That's great. I'm glad your mom's happy with him."

"Yeah, they belong together, one hundred percent."

I knew we were avoiding the topic of his actual father. As much as I wanted to know how everything had played out in the end, I didn't want to force Colton to talk about it. Some scars couldn't be discussed for years, and I had to respect that.

"Gavin," Colton said, calling my attention back. "What's it like?"

"Having a son?"

He nodded.

"It's...the most incredible thing in the world," I said. "You have this kid who you would do anything for, who you love unconditionally. It's magical."

"You never struck me as someone who wanted children."

"Well, I wasn't really thinking about it at sixteen."

We both laughed at that, and Colton sat back in his chair. I took note of how this felt, how sitting with him felt, and how it felt right.

"I've always wanted to be a father," he admitted then. "I want to help shape someone's life and have that connection. I mean, Heaven knows I'd be a better father than my own."

We both locked eyes for a moment, and I couldn't help the little tremble in my lip. Colton's scars...were they still there? Or did they heal? Could someone ever really heal from something like that?

"I'm sure you would be an amazing father," I murmured.

We stared at each other a moment longer before I forced myself to look away.

"Do you remember high school graduation?" I asked.

I didn't know where I was going with this, but he nodded.

"Of course."

"I wanted so badly to say goodbye to you because I had it

locked in my head that I would never see you again. And that scared me."

"Why'd it scare you?"

I tossed my hands out conversationally. "Because I was scared that I wouldn't find someone like you. You were my best friend for a long time and...it's just hard to give those things up. Especially someone like you."

I realized my mistake and could have kicked myself because now his eyes were liquid emeralds, and I felt my heart begin to gallop.

To break the ice, I said, "I mean, it's actually cruel—the fact that you've barely aged."

He chuckled. "You haven't aged either!"

"Are you kidding? Look at these frown lines!"

I didn't know why I was highlighting my flaws to him, but when he laughed, I laughed, and it was so natural that we had to smile and hold each other's gaze for a beat longer than necessary.

"You're still beautiful, Abigail," he said after recovering from his laughter.

When I smiled, it was only to be polite. I couldn't show him the smile I wanted to show him for fear of revealing my emotions.

I cleared my throat when the waitress returned and asked us for dessert. I ordered a strawberry cheesecake because I thought I deserved one after a brilliant performance...and partly because I didn't want to leave Colton. Not just yet. I liked talking about the past. I liked catching up. But when he flashed me his handsome lopsided grin, I had to force myself to focus.

"When I saw you at graduation, toward the end," he said, sloshing the end of his straw around in a cup full of ice. "I wanted to say something, too."

I felt my eyes widen. "Really?"

He nodded. "I was scared for the same reason, and I kind of wish I *would've* said something."

"We were stubborn," I muttered.

"Too stubborn."

My hand twitched to touch his. "But we're here now, talking."

"Just for tonight."

I cocked my head at him. "What do you mean?"

"I'm leaving to go to Arizona tomorrow to visit my cousin and help paint his living room. My flight leaves at ten, so I have to be at the airport by eight."

Something about having Colton on the opposite side of the country made my breath catch in my throat.

"A big job?"

"Well, the guy's a heart surgeon, and he lives in a mansion," Colton answered lightly, laughing. "So yeah."

"Well, I wish you all the best."

His eyes flickered to my hands and back to my face. "You, too."

Hearing it from him made my bones tingle.

"When I...saw you in Starbucks that one time," he mused, "I wanted to sit with you so badly. Beverly completely left my mind, and if it weren't for her, I might have left with you." He spoke with his hands, raising his eyebrows to give each word emphasis.

"Colton."

"But I couldn't because I thought it wouldn't be fair to you *or* Beverly. I was ashamed of my decision to leave you in high school, and I figured you wanted nothing to do with me."

"I wouldn't have said hi if I didn't," I retorted. "But I thought you wanted nothing to do with *me*—"

"How could I not, Gail?" His green eyes glowed, overflowing with emotion. "You were the love of my life."

"Stop," I insisted, flustered at his sudden confession. "I can't have this conversation."

Colton watched me shrink back in the booth, and fear registered on his face.

"I'm sorry," he murmured. "I didn't mean to bring it up."

Why was I being so bitter? Why couldn't I let the conversation steer in that direction? He was right here, my first love—the person who held my entire heart in the palm of his hand—ready to settle our differences and move forward, so why couldn't I do it? Why couldn't I forgive him like that?

"I don't know what I want," I admitted in a robotic tone.

I just felt numb. Nothing made sense right now.

"I understand," Colton said, nodding. "I needed to see you because I heard you were back in the area, and I couldn't stand another minute without talking to you. But that doesn't mean I'm...asking for you back." I frowned at him. "I just missed my best friend."

We both knew deep down that we could never be just friends. But it was a safer topic, so I accepted it.

"Thank you," I whispered. "It's nice to have you around, given what I've just been through."

Colton nodded. Then his Fitbit buzzed, and he glanced down at it. "Crap. I gotta go."

"To Arizona," I said dryly.

His grin returned. "It's not for forever. I'll be back in two weeks. Besides, you have my number, right?"

"Never deleted it," I said somewhat sheepishly, which only made his grin broaden.

"Call me anytime. If you ever need to talk, I'm here."

I wished he would've said that ten years ago when I needed him most, but I appreciated the offer just as much now.

"Thank you."

He set a wad of cash down for the tip, smiled that lovely smile, and sauntered out the door. His chivalry almost made me laugh. After everything he'd been through, Colton Reeves was still the gentleman kind enough for dinner.

For the next several hours, he danced in the spotlight of my mind. I replayed our conversation a hundred times, feeling goosebumps tickle my skin as I recalled the look in his eyes when he told me I was the love of his life. What a statement. What a crazy, terrible, frightening, beautiful, spine-tingling statement.

I sat on the edge of my hotel bed, bouncing my leg up and down, which had become a relentless habit. But I couldn't focus. Everywhere I looked, those gold-green irises stared back. I actually hated myself for it, but a softer part of my conscience told me to relax. *Hush, Gail*, it said. *Don't fret. God's got a plan.*

I laid down on my back and ran a hand through my long hair. I was suddenly bored out of my mind. I could call Seth and Veronica and see if they were up for a few more hours of shopping. I could call my father and see how Gavin was doing. But deep down, I knew those things were just distractions. Seth and Veronica had no doubt spent their energy shopping by now. And my father wouldn't let my son out of his sight. So, it was time to face the music: I missed Colton.

I wanted him here with me. I wanted to lock us in this hotel room so that we could talk forever and ever. Anything to hear his voice, see his face again. The realization overwhelmed me and I swallowed nervously.

Once upon a time, I had loved Colton Reeves freely. He was my rock, my world. At such a young age, I had never known anything but him. He taught me love and loss and growth. And as much as it *pained* me to see him drive away that day, I had since found a strength in myself that I'd never known existed. So thank God for first loves. Without them, we wouldn't know what love really was.

I showered without feeling the water. I read without making sense of the words. I settled in to watch *Friends* without seeing the TV. And sleep avoided me. Sometime within the early hours of the morning, I laid on my back and stared up at the ceiling while my heart went crazy.

Finally, a thin rim of color ringed the sky, and the sun materialized in the east. I knew Colton would be on his way to the airport by now, and I pushed myself up from the bed. I didn't know when I'd see him again. He tended to pop up when I least expected it, but I was hoping he would come now, appear out of thin air and come sit beside me again.

But that was unlikely.

An hour later, I met the Saratoga Strings for breakfast, and we all bonded over endless stacks of pancakes dusted in sugar and topped with strawberries. Tod Niles treated us all to hot chocolate, and I laughed out loud when Seth burnt his tongue and cursed. Still, I felt like I was missing something.

"Hey, sweetheart," Dad answered on the fourth ring. "How was your first performance?"

"Awesome," I replied, wheeling my suitcase to the hotel's front desk.

"That's great. And Gavin was perfect, we had no troubles whatsoever. I even taught him to say grandpa! Well, it doesn't sound like that yet, but he'll get there!"

I laughed. "Tell him I miss him so much."

I couldn't wait to have my son back. Leaving him was one of the most difficult things I'd ever done, but I knew he would be just as safe in my father's care.

"He misses you, too, Gail. So, how's Hanover? Did you go out shopping?"

"Uh..." I pictured Colton sitting in the booth across from me and failed to keep a smile off my face. "Not really. I had other things to do."

I didn't want to tell my father about Colton, not until I was sure of what I wanted. It was only fair given how much my dad suffered right along with me.

"Call me when you're close to home," Dad said, and I told him I would.

After checking out, I collapsed onto a bench in the lobby and clutched my phone warily.

Friends called friends. That was how it worked, so I shouldn't have been nervous to dial his number. I scrolled through my contacts, searching for his name, and froze when I found it. His contact picture was the photo I'd taken of him the summer after our freshman year of high school. We were at the pool, and he was bundled up in a towel, gazing at me with that same brooding look, only through a younger face. I couldn't believe I never changed the picture. It was actually kind of painful to look at.

I drew a deep breath and then brought the phone to my ear. While it rang, I wiped my sweaty palm on my knee and glanced at the receptionist at the desk. The operator picked up, and I felt my spirits falter slightly.

"Hey, Colton," I said after the beep. "Listen, it was really great talking to you yesterday. I loved catching up." I beamed as I spoke these words. "If you ever wanna hang out when you get back from Arizona, I'd love—"

Another beeping sound cut me off, and I pulled the phone away from my ear to find the source. It was an incoming call from Colton, probably just calling back. I exhaled and quickly answered it.

"Colton."

"Abigail?"

My heart stopped when I heard Sandy Reeves' voice instead, a voice that was filled with anguish and terror. I rose from my seat, feeling my lungs tighten in my chest.

"Miss Sandy?" I asked. "I-I'm sorry, I thought it was Colton. Is everything okay?"

"Abigail, Colton was in a car accident!" she wailed. "He was supposed to be on a flight to Arizona this morning, but he never made it to the airport!"

Every nerve ending in my body sizzled to life, constructing a raging, horrific bonfire. It split me open and charred me alive.

My body wasn't able to take the explosion. It would kill me right here, right now if Colton was—

"Is he okay?" I demanded.

Sandy sucked in a sharp breath and then sobbed again. "He had to be rushed into emergency surgery. They don't know if he's gonna make it."

I sank to my knees, unable to stand the flames as they swallowed me whole. Somehow, I noted that the receptionist had rushed over to help me as well as another stranger. They asked me questions, but I couldn't hear them; a terrible ringing had filled my ears, muting everything like I was being held underwater. But I welcomed the sensation. It was like the water was putting the flames out. And thankfully, the world went dark before my head hit the floor.

Chapter Twenty-Five

HANOVER, PA—SARATOGA SPRINGS, NY (2027—2029)

I called my father on the way to the hospital and he was off his rocker, shouting into the phone. It seemed like he didn't want me anywhere near Colton, but at the same time, he was fearful and wanted to know how Colton was doing.

"Are you sure you wanna do this, Gail?" Dad asked. "After everything he's put you through?"

I swung the wheel into the hospital parking lot, feeling my anger rise. "Dad, Colton's been through a lot more than I have! And clearly, life's too short to hold grudges!"

I parked crookedly and waited for him to answer. I was already starting to shake, and I needed my father to give me strength before I walked through those doors.

"You're right," he said at last, and his tone had shifted. "Call me as soon as you know."

Seemingly in slow motion, I sprinted into the lobby and slammed my palms down on the front desk. The woman peered up at me through her black corkscrew curls and feigned a smile.

"Colton Reeves," I said breathlessly.

"Are you family?"

"No, a friend."

She typed something into her computer and then pursed her lips. "It appears that Colton already has a visitor right now, and given his condition, the doctor is limiting the number of people who are allowed to be in his room. He just got out of surgery an hour ago." When I started to protest, she held up a hand. "You'll have to wait."

With that, her syrupy sweet smile returned, and she gestured to the waiting area.

"Help yourself to the vending machine, dear. Or the cafeteria on the second floor."

I sank into a chair, wincing as all the air left my body. Thankfully, I'd never known true torture, but this had to be pretty damn close. Knowing that he was up there somewhere, bandaged and broken, barely breathing — it broke my heart. Sandy had called to tell me he lived through surgery but that he would need to stay several nights in order to heal.

It had been a teenager. A careless, selfish, texting teenager. Could he not have waited to send that message? With one look down at his phone, he almost killed one of the most important people in my life.

My stomach heaved, and I squirmed in my seat. All of the what-ifs, the could've happens, they were syringes, piercing my skin and pumping poison into my bloodstream.

Welcome back, anxiety.

I ended up getting a bottle of water from the vending machine just to cool myself down. The waiting area was painfully bland with beige folding chairs, white walls, and pale tile. And everyone here looked as nervous as I felt. Had they all been on the brink of losing someone today?

I sat back down and twisted the cap off my water, greedily pressing it to my lips.

"You must be dehydrated," a man beside me observed.

I glanced over at him and lowered the bottle. "Oh, no. I'm just upset. Nervous. One of my good friends was in a terrible car accident, and I can't get in to see him yet."

"Huh," he said, scratching at his graying goatee. "Must be something in the air. My stepson was just in an accident, too."

My ears perked like a dog's, and I looked at the man again. His worn, olive skin framed the bright blue-gray of his almond-shaped eyes. His face instantly announced that he was a kind-hearted person, the kind who willingly sat in a waiting room just to make sure his new stepson was okay.

"Are you...by any chance Sean?"

He blinked at me. "Yes. Do we know each other?"

"Not officially." I sighed and stuck out my hand. "I'm Abigail Ferr. I've known Colton since high school."

"Oh my goodness! Abigail, yes! Sandy's mentioned you so many times."

A sliver of gratitude streaked through me.

I explained how I had been in Hanover for a concert when Colton caught up with me and how I was so, so sorry for what had happened. Sean's face grew dismal. It was clear in his eyes that he truly cared for Colton, and just for that, I wanted to thank him a million times over.

"It really puts things in perspective," Sean murmured. "We can't ever assume we have forever, so it's always important to say things now. Because tomorrow doesn't really exist."

I nodded, feeling a golf ball sized lump form in my throat.

Maybe it was time I came clean, to myself and to Colton. I didn't have anything to lose now. We were older, and our days were numbered. He deserved to know how much he meant to me all those years ago...and now.

"Miss Ferr?" the woman at the desk called. "Colton is free now if you'd like to head up."

I risked a glance at Sean, but he waved me along. "Go on. I'm sure he'd really want to see you."

I smiled and thanked him profusely.

210, 211, 212. The room numbers swirled past me as I hurried down the hall. My heart was hammering in my chest as each step brought me closer and closer to—

"Oof!" I grunted as I slammed into someone around the corner.

I stumbled back slightly and shook my head, but when I got my bearings, a coldness swept through my body.

Beverly Andrews' stark brown eyes swept over my face, and then crossed her arms. She was dressed in stylish capris and nude red bottoms, flaunting all of her wealth.

"What are *you* doing here?" she asked.

I leveled a glare at her. "I could ask you the same question."

She uncrossed her arms and heaved a sigh. "I'm here to see how my boyfriend is doing, *obviously*. So tragic what happened, isn't it? He was supposed to be my escort for a gala next week-end, too!"

"He dumped you," I said dryly.

She pressed a manicured hand to her heart. "He's just confused. And besides, how could he say no when I've offered to pay his medical bills?"

My nails bit into the skin of my palm. "You don't love him, you *use* him. And in case you were wondering, Beverly, there's a difference!"

She snickered and tossed a strand of copper-colored hair over her shoulder. "Oh please, like he'd ever go back to you. High school was so long ago, Abigail. You need to grow up. Plus, he would never get anywhere in life with a sorry middle-class reject like yourself."

The world went silent as my vision turned red. *Did that really just happen? Did a grown woman really just say that to me?* Something inside me boiled, begging to be let free. I was *done* letting people push me around.

I stepped toward her, so close that our noses nearly touched. She seemed baffled by my closeness but kept her glare strong.

"*Cut the bullshit.*" My tone dripped with acid. "You don't want love. You want reputation. Anything to boost your sick ego."

I knew I'd gotten through to her because she staggered backward a step, and her indifferent expression faltered. Her lips parted in shock.

"And I can't help but wonder if you've ever genuinely looked at yourself in the mirror," I hissed, moving closer still. "Yeah, you'd see the expensive clothes and the gorgeous face, but you and I both know that deep down, there is nothing but emptiness and *selfishness* in your heart. And that makes you the furthest thing from pretty."

She gulped, clearly flustered by my statement. Her back was pressed against the wall now, and despite the fact that her heels made her taller than me, I had all the power. Because nothing was more effective than shoving a mirror in someone's face.

"Colton almost *died*, and yet you're only here to win him back to save your own ass. I wouldn't call that love."

She blinked profusely and tried to speak, but I cut her off.

"You've said enough. Now take your overgrown ego and get the *hell* out of my face."

She exhaled, stung by my words. And in the silence that followed, she tightened her grip on her Michael Kors purse and stomped away down the hall. I actually laughed at her as relief swelled in my lungs. Who knew calling her out could feel so good?

I couldn't celebrate this small victory for long though. A woman rounded the corner and froze in her tracks when she saw me. I stopped, too, stunned by the memories that shot through my mind.

"Abigail," Sandy said, closing the distance between us. "Is it really you?"

She touched a wrinkling hand to my face, and I could only nod. The last time I'd seen her, she was in the stands at high school graduation, screaming for her son. Time had changed her.

"How is he?" I asked after we embraced.

She massaged her temples, and I could tell she was exhausted. "He's breathing, and that's all that matters. Right in there," she said, gesturing to the room behind me. "I'll give you two a minute."

I turned to the door, closed my hand on the knob, and felt my heart stop. What if Beverly had already gotten to Colton and told him she was paying his medical bills? And what if that somehow sparked his attention again?

"Shut up," I whispered to my anxiety.

Sandy turned around. "What'd you say, honey?"

"Nothing." I smiled.

Hesitantly, I pushed the door open and was hit with a waft of disinfectant spray. A soft whirring filled my ears along with the steady pulse of a heart monitor. When I saw him, I almost turned right around and walked back out the door because I couldn't handle the sight.

He was laying on his back with his right arm perched in a sling, and I thanked God he was wearing a hospital gown because I didn't want to see the extent of his bruises. His arms were already black and blue, and he had a long bandage stretching down his forehead. His cheeks were indigo and hollow, and his lip was split open. He appeared to be sleeping, though it didn't look like a very enjoyable slumber. His brows were furrowed, and every few seconds he twitched.

I took a shaky step forward, clenching and unclenching my fists. I tried to be quiet, but I didn't even make it half way before his eyes snapped open, and I was hit with those gold-green irises.

They glimmered in the fluorescent lighting, and I could see how much pain he was experiencing.

"Abigail," he slurred, and I shook my head.

"Shh. You don't have to talk."

He tried to sit up and winced with a sharp gasp. My heart plummeted.

"Please, Colton," I said, pressing a gentle hand to his chest. "Just rest."

His eyes flickered from my face to my hand, and I pulled away to sit in the chair by his bed. He watched me curiously.

Even though he was terribly battered and bruised, I was thrilled that he was alive. That he was *breathing*. I couldn't bring myself to play What-If right now because if the situation was worse...If Colton had...

"Are you okay?" he asked.

Something like a laugh escaped my lips, and I glanced up at him. "Are you kidding? Here you are writhing in pain and you want to know if *I'm* okay. Classic Colton."

This earned me an award-winning smile.

It was time to come clean. No more running.

"I couldn't stop thinking about you after you left the diner. I almost called you like eight times, but I figured it would seem weird," I admitted in a small voice.

His eyes never left mine as I spoke.

"And when I found out what happened..." I swallowed, almost unable to finish the sentence, "I thought I'd lost you...for good."

Colton shook his head slightly—a small, pained movement—as he scanned my face.

"And I didn't think I could live with that," I continued after clearing my throat. "I guess I should tell you what I meant to tell you and that...you've meant so much to me ever since I met you. Ever since that day in English class where you asked for my number 'cause we were partners for that stupid research project." I stopped to laugh. "I still remember that like it was yesterday."

He reached for my hand, and this time I let him take it. His hands were painfully cold, and a shiver slid through me, yet my heart was pulsing warmth. If someone would've told me that I would be sitting here next to Colton Reeves again, I would've laughed in their face. But this was real.

I stared at our hands, at his hand; I knew this grip like it was my own. And if I had learned anything, it was that we only had this moment because tomorrow wasn't guaranteed at all. We were selfish to think it was.

"Abigail," he whispered. When he looked at me like that, broodingly, even if his face was carved and bloody, time seemed to freeze. "I'm in love with you."

Evan had said the same thing. But that was nothing compared to this, compared to Colton. It was strange how two different people could say those five words, yet the one could make your heart burn and cry and squeal for joy so much more than the other.

"I'm in love with you, Colton," I replied.

Helplessly, hopelessly in love.

And then I felt a tugging in my chest. It was an orbit, a magnetic force, pulling me closer to him. He must have felt it, too, because his hand tightened around mine, and then we were nose to nose. I was leaning over him, careful not to touch his fractured body.

In the moment before our lips touched, I pictured us as sixteen-year-olds: young, in love, and free. Then I leaned in, and my soul lifted from my body.

My heart *pounded* for him. I never wanted this feeling to end. When the heart monitor increased its speed, I giggled lightly against his lips, and he drew me to him again. I was lost in my passion and close to bursting out of myself, so he had to be, too. I broke the kiss to spare his aching body.

I stepped back, slightly breathless. Our eyes were locked as if we were both saying, "If we weren't in a hospital for such dire reasons, I'd kiss you forever."

But we *were* here in a hospital, and Colton *was* clinging to life. I sighed and hung my head.

"You know we can't be together yet though. You need to focus on healing, and I need to go home and see my son again."

"We *can* be together," he insisted and flinched when he tried to move. "Beverly isn't—"

"I think she knows her place now, Colt. Honestly, I can't believe she offered to pay your medical bills."

He shook his head and ran a hand through his matted hair. "I guess I'll have to thank her someday."

I swallowed. "Yeah. But until then, you need to heal."

He hesitated before saying, "I don't think I'll be able to drive again for a long time."

"Make that heal and conquer your fears then," I added. "Get back on your feet and feel like yourself again. And then...when all of that is taken care of...come find me."

I hated seeing him in this condition. I only wanted to know the happy, healthy Colton from our youth, so he *had* to take time for himself to heal. He had to.

"What if you don't want me by then?" he asked fearfully.

I shook my head. "I don't think I've ever stopped loving you, Colton. And I doubt I ever will."

He brought my hand to his lips and kissed my knuckles tenderly.

"Besides," I said. "There's still a lot more we need to catch up on." I let my eyes shift down his body and back up to his face. "Your scars?"

Colton nodded once. "They've faded, but they're still there."

As much as I *despised* Mr. Reeves for what he'd done to his son, I realized in that moment that I could learn to love Colton's scars. They showed his strength and resilience. They were part of him and his past battles, and I wanted him to know that I would fight alongside him from now on.

"Don't you dare be a stranger," I whispered, smoothing his hair back one last time before stepping toward the door.

He watched me longingly, and it took all my strength to keep moving. But he needed to focus on his healing, and I needed to focus on my son.

"I'll see you soon," he said.

And I hoped to God that was a promise.

He rested his head back against the pillows and gently closed his eyes once more. I stared at him for a moment. My heart wanted to tow me right back into his arms. But then I pictured Gavin and slipped out the door.

Somehow, someway, time passed. The summer faded away with each sunset, and the days grew colder with each sunrise. The Saratoga Strings performed in November and December of that year, blowing our audience out of the water both times.

I became very close with Veronica and Seth. I had come to think of them like the siblings I never had. I even added their names to the sky-blue journal that I kept under lock and key.

Gavin and I attended church every Sunday. At first, he wasn't thrilled when I enrolled him in Sunday school, but he quickly got used to it and often sprinted to his classroom after giving me a hug.

Pastor David spoke of faith, perseverance, trust, and many other concepts that I took upon myself to research further. And I prayed every single night. My faith was like a butterfly; it had flourished over time.

It was for that reason that I wasn't offended when I never heard from the Caldwells again. Evan was nothing more than a fleeting dream, and I figured if he wanted nothing to do with our son, that wasn't my fault. If anything, I hoped he was content in the life he'd chosen; I was just happy I wasn't a part of it.

To my complete and utter dismay though, Gavin was growing up. When he turned five, he took his first brave steps into kindergarten. On the first day, he puffed his tiny chest out and assured me that everything was going to be fine. I was almost in tears over how adorable he looked in his vest and jeans. I wanted to keep him in my arms and protect him from growing up, no matter the cost. But in no time, he was having other little boys over for playdates.

Gavin was also quite the talker; he could chat my ear off for hours about his favorite dinosaurs and how he was already making a Christmas list for the upcoming holiday season. He was my little ball of energy, sprinting around the house, jumping on the couch cushions and using "The floor's lava, Mommy!" as an excuse. He was a risk taker, and when I discovered that he and his friend Andre planned to ride a skateboard down the street without helmets, I put a stop to it immediately, which earned me the evil eye for all of five minutes. Because for as adrenaline-seeking as my son was, he was also very loving and forgiving.

I had to learn from that.

But I was there for all of it — the good, the bad, and in between. I held him when he scraped his knee while trying to climb a tree, and I read to him every single night. Every once in a while, he even asked me to play my violin for him, to which I happily obliged. My life had become his life.

It had been two years since I spoke to Colton in the hospital. We didn't talk as much as I thought we would, but something told me he would still find me. It was an inclination, and a powerful one at that. Though I went out on a few dates, I hadn't met anyone that gave me the same chills as he did, and I took that as a sign. We were doing exactly what we said we would do. I was taking a part in my son's life, and Colton was coming to terms with all the monsters he'd faced. I wasn't exactly holding my breath, but one thing was for certain: Colton Reeves was the only man I reserved forever for.

I thought about this while sipping tea in front of the roaring fire one cold January night. Gavin called my attention when he stepped into the room all bundled up in his snow gear.

"Where do you think you're going?" I inquired.

He wobbled toward me, his pants making a swishing sound with every step.

"I gonna make a snowman w-with Andre."

I scooped my little troublemaker up into my arms. "Oh, and does Andre's mother know about this?"

He nodded vigorously, widening his large blue eyes at me, and I had to laugh. Andre lived a few houses down the street, and they ran back and forth almost every night.

"I'll come build a snowman with you," I offered.

Gavin stuck his tongue out. "No girls, Momma!"

"I hope you'll say the same thing when you turn sixteen," I responded solemnly, and he just stared at me. "All right, go play. Then we can make hot chocolate when you're sick of the cold."

He squealed and leapt from my arms, almost tripping in his haste to get to the door. I listened to the door open and waited for it to close, but the locking sound never came.

"Momma, someone's here!" Gavin called.

"You must be Gavin," a voice said.

And I shot up from the couch, nearly spilling tea all over myself. I stumbled into the foyer and froze when I saw him. "Colton."

He was whole again — no bruises coloring his skin, no split, bleeding lip, and no black and blue eyes. He was *here*, alive, breathing, standing. I shook my head, trying to clear it.

Gavin looked between us with a quizzical expression.

Just then, Andre clomped up the porch steps. "Hey, Gav!"

"'Scuse me," Gavin said, shoving past Colton and jumping off the porch into a pile of snow.

Colton laughed as he watched them.

I slowly walked forward, drinking in the sight of him, praying that this wasn't a dream. When he turned back to me, his expression hardened, and he gazed into my eyes like they were all he ever wanted to look at again. I always knew he would come back, but I expected a call first. Or a text message. I guess I should have known better though. Colton tended to play with the element of surprise.

"You're here," I whispered. I'd texted him my address at least a hundred times over the years, hoping he would turn up. But no amount of daydreaming had properly prepared me for this moment.

"I'm here." His smile shimmered.

A gust of wind whistled through the foyer, and I jumped at the cold's vicious bite. I hurried to close the door and gestured down the hall to the living room.

"Please come in."

The fire crackled and twisted, chomping at the wood. For a few minutes, all we could do was stare into the embers, but then I glanced over at Colton, hyper aware of his presence. The way his skin glowed in the firelight and the way the flames danced in his eyes, I wanted to lay my head on his shoulder and stay there forever. But then he was looking at me, too.

"I'm glad you came," I said.

"Yeah, finally. Treatment took longer than I thought," he answered dryly. "I had to spend days in that hospital, go through endless hours of physical therapy. I even had to have another surgery on my arm because it didn't heal right. The only thing keeping me going was you."

I couldn't imagine the pain or the debilitating amount of hours he'd given up just to be able to walk again.

"Talk therapy was the worst part." He shook his head and

groaned. "The guy went into so much detail about how trauma affects the brain and why PTSD keeps you from doing normal things. Like *I* need a lesson on PTSD after what happened with my dad." His face darkened.

"Hey," I said. "It's okay. You have every right to be scared after what happened."

Colton gazed into the roaring fire. "I was so...*angry*. I wanted to find that little teenaged asshole and give him a piece of my mind, but the psychologist only made it worse by explaining that revenge will never fulfill me." He air quoted that last part and then rolled his eyes.

"But he was right, Colt. You can't take matters into your own hands like that."

"I figured that out eventually, even though it took at least a year and a half. But I was just ashamed of myself that I wasn't healed yet, that *other* people could get into a car, but the very sight of a vehicle made me nauseous. And thoughts of my dad started coming back and..." He trailed off.

"But you conquered those fears," I reminded him, "which proves how strong you really are. And I'm so proud of you."

The firelight illuminated half of his face and shadowed the other. He looked so innocent and pure. Totally undeserving of the fate he'd received.

"Well, like I said...the only thing keeping me going was you. I can't tell you how many times I almost called just to hear your voice."

"Why didn't you?"

He paused for a moment and then shrugged. "Because you needed to worry about your son. Not me."

I was about to argue when a strange expression crossed his face. He shifted beside me, and I watched him closely, taking note of how his littlest movements sent my heart racing.

"Gail, I...I need to tell you something. I didn't tell you in the diner that day because I knew you didn't want to hear it, but then I got in the accident, and I realized that life's too short to keep my feelings to myself." He swallowed and then met my eyes again. "I've been in love with you since I met you."

A smile touched my lips. "Freshman English was—"

"No," he interrupted quickly, "in fifth grade. I remember you answering all the questions and twirling your pigtails. And I just...I thought you were super smart and pretty. And every day during recess, you always took Katy and went straight to the monkey bars, and when I wasn't in the foursquare game, I would watch you. You could do them so fast," he said, laughing breathlessly. "And one day I sprinted to the monkey bars before you and tried to climb across while you were watching, but you opted to swing that day for some reason. I could never get your attention. That's why our teacher hated my guts. I always said things to try to make you laugh, but I think I just ended up annoying you.

"Every single day since fifth grade, I couldn't talk to anyone else. I couldn't *do* anything when you were around. All my friends knew it, and I was the laughingstock of the group for years because I was too nervous to actually talk to you. I remember passing you in the hallway and having my heart beat out of my chest, praying that you would acknowledge me in some way. But...you never did. And then I would always get down on myself for not being able to make the first move.

"But all of a sudden, we were freshmen in high school, and I knew my life was over when Mr. Korrins made you my seat partner. Every day you came in, sat down, and copied the homework into your agenda. I couldn't stop thinking about...how organized you were, how *pretty* you were. More so because I'd finally gone through puberty." He stopped to laugh again. "And then we were partnered for that project, and I could *finally* get your number.

"I knew I was gonna ask you out the night we went to the Christmas lights. I told myself, I'm not leaving until she's my girlfriend. Being with you...was heaven, Gail. You were so kind, generous, and selfless. You showed me what love really was. It was like I knew you were the one for me. I couldn't shake it...

"And then my dad almost killed me. I-I was so *terrified*. I was scared he would come after me again, come after my mom! I was confused and angry and *hurt,* and I was lashing out like a ridiculous teenage boy would."

He paused to stare into the firelight, no doubt reliving the horror from his past. It nearly broke my heart in half to listen to this, to his side of the story. It felt like it was just yesterday, and that was the scariest part.

"Being *without* you, Gail...was hell. At first, I thought I would be okay because I had it in my sick head that you were somehow responsible for what had happened. But as the months went by, I started to crack. I didn't want to admit it to myself, but I missed you like crazy. It didn't help when Ashton and all my friends were saying to forget you and to be a man. I tried. I went out with them on weekends but then came home and cried. It was the worst summer of my life, I'll tell you that.

"I actually despised you for a little while," he said sheepishly, frowning at the carpet. "Well, no. I wasn't mad at you. I was mad at *myself* for not being able to get *over* you. And that's why I went after Destiny during our junior year. I was determined to do anything to make it seem like I was fine. Fake it till you make it, right?" He shook his head in disgust. "I would see you at lunch and in the halls, and I tried so hard to make it seem like I didn't care, but all I wanted was to slip into an empty classroom, pull you in with me, and tell you how much I loved and missed you.

"And trust me, I hate myself for not doing that sooner. All the precious time we wasted being stubborn, it makes me sick. But then we graduated, and I was happy to finally be out of high school. I thought Penn State would heal me, and it did...kinda. I met new people, met Beverly. Of course little did I know that was the wrong crowd to be in."

Colton's eyes touched mine, and the worry was clear on his face.

"I smoked and drank a lot in college."

My stomach somersaulted as I pictured Katy and Professor Autrie. "Colton, that stuff can hurt you!"

"I'm not proud of it," he said, holding his hands up. "But Beverly liked doing it, and I figured she wouldn't like me if I didn't. I was a little late on learning the peer pressure lesson. I knew it was bad for me, but...addictions are weird. You're in over your head before you even realize it."

"How'd you quit?" I demanded.

"Remember my friend who plays the drums and was at your concert?"

I nodded.

"He found out about it and sat me down to talk. It was the first time anybody had confronted me on the issue, and I was grateful. Levi saved my life. He said, 'Look at yourself, Colt. What would someone you love think if they knew you were doing this to yourself?' And I pictured you.

"Beverly wasn't very happy about it, and that's why I dumped her the first time. She was too into that stuff, and I needed to protect myself. I just kept thinking...Gail wouldn't do this. She wouldn't want me to.

"Of course, the Pulmonem Fever threw everything into wack. I went crazy in quarantine and needed to get high again to chase the nerves away. That was why I got back with Beverly because I knew she would hook me up with it." He swallowed and held his hands up defensively. "Again, I seriously regret doing that."

The fire hissed when he paused.

"Anyway, after I graduated from Penn State, I moved back home and got a job as a project architect. Beverly came to hang out every once in a while and dragged me out to clubs and stuff. It took me a few years to realize how toxic she was. And then I had a massive breakdown. Two years after college graduation—that was when I looked in the mirror and finally realized I was in deep shit. I didn't like who I was. I didn't like who I was spending time with. And above all, I missed who I was when I was with you.

"So, when I found out you moved back home, too, well...I had to find you. I was sick of living a lie, and I knew that you would set me straight. I love you, Abigail. I have always loved you. Even after our breakup when I said shit I didn't mean, I loved you. I don't deserve you, and I am so sorry for hurting you all those years ago."

My heart cracked when a single tear dropped from his eye. It was a lot to take in, yet I felt myself start to smile. I almost laughed. When he saw my expression, his features softened, and he held my hand against his chest, where his heart pulsed quickly.

"Even now, twenty-some years later...my heart still beats for you," he whispered.

And then I was in his arms, tackling him onto his back and kissing him like this was our last night on earth.

I held his face in a tight grip, drowning in his embrace, an embrace as familiar as my own skin. I couldn't get enough. I crushed my lips to his, and when he pulled me on top of him, a tsunami of heat coursed through my body.

After everything we'd been through, we deserved this moment. The universe had frozen for us, providing us a second chance. I lost myself in his touch, feeling the void in my torso fill to the brim. The happiness that rushed through me was nothing short of overwhelming; it *consumed* me. And as my mouth moved desperately with his, it occurred to me just how much I *had* missed him. Missed this connection, our friendship, our relationship. It felt like my past and my future were finally shaking hands, and I broke our kiss as my emotions got the better of me.

He cocked his head at me curiously. "What's wrong?"

I shook my head as tears oozed from my eyes. "You're just...here. This is real."

He smiled the smile that my heart adored, and I pressed my head against his chest, where he held me and gently caressed my shoulder.

Perhaps life was like a figure eight instead of a straight line. Your path was never set in stone; the tiniest glitch could throw you entirely off course, making things feel impossible. But with each twist and turn, there was a new lesson to be learned, a new opportunity to find happiness and peace. And when the time was right, you would circle back around and reconnect with things you feared were lost forever.

Chapter Twenty-Six

FEBRUARY 2082

Abigail was broken from her thoughts when a violent coughing spell attacked her lungs. She coughed harshly into her elbow, and her raw throat caught on fire. This had been going on all day. Or more like every day for the last year. She was eighty now, and her health had been deteriorating ever since the death of her beloved husband. She coughed again, wincing against the claw-like sensation that tore at her insides.

Her son Gavin wandered into the kitchen and broke into a sprint when he saw the slight greenish tint to her skin.

"Mom, are you okay?"

Abigail coughed once more and swatted her son away. "I'm all right. I'm all right." She cleared her throat and flinched.

"You don't sound all right."

"Oh, honey, don't worry about me." After regaining her strength, she gave him a brave golden smile. "An old bat coughing is not an unfamiliar sight."

Gavin narrowed his eyes at her, unconvinced, but Abigail's smile was so radiant he sighed and collapsed into the opposite chair. A beat of silence passed before Gavin noticed the sheet of paper Abigail was writing on.

"I can't believe you're still writing, Mom."

"What's wrong with that?"

Abigail reread her previous sentence, and her thoughts stretched back fifty-some years.

"Nothing," Gavin said. "I'm just surprised you haven't had terrible arthritis or something. It can't be good for your joints to be sitting and cramped up like that."

Abigail cocked her head. "Son, I go for walks every day and spend more time with my grandkids than I ever have. And they're even off living their own lives now!"

"It's not a bad thing, Mom," Gavin responded with a small chuckle. "I've just never seen you so passionate about writing." He crossed his arms and set his elbows on the table. "Dare I ask...can you tell me what it's about yet?"

"I think I hear your wife calling."

"Nice try. Hope's in the shower."

"Then maybe it was your sister."

"Aliana went out to pick up the pizza."

Abigail sighed. "Sweetheart, all secrets will be revealed soon enough."

"What kind of secrets are we talking about?" Gavin asked. "Did you murder someone?"

"No." Abigail thumbed the corner of the page, feeling a swell of emotion consume her when she glanced at the name of the person she loved beyond life. "I want to explain to you kids what my life was like growing up. I had some hard times."

The only sound between them was the soft *tick, tick* of the kitchen clock. Gavin uncrossed his elbows and sat back.

"I can't wait to read it," he said smoothly, and the smile that lit Abigail's face made his heart ache. "How many pages you got though? You must've written well over a hundred by now."

"More than two hundred actually."

Gavin balked. "Wow." His eyes flickered to the paper, and Abigail covered it with her hand.

"No reading till I'm finished."

This actually made Gavin laugh out loud. "You're *not* finished?"

"Not even close." Abigail stared down at the page, her eyes nearly drowning in fresh tears. She missed him — missed him more than words could even begin to describe. Her heart quivered when the memories returned. Sweet memories of a sweeter time. Abigail took a deep breath and glanced up at her son again. "The story is only just beginning."

THE STORY CONTINUES WITH
TO NOW AND FOREVER,
FEBRUARY 2023

Acknowledgments

There was never a moment in my childhood when I snapped my fingers and insisted, "I'm gonna be a writer when I get older." It was just a solid fact in my brain. What I *didn't* know was that my first book would be written during a global pandemic and in the midst of such a gut-wrenching personal loss. Writing saved my life, and as Abigail discovered herself, I was discovering myself.

But I didn't get through that dark chapter of life on my own.

The biggest portion of my gratitude goes to my parents for their undying love and support for both my book and my healing process. I also want to thank my closest friends a million times over for staying by my side and encouraging me to keep going, to keep writing. You guys own my heart.

And of course, this book would not be a book without Jodi Jackola, my outstanding, incredible publisher. I will never forget the moment you accepted my manuscript and made my biggest dream come true. You are amazing at what you do. Thank you for advocating for me, trusting me, and believing in Abigail's story. The same goes to Shonell Bacon for having the patience to edit my manuscript. You are a wonderful human being, and I am beyond grateful.

Last but not least, I have to thank God for not only giving me the idea for this book but for changing my life in the first place. You work in mysterious ways, but when I hold my book in my hands, I realize why I had to go through it. I have never been more thankful. May this book find the next person whose heart was just shattered, and may it give them some peace.

About the Author

Born and raised in Pennsylvania, Avery Volz knew she wanted to be a writer when she received her first journal at the tender age of eight. Today, she adores crafting stories that explore what it means to be human and what it means to be in love. Her mission is to make each individual feel seen and understood through the rocky roads that her characters walk. Outside of writing, Avery is an accomplished hip hop dancer. She also finds solace in her favorite romance novels, in her friends and family, and in her dog, Izzy.